25415258 9

AUTHOR	CLASS No.
LOTHAR . M.	F.
TITLE	BOOK No.
Rage of joy	17045921

Rage of Joy

RAGE OF JOY

The divine Sarah Bernhardt

by

Minda Lothar

LESLIE FREWIN : LONDON

25415258 9

ORMSKIRK

BR/BR

© Minda Lothar, 1968

First published in 1968 by Leslie Frewin Publishers Limited,
15 Hay's Mews, Berkeley Square, London W1

Set in Baskerville
Printed by Anchor Press
and bound by William Brendon
both of Tiptree, Essex
WORLD RIGHTS RESERVED

01762287

Contents

I

Seduction in the Morgue

In the time of Napoleon III of France those who were
ambitious to rise in the world became aware that the power
resided not in Napoleon the Little, as Victor Hugo named
him, but in his bastard brother, August Charles Joseph de
Morny, who was the brains behind the coup d'état of 1851.
The word had been passed around: 'to get a decoration; a
membership in the Jockey Club; a lucrative contract with
the government; an ambassadorial post – see Mons de
Morny.'

Since de Morny was a bon-vivant, a Brummell, a night
prowler, a dealer in fake art and in broken horses, he had
to snatch his few hours of sleep during the morning. Thus,
his day began near the noon hour. By that time politicians,
merchants, foreign ministers and young careerists had waited
patiently, hours on end in the antechamber of the Morny
Palace for their scheduled interviews. And by that time his
devoted valet, Henri, had brought out trousers, coats, ties,
perfumes, jewelled tiepins and decorations for that change
of apparel which was a daily pleasurable routine for him.
The vast collection from which Henri had made his daily
choice easily held as much haberdashery as the largest shop
in Paris.

The valet recognised signs of sleeplessness in his master
when he rose out of bed, and like a mother hen, brooded
over him as he emerged from his bath.

'Is there something I can do, Monsieur? Perhaps to rub
the back of the neck or the feet?' With a gentle tired smile,
Morny gestured for the full massage. His muscles were
aching with fatigue and as usual, had to be tuned up for a
day that was scheduled to the hilt.

He had dragged his tired self to bed about 4 am but the

excitement of a midnight banquet and a new mistress had keyed him up to so high a pitch that his sleep had been only fitful. These night affairs always exhilarated him to a high pitch and they might have killed him had he not put aside two days a week to join his wife and children at Nades, their country estate.

Like everything else he touched, even his pleasures turned out to be a fabulous source of income. Actresses and portrait artists, courtesans and countesses gave parties to advance their own interests. An inner circle of nobility and devotees of the creative arts flocked to these private gatherings like bees to a honey hive. There was always a 'newest member' who paid for a celebration where food, wine, flowers, waiters, and chefs cost a small fortune and sometimes bankrupted the donor. Since Morny was invited everywhere, the *nouveaux-riches* merchants offered him fat envelopes filled with crackling new bills for the honour of joining him.

Morny found the *jeunesse dorée* stimulating and the artists forever whetting his own rage to live. To share their kinship more intimately, he had taken to writing plays under the name of Saint Remy. The plays had no success, which earned him every playwright's gratitude, but it was sufficient to bring Morny the illusion of equality with his talented companions. In that night world only a select few knew him as the secret power behind the throne. Morny preferred to be known as a promising playwright.

He was still a little groggy from the drugs and the drinks of the night before as he examined the names of people waiting for the interviews. He checked off Metternich as the first to be called. While the valet was still dressing him he greeted the ambassador from Austria with a studied serenity, disarming him by inviting him to participate in the final choice of his attire.

'What do you think of these delicate black stripes on grey? Is it the correct costume for today when I shall have to persuade Monsieur Thiers to increase the tax? Ah no, come to think of it, the drape of the jacket will offend him as being too aristocratic. The steel-grey wool, Henri.'

Metternich protested impatiently that matters of greater concern were at stake. Morny shook a little finger at him: 'You Austrians should learn to play a bit, like the French.' As Morny chose a more sober cravat and had his valet tie it for him, he continued: 'It's all such nonsense, this scorn of proper dress. You should not overlook the connection between coat and character. Let the first grow shabby and the second totters. The very cut of a man's trousers affects his morale.'

Metternich was too astute a diplomat to argue with the connoisseur who set the fashions for men throughout France. Black waistcoats edged with gold thread and the hat pulled down over the eyes at an angle were *à la Morny* and had become *de rigueur*. Metternich remained silent as Morny examined a trayful of sparkling scarf pins. He dared not show his contempt for the frivolous brother of the Emperor who had just started a new social sport by importing the steeplechase from England; there were rumours that he demanded fabulous sums from those who yearned to join the Jockey Club, a mark of distinction almost equal to the Order of The Garter.

Morny slipped into his velveteen coat and reached for a delicate Sèvres *demi-tasse* as he blithely went on to discourse on the patriotic duty of lavish spending to provide for an army of retainers. Metternich came to the point of his visit abruptly: 'I am hearing that you propose a Savoy uprising against the Austrians. Why?'

Morny dropped his mask of gaiety and turned sombre as he retorted savagely: 'My dear Metternich, to earn thirty million francs. Does that answer you?'

'Is that your message for Vienna?'

'Yes!' Morny's eyes flashed a deep blue as he resumed his nonchalance to apply a touch of pomade to his eyebrows: 'If I were you, I would not betray my confidence to your Emperor. That good and simple man could not be bothered with trifles and he would not thank you for retailing the persiflage of a clown. Thank you for waiting.'

Metternich smiled wryly, bowed and left. Henri came in

9

and announced a 'special caller', giving a code name. The mysterious visitor was the Emperor himself. There was no ceremony between the two brothers; the Emperor was never completely at ease with his half-brother who despite his close resemblance, outshone him as a social charmer. He handed his rival some legal documents – subpoenas and suits for redress of payments – with the curt remark : 'What is the meaning of this?' Morny examined the briefs which accused him of being a swindler, a dishonest horse trader, usurer, and a dealer in paintings and antiques of doubtful origin. He handed them back to the Emperor with a shrug of his shoulders :

'Am I to blame if social climbers make giddy fools of themselves? It is they who should be required to answer for their greed. They push themselves forward, they bow and scrape, rob me of sleep to demand little favours. I simply make them pay.'

'Doesn't it occur to you that you might bring disgrace and dishonour to the throne?'

'On the contrary, Sire, as long as France prospers, the throne remains inviolate. I must have a bottomless purse so that France may glitter before the world. May I recommend to you the sage comment of our illustrious forbear. The Great Napoleon said "Great men are like meteors, they shine and consume themselves to illuminate the world." '

The cutting adjective 'great' was not lost on his brother. Louis Napoleon almost had one of his apoplectic seizures. But he was only too painfully aware of how he depended on Morny's advice. His crafty half-brother had a host of paid informers who reported to him on all affairs of urgent political or state importance. Baffled, the Emperor bit his lips and Morny had grace enough to pour oil on his smarting wound. His voice was gentle and apologetic : 'It would devour all my time just to add the figures of my transactions; it should require several dozen secretaries. It is all too tedious. But never doubt my loyalty to you. What I do is for the continued glory of your régime. I'll be seeing you shortly on this Savoy matter. Forgive me, brother, a lady is waiting.'

Morny smiled ingratiatingly and put a placating hand on the Emperor's shoulder. Louis Napoleon sighed and with a parting 'be more careful' left defeated.

The calendar for that evening had been marked off with the simple word – Julie. Of his several mistresses, Julie received the most generous stipend. She outranked the others with her dainty figure, classic profile and flawless complexion. What attracted Morny most of all was her consummate skill in bed. The amazing control of her muscular agility continued over the years to give him the little shudder of delight.

Though it was a lovely spring night, Julie had one of her headaches. Draped in a lemon chiffon peignoir, he found her reclining in a Récamier chaise-longue of gold velvet. The coverlet over her knees matched the chaise. The lovely composition was reflected in a Louis XV mirrored folding screen of five sections, the upper part decorated with Boucher scenes of happy child-like adults cavorting in a pastoral paradise under blue skies lit by random puffs of white clouds. It was one of Morny's gifts to her. He had acquired it when he bought up the entire collection of a bankrupt antique dealer for a ridiculous sum.

Julie gave her lover her most ravishing smile : 'It was so good of you to come; forgive me for a slight indisposition.' He kissed her gently on the forehead : 'But of course. Why do you permit these headaches to come?'

'Why indeed when you are so generous. These roses you sent this morning should have healing enough for any- thing – such a divine scent. And these earrings! Wherever did you find them! They must be worth a king's ransom.' Morny smiled secretively. The jewel box in his vault was piled high with oriental artcraft, a bonus he received from a jeweller for saving his son from a court action for unnatural behaviour. Julie flung her arms around him: 'You make me feel better already. I have only to look at you, August!'

She began plying him with those practised caresses that gave him such delight. Her gliding fingers soon touched off a storm of passion within him. The love ritual proceeded without dialogue. Her years as a courtesan had made Julie adept at pretending an excitement she did not feel. And Morny himself enjoyed the skilful artificialities which ladies of pleasure lavished upon him; making a comparative study of them like a disciplined sybarite.

Julie's cat-like massage brought back to mind the artfulness and coquetries displayed by the actresses at the late supper party the night before. Those cocottes who led double lives off stage and on were attuned to his own various theatrical roles he loved to assume in his daily round of politics and business. There was ginger-haired Florette, her jet-black curling lashes set off dramatically against the alabaster skin. And how she showed off that mole of hers, so far down on her breast that her *décolleté* seemed to be pulled askew! Lucie had the body of a potato-soup-peasant which she piled upon her guest like a rolling wave of flesh. Florette sang snatches of *risqué* ditties. Giselle followed the rhymes with the suggestive movements of her torso which caused a Marquis to shout: 'Formidable! easily worth twice the price.' And now Julie was nibbling him with her ivory teeth until he could hold back no longer.

After they gave themselves up to each other, Julie kissed him again and again, her grateful voice repeating with a slight guttural of a Dutch accent: '*Merci, mille fois*' – a hymn of praise reminding Morny of Handel's famous chorus, celebrating a more divine event. Conversation flowed more easily after the tensions were removed and they could sip their liqueurs with tranquillity. Morny relaxed sympathetically: 'You had a headache, *chérie*. Is something worrying you?'

Julie rolled her eyes with exaggerated hopelessness: 'It is Sarah; I simply can't fathom her. She is no longer a child

– near fifteen. I must think of her future but nothing appeals to her. She's an utterly selfish *ingrate*.'

Morny's hand automatically pulled at his moustache: 'Ah yes, I see. What is the trouble?'

'She refuses to marry. Already she's turned down four suitors. Even the poorest of them offered me 200,000 francs and 250,000 to Sarah. When she marries, she will receive the 100,000 francs which her father left her, altogether 350,000 francs. Oh August, may you be forever spared from having so stupid a daughter. Just imagine, she wants no money. She wants only to become a nun. Throwing away 350,000 francs to become a nun! What is a mother to do with a daughter like that. *Ma foi!*'

Julie's face was now flushed with anger and her head began to throb unmercifully. Morny was taken by surprise at this outburst of petulance. He betrayed his annoyance in the tone of his voice: 'Give her time. She's just out of childhood.'

'You don't know Sarah. She has a devilish temper. She swears she loves me and yet she deprives me of a fortune. Besides, our personalities grate. She tires and irritates me.' Julie sighed heavily. Morny tugged at his moustache nervously.

'Why haven't you confided in me? I thought you were amply provided for.'

Julie sensed she had made a bad impression. Morny was not at all sympathetic. She hastened to explain: 'Forgive me August. My sister has been running up bills at my dressmaker and hairdresser. I'm not too well and she can be depended on when I need her. I have two younger ones whose futures have to be planned. It isn't anyone's fault, your's least of all.'

Morny became his smiling self again: 'I shall give it my personal attention. If I succeed, you shall gain twice 200,000 francs.'

Julie was beside herself with joy: 'Please tell me more,' she pleaded. 'Is there any hope for such a girl!'

'It all depends on how we play the cards. We must

13

prepare the greatest party you ever gave; a débutante's introduction to society. The list of guests will astonish even you; it will be an event presided over by a prince of the blood. Sarah must have a gown that will rival that of the Empress. Spare no expense. It's a gamble, but well worth the throw of the dice.' Then and there he wrote a cheque for five thousand francs and handed it to Julie.

She threw grateful white arms around his neck and smothered him with kisses and caresses: 'My Lord and Master! My King! Your wish is my command!'

Morny winced. Though he quickly recovered himself, Julie had glimpsed the anguished distortion of his face.

'Have I said something wrong?'

'When you used the word king – well, how could you have known! I was on the way to the Royal Palace for an exhibition by that Scotsman, Home – he's the one I told you about who can float in the air; I have seen his levitation myself – my coach was stopped, all traffic halted by a police cordon. I was informed the Emperor had been shot. You can imagine how I felt. Twenty minutes later, I was told the assassination attempt had failed; you see Destiny had twice cheated me out of my rightful heritage. During those twenty minutes . . . how can I describe them to you? I relived my life with a new destiny!'

Julie had never seen him with so crestfallen a face. If Queen Hortense had legitimised his birth, the right to the throne would have been his instead of the younger Louis Bonaparte.

Their physical resemblance was so startling: the same imperial aloofness, the pointed cat's whiskers moustache, and even their slightly veiled look.

Julie had heard of the Emperor's jealousy. He had once called his half-brother a *faquin*, but not to his face. His paternal grandfather was the famous Talleyrand and yet August had to use the name of an old pensioner who had posed as the baby's father at the birth registration. He called himself Count de Morny, a title to which he had not the slightest claim. Unashamed in his boldness, the escutcheon on his carriage was a hydrangea (hortensia) barred, letting the world know of his Napoleonic, though illegitimate blood.

Ruthless with women, he had already consumed two of their fortunes and kept wide awake to fascinate and marry a third. He married the Princess Troubetskoi of Russia who was called the 'White Mouse' because of her silver hair and black eyes. She revenged herself on her faithless husband with the tempers, whims and caprices of a child of six.

Julie knew how important it was for her to comfort and flatter him; her lover needed solace for his luckless marriage. She divined the enormity of his ambition – his frustration and need for distraction. With a tinkling laugh, she swung his head onto her lap and cuddled him. 'Ah *mon pauvre petit*, let us both forget the stupidities.' Julie played with him and gave a virtuoso performance that had kept Morny enthralled and satisfied for years.

Morny's large cheque was no real assurance for Julie that the party would persuade Sarah to marry. When her daughter had said she would marry only for love, there was fanatic determination in her eyes against her mother; a fierce moral indignation – as if it were a horrendous sin to marry without love. How could she get a mere chit of a girl to understand that money was more important than love? She regretted now that she had let the nuns at the Grandchamps Convent educate Sarah. They had moulded her mind towards the incorruptible and the impractical only too well.

Though she detested playing the disciplinarian, Julie knew she had no choice. It was her duty to save her daughter from a stubbornness that would doom her to poverty. When Sarah returned from her classes at the Art School in the late afternoon of the following day, Julie called her into the parlour; the immaculate golden sanctuary reserved for serious occasions. The thin girl with the enormous liquid-green eyes sat down, anguished and anticipating the worst. Julie sat next to her on the couch and gently held her hand.

'Sarah, darling, I want to have a serious talk with you – I promise you – no harsh words, no tantrums. You are old enough to understand now. I want to tell you about myself when I was your age. It isn't a pretty story but it did happen. Just before you were born, I tried to kill myself; yes, more than once. And why? because I believed myself in love with a man who ran off with me to Paris and then deserted me. He was not Jewish and it broke my father's heart. He mourned for me as one dead and he never permitted me to see him again. Then I met your father and even he later abandoned me. You can imagine that it wasn't easy for a woman to make ends meet and to bring you up. I wanted to throw myself into the Seine but I had not the heart to abandon you.

'Your father came back a few years later. He had a little money and he insisted that I place you in the care of his former nurse who was living on a farm in Brittany. But your father could not remain in one place. He was a travelling salesman and as you know, we saw very little of each other after that. My love burned out to ashes. My heart never recovered from that shock. I vowed never to let myself fall in love again. You cannot know what humiliations poverty can bring. It took me years of suffering to realise how much more important was money.

'Your Aunt Rosine was more fortunate. She was provided for by a wealthy nobleman and she was able to travel to the fashion spas all over Europe. It was Rosine who opened the doors of society for me. I had learned my lesson and I found the protectors who made life more pleasant for me. I was no longer the oversentimental child you are. I learned to walk with grace, to carry myself with poise and to use a lorgnette. I had luxurious blonde tresses, dressed in the latest mode and I need not tell you how that changed my world. When I was presented to the Count de Morny, he kissed my hand and said simply, "May I call on you tomorrow?" Whatever comforts we have today, we owe to him.'

Julie rested a minute, patting Sarah's hand : 'Your father's family provided you with a legacy, it is true, but that 100,000 francs will come to you only if you marry. Rosine and I are no longer as secure as we had hoped to be. I shudder to think what the future might bring. Look at what I have to suffer – my heart attacks – just because when I was your age, very young and foolish – I believed in love and embraced poverty. My heart still suffers from shocks I had to endure. I want to spare you from this, so that is why I'm telling you all about me.' Julie sighed softly. Then she continued :

'Count de Morny will introduce you to a man with a fabulous fortune. We have a chance of dividing a million francs – think of it : my child, a million francs! We could all have everything our hearts desire. Do you see now why I'm in despair when you talk of marrying for love only? If you love your mother, you will listen to her. Take my words to heart. Believe that I know what is best for you. Promise me, please promise me you will think of marrying to secure your future. How can I make you realise what wonderful blessings will follow for all of us.'

Julie's eyes pleaded with her daughter. Sarah sat numbly, her sweating hand held in her mother's lily-shaped one. Tears slowly filled her eyes while Julie's long lashes lowered over hers, like curtains drawn after a performance. Nothing could assuage that inner ache of desolation she felt more poignantly now than ever. She could not think of her mother without that inarticulate pain. There could be no meeting of mind, no meeting of emotion, only duty and greed masking under a pretence of concern. If only her mother could love her. If only her mother understood her agony. Hopeless, hopeless. Despite that soft sympathetic drone of voice; despite the words that pleaded; that expressed concern for her future – yes, it was apparent that her mother could think only of herself – from now to doomsday.

17

Sarah withdrew her hand slowly. There was unfathomable despair in her choked voice as she said : 'There is only one solution for me. I shall go to the Convent and become a nun. Never, never will I have any peace unless I become a nun. I can retire from this horrible world. You can forget me and you won't need to be upset over me – ever again.'

The blood rushed to Julie's head. With difficulty she controlled herself. She gave a strangulated cry of fury like a dying animal. Her hand clutched the empty air as if strangling an imaginary throat. Sarah rose up in alarm and ran to call her governess, Madame Guerard. They rushed back to the parlour to find Julie stretched flat on the couch, gripping her head.

Sarah's hysterical cry rang out :

'Mother, mother, please forgive me. You are dying! It is my fault. I promise, I promise anything. Only get well.'

The words brought a vast sigh of relief. Julie sat up, a smile of triumph crossing her face. She stretched out her hands for her daughter who tumbled into them more dead than alive.

'I knew you would be a good girl.'

Sarah had a restless night and the following day she walked to her art class, her mind still seething with rage against those who were rejecting her deepest self. The older worldlings circled about her like implacable wasps determined to sting her if she did not conform to the prevailing way of life. She saw through their gently droning talk and knew it served only to camouflage the ugly reality. They were forcing her into a loveless marriage. A lifetime imprisonment in the name of love.

The world was a mocking façade of a triumphant Satan, that wily schemer who moulded all souls to his own pattern of the worship of comfort and money. The fifteen-year-old girl who yearned to model herself after the modesty and sweetness of the Mother of God felt tricked and cheated by her own mother and by life itself.

The very thought of her mother brought a fiery outburst of volcanic upheaval. No loving mother would force her daughter into a hideous marriage, not for all the gold in the world. If her mother were really fond of her, she would have known that she was crucifying her. All of Julie's maternal love went to the younger sisters who had blonde tresses and softly chiselled features, and who were models of correct deportment, moulded to make marriages of convenience with sweet complacency. Tradition demanded that the oldest girl be married first, and Sarah, who knew herself as the plain one, the rejected child, wondered if she was creating a serious obstacle for her sisters who might come to hate her.

Count de Morny provided enough money to permit Julie two guardians for her daughter : Madame Guerard busied herself with the household chores, and Mademoiselle de Brabender, who, a lady in waiting to the Czarina, had returned to France to become a nun-without-habit. She was hired as a lay sister to continue Sarah's religious education – to read prayers with her ward and to watch over her soul – these two gave Sarah the love she could not find in her own mother.

How could her mother, her own flesh and blood, sell her off to the misery of a loveless marriage! The outrage circled in her mind as an incomprehensible evil. Sarah could not free herself from the torment of that obsession. Her mother had never married, then why should she persist that her daughter do so. Never did Julie feel a pang of conscience about selling herself for money and luxuries. Sarah, perhaps because of her virginal innocence, glimpsed only too clearly, the duplicity in the faces of the men who brought her gifts. What hypocrites they were, pretending to be so respectful to the official mistress of Count de Morny.

Her own destiny would follow that of her mother. Sarah, like a trapped animal, yearned to flee from them all, as from a horror. How could she escape except to a nunnery? Only Mlle de Brabender understood her agony. The lay sister prayed with her 'to put on the whole armour of God' against the perfumed temptations of the world. How she prayed and with tears in her eyes, that God would grant her release by becoming a nun, for only the Beloved Bridegroom could love her and guide her with a sincerity that did not exist outside the convent walls.

She felt she was only a child but she had noticed how prominent her breasts had become. The pain and blood of her menstruation had brought panic to her. Being a woman seemed a catastrophe, for a new desire had entered her body. There was a fatal, shadowy side to her that yearned for a man. It came to her at night in her sleeplessness. The devil infused her with the fantasy of being the seductive woman with the furtive cloak and the secret smile that was so typically the expression on her mother's face. Now, the daughter too, yearned to be ravished. But is it not in this way that Lucifer, the Dark Angel who fell from Heaven, passed on the original sin to the race? Even as she tossed in her bed with desire, she sensed the presence of that strange and invisible being in the room. Two enemies confronted each other in the battleground of her mind : the virtuous goddess and the sinning mortal woman. That was why, despite all her good intentions, everything was going wrong.

The art class sickened her as did the cheap scent used by the professor. His theory of art seemed as absurd as his moustache, waxed à la Morny, and his long wavy hair falling straight back down to below his neck. Art, he preached, must be separated from life and have an existence of its own; it was the cult of Ideal Beauty compared only to the Ideal of the Ancient Greeks who kept their gods apart on Mount Olympus, far from the vulgar herd of men. Art must have no mortal blemish of stress or strain; no distortion of form, no depressing colours. The composition must be balanced, the forms classic, the colours sanguine. In short, a dream of Paradise that men amidst the bustle and dirt of life could glimpse for a moment, a flash of ideal perfection.

Sarah rebelled against painting flowers, animals and people as if they had no live counterparts. She despised the false notes of sunshine, joy and ideal perfection, when she herself could feel only continuous torment and frustration. In defiance of the professor, she chose colours that reflected the melancholia now habitual with her. The leaves of wild gillyflowers that she painted were made up of colours of a setting sun – heavy and sad-looking. All her drawings were steeped in the sense of doom that reflected her secret belief that she was a fated child of sorrow.

What was most disconcerting to the professor was that his one rebellious pupil so excelled in technique that he was obliged to give her first prize at the end of the last school term. Sarah had a good notice in the newspapers and hurried home in high spirits. But when her mother revealed no special enthusiasm for her accomplishment, the sense of glory vanished. With a leaden heart she continued stubbornly to master the techniques until she was far ahead of her class, but the paintings she brought home found a resting place only in her own room.

No one seemed to take her art seriously. It was just one of the accomplishments expected of the young ladies in the school for genteel females; the school itself was a mere prelude to marriage – the only goal destined for women. Time would gradually push her into the corner where the wild creature would be netted and dragged to the altar to become the slave of a master. In this barbarous institution, so agreeable to man who could lord it over wife and children, there was perpetual imprisonment for the wife. Only the Pope had the power to release her from such a lifelong doom. Marriage was forever.

Sarah's depression deepened at the end of the school day and she evaded her chattering classmates who wanted to walk home with her. She had to be alone – a splitting headache excused her, and so the moody young lady walked the streets alone, a portfolio of drawings under her arm. When she reached the rue de Seine her steps lagged as she approached the windows of the undertakers, Gannal & Cie.

Appearing to be fascinated by the coffins in the window, she peered in. Sometimes Monsieur Gannal left his apprentice alone while he went to the home of the bereaved to discuss arrangements. The apprentice, Hippolyte, was in fact alone and watched the window as if it was a kettle about to boil. Seeing Sarah at last, he hurried out.

The pale youth of twenty and the awkward girl greeted each other with the merest raising of eyebrows. A furtive smile showed her pleasure in seeing him, slightly guilty that she had told no one about his chatting with her in the shade of the Luxembourg Gardens several times, when he had instantly aroused her curiosity in his work: preparing bodies for display before burial. Perhaps she thought, the faces of the dead might offer a clue to their transfiguration! He had given his word to let her witness it at some appropriate moment. Why tell anyone at home her secret? It would only bring more disappointment as she would surely be forced to relinquish a specially intriguing friendship. His intellect constantly challenged hers; he was stimulating, exasperating, and unpredictable. Had she spoken of him her family would have reacted quickly: 'A young lady who was being courted by men of fortune associating with an apprentice!' How could they appreciate what it meant to her when he gave his word that Sarah should see him at work.

Perhaps that moment was now; this very afternoon! She followed him into the back room that was stocked with chemicals, coffins and basins of every size. And now at last here she was, among the most jealously guarded of secrets. If only she didn't feel so self-conscious.

While he busied himself with his concoctions, he shot furtive glances at her. She moved about in silence, staring at the mysterious coloured containers. For Sarah they might well have been the magical life-giving secrets of a medieval alchemist. The silence lengthened in the gas-lit room, and like elastic, as it lengthened, it tightened. Sarah shivered. She sensed a strange being in that sanctuary of death, whose presence had to be cut off.

Her voice echoed artificially as she felt the need to break the silence.

'I love silence. Flowers and animals are silent; I'm happier with them than with people. I don't like a crowd and I hate parties. It's better to be with just one person.'

'*D'accord. Moi aussi.* Crowds, ugh! and yet, loneliness drives one to just that. When I'm alone too much, I become depressed at what I'm thinking. Funny thing, isn't it, to be afraid of my thoughts? I hardly know myself. I make drawings like you do, just to see what will come out of the imagination. And what do I do? I see nothing but monsters. People without masks are monsters; what a terrible thing it is to look truth in the face; human faces become animal forms.'

Sarah had no desire to see his drawings: faces with pigs' eyes and slobbering mouths that resembled the corrupt priests of Hieronymus Bosch, too horrible to look at – grotesque obscenities. She had to change the subject. 'You promised to let me see an embalming.'

'Ah yes, morbid curiosity but it wears off. They're all alike – *néant* – nothing. The important thing is to pretty them up before they turn to dust – even those that go to the Faculty of Medicine. We prepare the corpses for the students in the dissecting theatre. It's just the right word – theatre – the spectacle of Humpty Dumpty shattered and the pieces are then put together again.'

'Then you have no body?' Sarah persisted.

'There's always a body.' He pointed to a covered casket in the corner. 'The chemicals are developing there and she is being preserved from decay by my boss's skill and compassion so that the sight of her will not pain her bereaved family.' He uncovered the casket and motioned to Sarah.

'*Voilà!* I'll show you one of his masterpieces – the secret of Monsieur Gannal – for which he was awarded one thousand six hundred francs to help him set up in his own business. A sculptor helps to make death more beautiful than life.'

Sarah was speechless. Before her in a satin-lined coffin lay the corpse of a girl no older than herself.

'Isn't she beautiful? About the age of the Sleeping Beauty,' he said proudly.

Sarah swallowed and choking slightly said, 'She looks happy . . . for having left this world. Yes, I see an intense joy. She must be with our Lord in Paradise.'

The awe in her voice caused Hippolyte to cackle with laughter.

'You really believe that? Are you strong enough to look truth in the face? I warn you; truth is like the face of the Medusa; it will turn your heart to stone. You have courage. You dared enter the mortuary without flinching. Yes, I'll tell you. She is *not* serene, she is *not* in Paradise. What you see is Gannal's art of embalming; the work of a great artist. He, more than anyone knows how to make death look beautiful. Were it not for his genius, you would see a green face with sunken cheeks, spotted with corruption; a girl of fifteen turned into a hag overnight.'

Hippolyte's words poured out as if he expected opposition to everything he thought and said. Sarah's first impulse was to leave in disgust but the odd slant in his eyes, his almost girlish features held her. She sensed the two great devils within him – Leviathan, the demon of pride, and Behemoth, the Lord of all blasphemies. Sarah recalled the words of the Mother Superior in the convent, 'It is God's grace to permit the two great devils to possess a soul which He wishes to save later in life, to a high degree of holiness.' She knew that his blasphemy was a form of passion. He burned with desire for her and he relieved himself by spitting out the venom of his disbelief.

She spoke quietly to him as her Mother Superior once spoke to her. 'You love darkness. There is a raging of sin in your blood and you call the devil father.'

His smile became even more sardonic.

'It's all made to order for you, isn't it – life and death *à la mode* – midwife at birth, Mother Superior at confirmation, priest at marriage, and the mortician at death – and why not – He is the most powerful of Gods – the only God.'

The diabolical side in him called out the missionary in her – in the presence of evil, put on the whole armour of God.

'Poor, poor boy!' she murmured. 'I was warned I should find such lost souls as you. There is only one Truth, and that one is God. How can I, what will make you believe? Change you heart and He will cross the universe to meet you this very moment. I shall pray for you.'

Sarah's musical, impassioned voice had its effect on him. He turned to the body in the coffin and said more softly, 'You should have said – poor poor girl!' He shook his head sadly and incanted some lines of poetry.

'Slaughtered youth, for here lies Juliet
And her beauty makes this vault a feasting presence
full of light.

'There she is without a memory, without an identity, only a body that will be eaten by worms. Nothing will remain of her but a skeleton and even that will disappear and become nothing but dust. In twenty years no one will remember her. Like the wind she came; she laughed, she sighed, she disappeared. What remains right now is the art of the embalmer and the priest who will chant a few words in Latin. Some tears will be shed and then the memory will fade away as a flower picked two days ago and now tossed into the compost. Perhaps you can now really appreciate the art that transforms her for a last glimpse into – what was it you said – a child of Paradise.'

Sarah remained speechless, chilled to the bone by his incantatory recitation as if he were composing a lamentation, a poem of being and non-being. Not to believe in anything, not to believe in the hereafter; why was she attracted to this monster? Yet she sensed in him a familiar, even friendly spirit, lonely and rejected as her own. He held the fascination for her of the fair Lucifer who defied the world, rejected all ties whether human or divine; he had sunk into a despair far deeper than her own. He belonged to the homeless ones who had turned away from tradition and beliefs of their elders; there was nothing for him to hold on to – neither honour, nor virtue, nor faith, only the courage of defiance. She determined to dispel the darkness in him with the light of her own belief.

He mistook her silence and went on enthusiastically 'What a masterpiece! Master Gannal thinks the idea first came from seeing bees perfectly preserved in honey. The Egyptians drained the body of its blood and then immersed it in honey. Incisions were made to hold the aromatic herbs and spices which were soaked in alcohol. This had been going on for ages until my boss discovered that a cheap aluminium salt preserves the body for six months and is more effective. Now that is a blessing for mankind – to make the transition from one state to the other tolerable, even enjoyable for the spectators. She is more beautiful in death than she was in life.'

Sarah's eyes turned in hypnotic curiosity to the rouged corpse, a rosy glow against the pale satin of the coffin and the long black hair, her interest suddenly absorbed in something she had not learned at the convent, nor in art school – something that no one had told her about.

'When will you let me see something, an autopsy? Will you let me see it?' She coaxed eagerly; he must feel that he would be conferring the greatest of favours upon her. Her eyes were now staring unflinchingly at the corpse as if searching for a clue to what was going on beyond the veil. He shook his head.

'You would faint away. Only those who can endure incisions and blood can become nurses. An autopsy is like an operation in surgery. You won't be able to stand it.'

Her voice became insistent. 'You must let me see it. A body is only a temporary tenant for the spirit. Why should I be afraid of what is done to the body? It is only clay. If you won't let me see it, you'll never see me again.'

The possibility alarmed him.

'But how? Monsieur Gannal would never permit it.'

'I will hide.'

'Where? Show me where you can hide.'

She pointed to the coffins against the wall. 'I can hide in one of those.'

'Are you crazy? You wouldn't dare.'

'I can dare anything, *quand même*.'

Hippolyte appraised her calmly and quietly. A bounding hope stirred in him – the pang of a desire he had given up the moment before. If she dared anything, she would not hold back a delight from him. Was it possible that she was not afraid – to make love? He studied her coldly, seeking the vulnerable spot that would disarm her. Suddenly her yearning to become a nun held a new meaning for him. It was not an escape from the world but a cry from her heart for a love that she could lavish boundlessly. What role should he play? The answer came in a nervous fit of coughing. He covered his mouth with a handkerchief, and coughed up again, hardly able to catch his breath.

Sarah's maternal instinct stirred once again.

'Hippolyte, are you ill? You never told me. Poor, poor boy!'

Hippolyte swung back to his sardonic role as if to mock the weakness in his body, 'Yes, I am poor and my life will be short; I'm only an exile on this earth.' An unreal smile played over his lips to show his high scorn for the harsh role that Fate had assigned him. 'Perhaps I am different from others . . . destined to live in perpetual loneliness and anxiety. That may be the reason for my apprenticeship in a mortuary. I too, will be a slaughtered youth. I have no hope, and what can I hope from you? From what Olympian heights are you now pitying me?' His eyes glowed accusingly.

'I am praying for you. It always helped me.'

'Pray and be damned. You refuse me any real comfort.' His pitch lowered, '*Dame d'amour*, you're a witch, you fire my blood. I envy the men who can dance with you freely, caress you, while I must steal a few furtive glances in this ghastly room, where instead of attar of roses, odours of death insinuate themselves into everything. You will sell yourself to a greedy bourgeois and feast at the banquet tables whilst I, because I haven't a sou, though I love you more than life . . .' he began to cough again and covered his mouth with a rigid hand. Sarah's heart went out in sympathy, the parallel image of the rejected ones – he and she – stamped itself once more as a bond between them.

Just then the doorbell tinkled. Hippolyte turned pale as death.

'Not Monsieur Gannal, dear lord! He said he wasn't coming back.'

He peered through the door of the back room and confirmed his worst suspicions. Quickly, he replaced the lid of the girl's coffin and whispered desperately to Sarah, 'Be very quiet. I'll lose my job if he finds you here! Quick! Quick!'

He opened up an empty coffin, 'Please, please, lie here. It won't be for long and you will save me.'

Sarah shrank back but his face pleaded so pitifully, she pulled herself together and climbed in; *quand même*. Hippolyte replaced the cover loosely to allow for air.

Gannal came in breathless with haste as he called out orders to his apprentice, 'Everything is arranged for the Count's funeral. Has the sculptor been here yet?'

'No, Monsieur Gannal. No one.' He dropped his voice and busied himself stirring a mortar-pestle furiously. Gannal clucked his disappointment, 'Then he won't come till after six. I must see to ordering flowers; I might as well order the engraved invitations as well.' He looked about to see if all was in order, opened the lid of the coffin in which the corpse of the girl rested and peered closely. Satisfied, he replaced the cover and then observed the slightly open cover of Sarah's coffin. He was about to peer in when Hippolyte nervously distracted him by holding up a vial and asking, 'The precipitate takes a long time coming.' Gannal pushed the coffin lid to close it tightly and took the vial from Hippolyte's hand to examine it. 'You should add more bichloride of mercury,' he said and proceeded to leave with a last instruction to fill a glass bottle with alcohol from the five gallon canister.

When he closed the door after him, the bell tinkled again

as if to signal the end of the alarm for Hippolyte. He was in a sweat of apprehension and filled a glass with a solution of wine and tincture of hashish. He swallowed some and looking at Sarah's coffin, abruptly decided to fill the glass again. Opening the lid of the coffin, he found Sarah almost asphyxiated, and gasping for breath. He lifted her up to a sitting position and held the glass to her mouth.

'Drink this quickly. It will revive you.'

Sarah gulped down the draught and sank back into the coffin more dead than alive, to regain the energy exhausted by her shocking experience.

When Sarah first lay in the darkness of the coffin, she had shut her eyes tight, exerting all her will not to shriek. Her slim fingers found the crucifix on her throat. A clammy perspiration covered her entire body, the same nauseating horror she felt in her childhood nightmares when she had first entered the convent, and the bliss that followed – the enfolding arms of Mother St Sophie – the compassion glowing tenderly in the eyes of the communicant who called her 'my lamb'.

The nightmares continued. She would sit bolt upright after these frightening dreams, soaked through with perspiration and shrieking at the top of her voice. Her dormitory mates mimicked her outcries and then hurled themselves upon her, pummelling her, pulling her hair and shouting.

Over and over again the nuns complained that 'this one contaminated child was undoing all their discipline and order'. Mother St Sophie took it upon herself to cure 'the possessed one'. Sarah learned about God's tender loving care. She need only to pray and He would radiate his healing power and make her whole. How often had she recited the memorised lines of the Canticle of Canticles.

Together on her knees with the Mother Superior, she would recite the dialogue of the love of Christ, 'My sweet daughter, my daughter, my beloved, my temple, love me, for I love you much, much more than you are able to love me. O my God, if you would make the most sensual of women feel what I feel they would quickly forsake their false pleasures of the flesh for the enjoyment of so true a good.'

In the sepulchral darkness, Sarah clung to the image of her spiritual teacher, who showed her how life is surrounded by mysteries. Somewhere in the world of darkness, unseen by mortal eyes, was the radiant world of the saints worshipping and adoring Christ and the Mother of God. Death held no terror; on the contrary, a marvellous rebirth.

The Mother Superior would be looking for her to take her by the hand and lead her over the flowery meadows to the shining celestial city. And when Sarah left the convent, her parting words were engraved upon her heart.

'Be at peace with God, whatever you conceive Him to be, and whatever your labours and aspirations; in the noisy confusion of life, keep peace with your soul.'

Ah, those happy years at the convent, the only place where she found kindred souls; what though she was only an anonymous number 32. The numerals were embroidered next to her initials on each article of her personal wardrobe as symbols of honour. The nuns never wearied of telling her they had no identity and no desire for worldly pleasures; they had no hope of marriage and children. Their destiny was to prepare themselves for their Heavenly Bridegroom. Someday, they prayed, Sarah herself would take on a new name, wear a wedding ring and pledge devotion to the One Spirit.

Her images grew and became more vivified. She was lying prone on the ground, covered with a heavy, black cloth. Four candles in massive candlesticks burned steadily sombrely, at the four corners, while the pungent scent enveloped her like a fog. She accepted the mystery of dying in all its shadowy tremors and expectancy but without the nightmare terror of her previous dreams.

Another episode of the past flashed before her. She had lent her doll to a classmate who dropped it and broke the china head. Trembling with anguish she cried out 'Papa is dead.' She had secretly worshipped her handsome father who saw her only in intervals of years but who had solemnly promised he would return from his travels and then take her everywhere with him to see how beautiful the world really is.

Julie learned of the dream and soon after came the fatal news. It had seemed to her mother that Sarah possessed unholy powers which further alienated her from her child. The child herself became fearful of her extraordinary revelations.

Perhaps she had the power to have a glimpse of Paradise? Sometimes she thought she saw it under the ghostly light of the candles which gave a luminous transparency to the faces of the nuns and the children chanting around them. The Convent itself became a haven that brought her peace, . . . a peace she never knew before, a peace she yearned to have again. But a true glimpse of Heaven would come to her, she was promised, only at the transition of death into the second life. She had fallen in love with death that promised so much ecstasy. If only she could die now and see the apparition of her beloved Mother Superior holding out her welcoming arms to her.

Sarah became aware of the murmurs of voices. Hippolyte was still talking to his master. Suddenly the slightly opened coffin-lid was clamped down tightly over her. She suppressed a cry of fear. Now she was completely cut off. She had entered the Shadow of the Valley of Death. The very silence shrieked. She was one of the dead. Seconds ticked by but the darkness revealed no more visions. Fear gripped her again and she shook with terror. Compulsively she pushed up the cover an inch and gulped for breath. She could hear Gannal stalking out and the tinkle of the doorbell when he left.

Hippolyte quickly lifted the lid, helped her to sit up, and stared down in alarm at the chalk-white face. She drank the glass of wine he had placed against her lips. A deep sense of relief brought back the first slight flush to her face. A strange lethargy overcame her.

'How brave you are,' Hippolyte was murmuring, lost in admiration. 'And how beautiful!' Seeing her in an entranced lethargy, he waited for her to recover. His hand strayed to her hair and his fingers combed gently through it. Under

31

the spell, he began to recite a poem almost under his breath.
As if from a distance, Sarah became aware of the words:

> Come to my arms . . .
> For I would plunge my fingers in your mane
> And be a long time unremembering –
> And bury myself in you –
> Lavish without shame caresses upon your body
> Glowing and dark.
> Forgetfulness lies indolent on your red mouth
> And the flowing Lethe is in your kiss.

'The words are lovely,' Sarah murmured drowsily. 'Are they yours?'

'I wish they were. But they belong to all lovers after Baudelaire wrote them. Priceless, isn't it . . . and to think the police confiscated the entire edition. There's not a copy of the *Fleurs du Mal* to be found in any shop. I bought one just in time – it's yours – if you want it.'

Sarah was in the grip of the drug and she hardly heard him. She moved languidly in the yielding softness of the coffin cushioning, 'If only my dreams were to come true, as St Sophie promised,' she whispered.

Hippolyte sensed in her a seductive woman who secretly wanted to be ravished. The mystical aura deepened and like a great magnet drew the helpless young girl to itself and Hippolyte with her. Sarah continued as in a trance:

'I feel my life depends on going to sleep. Would you – you know what I mean? Drink the vial that Romeo and Juliet drank?'

Hippolyte wondered if he heard aright. 'Do you mean – but why – why – you of all people with so much to live for?'

Sarah's eyes lost their drowsy look and confronted the eyes that looked down at her, this time so very close. Hippolyte found himself irresistibly approaching her lips. She was saying: 'What is there in this world to match the bliss of being with the Lord. I feel so near to Him, like St Therese of the Cross. She too felt the pain of His love penetrating

32

deep into her body as if He had pierced her with a long golden arrow.'

Hippolyte was speechless . . . as their eyes held and held.

Caught off guard, her concern for him dissolved into a physical hunger that rose to an excruciatingly white heat. She found herself heavy and torpid in his arms, helpless to resist. In her veins, she felt the life and sap and gladness of the world rising like an intoxication. The misery and loneliness of his soul twisted through her mind, meeting and mingling with her own despair.

He was breathless; beside himself. Nothing else mattered. She made little sounds with her breath, low moans. She called to him as if to protect him from the demons that lusted for his body.

They lay nestled together in silence. Her mind had become a blank. Slowly it awakened to reality. She stared at a Hippolyte who radiated gratitude with a tinge of triumph – a fisherman who had cast his line skilfully and had caught an angel fish; no common creature this one from the connoisseur's pond. Thoughts of dying and death had completely evaporated from his mind. But Sarah had become aware of a gnawing guilt, an undercurrent which had begun a slow torture.

The angel fish, now plucked out of the water of innocence was pathetically losing its iridescence. She nervously smoothed her clothes with methodical strokes. She fixed her hair in the one small mirror of the room and saw a flushed, shamed face made all the more vivid by the enlarged luminous eyes.

He peered at the reflection over her shoulder and wrapped his arms round her waist. Baudelaire's words again filled the void :

> Dame d'Amours, you're a witch. You fire my blood.
> Your health is radiant, infinite.
> Superb! When you go down the street
> Each mournful passer-by you meet
> Is dazzled by the blaze of it!

The flattery this time echoed hollowly in Sarah's ears. It flashed upon her that Hippolyte was at bottom an actor. Believing nothing, he could believe everything; not knowing where his vagrant fancy would turn next, he played his roles convincingly. There was an emptiness in the pit of her stomach. A feeling of having been cheated rose in her. She spoke harshly to puncture his bubble of invincibility.

'Your Baudelaire must be sickly, or he wouldn't be dazzled by a healthy girl. The words might fit my aunt or my sisters. I know I'm plain.' Her last words dropped flat. Reality had come back harshly.

'You surely can't believe that! There's something about you that inspires lust, and I mean that as a compliment.'

In the mirror, Sarah's eyes turned upon herself accusingly. The fallen woman – like her mother! She wanted to shrink, to become a worm and crawl out under the door-slit; to crawl away unseen to a swampy pool near the foot of the birch tree at the end of the Convent grounds. There, when desolation overwhelmed her, she would spend her passion in sobbing. Then, limp as a wet leaf she would fall into a stupor and stare into space through the lacy branches until at last she was missed and someone was sent to bring her back to the warmth of humanity.

She grasped the crucifix hanging round her neck and repeated a prayer under her breath. Someone would come to fetch her back to the lost innocence. Everything the devil does, God soon turns to His own purposes.

Firmly, she disengaged herself from Hippolyte's embraces. She recalled that her mother had been taking Dr Olliffe's pearls; the gelatine beads held a trace of arsenic, stimulated the heart and brought a quick sense of well-being which however, was not long sustained. Her mother now believed that the use of the pills, instead of lengthening life as the doctor claimed, shortened it. Hippolyte too, had been feeding her poison with his diabolic cunning. She was fighting back tears and using all her resources to prevent him seeing it. She snatched her portfolio and fled to the door.

34

As it slammed behind her, she had one quick glimpse of Hippolyte, who stood rooted in dismay; his face frozen in bewildered incomprehension, knowing she had fled never to return.

2

The Reluctant Debutante

Sarah had walked home with laggard steps, trying to tranquillise the seething cauldron of her mind. She had been transformed into a woman too unexpectedly, had stumbled into a trap unwittingly and had climbed out bemired and confounded. Sex and death were to become curiously commingled in her mind as though one were impossible without the other. There was no doubt however, that the experience had awakened a sleeping monster within her. She was aware now what men wanted and something deep within her rebelled against a physical appetite that was no different from animal desire. The Bridegroom of her dreams had now become infinitely more desirable. No one must know what had happened. God alone was capable of understanding and forgiving.

Mlle de Brabender was waiting to let her in that late afternoon and led her quickly to her room. Weariness and exhaustion suddenly came in a flood and Sarah dropped heavily on her bed, sinking into her downy quilt without a word. The nun, fearing that her charge was down with a fever quickly peeled off her clothes and shoes, deftly twisting and turning her while she removed the garments. All the while murmuring prayers, she put each piece in its proper place, then sat near the bed and began to rub Sarah's feet between her palms. Sarah sighed deeply and drowsed off into sleep.

When she awoke an hour later she was ravenously hungry. Marguerite the cook, anticipating the 'odd one's' habits had prepared a tray which the nun brought and placed before Sarah, while filling in the events of the day to make small talk. Having satisfied her hunger, Sarah was more cheerful. Now the nun closed her eyes and clasped her hands over her breviary.

'My dear, I have something serious to discuss with you. I have been chosen to speak ... about your future.'

Sarah nodded absently, her face taking on a cast of gloomy resignation, 'Ah yes, marriage ... Mother can think of no future for me except marriage.'

A muffling of squeals was heard in the kitchen; a hand had been clapped on Regina's mouth to keep her from calling to her sister Sarah, and interrupting the moment of preparation, so important to the scheme of things.

Mademoiselle fussed with the folds of her dress.

'I still feel you would make a perfect nun; the Lord has given you a mystical nature and a sweet voice, but it seems the entire family is set against it. We must face our duty as it lies before us, mustn't we dear? New wonderful plans have been made for you.'

'So that's it,' Sarah reproached the nun. 'So you too, along with the rest, now think marriage is best for me.'

'*Alors*, you must realise how delicate you are, the sudden fevers; you fall ill far too frequently. Were it not for the special foods prepared for you, since you can't eat meat which you detest, you would surely become an invalid. You are surely intelligent enough to agree that the future might be most painful unless you have the service and comforts which an advantageous marriage can bring you. Now listen carefully; there's more to it than just this; there's a wonderful surprise for you tonight. How fortunate you are. There is one who knows of you and admires you.'

The nun paused to let her words sink in. Sarah was silently disdainful. Another man! Was there a man alive who could even approach the matchless grace of the Christ? Mademoiselle's eyes were shining. In her heart rang a triumph : she suddenly realised God had entrusted her with a task whereby the weakness of the flesh might be turned to do His Will.

'Darling, you are to meet a young man, a real prince, at the party tonight. Do you realise what it means to be married into one of the great families of Europe? You will live in a palace, wear gold satin slippers; twenty attendants

will serve your slightest wish. And most important of all –
you'll be able to do as you please and no one shall order
you to do anything which you do not want to do. And I
know you'll find your greatest joy in driving your own
carriage everyday to the Convent, there to spend as much
time as you please.'

The prospect was too dazzling to be taken in all at once.
Was it real? Mademoiselle went blithely on adding even
more enticements:

'Think of the example you will set for the many girls
growing up in the convent. Remember, like you, many of
them feel unloved and abandoned. What hope you will
bring to them! You will be their model: a lonely child who
grew up to be married to a prince! And yet, in spite of
position and wealth, you care enough and are modest
enough to visit them, bringing them gifts and courage. God
will reward their faith as He is surely rewarding you now.'

Sarah agreed to be dressed and presented. The nun's
prayers would give her the strength and confidence to carry
off the role that would delight her mother. But this time,
Sarah knew she could not confide in the nun.

How easily Satan can corrupt the devout souls. He need
only display a prince and unlimited wealth to have the
mademoiselle become excited over worldly success.

Mademoiselle assured her of the virtuous road she was
taking, removed the tray and brought chocolate, steaming
hot on an exquisite Limoges tray set with its matching
pitcher and cups. Elated over her victory, the nun hastened
to tell Julie.

Tante Rosine had come early expressly to help Sarah
choose the most becoming gown. Only that afternoon she
had called for them herself just to be sure all would be in
order. A white Alençon lace over a gold satin slip which
made her look childish; a striped Biedermeyer in the
Empress Eugénie mode which gave her a stiff look; and
lastly, a soft pearl embroidered satin sheath. Of the three,
it was decided she looked best in the last – the sky-blue
sheath which the dressmaker, under Rosine's instructions,

had cleverly padded at the bosom and hips to enhance the youthful slenderness of its wearer. Tracings of seed pearls in artful outline did wonders in giving the illusion of curves while the heavily encrusted hemline gave it the elegance of a royal presentation gown. She wore her first high heel slippers, embroidered with the same pearls in rosettes.

Rosine's fine hand at make-up and a hairdresser who knew how to please a curly-haired fifteen-year-old did the rest. Julie hung a double strand of pink tinted pearls with a diamond clasp round Sarah's white throat, and like the fairy godmother, touched with magic perfume the dimples in her elbows and behind the ears and thus, armed by her mother and aunt, Sarah seemed one with the candour and exquisiteness of the flowers in the Louis XV salon : a flower tempting enough to be plucked by a prince.

Giddy with the fabulous opportunity Julie splurged extravagantly, not only for special gowns, but went into debt to redecorate her duplex apartment. Sofas, chairs and footstools were recovered with Beauvais tapestry to match the sumptuous window draperies. Such bibelots of the period as jewelled snuff boxes, Meissen and Limoges figurines, and marble pedestals with Greek statues shone and glinted under the lights of candelabras refracted by massive crystal chandeliers. Julie's gown, modelled after the classic figurines, displayed a marble-white bosom, nestled in folds of sheer rose velvet, a marvel of the weaver's art. As a final touch, the rarest of flowers graced new vases from China and Dresden. Only then was Julie satisfied that the setting was worthy of a prince.

Count de Morny did not bother to reveal to Julie the nature of his own machinations. He was too much a realist to believe that a prince would marry a commoner. He would have to make use of the prince to bait his trap. The prince was one of his cronies and Morny knew that he would not turn down such a *bon-bon* as a pretty fifteen-year-old virgin just ripe for the plucking.

The real *pièce de résistance* for Morny was Marcel Bombois, the fabulously wealthy planter from Martinique, owner of vast plantations, where yearly holidays to Paris had set a standard for orgies to equal the libertines of ancient Rome. Morny simply suggested to Bombois that he take back to Martinique a certain ripe virgin as a bride. The planter would be rewarded with the monopoly of providing the vast French army with enough sugar for its needs. The deal could earn millions for Bombois who would discreetly hand over one million francs to his benefactor. Morny revealed his personal interest. He wanted to save the fifteen-year-old daughter of his mistress from the dismal fate of becoming a nun. The understanding was consummated with a handshake.

As Morny once said of himself while smoking a panatella, 'he always placed himself at the side of the broomhandle.' The planter would sweep Sarah into his lair, while Morny pocketed the sweepings of gold. It was a typical scheme for Morny who had made a career out of his one goal of enriching himself. His greatest success of course was the *coup d'état* he had engineered for his brother. He had persuaded Louis Napoleon that it was destined to succeed. 'Constitutions are too subtle for the peasant who believes only in what he can see and hear. There are millions who desire nothing better than to shout "*vive l'Empereur*". The masses need something tangible round which to rally and the standard of Napoleon is the only one there is.'

The *coup d'état* was simple enough, but Morny craftily prepared himself for the inevitable fighting that would break out three days after. He exiled the leaders of democracy with a twenty-four hour notice. Those who failed to flee met with fatal 'accidents'. While Louis Napoleon nervously chain-smoked packs of cigarettes, Morny's secret police-actions made France safe for the Emperor and inaugurated the age of unprincipled, cynical, pleasure-loving dandies.

Louis Napoleon rewarded his half-brother by making

him ambassador to Russia. When Morny failed to take with him his mistress, Madame le Han, a banker's daughter who had loaned him millions, she said bitterly 'I found him a sub-lieutenant and left him an ambassador.' Morny went on to his next *coup* returning to France with a bride and a fantastic dowry from the Czar. The fact that she turned out to have the tempers, whims, and caprices of a child did not disturb his unruffled calm. He found solace in Hortense Schneider, a famous actress, and in Julie Bernard who worshipped him. All important to Morny was that his actions should bring financial reward. He had already acquired twelve millions in gilt-edged bonds for his children. Thus, his imagination appreciated the chance of a million more francs for himself on so innocent an occasion as a débutante party for Sarah.

Julie, of course, was overwhelmed that an illustrious scion of royalty had been invited to meet her daughter. She had no doubt now that temperamental Sarah could thus be transformed into the tame pigeon eating from the hand of a prince. Julie of course, was certain that she herself would be the recipient of a deed to a baronial estate. Here was security heaped to overflowing for herself and her daughters. Julie's eyes were shining with anticipation as she greeted her distinguished guests with Morny at her side. It was to be the triumphal evening of her career.

When the time was ripe to fetch the débutante, Morny, immaculate in his evening blue-black, climbed the stairs to Sarah's room. He bowed to the lovely vision and said, 'I hardly know you Mlle Bernard. We are proud of you. You'll be a great success. It is possible we may have to bow to you as, *la Princesse*.'

Count de Morny had the veiled look of a man accustomed to hiding his real feelings and Sarah felt the unnerving coldness in his glance. In spite of her composure she experienced an inner chill. His manners however, were so charming, it was difficult to imagine him as the incarnation of the arch fiend. Morny hooked his elbow and Sarah rested her hand on his arm. She was gloved in the finest of silk kid, opera length, against which her jewelled bracelets, lent by Aunt Rosine, glittered in splendour. With a glazed look Sarah walked down the stairs, through the mirrored rug-cushioned corridor, to enter the brilliantly lit salon where the guests were already imbibing wine from crystal goblets amidst the hub-hub of conversation.

The voices perceptibly stilled when Sarah entered. Lorgnettes were raised to stare at her. Morny introduced her to the group nearest the entrance. As he rattled off such famous names as Dumas *père*, Delacroix and George Sand, Sarah held out her gloved hand as she had been instructed, nodded and smiled. But panic gripped her when George Sand kissed her on both cheeks and whispered her wish to have a nice chat with her later in the evening. It was difficult to believe that this diminutive woman was the famous author of *Lelia*. Only the tremendous eyes with their searching gaze and the luminous black of her hair suggested uncommon powers. Looking into her eyes, Sarah was drawn to her; the eyes had the kindly compassion and understanding of Mother St Sophie. And yet the Mother Superior would never permit her to read the words of an author who was on the 'forbidden' list for Catholics.

The confusion of these contradictory thoughts made Sarah uneasy as she made the tour of the salon, mechanically smiling and raising her hand to be kissed. When she reached the group surrounding the august presence of the prince, Morny introduced him with elaborate decorum speaking in glowing terms of his illustrious grandfather, the Grand Master of the Congress of Vienna and famous in literary history as the patron of Casanova and his companion in amorous exploits. The innuendo was lost on her; she forgot to curtsy and only offered him her hand to be kissed. The signal had been given and the musicians struck up a polka.

The prince circled her waist with his arm, and without asking permission, swept her off to orbit within the narrow circle. The dancing couples stepped aside in deference to royalty. The prince held her tightly, his faced turned to hers, gazing disconcertingly into her eyes whenever she looked up. He whispered, 'You are as light as a feather. I could dance with you all night.'

She was conscious of the numerous lorgnettes that were concentrated upon them. The prince was an expert dancer and it was exhilarating to be whirled about. It helped unwind the high tension she always felt when she had to pretend. In contrast, the prince was completely relaxed and when she glanced up at him, she caught the half-lidded eyes that were appraising her appreciatively as if he were stripping her for his bedroom. She hesitated to reply.

The bland, good-looking prince, believing that Count de Morny had tutored Sarah in the role she was to play, began speaking to her in the confidential manner of a fellow conspirator. Her modest maidenly air; the expectant trustful attitude of the inexperienced girl did not fool him. When he began telling her about the *fêtes galantes* of his châteaux in Belgium, he felt no need to conceal the bawdy side of it. He had persuaded the judges to give the first masquerade prize to the Duchess of Chambrun whose seven diaphanous veils barely concealed an Eve in iridescent flame colours.

'I can't imagine anything more daring, can you? What kind of masquerade would you prefer?'

The question took her by surprise, but she recognised instantly that the débutante of the party was mistaken for a demi-mondaine – a true child of Morny's mistress. She was not even the wild fox which required skill and horsemanship to be hunted down. She had been tamed, powdered, painted, dressed to be served up as the *pièce de résistance* in a banquet to honour the prince. He was making a pretence of trying to win her favour, knowing all the while that she would be his by right of *seigneur*. The only thing that remained was to haggle over the price.

She found herself enjoying the whirling motion and nodded, but she could not look in his eyes. They were the half-lidded sensual eyes she had caught in Hippolyte when he looked at her with a side glance. The prince was a good dancer and since she did not know what to say, he kept up a bland patter of conversation as if dancing were incidental. He was describing a masquerade party at his ancestral estate in Belgium and spoke of the lack of originality in the costumes – the same pierrots and pierettes, the same glitter of Versailles court dress, the same shepherds and shepherdesses – infinitely boring! It would have been far more pleasant if he could have danced with his present partner.

The music stopped and the prince waited for it to recommence, continuing his monologue as if to make her feel at ease by a soothing flow of conversation. Sarah looked about her and noticed Rosine and Julie kissing each other in mutual congratulations for their success with Sarah. Her mother, in fact wafted a melting glance of approval at her daughter and suddenly, inside Sarah something snapped.

To be a lovely plaything for the prince was all that her mother desired. But she was conscious of being a person and to desire for herself all that that implied, independence, freedom, the right to happiness and the right to be herself – just as the prince did. She began to sense an undercurrent of hostility towards him simply because of his privileges; his easy assumption that the pleasures of life were his due by right of his royal blood. Beneath that façade was a human being like herself who could suffer pain and humiliation the way she did. She despised the hypocrisy of the role she was playing: the shy young virginal girl bedazzled by a prince. She would reverse that role. She was no longer a girl, she was a woman; she was the despised harlot who expected nothing from society and could do as she pleased. The thought of playing such a role shattered the stifling ennui that had been paralysing her. She had been encased in her evening gown like a sheathed slave, capable only of mechanical gestures and polite phrases; held up for exhibition, lacquered into immobility, to be sold to the highest bidder. She tossed her head defiantly and stared boldly into his eyes. The music started again and this time he was waltzing with her.

She had promised her mother to be 'nice' to the prince, but her gorge rose at the smiling face and the white teeth that had nibbled so daintily at the banquet table of life, all his life. Was there ever a time when his slightest wish had not been fulfilled? The yawning gap of her own misery would forever separate them. She became conscious that there was only one guest at the party who could ever understand her and she recalled the penetrating scrutiny of George Sand that seemed to read her heart. It gave her courage to drop the role that was betraying her sex. She would be the schoolgirl no longer. Hippolyte had sprung a trap and she was alert now to the designs and stratagems of men. No one would ever get their hooks into her again – not her mother, nor Count de Morny, nor the Prince de Ligne.

'Do I need a masquerade?' she replied flippantly. 'I can come as myself without a disguise. Oh, that would really make them notice me.' There was a hard glint in her eyes now and she stared boldly into his. The transformation startled him. The soft, shy, virginal look had become something hard and glittering. It roused him into a deepening interest. The prince shook his head and pretended to frown.

'Oh no, that would be against all the rules. It would arouse too much anger.'

'And why?' Sarah shot back. 'Because no woman dares show herself as she really is. They all have to pretend to be what they are not – all the time.'

How stupid of the prince to lump all women under the same category. She shot a hostile glance at him. She would take him off his high horse and be rid of him. She felt the pressure of his hand holding her more tightly. He lowered his voice to whisper into her ear '*Sans doute*, I'll invite you to my next *bal masqué* if you'll tell me what disguise you'll wear'.

'How would you like to see me covered in a snake skin and invoking blasphemies?'

He looked puzzled. She went on to say, 'Since I have to choose a masquerade, I would dress myself as Lilith, who persuaded Eve to eat the apple. Lilith was a snake, of course.'

The prince showed his bright teeth in a delightful smile.

'I'll see to it that you win a necklace of gems – what a stunning idea! *Ma foi*, you fooled me completely. You're an interesting young lady – probably Lilith herself! I'm sure you can persuade me to eat the apple. Do I need your mother's permission to call on you or can we meet at the Café de Palais Royal for an ice?'

She felt a pang of triumph – to have a secret rendezvous with a prince – her classmates would never believe it. Then recalling her resolve to humiliate him, she froze up.

'Since you think it depends on my mother – you know very well she will be honoured.'

'And you?'

'I will have to think about it.'

The music stopped. 'May I have the next dance?' the prince asked eagerly.

'I'm sorry. I am committed to so many others. Thank you for the invitation.'

She curtsied and left him abruptly, dangling like a fool. Her face was flushed. She had succeeded better than she had imagined and a sense of her own power surged up in her. Other men would be collecting around her like bees to a honey pot. She would flirt outrageously with them all. Prince Popinjay would squirm with jealousy.

She took her place beside her mother and Rosine, who were all agog to hear what she had to say. She felt the sweet compulsion to speak of her triumph : 'He invited me to his château for the Easter holiday,' she said loftily as if it were a mere bagatelle. The effect was sensational. Julie was in ecstasy. She threw motherly arms about her and kissed her fervently. 'How simply wonderful! Did he ask you to dance with him again?'

Sarah stiffened. She could earn her mother's love only if she gave herself completely to a man who would use her only for his pleasure. She resumed her lofty tone. 'He wanted to, of course, but I should like to dance with some others.'

Rosine's face was frozen with shock. She spluttered out her outrage.

46

'What have you done? One never turns down a prince? How stupid can you be? It is never done!'

'*Quand même.* I am doing it.' There was defiance in her words. 'Despite everything!' The words were stamped on her stationery. She had first used the words at the age of seven when she had jumped across a creek and fallen into the water. But *quand même*, she did get across. At the age of nine she jumped from a second storey window just as her Aunt Rosine was entering her carriage after saying goodbye to her. She had wanted Aunt Rosine to take her back home, back to her mother, who had left her with strangers. In the fall, she had broken her foot, but *quand même*, Rosine had to take her away. She had been expelled three times from the Convent for breaking rules, but *quand même*, she was brought back and finally made the nuns accept her on her own terms. Despite their black garb, the nuns were sweet and loving, and had hearts that had not turned to stone, unlike those at the party. If her mother or her Aunt Rosine insisted upon having their way, *quand même*, she would become a nun herself, far away from the false life of 'gay' society.

Julie moaned and muttered to her sister: 'She will ruin everything.' She stood up abruptly and walked over to the group that was surrounding Count de Morny. He was the only one who might save her daughter from folly. Beckoning him from the group, she managed to whisper a few words about the dangerous turn that Sarah had taken.

Count de Morny with his usual consummate skill in public relations, had prepared himself for such as emergency. Marcel Bambois, the planter from Martinique, had just arrived – in the nick of time, it seemed. After all, Morny had only meant to use the prince as a decoy, albeit a gilded one. The dividends would have to come from Bambois. The count hastened to bring the swarthy plantation owner to Sarah. He whispered some last minute instructions to Bambois, warning him that Sarah had a combustible nature that could explode for the slightest reason. He was to mix his cocktail with a bitter dash of religion, the piquant flavour of exoticism, and a good stiff measure of passion with a suggestion that he was prepared to lay his entire fortune before the feet of the beloved.

Morny congratulated Sarah on the good impression she had made on the prince. 'I hear you would like to dance with some others. May I introduce Marcel Bambois who has just arrived from Martinique and who has asked me to introduce him.'

Sarah smiled artificially as she extended her hand, barely concealing her distaste for the huge swarthy man that loomed over her. His lacquered greying hair was parted in the centre; his coarse sensual mouth seemed to be made of rubber. When he smiled, the thick upper lip stretched the straggling moustache above it. But what mattered the looks of a man if she could snub that conceited coxcomb of a prince. From the corner of her eye she could see him in animated conversation with his admirers, dribbling and joking around him. She had not failed to notice though, that from time to time he shot a quick glance in her direction. She would dance with a buffoon if necessary, to puncture the vanity and invincible smugness of his Highness.

As the band struck up again, she accepted the invitation of Monsieur Bambois to dance, but he had less interest for her than the prince for whom she found herself looking about to locate.

'I have been told you have a great interest in matters of religion – a dedication I admire immensely. How the world needs the soft ministering hands of the angel of mercy.'

The man from the French colonies had a flowery way of talking she thought surprising in one who had lived among the savages. She had to answer and so she replied mechanically,

'If I were worthy of being a nun, I might devote my life to missionary work.'

'What a waste of loveliness,' he said 'and yet my island of Martinique, beautiful as it is, is badly in need of an angel who can convert the people from practising the devil's art.'

Sarah saw the prince dancing with another and caught

48

the glance that he shot at her. It was a look of reproach. She was sure of it. She was making him squirm and she found a strange delight in it. 'The devil's art' Monsieur Bambois had said.

'Yes,' she said bitingly, 'the devil's art, they must practise it because they are unhappy.' She recalled a sentence that she had read in one of George Sand's novels and repeated it. ' "The corrupt and wealthy libertines are always ready to tempt the hungry and debauch the innocent" – and nobody cares, least of all a heartless, self-righteous society.'

Monsieur Bambois was startled by the phrases that smacked of a dangerous revolutionary spirit. And yet the girl in his arms was a picture of innocence and purity. Startled, he replied, 'Ah, you do not like life here in Paris. I would like it very much if you said you were unhappy here – then I could show you how beautiful Martinique is.'

'It's an island of black savages. You just said so.'

'Ah, you misunderstand, *chérie*. My island is so beautiful we call it – the Earthly Paradise. How can I describe it to you? Imagine a full moon in a violet sky. Impossible to sleep on such nights. Here, you say, the night falls. There – the night rises like an apparition. I do not know the words to say it. One must go there to see it. I have a castle near the top of a mountain. At sunset time I drop everything just to drink in the elixir of nature. I lie in my hammock and I can see the coastline darkening first. I have a mountain view and I see the gloom creeping up the heights – so slowly – not even a bottle of rum can give you that feeling. Even when the whole view turns deepest black, I can see the glow of the mountain peak like a candle in the darkness. The stars are bits of fire. It all steals into your soul – oh, words cannot describe it. It is well named Earthly Paradise. You must visit me sometime – yes, the Earthly Paradise, I will show it to you.'

His eyes rolled with ecstasy and in his excitement, he whirled her more giddily about the floor. Sarah could not help feeling intrigued. But even as she felt the desire to visit that mysterious island, the fear rose again that she was being trapped. Dark forebodings, never really absent from her mind, obtruded. Again she felt the pain of the rejected child, who saw her Aunt Rosine driving off without her. The faces of the other orbiting couples glowed with joy as their speeding feet barely touched the floor. She alone nursed that hidden misery, the terror of exile from home and family. Oh, she knew what those invitations meant – to castles in Belgium and Martinique! One of the sentences George Sand had written had burned itself into her. 'To marry without love is to serve a life sentence in the galleys.' Her mother wanted to turn her into a galley slave so as to assure herself of a supply of luxuries and a life of pleasure. 'No woman should allow herself to be used as a chattel.' She was being cheated out of love. She had permitted herself to be seduced because George Sand had whispered to her in one of her books, 'why should a woman remain chaste, while a man was free to wander at will and indulge in the coarse tastes of a libertine.'

Bambois whirled her so rapidly, Sarah had to clutch his collar to maintain her balance. Mistaking the gesture for an enticement, the libertine blood of the man flared up and he clutched her wildly, whispering hoarsely, 'Come to my island Paradise with me. You will be a queen over thousands. You will have everything your heart desires.' His lips brushed her cheek lightly. In the strength of his grip she was helpless to protest her feeling of outrage.

Fortunately, the music stopped after its last wild burst.

'Please,' he pleaded with her 'let me talk to you privately. Can we go somewhere now. When can I see you?' The butlers began circulating with silver trays of glasses filled with sparkling champagne punch. Bambois took one and passed it on to Sarah. He clinked her glass against his and swallowed it in one gulp. The excitement of the dance had wrapped his creole blood in a blaze of dark lightning. As she sipped her champagne, she noticed the prince approaching her with that smiling assurance of his, to ask her for the next dance.

It was the Prince de Ligne who had brought George Sand to Sarah's début. She was the banner head of those who dared to revolt against the institution of marriage which sanctioned a life of slavery for women, while it ignored her complaints. The prince frankly admitted to her that he was in love with love, and that he preferred women who were similarly inclined. He discovered, he said, that in every woman who is in love with love, there is, unknown to herself, something of the bawd. George Sand tolerated such talk from the very young because it brought her back to her salad days when she was the firebrand of her generation. In those divine years of youth, there was no fear on her part in being excessively frank. Her love affairs were trumpeted to the world in book after book.

But now that she was long past fifty, she treated her heart as aged libertines treated their bodies, hiding it behind a disguise of fresh paint and subterfuge, but since those halcyon days, she had seen that the road to freedom had been a way to ruin for too many women. She had travelled from certainty to doubt and become far more cautious about advocating unlimited freedom for the individual, whether male or female. And yet something about the débutante of the party brought back the itch to be friend, guide, and counsellor to the very young. She was watching for the opportune moment to have a chat with Sarah.

If Sarah's behaviour toward the Prince de Ligne was incomprehensible to Julie, Sarah herself found it difficult to explain her perverse mood. Some instinct within her – stronger than her will – drove her to fight a lone battle against all pressures that she believed were forcing her into a loveless marriage.

It was a battle against overwhelming odds, enough to drive her to despair. She was debating in her mind whether it might be best to be 'nice' as she had promised her mother, when her heart leaped on seeing George Sand standing before her. Ignoring Bambois and the approaching prince she moved towards her and thrust out both her hands. How she admired the woman who had succeeded in defying the male world, yet lived a woman's life, with love and children in the midst of it.

Madame Sand saw Julie's empty chair and seated herself, gripping Sarah's hand and drawing her down.

'I promised you a chat. You made a charming picture with the prince. I hope you are happy.' There was a questioning doubt in her voice. It's penetrating softness and sympathy opened the floodgates for Sarah. She burst out: 'I am so bored. I have always loved your books. If only I could live as free as your heroines lived. How vividly I imagined myself as Indiana, Lelia, and so many others.'

The famous author gripped Sarah's hand again appreciatively.

'I suspected you have the touch of the rebel in you. I always recognise an original. Evil is everywhere. It devours every human heart, and at your age, rebellion is natural, like breathing. Still, the hottest of us, when we grow older are inclined to preach resignation to our young. Get married, become a mother – as if it were the be-all and end-all in the life of a woman.' She lowered her voice and added: 'Do you feel you are being put on the auction block to be sold to the highest bidder?'

To hear her thoughts expressed in words comforted Sarah:

'You understand! I knew you would. You are the first one who can truly read my heart. I feel that I can tell you everything!'

As if echoing Sarah's feelings, George Sand sighed and said, 'What weariness to suffer in the struggle against venomous intrigues. But you may as well study and learn it well; all of life is saturated through with it.'

The only answer to this universal ill seemed a certainty to Sarah who wailed, 'I can't convince my mother I should become a nun. I am sure it would cure all my unhappiness – to be out of this evil world. I ask for so little.'

Madame Sand clasped her small hands together. They were hidden in the lace of her sleeve. The peace to be found in the resignation of the cloister? She shook her head and said slowly, 'I thought so too long ago, but I am not so sure now. I have found there is only one happiness in life – to love and to be loved.'

Eagerly, Sarah whispered.

'I love the Lord and I can become worthy to be loved by Him.'

George Sand felt a moment of embarrassment. She dared not tell the child that the novels Sarah loved were proscribed by the Church. She had become anti-clerical but not anti-religious.

'Sarah, my dear. I believe you are following a private impossible dream. I must warn you that later in life your beliefs of today might become sour with experience. Hope and expectations that cannot be realised create bitter feelings. God keep you from such suffering. If you busy yourself in a convent you might become contented, but you might wish that you had thrown yourself into challenging the world – the way a man does – without reservation.'

Sarah looked confused. What undertakings were permitted to woman? She could think of none. George Sand recognised her silence as doubt, and she went on persistently, to win over the neophyte to become a standard bearer of woman's liberation.

'I would like to see you become a "personage", a "banner". I sense an amazing energy in you. I can feel the fires within you that have to be released. They will die out if you bury yourself in a convent. Ah, those bitter ashes, how you will regret them! You will never stop feeling resentful and indignant. You will distrust and hate everybody. And when there is such perpetual hate, where in your heart will you find room to let the seeds of love grow into flowers? Then, oh then, you will have cursed yourself for not having listened to me.'

George Sand sensed she had gone too far, having permitted herself to be carried away by her eloquence. There she was – the preacher again – despite all the doubts about truth that had begun to shadow her speculations. She hastened to modify her outburst.

'And yet it might prove to be a happier fate for you than that of a married woman, who is forced to live a life of humility. As a married woman, no matter who you are, what you say, you can't win. If you are ignorant, you are despised. If you are learned, you are mocked. If you are unfaithful, you are branded by your neighbours, and yes, you can even be imprisoned, while your husband can indulge in the coarse tastes of a libertine. And there is no escape. Your freedom to divorce and marry again is non-existent. What a fate for most women!'

With startling abruptness Sarah jumped up, went up to Bambois and whispered:

'Come with me. We can skip the next dance. I know a place where we can talk.'

With Bambois holding her elbow, she passed the prince, offering him a proud, frosty smile, intended to tease and torment him. She led him into one of the smaller rooms stacked with coats and hats, where two chairs were available. It was a quiet sanctuary amidst the hubbub of voices and dance music. She was pleased with herself for having brushed off the prince so pointedly. Morny, who had been keeping one eye on her, was delighted. Sarah's exit with Bambois was most auspicious. He reported to Julie that Sarah's engagement announcement might come sooner than expected.

Amidst such intimate surroundings, Bambois, flushed with a sense of imminent victory, was soon transforming the chat into a whirlwind proposal.

'You are a woman after my heart, *Mademoiselle des yeux bleus* – so audacious, so *sportive* – a woman with spirit, someone I have been yearning for all my life. I beg you to marry me. No, don't give me an answer now. You must have time to think and I must talk. I offer you everything – my five thousand sugar cutters, my molasses mills, my ships, my castles. They are all yours. Come back with me to Martinique. You will be the queen of a domain. My people will love you. They will build statues of you – more than of the Queen of Heaven, more than of Josephine who was

54

born in our drowsy dream-isle, *les Trois Islets*. I will build the most beautiful chapel for you – all marble and gold.'

He kept on talking impetuously, not even noticing the shocked face of Sarah. It was the last thing she expected, so quickly did the thunderbolt come. Marry him? *Ma foi*, his face was repulsive. His huge hulk could crush her. How could she love such a madman? She raised a hand to check his onrushing flowery speech.

'But Monsieur Bambois, you don't understand. It is impossible. I don't even know you. We have just met.'

Bambois gestured her protest into the wind. He could see only a small girlish figure that ensured his entrée to the seats of power. He would sweep her with him into the inner Napoleonic circle.

'It's all been arranged, my kitten. Your mother, Count de Morny, gave us their blessing. Trust the wisdom of your elders. Rest assured. I am an *amant* who can satisfy!' The closed-in intimacy of the room aroused his libertine blood. How often had he been thrown the beautiful creole native girls under such circumstances. But he was in Paris and had to curb his compulsion.

'It's all been arranged!' Sarah burst out in hysterical laughter; her face was suddenly contorted with rage. 'How dare they! What am I, a piece of merchandise to be bought and sold? It's shameful. Do you take me for a fool? Once I was your wife, you would treat me as a servant. As for being my *amant*, I would merely be one of your concubines.'

She jumped up, intending to stalk out of the room. Bambois was on his feet even more quickly.

'Don't you know who I am?' he roared. 'You can't do this to me.' He gripped her and rained kisses on her neck and bosom. 'Let's slip away,' he whispered hoarsely, 'just the two of us. No one would miss us now.' She realised she had been playing a dangerous game with the two men and she became frightened. He was burning with desire and kept repeating, 'I am madly in love with you, my kitten. Let's dash off together. My carriage is waiting outside.' She felt his prickly moustache against her mouth.

55

Panic stricken, she bit his lip sharply and screamed. Bambois was shocked out of his maudlin state and he slapped the palm of his hand against her mouth to stifle her screams. Her freed hand clawed at his face, drawing blood. In her paroxysm of rage, she bit his fleshy palm savagely.

At this moment, the Count de Morny and Julie rushed in. Bambois released her. His face was bleeding and he covered the scratches with his handkerchief. Rising to his full ruffled dignity, he began ranting his suppressed rage against the two conspirators.

'What kind of a devil have you thrown at me? Do you call that – an innocent girl who wishes to become a nun? *Ma foi!* she is possessed by the devil. I know that type – only too well. There was one in the island who had dangerous powers and I ordered three hundred lashes and a bath of stinging brine. That's what *this* she-devil deserves.' He shook a finger at Sarah. 'You call her a ministering angel. Don't you know she is a devil in disguise. What she needs is a good lashing on her behind.'

He thrust his way out of the narrow room in high dudgeon with the air of a man whose honour has been affronted. Julie, with a strangled cry, raised her hand and slapped Sarah so hard that her daughter reeled and broke down in sobs. Moments later, strangling her sobs, she ran out and through the salon of dancers who stared at the débutante in embarrassed silence.

Sarah mounted the stairs and ran down the corridor like a demented being. When she reached her room, she flung herself on the bed face down. Here she gave full release to the violent sobbing which began to fill her mouth with blood. Catching sight of the blood-stained handkerchief, she cried out in her agony, 'Oh, let me die, dear Lord, please let me die!' Although she knew there was a history of tuberculosis in her family, this was the first time she had given it a thought.

Rosine, Mademoiselle de Brabender and Madame Guerard rushed into the room. On seeing them hovering over her and seeking to placate her, she jumped off the bed and with the energy of maniacal fury, pushed them out of the room, screaming: 'Get out, all of you. Get out. Leave me alone, do you hear, leave me alone.' They closed the door behind them so as not to let the guests hear the screaming.

Alone once more, Sarah dropped heavily on her bed and let her eyes stare vacantly at the ceiling. She became still as she plunged into a depth of hopelessness. Nothing remained but suicide or the convent. A mother who had rejected her, a father who had abandoned her. A world of men who were merciless tyrants. No matter what you do with them you rouse in them the beastly snarl and snap of wolves. A world of beings who are less than animals. Yes, it would have to be one or the other, suicide or the convent.

She became aware of footsteps. She gritted her teeth when the door opened. She was set to snarl at anyone, no matter how they might pretend to be kind. Then George Sand, her face sad and humble, dropped on her knees beside the bed and said softly:

'Because I have known your suffering, I know how to guide you out of it. Will you let me?'

All of Sarah's hatred and despair was dissolved in the few words of genuine love. She burst into tears and threw herself into the arms of Madame Sand who sat up on the bed and rocked her gently in silence to give her time to subdue the anguish. George Sand alone understood the agony of youth. Had she not experienced it herself? She recalled the tragedy of her own youth – the time when she had broken entirely with the world in which she had formerly moved. She had run out of her home, left her husband and moved to Paris. She remembered her first breath of freedom, when she had ceased to be a married slave. Dressed in boots, trousers, and redingote, what joy at last to actually play the heroines of her own creation in the masculine world. She was Lelia, the woman who craved pleasure even at the cost of eternal damnation. She was Indiana, the symbol of a woman whose passions had been suppressed by human law. She was the woman who would

57

pretend to love two lovers and belong to neither. She had butted her head blindly against all the make-believe conventions, daring to claim the right to live her life as she chose. She had proved to the world that the destiny of a woman need not be the slavish goal of pleasing a man. She proved that a woman had the same right as a man to independence, freedom, the right to happiness and the right to individual development.

Sarah's sobbing had subsided and George Sand was saying, 'How well I know your heart. I too had a disposition to melancholia at your age. I could not find the love in others that I was capable of giving. I too was in despair. My mind dwelt sometime in the cloister, sometime on suicide. Yes, at your age, even earlier, I embraced death passionately. My diary bears witness: "Oh enlighten me, Infinite Light. Why hast Thou permitted that from my tenderest age death has always appeared so beautiful and so attractive." But I made one mistake. I plunged into marriage simply to escape the torment. If I have serenity of mind now, it was gained only at the cost of much cruel experience. You are living in a more enlightened day. Your generation is swept by a desire for love. They know it is the only honourable way men and women can be united in marriage.

'Now, I know that the Prince de Ligne likes you. He told me so – yes, and despite your coldness towards him. Do not be surprised if he pursues you in the future. But the prince is only a few years older than you, still very young, and he doesn't know what he wants. He simply follows every vagrant fancy. Ah, my poor bewildered child, what can I say to you. I can only tell you to offer your untouched body and your innocent heart only to the man you love – only then will you attain a joy unparalleled.'

The words stabbed into Sarah's heart. Without knowing why, she blurted out, 'My body is not untouched. I have never confessed it.'

Madame Sand tightened her protective arm around her. 'I should have suspected it. You take after me. You are not a child of sin, but a true child of Nature.'

'You don't understand,' Sarah almost whispered. 'I did not love the man. I was overcome by curiosity.'

'I am glad you are confiding in me. Very few would understand and forgive. But I must warn you that if you have too many lovers, you will become like Marie Dorval. She's a marvellous actress and I love her. But she has a terrible weakness. She can never fall asleep unless there is a man at her side. Yes, I will repeat what she told me, for your good. One must not step aside from knowledge. She said, "Do you know, the older I grow, the more sure do I become that the only man one can really love is the man one does not respect." How she will continue to suffer. We should not lavish our greatest passion on weak souls who are dependent and forever whining about their fate. I am glad I broke away from such men. I chose men who were poor, it is true, but they were proud and independent.'

She stopped talking suddenly. She thought of her own daughter. She had used the same words to Solange. She had given Solange every advantage, every freedom. But she had seen Solange and other women commit themselves to sexual release only to meet catastrophe. She had seen them become alienated from family, friends, everyone. She had seen them develop the slouch of a drug addict. And yes, even her own daughter was beginning to strut like a prostitute. Solange had written her only the week before, threatening to step into a life of pleasure and vice. The letter she wrote back to her daughter was blunt and cruel, possibly too strong for Solange.

Just try being a prostitute! I do not think you would make much of a success of it. You haven't the skill to feign your passion, nor experience in the art of making yourself desirable. Men with money to spend want women who have learned how to earn it. The kind of knowledge you need, if it were told you, would make you feel physically sick.

There were dangers on the road to freedom and George Sand, at the age of fifty had become more cautious about sexual freedom. She spoke more soberly as she added:

'If I had to start my life over again, I should choose to remain chaste. But I cannot expect you to follow such an ordeal outside of a nunnery. I can only plead with you. The sexual act should not be a service to be paid for. A woman should provide herself with other ways of earning a living.'

Sarah lowered her head, crushed by her feeling of inadequacy. Not being of age, how could she challenge the world?

'If only I had the power of your pen, then I could afford to be independent. How can I earn my living? I can't be a servant or a seamstress.' Tears of despair gushed out.

'Chérie, why all these tears. You belong to the company of rebels who are too proud to cry. Have patience, darling. A higher redemption lies ahead of you. It will justify you and give meaning to your life. I will do all I can to help you find the living strength to wrest from the world what rightfully belongs to you. Put your trust in your good heart and your good sense. The heart can never be wrong.'

Madame Sand smoothed Sarah's hair, stroked her forehead, wiped away her tears . . . like a miraculous cleansing. Sarah became serenely calm under the spell of this remarkable woman. If only her own mother could be so loving! Somehow, Sarah found herself undressed and tucked under the covers while Sand's magical voice continued to soothe her.

'You're not a child of sin but a true child of Nature. Because I have known your suffering, I shall teach you to know yourself. Will you let me?'

Never had anyone spoken to the 'stupid child' in such terms. Mme Sand was pleading for the privilege of teaching her. When they embraced for Sand's departure, a lifelong bond was forged between them. She had become the godchild of the most famous woman living in France! With George Sand's help she would never, never marry without love. Repeating the words brought her the peace she needed and profound slumber.

In the salon below, Morny displayed the rapier mind for which he was so famous. Not for a moment would he be foiled by the hysterics of an adolescent female. He smiled his gayest, ordered a gavotte, leading off himself, to the relief of all the guests who, only moments before, had panicked at the thought that the party – so extravagantly prepared for – was ended so soon.

When the guests had danced enough, he regaled them with his choicest *risqué* stories. His expert talents were never wasted. His audience, now rocking with laughter, had nearly forgotten the incident which had almost put an end to their high expectations. Having plied them liberally with champagne, Morny now begged to be excused.

'If the young lady has recovered, she will surely wish to return to the scene of her first crime.' A new outburst of compliments and laughter greeted him as he indicated his next duty. 'We must remember her youth, the sensitive years, *oui*?'

The ladies adored his delicacy and never tired of repeating 'Such subtlety! He thinks of everything. So considerate and so suave.' The men heaved sighs of relief. It would have been so awkward, such a bore, had the evening been irrevocably spoilt. *Oui*, Morny was a genius! All were deeply grateful to him.

His timing was perfect. Julie was on the verge of hysterics herself. 'How would she return and face her guests?' Rosine's ministrations were useless. Morny's appearance now calmed her. In his presence, she could never feel entirely without hope. She searched his face. Yes, he had thought of something. She said Madame Sand had talked to Sarah who was now asleep.

'Good.' He turned to Mme Sand, 'We are already deeply in your debt but for Sarah's sake, will you be our confederate just a little longer?'

'You can turn off your charms if you expect me to assist in leading your lamb to slaughter.' Sand laughed.

'Certainly not, Madame Sand. But it occurs to me that a sensitive young woman such as Sarah would never be able to face a reception or party again unless repairs are quickly made this evening. You see, I have already prepared the guests who are waiting for her to rejoin them at the buffet. I have succeeded in minimising the disturbance her departure caused. She will be received as though at her age nothing could be more natural.'

'Ah, I see,' Sand agreed to everyone's relief. Julie was so reassured she clung to Morny's arm, and they returned to the salon below.

Sand returned to the beside of the sleeping girl. By instinct, she knew just when to whisper 'Sarah, dear, time to wake up.' Strangely enough, Sarah opened her eyes, fully refreshed. She stretched and asked:

'You've been here all the time?'

'I'll help you dress. Everyone's waiting for you downstairs.'

'I can't! I simply couldn't bear to have all those people stare at me!' Sarah cried out.

'I'll see you through your début. It's usually a crisis for every young woman. You must trust me. You know that I shall never betray you.'

Sand's firm tone and deft movements as she dressed Sarah left no room for argument. Rosine's powder puff and lipstick made the necessary repairs while Sand's eyes held Sarah's, infusing confidence.

Morny was entertaining his guests again while Julie smiled away their queries, 'I do hope she won't revert to childhood completely. She loves to dance and I'm counting on the music to bring her down.'

The prince added by way of ending the episode 'She promised to give me the last dance.'

No one referred to Sarah again, and when she entered, absorbed in Sand's conversation, nothing could have been less conspicuous. The ensemble struck up a waltz with such brilliance, that Sarah's recent outburst seemed like a passing clap of thunder which had died away in the far distance.

Like a flash, the prince was at her side, claiming his dance. He cradled her in his arm again, whispering hotly.

'Thank you for coming back. My evening would have been ruined if you hadn't.'

She closed her eyes; a slight shiver of satisfaction leapt through her.

'If Morny had not assured me you'd return, I would have left long ago. The fact is, and I know I should not admit it, but when you went off with my rival, I almost made the fatal error of leaving then.'

So! She had succeeded in making him humble – it was balm for her wounds. Sand was right. Sarah looked for her and beamed the message toward her with triumphant smiles.

'I adore you. You're so exciting. You haven't yet agreed to accept my invitation. I'm waiting for your answer.'

She glanced round the room again as they whirled, catching glimpses of expectantly smiling faces. She expanded in her new role of the successful courtesan. She had won this round. She must be careful how she played her next hand.

Loftily, she told him, 'You seem much more human; if you assure me it isn't a masquerade, I might consider accepting. You see, I'm quite spoiled, and like to have my own way.'

'I adore spoiled women. I always spoil my friends – can't abide proper ones.' He laughed, following her lead. Her pulse responded to the leaps his were taking. He held her tight and never took his gaze from her.

Julie was unable to resist occasional glances in the direction of the young couple, as if it seemed too much to expect Sarah to go through the rest of the evening without creating another crisis. But this time she was wrong. Sarah's self-assurance had been given a secure footing by someone she trusted. It would serve her until the end of the evening anyway.

Sand wrote in her diary that night, 'Dr Piphoel prescribed wisely.'

The buffet was announced and the folding doors rolled away to display a Lucullian feast, the artistry of a chef who catered only to nobility. Butlers stood ceremoniously at the ready to serve the guests.

When all were refreshed, the entertainment commenced. An actor rendered a few favourite scenes, after which a conjuror amazed the company with his magic. It was Sarah's turn next to recite a poem in strict keeping with the protocol of the time. She was accompanied on the piano by Madame Guerard with whom she always felt free to reveal her true self. Petite Dame adored her.

Sarah was surprised at her own composure. She looked at the prince. His face was alight as he held her gaze. A sharp memory caused her to catch her breath. A distant image seemed to clothe the young man, superimposing itself on him. It was Sarah's memory of her father who had presided over another party given in her honour. She adored his memory and secretly hoped some day to meet his counterpart in life. She remembered his glow of pride in her at the dinner party in honour of her entrance to the Convent. The dinner was given by Uncle Faurre who gently stroked her hair while Papa held up a glass in his elegant hand and called the family to attention: 'Sarah dear, you must study seriously from now on and be a good girl. After four years I'll return and then you shall travel with me and see how beautiful the world is.' Her mind wandered to her first part in the Convent play – the childish fun of making costumes, scenery, and rehearsing. Her morale heightened and she began.

Mme Guerard had improvised a few chords of background music and Sarah recited *Les Deux Pigeons* in a voice so changed, that everyone sat bewitched. Could those pure bell tones be coming from that tiny throat? In spite of themselves, ears pricked up and eyes dropped to the floor, studying the roses in the Aubusson rug to readjust to the amazement while the musical voice continued.

Mademoiselle de Brabender had stolen down and hid behind the drapery in the cloak room, unable to abide her curiosity any longer. Sarah's voice was of a pure lyric quality, and she could hardly contain her delight to the end.

64

Julie peered through her lorgnette, inspecting Sarah's dress, hair, pose, and then turned her gaze to Rosine. Both sisters were non-committal.

One guest, deep in thought, undoubtedly the only one qualified to judge, twirled his pointed moustache; as if an electric current had been activated, it set in motion in Morny's mind, recollections of gay supper parties graced by talented artistes. When Sarah finished, tension filled the room ready to explode. The count rose decorously and his gesture signalled the moment for applause. He applauded and then walked to Sarah to congratulate her on a superb performance amid echoes of '*Ah bon! très bon!*' The prince followed up and escorted the débutante back to his side on the Beauvais tête-à-tête. George Sand made a mental note.

The count returned to Julie and whispered as he kissed her hand, 'You know what you ought to do with this child? If all else fails, take my advice and send her to the Conservatoire. Meanwhile – *voilà!* without any effort. De Ligne has asked permission to invite her to Brussels. What do you say?'

'Whatever you think, your judgment is always best. The point is, will she accept?'

'Only if she thinks it's her own wish. That's the secret, isn't it?'

'Yes, to be sure. But how shall we cross this bridge and still maintain our position?'

'Leave that to me.'

'What should I ever do without you!' The fine lines between Julie's delicate brows disappeared.

'At the next interval, you take Sarah with you to the powder room.' The count led Julie off to finish the dance as the ensemble wound up the last bars of a polka. With a turn of her fan Julie signalled Sarah to join her, while Morny casually approached de Ligne to join him in a crème de menthe. Morny turned the conversation to casual matters, but the eager prince brought it back. 'Has Madame Bernard given her permission?'

'Oh, so sorry, I haven't had a moment in which to bring it up. But I dare say she could hardly refuse. Suppose we say I'll take the responsibility for it. Good luck, old chap.'

'Thanks, I'll ask her during the next dance.'

Just as Julie and Sarah returned, the band commenced the first bars of another polka. De Ligne bowed to Sarah and led her back to the glassy surfaced parquet.

Sarah awakened next day in great spirits. She went over each event, retasting the excitement, the bitterness, and the balm of her success. Why not accept an invitation to a Palace? It had so many advantages, so many new excitements to experience. But before taking such a step, she must confer again with George Sand.

But George Sand had left her country estate in Nohant to await the birth of her second grandchild, by her son Maurice. Sarah postponed her trip, expecting to pay the visit within a short time. But George Sand was needed at home, and the delay stretched out into months.

She remembered the prince's parting words, 'I'm returning to the Palace tomorrow. It would be my pleasure to have you as our guest, if you would do us the honour. I promise you won't regret it; I shall place myself at your service. We have much to show you. Have you ever been to my country?'

She had seen this as an opportunity to indulge her whims. She would use the prince as her mother desired, and would revenge herself on all men by asserting her independence of them. Already, it was he who was the tame pigeon, eating out of her hand.

While the weeks stretched into months, Sarah's life resumed the routine as before, and ennui and boredom grew in proportion as time passed.

3

Brief Glory in a Belgian Palace

A new world was opened to Sarah one day, when a class-mate at the Art School asked her go to to the Odéon to deliver a note for Mlle Dorval. Afterwards she frequently did errands for the famous actress and her cheeks would flush in anticipation of walking the back stage corridor, to speak the name of Mlle Dorval who would be eagerly waiting for her. Sarah would then do her a favour in exchange for a ticket to the performance.

The time arrived when she got over her timidity and stood close to the stage. She could hear every word of the rehearsal. As in the Convent, she retained not only the words and gestures, but also memorised each detail of the dimly lit stage. Something about it seemed oddly familiar but she was too absorbed to dwell upon it. The actress had begged her to hurry but Sarah could not tear herself away.

'You're lucky to be so impressed, my dear. I envy you. It's a matter that I have taken for granted too long. Do hurry, won't you.'

Half-dreaming, Sarah left. Mentally, she reset the stage; the lamps smelling of kerosene, the simple wooden benches and chairs; cardboard trees; flickering silhouette shadows; the prompter's pit, and even the cracks in the boards, when suddenly – she knew why it was all so familiar – and a happy cry escaped her. Her steps quickened as she flew between two huge *camions*, the exasperated drivers swearing at her 'Maggot! to the Seine if you wish to die!'

Sarah heard nothing. Memory placed another scene before her mind's eye: the altar of the Convent; the flickering candles which gave the same chalky effect to the faces of the nuns and children chanting before it; the silk and velvet hangings with fine handloomed laces displayed on high holy days; the processions led by priests or altar girls; even the crypt had its parallel in the prompter's pit. She could think of nothing else. She had discovered the reason for the sense of security and fascination which she felt in the theatre. Perhaps she might find the haven here which she had looked for in the Convent. Now, if Julie would agree, her problem would be solved.

The Conservatoire among its several functions was the preparatory school for the Comédie Française and if Sarah was accepted she would be paid a yearly salary while training. Its prestige would open doors which she could not otherwise hope to enter.

Aware of de Morny's influence, Julie decided to make the most of it before turning elsewhere. With the help of the count's introduction, Rosine arranged an interview for Sarah with the celebrated Auber, the Director.

'You're fond of the stage?' Auber asked the nervous débutante.

'Oh yes Monsieur. Next to the Convent, I love the theatre best.'

The kindly Director was surprised and looked to Madame Guerard for the explanation. She made a few discreet remarks, and the interview concluded, they left with Auber requesting, 'Please give my compliments to Mme Bernard.' Secretly, she could barely wait to tell Julie that Auber had kissed her hand, but Julie hurried her about her business, 'Yes, yes, Thank you. Now we must make all the necessary preparations.'

Sarah's godfathers, Regis and Meydieu, took charge as if a full scale emergency had struck. Regis insisted Sarah must learn *Phèdre* to the utter horror of Mademoiselle de Brabender.

'If I am to teach her anything as offensive as that, I refuse.'

The house was soon in an uproar with Julie beside herself.

'She's right,' Meydieu argued. 'She should learn the part of Chimène in *Le Cid*. It will help to open her O's more and unclench her teeth. Here, I'll write out an excercise for you. Before breakfast, repeat forty times: *Un-tres-gros-rat-dans-un-tres-gros-trou*, in order to vibrate the R.'

Since there were already so many teachers in the house, why call in a professional? Everyone had given advice but no one was really helpful. They all argued over the way the lines of a poem should be read, where its stresses should by put. Meydieu argued incessantly with Mademoiselle who fairly bristled under the barrage. Her reddish moustache stood on end, menacingly, as she tried to control her temper, pinching her lips tightly together in wrinkles over the gaps made by her missing front teeth.

Sarah tried to practise her lessons in diction only to find herself in conflict again. The syllables Te – de – de insisted on becoming the Paternoster, the recitation of which had been meted out to her as a punishment at the Convent.

When the day of the examination arrived – and for Sarah it was too soon – she awoke with a heaviness. How would she face this most important day of her life? The confusion of all the advice-giving, the elocution drills, the parts she had tried to memorise, and the books she had tried to read kept whirling about in her head.

Absentmindedly she washed, and put on the black silk dress with its gathered lace bertha softening and flattering her neck and shoulders, billowing out in fullness above and below her waist to camouflage her thin body. Beneath the skirt, her embroidered drawers showed, reaching to the top of her brown kid shoes. Julie slipped a white *guimpe* into the black bodice of Sarah's dress for a touch of sophistication. Happily, it was just the right frame for her delicate face.

Between her two guardians, Sarah was squeezed into the carriage for the drive to the examination hall. A silence fell upon them, exhausted as they were from the ordeals of the past months.

The atmosphere exuded tension as young men and women came out through the red baize door, their voices high-pitched, in an excited state, chattering away in discussion of what had just happened in their audition, while others went through at the same time in answer to their names.

Monsieur Leautaud, in charge of the list of names, explained the procedure to Sarah and asked her if she needed someone to give her the cues. He would provide someone among several young people if she would care to choose.

'Oh no,' Sarah quickly rejected his offer. 'I don't know anyone here and I won't ask.'

'But if you are to do Agnes, you will need someone to cue you. What will you do?'

'In that case, I will recite a fable.'

Leautaud burst into a loud laugh as he crossed off Agnes and wrote down Sarah's name and the title *Deux Pigeons*. Sarah, showing signs of feverishness, walked back to her guardians, who, aware of her delicate constitution, wondered if it was all worth the pain and panic it caused her. Madame Guerard cooled Sarah's brow with a drop or two of eau-de-cologne.

Finally her name was called. Her governess quickly smoothed her hair and dress, and gave her a final admonition about her O's and R's. Sarah walked alone to the red baize door and, holding her head high, entered the audition hall. She had never felt so alone in all her life.

Resolutely, she walked toward the forbidding platform at the far end. In the middle of the room, around a large table crowded the judges. Among them a loud-voiced woman made herself conspicuous by dropping her monocle which she was holding, and picking up a pair of opera glasses to scrutinise Sarah. The girl walked up the few steps to the platform and turned in the direction of her audience when Leautaud, who had forgotten to give her final instructions, bent over and whispered; 'Make your bow and commence. Then, when the chairman rings, stop!

When Sarah noticed that Auber was the chairman, she

wondered what he was doing there. In her fright she had forgotten everything. Suddenly she remembered: he was the Director of the Conservatoire. She bowed and began:

> *Deux pigeons s'aiment d'amour tendre*
> *L'un d'eux s'ennuyant au logis* . . .

Through the audition hall, the ventriloquist, Beauvallet, that thundering tragedian, could be heard muttering: 'This is no elocution class. Where does she think she is, reciting fables here!' Sarah's heart beat wildly and for the moment she could not continue.

The silver-haired Provost, one of the teachers, said: 'Go on, my child.'

'You're right, Provost, it won't be as long as a scene from a play,' agreed Augustine Brohan, the woman who had looked her over with the opera glasses. Thus encouraged, Sarah repeated:

> *Deux pigeons s'aiment d'amour tendre*
> *L'un d'eux s'ennuyant au logis* . . .

'Louder! Speak up my child!' Samson, a little man called to her, shaking his curly white hair. His interruption confused her, and a moment later he urged her to continue: 'Come, come, we're not ogres. Begin again.'

But Augustine Brohan objected: 'No, no. If she begins again it will be longer than a scene.' Everybody laughed.

Angered by their rudeness, Sarah gathered new strength. By a great effort she shut out all distraction. Her voice became liquid silver and took on resonance. Never had she been more fluent or effective. Not once did she falter. The judges fell silent. Before she reached the end, the bell rang. Sarah stopped and walked down the steps, thinking only of gaining the safety of her two waiting friends. As she passed the judges' table, Auber took her hand and stopped her: 'That was very good, little girl. Provost and Beauvallet both want you in their classes.'

He pointed out the two men, making it easy for her to choose. She realised it was Beauvallet who had frightened her with his voice-projection. Without a word she pointed to the white-haired Provost.

Auber laughingly consoled Beauvallet, 'That will teach you to keep quiet next time.'

'Then I have passed!' the surprised Sarah told herself aloud.

'Yes, you have passed,' Auber said, 'and I only regret that such a pretty voice is not to be used for singing.'

But Sarah heard nothing more. She dashed from the room without stopping to thank anyone : '*Ma petite dame! Mademoiselle!* I have passed!'

'How do you know you passed? No one knows before-hand.'

'Yes, yes,' she repeated, 'I know. Auber told me. I chose Provost. Beauvallet also wanted me but his voice is too loud for me.'

'Well, well, imagine!' an envious girl exclaimed. 'They all wanted you!'

Sarah enjoyed her period of training under Provost and there came the day when she was to make her first public appearance, in a small part.

Julie went to the theatre, but Rosine, the fond aunt who was so excited over having an actress in the family, was not even in Paris. She was recovering in the country from an outbreak of jealousy over Sarah's success at a party Rosine had given in her honour a few days before, never suspecting her thin, childlike niece had charms with which Rosine could not compete.

When ready, Sarah left her dressing room with teeth chattering, in a cold perspiration, verging on a faint; she waited for the curtain to be raised. The touch of a reassuring hand on her elbow sent chills of fear through her, but it was her professor, Provost, whose deep, gentle voice again spoke words of encouragement. Her cue was given, and Sarah was pushed on stage.

Once there, she went through her part as in a dream, her ears buzzing, her head pounding with the throbbing of her blood . . . each throb a threat.

At the end of the first act, she rushed upstairs and feverishly began to undress. Madame Guerard stopped her as she reached for her street clothes. 'Are you mad! There are four more acts!' Sarah dropped her arms and pulled herself together. She braced herself before her mirror : 'Brain, take control away from my nerves. They will be my undoing. I must finish the play!'

Mystically intuitive, she used self-suggestion to fortify herself, adopting the slogan *quand même*, so that she could finish what she began. The suggestion always succeeded. Sarah finished the play.

The strain of the début told on her and the reviews were candid; she had been insignificant in the part, but was gracefully tall and slender, with a pleasing expression. The upper part of her face was remarkably beautiful. This was about all that was said for her except that her enunciation was perfectly clear.

Unbelievably, this time Julie rose to defend Sarah, gaining stature for herself and a burst of pride from Sarah. Commenting on the article by Sarcey in *L'Opinion Nationale*, Julie spoke two sentences : 'The man is an idiot. You were charming.' She even prepared a small cup of coffee for her daughter, whose emotions by now, were overwhelming her.

Could this possibly be? Julie complimenting Sarah? Running down the critic, the man who, next to Louis Napoleon, wielded the greatest power in France – for her? Surely Julie loved her oldest child! Sarah was content. Besides, she now had a career and this made them both content.

Regis had explained to Julie during the early months of her career, 'The child will receive so much during the first five years, then, so much afterwards and at the end of thirty years, she'll be given the pension for an Associate,

– that is, if she becomes an Associate.'

It was all very comforting to his bourgeois soul.

The ceremony for the Molière Anniversary was at hand, and Sarah's invitation to take part caused great excitement. Her younger sister, Jeanne, begged to go with her, and seeing no harm in it, Julie consented. Holding the child's hand, Sarah led her in the procession behind the fat old *Sociétaire* of the *Comédie*, surly Mme Nathalie. Jeanne accidentally stepped on the hem of Mme Nathalie's cloak, and the spiteful woman pushed the little girl violently against the wall.

Sarah caught the screaming, frightened child in her arms, and said to the actress: 'You miserable creature!' The woman turned slowly around, but before she could reply, Sarah slapped her face briskly. The ageing actress pretended to faint, and, as a group formed itself around her, a young, severe-faced *Sociétaire* began to sprinkle her with water. At this, the actress rose up, covering her face with hands, muttering angrily, 'You stupid fool! You'll spoil my make-up!'

A well-known comedian, Bressant, whispered to Sarah as he comforted Jeanne: 'We must arrange this little matter, Mademoiselle. Nathalie's short arms are really very long. Just between us, you were a trifle hasty, but I like that. And your little sister is such a pretty youngster.'

'You certainly have nerve!' murmured Rose Baretta, a fellow-actress, barely able to control a burst of laughter. 'How dare you do it? She's a *Sociétaire*!'

Until this moment, Sarah had been enraged. Now, calmed by the attention of her comrades, she knew only too well what a price she would have to pay, but she didn't know she still had a lesson to learn. If only she could keep it from Julie!

Post haste, a letter came from the theatre manager asking Sarah to be present next afternoon at one o'clock, 'in regard to a personal matter of great urgency'. As if lightning struck, everything happened at once. Jeanne was questioned by Julie, and in telling about how her cheek was cut, the child exaggerated everything and the whole family turned on Sarah in consternation.

Julie's reproach was in the form of silent suffering, refined distress; her godfather tittered in bourgeois embarrassment; Aunt Faurre needled her triumphantly, her ready abuse always being: 'I knew it, that terrible child!' Mlle de Brabender's little eyes shed tears on her drooping moustache, then fell on her clasped hands. Only Madame Guerard argued with everyone, defending her charge to the bitter end.

Sarah cried that whole night, and next day presented herself, swollen-eyed to the manager Thierry. He dispensed with ceremony and emphasised the enormity of Sarah's crime, ending curtly: 'I have asked Madame Nathalie to come here. You will apologise to her before three Committee *Sociétaires*. If she consents to forgive you, the Committee will then consider whether to fine you or cancel your engagement.'

Speechless at this unjust demand, Sarah stared belligerently until Thierry became restless. Impatiently, he prodded: 'Well mademoiselle?'

As she still made no answer, he took it to mean agreement.

'I'll go and ask Mme Nathalie to come here, and please, let us get this over with as soon as possible. I have other matters waiting, far more important than teaching you how to get along in this world.'

Once more, at the mercy of her emotions, Sarah shouted: 'No, don't bring Mme Nathalie here! I'll slap her again if I see her!'

'Very well. Then I must ask your mother to come.'

'My mother would never come!'

'Then I'll go and speak to her.'

'There's no need for that. My mother permits me to make my own decisions, so I alone am responsible for myself.'

'I see. Then I'll think it over. Good-bye.'

Overcome with panic but determined not to yield, Sarah

left. At home she found Rose Baretta, come to persuade her to use discretion.

Nothing moved Sarah. The arguments of her family only made her more stubborn. They reproached her in a hundred ways, diluting their arguments with advice, all of which she rejected. Finally, no one would speak to her. Forced to go to her room, she shut herself away and fell into a deep, merciful sleep.

But with awakening came all the ugly memories, returning stronger and uglier, it seemed, than the original. For comfort, she stole up to Madame Guerard's room. But this time Mme Guerard's attempts to bolster her morale fell short of the mark. Sarah went back to her room, entered it silently, and let her mind drift into thoughts of suicide.

Moments later, Madame was back. She had the solution. Now was the time to accept the invitation to the palace home of the Prince de Ligne. 'Your mother will be delighted and it will be a refreshing change for both of you.'

Sarah agreed. She searched for the contract with Thierry's signature and sent it back to him.

Marie Columbier, another Théâtre Française actress who had just made her début, took Sarah to The Literary Salon, a mock title given to the tiniest café in Paris where no drink cost more than five sous. Its patrons discussed art, politics and newspapers as if they were baudy bedfellows in the national triangle. Sarah's views were quickly broadened and her wit sharpened.

On entering, one could have sworn the place was on fire, but Marie nudged her in through the fog of smoke and began to introduce the regulars – Rudolphe, Casimir, Jules, Oscar to name the leaders, and their honoured guests – a Sorbonne language graduate; Iliana, whose long black hair, through which the heavy smoke was curling, appeared to be alive with grey snakes; she listed phrases in her notebook, and worked on simultaneous translations in the

76

languages she knew. Among them were to be found quite a collection of juicy *bon mots*, and Mercredi, so named because she could come only on that day and could be counted on to bring a bottle of the finest Napoleon; a gift from her 'Uncle' who was paid in brandy by an impoverished nobleman for whom he butled.

'Did you say butle or burgle?' Satan asked. He was the acknowledged Master of the Cenacle.

'We're all Satanists, you understand, and each must earn the title in his own way; your membership is conceded as you have met the regulations,' François remarked, scanning Sarah with lightning speed; a compulsive talker, he earned his membership by out-talking all opposition in stentorian tones interlarded with legal terminology.

Sarah nearly choked for air but heroically stifled her coughing. At the far end, Paul in an artist's smock sent billows of odorous Egyptian tobacco smoke directly before him like the snortings of legendary dragons; the rest merely set up a joint smoke blanket from the miniature chimney projecting at the corner of each mouth. She managed some grace in refusing proferred cigarettes. No one insisted.

'We salute you as spokesman for your generation. You have rebelled in the proudest tradition in your personal life and career,' Casimir interrupted, 'A toast! to our illustrious one, the Jeanne d'Arc of our day! *Vive* Sarah!' She was handed a shot of brandy which she was obliged to sip.

Despite herself, a deep sense of satisfaction made her glow as she pictured Regis's and Meydieu's faces, their bourgeois hearts shocked should they learn of her in this company 'the dregs who hadn't a *culotte* between them.' Indeed, it was true that they wore each other's scabby rags, dignifying them by names as if each one were a family member. Paul's overcoat was fondly referred to as Siberia, it was fur-lined. Casimir's shirt, La Bastille was striped. Iliana's short gold-trimmed jacket was Napoleon after the Little Corporal.

'You have the genius of Napoleon, our first Emperor,' Jules said. 'His secret lay in one dimension which no other general, no previous military genius happened on; all others were great in strategy, deploying of forces, knowing when to sue for peace. But Napoleon added a simple element which none before had thought of, in a word: speed! That's how he triumphed over one hundred thousand Austrian soldiers with only twelve thousand Frenchmen. Ergo, you too by one stroke triumphed in mocking aristocracy and autocracy.'

Sarah recoiled. She could not help wincing when she thought of the price she paid for her 'triumph' and every time she heard the word Satan, she shuddered. It was what she had called Hippolyte when he sneered at her faith and mocked her ideals.

At these cenacles, Sarah learned to appreciate modern poetry and was brought up to date on the industrial expansion going on across the Atlantic. Giants named Edison, Carnegie, Gould, Vanderbilt were changing the face of the world. But she could not keep a cool detachment when they ridiculed Napoleon during their admiration of Americans. She loved their nonchalance but questioned their loyalty.

It was here that she learned about the Jewish background of Élisa Rachel, the great First Actress of the Théâtre Française. How a man called Charon discovered the magic harp in her throat when she sang in the streets of Lyons, and got her father's permission to give her voice lessons. She had recently died in Provence after a fatiguing tour of America. All France mourned. The art of the tragedienne had died with Rachel.

Arrangements for Sarah's visit to Belgium were completed and now Petite Dame was busy packing her prettiest party clothes. She chatted happily and interposed cautions 'Forgive me, dear, but remember, you will be a visitor without title in a palace. Among royalty! You have the graces but please, do not lose control. There will be no one to rescue you and we'll never hear the end of it from mama. *Compris?*'

Sarah agreed lightheartedly. Petite Dame made ready to go to the depot with Sarah and ride as far as the border, but Sarah put her off gently.

'It's about time I learned to be on my own. It will be good practice to make the trip alone, all the way.'

'Bravo! Now I'm sure all will be well. I'm so proud of you.'

The prince himself met her on arrival and tucked her into the royal coach while her luggage went in another one; yet it seemed to have preceded hers, since upon being ushered into her room, her clothes were already hung up or stuffed into the bureaux by the maids.

'My mother is waiting tea as soon as you are ready,' the prince said. 'She sends you her compliments and is so pleased that you've arrived safely. Confidentially, I think I'm dreaming. Are you really here?'

The weeks flew by as the round of parties, teas, sightseeing, skating, drives through the woods and tours of the palace and mansions followed each other. But her most intimate delight was in using the palace stationery to write to those who would react most enviously.

De Ligne was positively entranced with her wit and feminine whims, and made the most of her brief acting career in speaking of it to his mother.

'Only the specially endowed follow their impulses spontaneously; it is the mark of genius. She has won distinctions in art as well and is quite serious and sensitive.'

His evaluation was affectionately accepted as a vision of a love-struck youth. The prince was hurt by the cool reception. He wanted Sarah to be accepted by them. He had indeed fallen deeply in love with her. Sarah herself felt an increasing affection for him, and when he began to visit her suite at night, she clung eagerly to his passionate embraces.

In Paris, Julie relaxed and breathed a prayer of deliverance in her ample chaise longue, now dressed in handloomed Chantilly lace, her tiny feet encased in black satin mules.

'What do you suppose is happening in Brussels, my love?'
she asked Morny. 'Will I be free of Sarah, or am I to be
plagued by her after her return?'

'Just what I was thinking, my kitten. I have been waiting
to receive news from an envoy, but trains are unpredictable
at times.'

'Did it seem to you that de Ligne would be able to sway
my headstrong one? Maybe the lure of a foreign country?'
she questioned hopefully.

'It is a year since the night of the Salon début. Sarah has
matured in some ways since then', he said doubtfully. 'It is
not an easy question to answer.'

Morny knew his cronies well and it was a matter of
indifference to him whether Sarah became de Ligne's
mistress. Morny could not hope to gain anything from that
liaison, but he also could not see Sarah overwhelmed by de
Ligne. What Morny was sure of was his own judgment of
Sarah. She was a veritable fire-goddess and she had an
incendiary effect upon everything she touched. It would
require Vulcan to fully ignite her passions. Morny could
not see Sarah in Julie's role, complacently performing for
her lover.

Sarah had the fiery Napoleonic temper which he knew
so well. It would be she who would command the masses,
she who would wield the sceptre of authority. If only she
knew and would realise her inner power!

This time he was wrong.

De Ligne had succeeded in becoming her lover.

One night they drove home from a soirée given by a
countess; the party had gone on into the early hours of
dawn and Sarah was worn from lack of sleep, her frail
health unequal to the activities. She stepped out into the
cool damp air and began to cough. De Ligne quickly
wrapped the carriage rug round her, snuggling her to his
wildly pounding breast. By the time that they reached the
Palace she was asleep.

He carried her up asleep to her suite to be undressed by
her maids while his valet prepared him for bed. He then

returned and awakened her. Quite refreshed, she clung eagerly to his passionate embraces.

While the prince prodded his family on the matter of accepting Sarah, a letter from Petite Dame gave the news of a serious heart attack that Julie had suffered. She added her belief that it was urgent that Sarah return as early as possible. There were also offers from theatre managers to the celebrity who had been summoned to Belgium by the royal family.

Sarah was full of anxiety. While she was holidaying, Julie was suffering. And what about those managers? Why now of all times when she was at peace and contented? A dull conscience began to thud against reality: the prince was attractive but what of the future? She was not blind to the invisible line of demarcation between his family and herself. Against this, she argued with herself over her stage career. 'You'll have nothing but failure and disappointment in that life. When the present publicity has been played out, you'll find yourself tossed on the beach once more.'

A mounting sense of loneliness overtook her and she knew she was homesick. It was useless to argue. She missed her family, Petite Dame, and even her mother's two cronies, Meydieu and Regis. Home was irresistible. Next morning she told de Ligne of her decision. He pleaded, begged, bargained, but was forced to let her go. Many promises were given between passionate embraces.

Sarah was charged to deliver gifts to Julie along with the proper messages from the royal house. When she arrived home Julie was over the worst, so Sarah sat on the pink satin slipper chair near her bed. Morny of course, was on hand eager to know from Sarah's own lips what had transpired in Belgium. He prided himself on his knowledge of the famous *Memoires* of the present heir's grandfather.

'Oh yes, the prince takes great pride in the scholarly reputation of his royal grandfather, and the queen made a great deal of it in order to impress me with the difference in background. At times, I almost felt like slapping her, she reminded me so much of Mme Nathalie. If the prince had not been facing me, reassuring me, I might have forgotten myself.'

Morny asked: 'Were there any references to Casanova?'

'Oh yes, the prince told me about one or two of his escapades – a sleight of hand artist – because witnesses swore to his presence in one place while at the same time, his unique handiwork was unmistakably visible elsewhere. It was very amusing.'

Julie beamed over her daughter's success: such an important connection! She hoped to hear that Sarah had at last found a milieu in which she could live contentedly. Julie returned to her train of thought.

'Did you have all your meals with the family?'

'Only dinner. They're forever eating and you know my crazy eating habits. Nothing but teas, parties, luncheons and in-between snacks. It was a relief to have breakfast in my suite. The maids, Gusty and Marya, opened the window drapes, put fresh flowers in the vases and bowls, drew my bath, not to mention the hundred other little chores. They could spot clean a dress so that you'd never believe I had spilled a saucer of cream on it. What a help they'd be backstage.'

'So you did enjoy your visit?' Morny smiled.

'Yes, it was perfect. Now I know why everyone wants to be a princess. It's so easy, even a child can learn it, even a stupid child.' They all laughed together like children.

'Tomorrow we shall write the letters of thanks for the gifts,' Julie said.

Morny studied Sarah. Was she deliberately avoiding the question, or had she returned as innocent as when she left? Did she find the prince as attractive as his reputation supposed him to be? He saw new facets developing, none of which had been noticeable in her childhood; she captured his imagination; intruded on his thoughts at the least expected moments; it happened only the previous night when he was again sleepless. Sarah, the illegitimate, unwanted child, a parallel to his own childhood; her proud assertions of her personal integrity; her passionate devotion to her beliefs; the mystic musical voice; invincible courage and belief in herself at all costs – if only she would permit life to smooth her rough edges she would be formidable! With his guidance she would conquer the world: an incipient Napoleon! And the oddity of her birthday falling on the same day as his own!

His thoughts turned to his beloved Julie who had not the wit to realise that her odd one was perhaps another Jeanne d'Arc, for, he mused, given the opportunity, she would overthrow all bigotry, spit in the eyes of those who judged her, and choose the pyre to pretence. What, he wondered, would she do next? Tear down barriers or, would she kneel at the shrine of diplomacy? There was a new look in her eyes; a tender glow of inner fire; a magnetism; an incandescence; had someone kindled it? Was she in love? With whom? Decidedly, there was more to this illusive female than met the eye: a vertitable volcano!

Sarah's arrival, just as Julie passed the crisis, gladdened the entire household, but especially Mme Guerard. She had not left Julie's side during her whole illness and was afraid Sarah would be too late. Marguerite and Sarah's two younger sisters were delighted to have her home again, because with Sarah there, something exciting always happened to enliven the household.

Sarah had indeed brought a surprise gift from abroad of which she was as yet unaware. She busied herself with a new wardrobe and presented herself to those managers who had expressed an interest in the young ingénue whose chief talent lay in her publicity value. For a time box office receipts were given a needed spur whenever she was billed, but as the novelty wore off, she was out of work again.

Time hung heavily and at first she stayed away from her former friends in art school and the cafés out of delicacy, hoping that their sabre thrusts would lose their edge so that she could again feel right with them. She longed to be one of them; to belong, as it were, to a family, not to be despised for whatever she did; would they accuse her of seeking status? she wondered. She stayed away as long as she could bear until, having exhausted all the theatres and even the burlesques, after two months she put on her tailored blue suit and a beret, and went, hoping to crawl in unseen under the smoke screen in the Literary Salon. She was immediately detected. 'Ah, a spy in our midst!' Rudolphe laughed, 'On guard, everyone.'

She was warmly welcomed. '*Entrez Mademoiselle Sans-Souci. Prenez une place ici, s'il vous plaît, près de moi.*' Paul bowed and indicated half his chair. '*Mais non*,' Oscar interposed '*Je vous prie, près de moi*,' and this went all round the table until she broke into delicious rowdy laughter.

Paul and Oscar pulled her down between them and, affectionately, each kissed the cheek facing him. A beer was ordered and in the best king's French – 'Mademoiselle Princess, it is most unfortunate that you arrived just as the last bottle of champagne was finished. We've sent Gaston with the keys to the wine vaults of the Louvre with instructions that should he for some reason be unable to fulfil his duty, in short, return empty-handed, he shall suffer immediate excommunication and a cold bath!'

Sarah laughed until she verged on hysterics; the caustic humour, the smoke and the beer which she forced herself to drink in gratitude for the welcome made her hiccough and she could not stop. A medical conference unsurpassed in history was instantly called: 'Madame, your symptoms require immediate attention. Do as we direct and follow our example. Hold the nose and the breath thus, inhaling quickly and exhaling slowly for one week, then relax thus.' They all fell over each other in a heap. Sarah by now could hardly catch her breath, tears rolled uncontrollably while she laughed, hiccoughed, held her sides and tried to stop herself. But her youthful companions were irrepressible, '*Bon Dieu*, Pasteur, you have overlooked the washing of the hands. We must settle this matter quickly before you are called to account for being remiss in your hygienic duties. *Voilà*, my washbowl!' He pulled off Paul's beret, placed it in front of Paul and with a broad flourish, poured his beer into it.

Sarah's hiccoughs became so bad she was unable to breathe and felt a painful stab in her side. Oscar saw her agony and lifted her out into the air until she recovered, patting her back and shoulders all the while to relax the tension. Then he apologised sadly. Impulsively Sarah embraced him; they returned to their chair arm in arm, but as soon as she sat down, she again broke into hysterical laughter. This time, she stepped out without waiting, retched at the kerb, and after some time, breathing came easier and the laughing stopped. Sarah was a pitiful figure as she apologised for disturbing the fun.

Oscar wanted to see her home but she declined. 'I'll take a taxi and see you tomorrow. *Merci, mille fois. Au revoir.*'

This time she welcomed the privacy of her room. It was time to tell Julie what was haunting her . . . she knew why she had become hysterical. Anxiety over her joblessness had turned to terror when she realised that she was pregnant. If Julie rejected her chaste, how would she react to her pregnant daughter . . . she dreaded to speak of it. . . . Julie might have another attack.

When Petite Dame came in ten minutes later, Sarah confided in her. '*Ma Petite Dame*, the palace was big and full of strangers, and no one had a sense of humour, or played the way Regina and Jeanne and I play. I missed you all, and the only familiar face was the prince's. When he put his arms around me, it was as if my own papa was protecting me, as he did when we drove to the Convent and he registered me there. I simply could not refuse him, and Rosine and mama had told me, one never refuses a prince.'

When Julie learned of Sarah's pregnancy, she was certain she should marry. No other solution was possible. She had no career, no ability for anything practical, not even common sense; she would have to marry.

But again Sarah refused.

'But what then, do you propose to do? And why do you refuse to tell the prince? It is his obligation to care for you and his child, and he will be generous, you may be sure.'

'No, I don't want anyone to know, and I don't need anyone to care for me, nor to tell me what to do. He didn't come for me; he didn't keep any of his promises; I never want to see him . . . never.'

'Then what will you do?'

'You needn't worry your head about that; you never wanted me either and now, worse luck, you certainly don't want my baby here.'

Hearing voices from Sarah's room, her Petite Dame came running just in time to hear Sarah reproach Julie with: 'Your home is just a beautiful doll house, and you play at being a mother; I'm used to strangers so I'll leave. With me out of your sight, you can play all the time.'

Mme Guerard tried to calm Sarah, and felt embarrassed for mother and daughter. Julie was saying: 'How can you be so ungrateful? Who has ever done more than I to make a proper woman of you? Were it not for my care, you would have died long ago. Is it my fault that you can't appreciate anything? That you destroy everything?' Julie walked out in despair and Sarah dissolved in tears.

'I'm here, dear, as you know. You can depend on me, my dear. I have a plan; we'll find a little flat just big enough for you and the baby and we'll pick and choose and furnish it to your own taste; it's lots of fun and something you've never done: building a nest of your own. It will give you a new experience. I wish I had it to do again for myself; I still remember how I lost sleep, unable to decide between two dining room tables. Come now, hot chocolate and rest for now. The latest copy of *La Femme Chic* has come so you might get some ideas from it. I enjoy looking through it and picturing myself in the clothes and hats. And I have a few boxes of extra china and other useful things which will save money for other things. You can have the blue organdie curtains from my bedroom, your mother won't mind.'

When the flat was ready, Sarah begged Julie to let her take Regina to live with her to keep her company until she got used to being on her own. Regina loved being with Sarah because she could do just as she pleased.

86

On 22nd December 1864, baby Maurice was born. The ordeal past, Sarah had a beautiful blonde baby boy to play with; her joy was inexpressible. Julie remarked: 'I hope you won't spoil him as you have Regina; she is a veritable *enfante terrible!*'

Prince de Ligne had bowed to his mother's plans: a marriage liaison befitting the station of the family. He married a countess. The royal father offered to give his natural son his name on condition that Sarah should give up her right to him, and let him be raised by his father as a member of the royal family.

Sarah reacted violently, calling it an insult and refused all his offers unconditionally. Several attempts to kidnap Maurice were thwarted by Sarah. 'I shall raise him like a prince myself, all alone, as I wish – *quand même!*' Through her own will power and sacrifices, she kept her word.

He was for her the culmination of all her life's yearnings.

4

Actress and Mother

Sarah's courage grew more resolute by the stimulation of her maternal responsibilities; even before Maurice's birth, signs of maturity were evident. She made plans for raising him and then to return to the stage while he was growing. She busied herself learning to cook simple meals, accompanying Mme Guerard to the markets; 'It is well to have several types of salad dressing to give variety to the palate. One can improvise endless flavours by using a bit of imagination: a sprinkle of nutmeg, paprika, anise, cumin, and rubbing the salad bowl with a kernel of garlic before making the dressing in it. Always buy those greens which are in season as they are not only more flavourful, but economical as well.'

Petite Dame now turned Sarah's attention to the decoration of her little flat, and taught her appreciation of antiques and bibelots. To her delight, Sarah suddenly developed a love of luxury, but she kept her life to herself, going and coming as she pleased, leaving Maurice with a young girl who was hardly more than a child herself; Sarah could not afford efficient mature help. A few friends, admirers who had met her at the Salon party, showered her with lavish gifts, some of which occasionally paid for Josephine's salary by means of the Medici exchange plan – the neighbourhood pawnbroker.

She began to appear in public again. When the great Alphonse Daudet heard of her courage in keeping her son, he heartily approved of her decision: 'Ah, she is truly a woman!'

Shortly after the birth of Maurice, Sarah was offered a three-year contract with the Odéon by her old friend, Camille Doucet, Minister of the Beaux Arts. He pulled up a chair and reminisced what a terror she had been.

'Come now, you must be calmer. It will never do to waste all those admirable talents in voyages, escapades and boxing people's ears!'

Moved to tears, she sobbed softly.

'Now don't cry, my dear, let's see how we can make up for all this folly. Youth makes many blunders.' He opened a drawer and took out a letter: 'Here, this is your pardon! Duquesnel has just been appointed manager of the Odéon along with Chilly. He wants me to send some young artists to make up the company. Well, we must attend to this. Shall we succeed?'

In high elation, Sarah hurried home to the comforting arms of Mme Guerard. She spent hours with Sarah listening as she rehearsed parts of Racine's plays. After several days, the letter from the Ministry arrived and she lost no time in presenting herself to Doucet. He beamed his usual smile: 'It's all settled then. Good. But don't think it was easy. You're notorious for your headstrong wilfulness. But I gave my word you'll be as gentle as a lamb.'

'I promise if only out of gratitude. Please, what must I do?'

'Here's a letter for Felix Duquesnel. He's expecting you.' Then, acknowledging Sarah's thanks, he continued: 'I'll see you again less officially at your aunt's on Thursday. She sent me an invitation to dinner. You can tell me then what Duquesnel says.'

Rosine kept on friendly terms with Doucet. She had told him of the birth of Sarah's child and of Julie's despair over her daughter. The only thing they were sure of was to keep her occupied with something she liked. Perhaps another try at the theatre might turn the tide.

Rosine was right.

Sarah did one more thing. She changed her name to Bernhardt. She used the first part of her father's name and added it to her mother's maiden name Hardt, combining the two. She hoped this would somehow change her future.

Sarah and Duquesnel found immediate rapport but his

partner, Chilly, eyed her coldly, pretending he had never heard of her. Rudely handing her a pen, he told her to sign the contract. Mme Guerard, seeing Sarah's colour rise, feared an outburst. She gripped Sarah's hand and cautioned her to read it first. For a moment Sarah was distracted.

'Yes, yes, do, but hurry. Read it and sign or leave it alone. I'm only doing this to go along with Duquesnel. It's his idea. I'd never hire you.'

Duquesnel quickly whispered to Sarah: 'He's all right. No ceremony about him. Don't take offence.' But she retorted: 'And if you offered it to me purely on your own, I would not accept.'

When the three left the office, Sarah related to the others that she had played a shepherdess and did particularly well in the role. Afterwards in the foyer, she had been surrounded by the author himself, the theatre manager and others who all commented favourably.

Chilly had stood aside for some minutes, listening, then had stepped up and said sharply: 'Thiboust is mad. No one ever saw such a thin shepherdess!' He had not only seen her, but had condemned her.

On a day when the sky over Paris was full of promise with flamingo pink streaking the pale blue, Sarah set off at top speed in a carriage drawn by a pair of spirited horses, for her first rehearsal. Seeing her niece at nineteen a personage with a few worldly credits, Rosine had swallowed her envy and judged it would be more sensible to be on friendly terms with her. Now that Sarah was back in the theatre with a three-year option, Rosine, trying to mend her bridges, sent her a pair of fine young carriage horses explaining that they were too spirited for herself.

In tune with July's brilliant sunshine and flamboyant colours, Sarah ran up the old cracked steps of the theatre, joyfully giving 'good morning' to everyone.

Tossing off her hat and gloves, she stepped into the

cavernous black of the stage, spottily illuminated with a lantern hung wherever a peg or nail was to be found, or set on a low bench where it lit up the faces of the players. To Sarah's imagination, this ghostliness was intensely vivifying; it bathed everything in a mysterious luminescence more dazzling than the brightest sunshine.

On 15th August 1866, in honour of the Emperor's birthday, a free performance was given in which Sarah appeared. She played Arici in *Phèdre*, a small part hardly noticeable in the overpowering drama in which the leading players gained all the attention. Having been chosen to replace Dicat Petit in the second offering, and determined to call attention to herself so as not to be mistaken for the other actress, she adorned her white skirt with rosettes in red and blue. Even though she played with the coquettishness and affection that the role of Sylvia called for in Marivaux's *Le Jeu de l'amour et du hasard*, the sight of her costume brought the house down with laughter, some even shouting above the noise: 'When will you sing the *Marseillaise*.'

One morning, with a confidence which he was far from feeling, Sarah's champion, 'Duq' strode into Chilly's office: 'I propose Mlle Bernhardt's contract be renewed,' he said.

As expected, Chilly leapt up and shouted: 'You're mad! You're just as crazy as she is! She's not worth a hundred francs! She's too thin and looks ridiculous in any part!'

Duquesnel waited until the storm blew over, then: 'You may be right at that, Chilly. Maybe she isn't worth a hundred francs, but aside from that you have no other objections, do you?'

Chilly stared and, not knowing what his partner was up to, nodded his head in agreement.

'Well then, please deduct a hundred francs from my salary and take up Bernhardt's option.'

Chilly reluctantly bowed to Duquesnel and left it at that.

Sarah knew nothing of this, Duquesnel carefully seeing to it that she was spared the embarrassment.

Next afternoon before driving to the theatre, Sarah read

the unfavourable reviews of the previous evening. By the time she reached her dressing room, her depression over them was intense. Unable to restrain herself, she screamed out as she struck her fists against her dressing table: 'I'd rather die! I will die! Anything is better than this torture!'

Quietly, Duquesnel entered Sarah's dressing room and begged her not to give up, and with his encouragement, Sarah continued in her various roles throughout the summer.

In the audience on the day of the Emperor's birthday sat France's most distinguished woman of the century. She had come backstage to see the girl she had comforted on another occasion, and again heard through the door the same anguished cries. She waited until Sarah spent herself a bit and entered. For moments she gazed in compassion on the distraught actress, then said gently: 'You remind me of myself at your age. Do you remember me?'

'Ah, yes. Forgive me,' Sarah stammered. 'I was so upset I didn't hear your knock. Please sit down.'

'Never mind, there are times when such things don't count. What troubles you?'

'All these stupid plays ... and the awful parts. If I can't be someone, something great, I'd rather be dead!'

'Not any more. Now you must make up your mind to live. You have a great future ahead ... worth a lifetime of suffering if need be. One is not given such a gift as your voice without having to pay a price, *n'est ce pas*? I shall write a play which will bring out all your talents; it will fit like a glove. I promise you great success.'

Such predictions from the lips of George Sand herself! Sarah went home not to die but to live, *quand même!*

Duquesnel's confidence in Sarah was vindicated the following month. In September 1866, at her true début, Sarah carried off a small triumph.

Until now, the tight-lipped Chilly gave her only understudying or triflingly unimportant parts. Sarah bit her lips and remembered her pledge to Duquesnel. She was beginning to grow on the public who previously came out of curiosity in the hope that with luck they would catch her displaying one of her 'mad originals'.

Her devoted claque greeted her entrances with vigorous applause. Patiently, Chilly watched her carry off triumphs in larger, more important parts until in the *Testament de César Girodot*, she had the part of Hortense. The great critic, Sarcey, wrote :

> Several times I found myself admiring in this unknown girl, a singular exactness of intonation, and unstudied elegance, and a sense of the stage which is really remarkable . . . She abandons her charms to the grace of God – what a pity that this young woman has not yet consented to take either life or her art seriously! She has the makings of an actress, if she would.

Duq beamed with satisfaction as he read, and enjoyed the embarrassment of his partner who was still far from admitting anything, while he was vindicated for his loyalty to Sarah. Without a word, Chilly gave Sarah the lead in Dumas père's *Kean*; the role of Anna Danby. It was her first important role and played opposite the idol of Paris, one of the handsomest, most distinguished stars of the Théâtre Française, Pierre Berton.

He fell in love with her almost as soon as they met; with the enchantment of her voice, her grace and inner hunger, her feminine appeal. They rehearsed privately all the important roles, and he taught her how to overcome the stiffness that Sarcey had lampooned. What Sarcey could not know was that Sarah had stagefright almost every time she performed. In spite of it, nothing seemed to spoil her voice, with that strange magic, already a legend.

Berton truly adored Sarah and was a regular visitor to her flat, playing with Maurice and feeding him *bon-bons*.

The night of her first appearance in *Kean*, the great Dumas was seated in his box with his current mistress, Ada Montrin. All Paris seemed to seethe at the sight. The audience felt it an affront, their sympathies still with the

exiled hero, Victor Hugo. As with one voice, they shouted :
'Send that woman away! *Ruy Blas! Ruy Blas!* Victor Hugo!'

The middle classes were furious with Napoleon III, and
their anger over the enforced exile of Victor Hugo was an
issue which became confused with the artists and writers
of the period. They wanted Hugo back and in their anger
remonstrated against Dumas. Helplessly, Dumas tried to
calm them, pounding his big fists on the brass railing of the
box, but they would not listen; instead, they sent up cat-
calls and volleys of thunderous shouts.

Unable to cope with the uproar, Duquesnel decided to
raise the curtain in the hope that the tempest would then
subside.

Dumas' mistress left while he was trying to speak, and
her departure plus the rising curtain subdued the crowd
somewhat. As he turned to sit down, Dumas saw Ada
Montrin had disappeared, so he followed suit.

With the noise still roaring, Sarah made her entrance.
Speaking her first lines, stage fright gripped her so hard
she nearly fainted. Her eyes turned backstage. Duquesnel
notioned to her to continue as the words formed on his
lips, words she could not hear : 'You may die of fright but
you must act! Proceed!'

Part of the audience laughed at her costume but her
faithful ones applauded to impose silence. Her voice captured
the most hardened by the clear tones which rose and fell
as enchantment and distress followed each other. The
audience fell silent so that even their breathing seemed
abated. It would be sacrilege to disturb the air – to miss
one syllable or nuance. When she finished the speeches –
interminable, but adored by Dumas' public – the audience
seemed unable to rouse itself from the rapt attention into
which it had fallen, and appeared utterly hypnotised.

Finally realising it was time the artist knew their reaction,
they roused themselves and sent up a 'Hoorah! *Ah bon!*'
whistling and applauding. Upwards of sixty students locked
hands and dashed up and down the aisles, looking as if
they meant to invade the stage. Thinking this a demonstra-

tion against her, Sarah rushed off the stage and up to her dressing room to hide. Berton quickly followed to reassure and call her back. Encircling her small waist firmly he swept her up in his arms and carried her down again: 'Come, they want you. You were eloquence itself.'

'I was frightened stiff,' she said still shivering.

'No, no. I tell you they want you. Listen!' He waited a moment. 'Can you hear them? They won't let the play go on until you acknowledge them yourself.'

'Then it isn't another failure?'

'*Mais non, ma chère*. You've scored a triumph! Go out and take a bow.'

Pandemonium again broke loose when she stepped out: 'Sarah! Sarah! Our Sarah!' over and over they repeated. She stepped into the wings and brought Berton out to share in the glory which he had helped her to earn.

Next day Dumas was gracious to her in his thanks for saving the day for him and raising his play to success. He had the distinction of being the first of dozens of great authors who were indebted to her for inspiring their work beyond anything their imagination had conceived.

Young Sarah was the idol of young Paris; her unique interpretations fitted the mood and restlessness of her generation; the new and young France which spat just as easily in mocking mention of their Emperor's name, Napoleon-le-Petit, as when they spoke hers lovingly.

Though fond of luxury, Sarah accepted matter-of-factly the ugliness and disorder of backstage life; the constant contact with the raw materials of make-believe so essential in theatre: the wig-makers whose skill was classed with the great artists'; make-up artists who could transform an adolescent into a dwarf or an octogenarian; the dressing rooms that reeked of perspiration camouflaged by perfume; costumes of every fabric and colour racked up like rags; no one would suspect their transformation when clothing a softly curving female form. Animals, pets belonging to actors or strays, mysteriously darted up and down the stairs and corridors between the stream of human traffic without causing accidents; by the same token, they prevented those same stairs and halls from being scrubbed, and débris of every sort was crushed into the wooden surfaces. Peeling paint hung like fungi on walls, and cracked or broken windows allowed Nature's small squatters to enter for shelter and build nests so that spiders, hornets and even pigeons laid a few eggs and raised a brood. Amid this modern Noah's Ark the scent of roses or violets in season, and sometimes heliotrope freshened the mustiness when an admirer's bouquet was stuck in a vase.

After her success in Sand's delightful comedy, *L'Autre*, she played a young male in Coppée's *Le Passant*, and earned enthusiastic praise for this interpretation which she carried off easily with surly boyish grace.

She was summoned to give a command performance at the magnificent Tuileries which ended in high excitement when the Emperor approached Sarah, kissed her on both cheeks and pinned to her shoulder a diamond brooch set with the imperial initials. For that evening, Sarah was queen!

Berton looked on with mixed feelings, brooding. In the midst of all the excitment, none of it eluded Sarah. Intensely involved with the politics of the day, he sat silently moody as they drove home. When he could spare time from his acting, he attended political meetings where he met rebel artists and writers; conditions were coming to a head; Napoleon was heartily disliked by more than half the population. He remembered that whenever he mentioned this subject, Sarah exploded, 'You know I hate politics! It is an invention of *vulgaires* who like to argue; envious of those whose places they'd like to have. And the worst of it is, it makes enemies of the dearest friends.'

'But you should know the truth about your own Emperor,' Berton insisted.

'I know what I have to know . . . I'm a Frenchwoman!'

'That should be more than enough, under ordinary conditions. But our stupid Emperor is flirting with war and if we keep quiet, he'll think we approve. If we don't stop him, every Frenchman will have the guilt of war on his own shoulders.'

'Very well', Sarah shouted. 'If he asks my advice, I'll be happy to give him your report. And now I'm tired and I'll thank you never to mention this again.'

Similar heated discussions ran through Berton's mind as they drove along while Sarah, exhilarated by her thrilling evening, coquettishly reminded him, 'I told you my luck would change, but you don't seem pleased.'

Her words stung as he put his own interpretation on them.

'This brooch should bring a small fortune at Uncle Shylock's, and it will never be missed as I'll have it copied. And pay Maurice's tutor for a year, I should think. Why do you look so gloomy?'

'I was jealous; to think a mere accident gives that imbecile the right to command. It's monstrous!'

'*C'est la destinée,*' she attempted.

'*C'est un canaille!*' Berton hissed.

With Berton at her side and her career well established most of Sarah's inner needs at once found fulfilment, emotionally and artistically. Spearheading her popularity, her small public argued over her press notices and drew with their probing analysis the attention of busier but not less interested spectators from every level in the boiling-pot which was Paris in the reign of Napoleon-le-Petit.

Mme Guerard had put in order the first floor flat at 16 rue Auber, arranging the antiques left to Sarah by her Dutch relatives, the survivors of whom had moved to Paris to be closer to the few remaining relatives. They adored playing with little Maurice, but watching the fascinating career of the young actress was their chief interest.

There was a drawback, which brought hardship and inconvenience to Sarah's early career days. As she was very poorly paid, there were always debts. Mme Guerard was more busy with her own affairs and the distance between their flats also added inconvenience. Sarah could afford only the cheapest help, and had to be content with a stupid girl to look after the flat and to take Maurice out to the park for a few hours. Dishes and disorder were always in view because after the maid marketed, cooked and fed the child and herself, she had very little time to clean. With all his affection for Sarah, such an untidy setting was depressing to Berton.

'I wish there was something I could do, some way I could help take care of you,' he told her. 'There's only one way. You must marry me.'

Sarah loved Berton passionately but she refused. Before meeting her, he had lived with another woman who was the mother of his four children.

'No, *cher*. Your obligations come first. For me, you can't help anymore, so let's count our blessings. I'll manage. It won't be like this for long.'

He argued with her but she put him off:

'Apart from my mother's health, I only worry about my baby. I can't rely on Josephine, that's why I rush home from the theatre.'

'*Ma pauvre petite*. You see, I am a worthless wretch, and there's very little chance of things changing for me.'

'How can you talk like that? What would have happened to me the night we played *Kean*? And you're forgetting your writing. Some day you'll be among the great, as famous as Dumas, and I'll be proud of you. An artist never despairs. Chin up, *quand même*.'

'You are adorable, he murmured. 'Without you, I too don't know what I'd do.'

Sarah was given the lead in *Adrienne Lecouvreur*, the famous tragedy by Voltaire. Adrienne had been Voltaire's mistress. Berton taught Sarah the history of the heroines along with the history of the theatre.

'When you play Adrienne, remember she was a real woman as well as a great actress who gave her life for her lover's; he was an aristocrat who worshipped her, but his mother came between them. They had a son who grew up and in his turn fell in love with Rachel, another great and famous woman; our greatest tragedienne. Rachel bore him two sons.'

'It is poetic, *n'est ce pas, ma chère*? The son and the father both lost their beloved in their youth. Both had sons to remind them of their loved ones.'

Sarah and Berton were inseparable through the months of her developing career. Five months later after a performance, Sarah had one of a growing list of presentiments; a foreboding of doom. Anxious over her baby, she came home alone, Berton having had to stay on to discuss the staging of a new play. 'I'll be along as soon as the first act is set. Don't wait, I know you're worried.' Berton sent Sarah home in a cab and returned to the work in hand.

As the cab turned into rue Auber, she saw a fire engine hosing a burning building. A young woman trying to break through the crowd which had collected, was screaming in front of the building. The young woman was Josephine. Her efforts to get into the building were being repulsed by the fireman.

Sarah was close enough now to hear what was going on. One woman, her arms akimbo, was sneering at Josephine. Laughingly, she looked to the others for their tacit agreement:

'So Mlle Bernhardt's baby is in the apartment, eh? Very clever. Set a fire to collect insurance on a lot of old rags so she can pay off all her creditors with someone else's money. G'wan, we've drunk from that bottle before.'

'But how can that be? Would I try to get in if that were true? Please? Please let me in. If you won't let me in, please,' she turned to the fireman, 'please won't you go in, the baby is sleeping in there!'

'Really? You expect us to fall for that? No, dear lady, we don't throw away our lives so stupidly.' The fireman held her firmly. The fire had spread in so many directions it threatened the foundation. 'You can't go in. The stairs are on fire. What did you forget there? Your sleeping lover?

Had one too many, eh? Never mind, you're young. There'll be others. We're not crazy enough to believe your story.'

Sarah rushed up to Josephine who fell upon her, crying and talking in confusion. 'Madame, your baby! They won't believe me! He'll burn . . .!'

Without hearing the end, Sarah dashed away to slip between the firemen whose hoses soaked her through to the skin. Her cape thrown over her curly hair, her slim ferret-like body slithered through before they knew what had happened. They heard a cry of anguish from the burning stairs as she disappeared into the thick smoke; they cursed, concentrating their hoses on the doorway, unable to do anything but to continue playing the pitifully inadequate water on the spreading flames.

The crowd of Frenchmen stood silent, suddenly aware of a tragedy being enacted before their eyes – they who had laughed and sported a moment ago. They began to console Josephine, apologising as the moments passed, each one an hour, while the crowd tried to keep hopeful of the outcome.

Finally, a darkly-shrouded form, thickened out around the middle, was seen emerging from the smoke, feeling its way with shuffling feet as if blind. A shout rose from the crowd and they all surged toward it. The firemen held them back while one of them quickly lifted Sarah with the sleeping baby in her arms and carried them to Guaducelli's chocolate shop just across the street. The crowd moved along sympathetically, following the fireman and his bundle, taking charge of Sarah and her baby as soon as they were deposited on chairs. Some women took the sleeping child and held him, while others brought a bottle of cognac and poured a drink, urging Sarah to sip it.

The fire continued to burn until everything was destroyed, including all the priceless Dutch antiques which her grandfather had cautioned her to insure – they could never be replaced – and her pets, Chrysagere and Zerbinette, tortoises which she had allowed to roam about the flat to everyone's amusement. Chrysagere had been her special delight because its back was covered with a shell of gold, set with small blue and pink gems and yellow topazes that flashed and reflected the sunlight or the moon.

Sarah had to go to Julie's, and lived there with her princeling, Maurice for some time. None of her rich relatives offered help of any kind. Uncle Faurre came to visit Sarah but his wife, Aunt Henriette, would not allow the actress's name to be mentioned. She thought it scandalous that Sarah had become an actress, and agreed with the widespread notion that she was wildly extravagant. She even seemed satisfied that in a way her predictions had come true and that this was just what she had expected. Rosine laughed to think that with all her success, Sarah was still too stupid to find herself a wealthy protector. 'Why ask me for help?'

Hearing of the debacle and the young actress's suffering, Adelina Patti, the Nightingale, offered to sing at a benefit performance. As soon as the announcement was made public, the house was sold out. All Paris had but one idea – to restore Sarah's home as quickly as possible so that she could devote herself to the stage. Clearly, Parisians had a double duty in supporting this concert. Total receipts more than paid the claims made by the landlord in the negligence case, but Sarah still needed money for a new flat and furnishings.

Now, when all her close relatives turned their backs on her, still another stranger, the last person from whoms he would have expected help, her late father's notary, came to offer his. He called quite unexpectedly and explained he had read the story of the fire in the papers. He wanted to know every detail of how the fire had started. Sarah surmised it must have been the candle by the bed which caught the lace curtains. The maid was always being cautioned, but always forgot. Sarah had carefully moved it away many times, but Josephine pushed it back.

'Then you mean you were not insured?'

'No. I meant to be, but my papers lay in my dresser drawer, and I didn't have the money for the premium.'

'Oh, I see. But I can help you. Since your grandmother

left you an annuity, you can raise a lump sum on it by agreeing to insure your life for two hundred and fifty thousand francs for forty years for the benefit of the purchaser. I will then give you a hundred and twenty thousand francs in cash.'

Sarah agreed immediately, since she was penniless and this would save her from having to beg or receive charity from her relatives. When he left, Sarah recalled her childhood aversion of him and marvelled at Fate.

The fire which nearly took her child's life recalled a parallel, the story Julie often told her of the fire in which Sarah was burned at two years of age, and which Julie often blamed for Sarah's fiery temper. Though Sarah quipped lightly that she and Maurice were under special Grace, having 'both suffered baptism by fire,' she became a fiercely possessive, fear-ridden mother. From this experience, Sarah grew aware of repetitions – as though the appearance of one event foreshadowed a second – not only in her life but in history and its historical figures.

Hugo, Sardou, Dumas and other great personages of the period were known to be intrigued with and studied occult phenomena. Some met regularly and sat in séances. They exchanged experiences and George Sand, born under the first Empire, pointed out the uniquely identical career of the Great Napoleon with that of his nephew. His entrance in Paris from obscurity to dictator, to exile, after military defeat.

When Sand crossed Sarah's path – like a huge dynamo sparking and infusing energy to a stalled motor – her life took on vigour, direction, and continuity. All the great of the period: makers of history, drama, finance, art and philosophy gravitated to her and became life-long friends. Sarah's attraction was undefinable but very real. That she survived the cycles of high good fortune and the aftermaths of destruction were due to an accidental discovery. Anaemia and nerves drained her, so that her voice did not project; in despair that this would damage her success, she determined to go on stage for the next performance and raise her voice to an angry pitch and give out with all her strength, then stalk off. To her surprise, this forced exercise opened her throat, deepened her breathing and exhilarated her so that she gave a superb performance. Afterwards, she had no ill effects, quite the contrary – she never felt better. From this she learned that her body was a mere robot which she could command to do her will.

Her success dated from Sand's comedy, *L'Autre*, and brought new glories to Sand. Patiently the actress listened when Sand questioned her why she had previously played the roles she detested.

'I had no choice.'

'I see. Remember this, an experienced player recognises a poor role and would never play it, since it would only give the critics the chance to tear him down.'

'But how can I avoid them?'

'Pretend you're ill and send a message just before rehearsal. But you'll find your own ways I'm sure.'

With the money her father's notary had sent, Sarah took a studio-flat at the corner of the rue de Rome, almost opposite the one which was recently burned. The studio-reception room where she entertained while working became a mecca for all Paris; its Bohemian cosiness, the spacious bare floor nonchalantly strewn with damp clay, easels, slabs of marble, and animals delighted patrons, artists and friends, and Sarah's menagerie featured in the brilliant conversations.

At the entrance, her huge dog, Caesar, snarled at everyone, even the 'regulars'. At the end of the long hall to the studio, Darwin's retreat at the far corner came into view; the monkey's leg was fastened by a light chain attached to the badly worn Louis XV settee; a little table stood on the white bear-skin rug, bearing rosé wine sparkling in a crystal decanter. Above the settee, two cages hung, one housing lovebirds, the other Sarah's favourite brightly coloured parrot.

Watching for a dull moment, she would set the birds loose and wave them toward the guests who soon scattered in panic when the dogs and cats made a wild chase after the birds, climbing up the cross-trees, knocking busts of celebrities into wet palettes, while Sarah laughed uproariously and entered into the chase. Her white pyjama-like smock and trousers, her own design, made her look like a snowman cavorting indoors.

High on the list of celebrities was the famed Baron de Rothschild who had promised Sarah ten thousand francs for his likeness. This restless man furrowed his brows first in a straight line, then raised them, changing expressions as he turned over papers and reports, ignoring the pose Sarah had taken so long in choosing.

Patiently, she tried: 'My dear baron, I would so appreciate it if you would lift your distinguished head long enough for me to finish. It would save you time too.'

The baron stopped long enough to say: 'I would indeed be happy to oblige but we are on the verge of a crisis and my responsibilities are great; this is not the time to sit and stare into space: we may be at war any minute.'

'Very well. Everyone agrees it's an excellent likeness, so I too should be satisfied.' But Sarah scraped and smoothed a bit longer, reluctant to stop. '*Voilà!* Finished. You may look at it, baron.' She stepped back wiped her hands and picked up a little dog who waited at her heels.

The baron rose elegantly and walked round the sculpture, smoothing his beard and trying to focus attention on his bust, but failed: 'Is that me?' he asked at last. Still absent-mindedly he took out his chequebook and began to write, unmindful of the effect his actions produced in Sarah. She, indifferent to all except her world of art, mistook his attitude competely. One of her blind furies was touched off. The next moment the baron's likeness was raised high overhead, then it came crashing to the floor at the feet of the sitter, thundering and echoing into a thousand splinters.

With magnificent control, he finished the cheque and looked up into a pair of enormous flashing eyes. Without a word he picked up his hat and left, Sarah's breath scorching the air. 'Sir, you owe me nothing, you b-b-banker, you!' he heard as she tore the cheque strewing the pieces among the bits of plaster on the floor.

Passing the baron, Clairin, the famous muralist, entered with Duquesnel. Both looked ruefully round the room, imagining what had happened. Clairin understood the young artist's suffering and comforted her. 'Never mind, dear, it's a pity of course; it was one of your best.' One of his favourite pupils, he adored her. She hissed: 'Ugh, bourgeois millionaires! All they know is money; thought he could pay for the privilege of insulting me.' Duquesnel silently nodded agreement.

Sand paid an unexpected visit to Sarah's dressing room. 'Mind my smoking *chérie*?'

'Never in your case. It's so good to see you; so much has been happening. That new sentry-box suit is stunning and so becoming, especially the stove-pipe hat. I have so many questions about your new play.'

'Don't feel much up to it today.' She sighed heavily 'Forgive me but I sense a storm and feel low. I came for a lift. How's Maurice?' she spoke slowly as if by such tricks fate would be propitiated.

War rumours were in the air, growing louder with each passing day since the New Year of 1870, but Sarah refused to let herself hear. 'He's very naughty but I love him too much to punish him; Mme Guerard warns me I must discipline him or he'll be impossible. He's such a baby, I can't.'

'I know, easier said than done. I too, spoiled mine but it was partly due to the times; do you realise I was born just before the end of the first Republic, Napoleon I was still Emperor. Then there was the restored monarchy; the Revolution of 1830 followed which brought back Louis Philippe until 1848 when our country nearly turned communist.'

Sand laughed, 'Sounds like a Dumas novel – next instalment – I sat in many groups, listened to all sides, helped with pamphlets. Ah, that unforgettable Lamennais. He was like a Greek god turned philosopher, only his writing was sheer poetry. Let's see, after that came our Napoleon-le-petit who began as president and is now Emperor. *Bon Dieu*, what next!'

Apprehension gripped Sarah as she heard Sand's courageous recital. Sarah's life had now reached beyond the delta. On 10th March 1865, Morny died suddenly after a short illness and left Julie almost penniless. She had taken a very modest flat, and to save expenses, Mme Guerard took the year-old Maurice to Julie's so that she could care for both, but the baby's prattling irritated his grandmother, who was feeling ill and sorry for herself. She complained continually and ended by spoiling the baby in her efforts to keep him quiet.

'I'm frightened. I hate political quarrels. Nothing is ever settled. How did you get drawn into it, you, The Romantic?'

'I knew everyone through the papers I wrote for and they considered me an intellectual, a wise woman, and of course a rebel. Each tried to drag me over to his side, even de Tocqueville, that pompous snob.'

'And what came of it?'

'Bloodshed; nothing but bloodshed. I soon realised it takes more than wisdom or talk to make things fall right. We're a long way from our goal yet, so you see, we had so little time, so few moments of peace, one hated to miss them. Life itself is the best discipline here in France.'

Morny's death threw all France and its colonies into a panic: Maximilian was executed and Mexico was lost; his widow returned home insane and lived until ninety in a child's world of fantasy. Those who had blindly put their lives and fortunes into his hands awoke that fateful 10th March to curse him for having by his death led them into poverty and betrayal. As if to taunt them, his funeral was as opulent and stately as a king's and mourning lasted a month.

His circle of intimates and close friends, as well as the merry-minded joy-seekers were bereft of their leader. His young wife mourned him deeply, but remarried soon after to a wealthy nobleman. Julie and his other mistresses were impoverished; without status or credit.

Napoleon III, now left to his own counsel, blundered into Bismarck's trap and threw France into war, knowing it was suicide, yet unable to find the diplomatic key to avoid it without the aid of de Morny's statesmanship. The greatest tribute paid to his half-brother came from Napoleon himself, in his self-pity: 'Ah, if only Morny had lived, this would never have happened.'

For Sarah, the war's untimely interruption was boiling up angers and conflicts to confuse her. One evening, after supper with her little son and Berton, she asked; 'Berton, please tell me *why* we are at war?'

'It's all very simple; we're at war to save our Emperor's vanity.'

'Go on, what has he done?'

'He has insulted our strongest neighbour by impossible demands on Bismarck, whose only interest was in uniting Germany. Napoleon feared a strong Germany because he has no confidence in his position at home. His thieveries have made him many enemies.'

'Enemies?'

'Yes, enemies. This Napoleon has the gift of staging a *coup d'état* at the drop of a secret; he expected to show how clever he was by taunting Bismarck; he has tried to effect an alliance with Austria and Italy against Prussia since 1867, but they turned him down. No one, it seems, trusts him. Naturally when Bismarck heard about this, he doubled his efforts to strengthen Germany.'

'Go on, I'm listening,' Sarah whispered.

'Then suddenly, Spain expelled Queen Isabella and offered their throne to Germany, asking that it be filled by a German Prince. At first the Germans hesitated because they knew it would only raise issues with Napoleon, and they were anxious to avoid war. Is this clear so far?'

'Perfectly. Then what happened?' she asked.

'Our little tyrant mistakenly thought this was a show of weakness and pushed his luck too far. He insisted that Kaiser Wilhelm put himself on record as being opposed to the whole thing, which he of course, refused to do. If Napoleon had simply accepted the Kaiser's word for it, everything would have quietened down. Napoleon took the Kaiser's refusal as a rebuff, with no other alternative except to declare war.'

'My God! Is that all? That's awful!'

'In a nutshell. The man is an imbecile!'

'But Bertie, whatever the reason, I'm on the side of France. I'll not call my Emperor imbecile or stupid. This is my country and I'll do my part in any way I can.' In spite of his mean reputation, the Emperor had been kind to her and secretly, she thought of him as the one man, the only man who could fill the void left by her father. She had childishly thought her troubles were past – never to return. Ahead lay one goal – art and its shining rewards! Instead, despair and disappointment dashed all her hope to bits, just as she had, a few days ago, smashed a perfect work of art in her studio.

Sarah refused to be convinced. Stinging with resentment, she tucked her baby into his crib and left in high dudgeon with Berton for the Odéon.

Promptly at seven, the company on stage were receiving last minute instructions from the managers, each one agog with the news of war, whispering their worries over the unknowns facing them and what to do about their families. Impatiently waiting for the two stars to arrive, the managers sent out for the latest papers. The clock ticked away; more than half-an-hour passed with no sign of either one.

Messengers were sent to Sarah's home, pages dispatched to search the dressing-rooms, wings, and any likely spot.

The audience was growing restive under the double impact of the war tension and the late curtain. Feet began to stamp and whistles pierced the air. Duquesnel looked at Chilly and opened his palms in resignation. One minute more and Chilly would lose control.

'I suppose we'll have to begin without them. You go out and make the curtain speech while we take advantage of the next few minutes. Maybe they'll yet appear. Sarah is one thing, but what has happened to Berton? At least he is always dependable. He knows what is proper.'

Chilly was just about to do as his partner suggested when Sarah came in, hurrying ahead of Berton, both flushed in angry silence. The signs of their violent disagreement were only too apparent, but as yet, no one suspected why they had quarrelled. For a few moments the war and the chafing audience were forgotten as whispers passed through the company. 'They've had a row. Sarah's quarrelled with Berton!'

Sarah, straight as a cliff, went to Duquesnel in her most imperious attitude, her eyes blazing, but he spoke first, thoroughly out of patience:

'Where have you been and why, of all times, are you late tonight? Explain, but please hurry! An audience is waiting!'

'I have acted with this MAN for the last time!' she uttered hoarsely, pointing a finger at Berton, who looked on bitterly.

Chilly interposed himself, unable to restrain his impatience:

'What's the matter? WELL! Must the war be over before we know what's happened between you two!'

Sarah went on in the same tone, her voice rising as she denounced Berton:

'He is disloyal! He is a pro-German!'

Berton could no longer let her go on. He came forward a step, his face pleading intensely for understanding and said simply:

'It's a lie! It's a lie! She asked me to come on stage and

sing the *Marseillaise* with her and I refused because I disapprove of the war and the crazy Emperor who declared it. Every sensible man in France agrees with me. But I am not disloyal and I am not pro-German!' Berton dropped his arms while Sarah continued flinging her remarks at him with the lash of a whip.

'You hear him? He admits it himself! I will not appear with a traitor! I will never act with him again!'

Berton looked round him at the managers and the company, then in a hoarse voice spoke as if to himself:

'I have loved a wild eagle, and now she tears out my eyes with her sharpened claws.' He turned away and walked off stage.

Sarah felt a deep twinge but she fought it down. The company and the audience were waiting for the curtain. She could do nothing more now.

Chilly gave the order to raise the curtain. Hardly was it lifted three inches, when the audience exploded with a thrilling shout: '*À Berlin! À Berlin! Vive la France!*' Sarah stepped forward, the company closed about her as the orchestra struck up the *Marseillaise*. Her bell-tones soared, resonated clearly above the public as if only she sang, its quality defying any sound or vibration to mingle with it.

At the sound of her voice everything was forgotten. Her audience and the company knitted together into one whole, one entity with a single core. Sarah's dark cape slipped off her shoulders revealing her slim figure in a dazzling white robe with a girdle of brilliant green circling her tiny waist. She was the Spirit of France. The audience was carried away, frenzied with emotion and exultation. As her singing ended, a band of young students rushed on stage, shouting '*Vive Sarah!*' raised her up on their shoulders and carried her off heading towards the Boulevards.

The audience sang provincial tunes, chattered as they milled about not knowing how to escape the feeling of confusion and desperation which tugged at them like an undercurrent. Speeches were made by important men, after which there was more singing. The crowds left the theatre for the neighbourhood cafés.

Chilly and Duquesnel read from several papers, searching headlines, despatches and theatre news, making a weak attempt to discuss what the next practical step should be. The war crisis left them utterly helpless.

Chilly wearily remarked, looking up from his papers: 'Well, it seems the morale of the troops is high. That's good news. Macmahon is at Reichshoffen and expects to be in Berlin in a few weeks.'

'Yes, yes.' Duquesnel nodded absent-mindedly. 'I think I'll go home. Enough for one night.'

'Me too. *Au revoir*.'

'*Au revoir*. See you tomorrow.'

The beginning of September brought an epidemic of patriotic anguish, of fanatical suspicions, and of rage against the perfidious indifference of other nations. Sarah saw before her, the spectacle of a heart-sick nation.

The Battle of Sedan had been fought two days before. The results were such that the government judged it best not to divulge the news, hoping for a miracle to save the nation's honour. But finally, private telegrams from London and Brussels brought the first rumours of the debacle. It began with Bazaine's treachery which resulted in the butchery of Canrobert's men; the battle at Gravelotte, with thirty-six thousand men, French and German, cut down in three hours; the great Macmahon left powerless; repulsed as far as Sedan; then the loss of Sedan itself!

To make matters worse, it was felt that amidst that terrible anxiety, the news supplied was unreliable; newspaper statements were more or less fantastic and conflicting; even the official telegrams posted by the Ministry of the Interior were regarded with suspicion. The struggle between fear and hope went on but beneath was the national conviction that France could not be beaten. Yet at four on that lamentable Saturday in September 1870 the Empress received a dispatch:

L'armée est défaite et captive; moi-même je suis prisonnier.

Napoleon.

but not until seven that evening did the whole awful news burst upon the people.

Foreign nations speculated whether this was the end of France. Reality surpassed all imagination. The Emperor and his whole army taken! Like a death knell, it echoed and re-echoed dully in Sarah's whole being. She must ask, talk, see what others were thinking and doing. In the nearest gathering, she saw a concierge. She heard her own voice asking, as though coming from the end of a tunnel:

'And what is going to happen today?'

Wearily, the concierge fanned out his arms leaving the answer to one of the group who muttered savagely:

'They're coming down from Belleville; we shall fight on the Boulevard, and by tonight there will be no more Empire left. Curse the Emperor!'

It was not a day for neutrality. Each one had to stand up and be counted. Even artists and *petit-bourgeois* whose interests set them apart had to take a stand. Destiny helped. Napoleon was done for, so they all rejoiced over his fall. All cursed Napoleon, but no one mentioned France.

She joined another group. This time she heard passionate denouncements – the Emperor must be dethroned at once and another government, any government, it mattered not which, be set up if it would end by beating the Prussians. Only a victory, a total victory over the Prussians would set France back on her own throne as Queen of Culture, courtesan to all of Europe and playground of the world.

Sarah tried not to look at the coming catastrophe. France, her homeland, obssessed by maniacal passions. The disposition to be an onlooker to history's undoing of her country was not within her. She could close her eyes so as not to see the smash, but it was a certainty that she would be present during the irreparable fall of France.

From this moment, France appeared to her as a living goddess who had been raped, betrayed, and torn asunder limb from limb. A fierce kinship was forged in the young woman's super-conscious self which turned her into an instrument of personal vengeance for her Nation. She would not eat, sleep, nor rest until her country was purged and vindicated, and again restored to honour and dignity among the nations of the world. She berated herself for having ignored politics; perhaps if she had listened to Berton, Sand and the others, she could have been the instrument by which this might have been averted.

But now the mobs were fomenting a waking nightmare of wreckage in the name of politics. On 4th September, she reached the rue de la Paix, just in time to see a part of the crowd that had been urging on the National Guards to attack the Chamber. They wanted a government of lawyers to be proclaimed. Sarah was wild with anger. How the enemy would laugh to see the French so eager to destroy themselves!

The demerits of the Empire did not excuse those who made the unpatriotic revolution of 4th September. That should have been left for the time when the last German had left France. She could not forgive the half-dozen deputies who on this day thought fit to seize the government for their own use. With the Empire lying in the gutter, the army almost annihilated, and the remnants demoralised, she hated the triumph of the radical barristers.

5

The Siege of Paris

The Odéon closed for a time in order to give the company a chance to offer their services to the defence department, but news from the front was so discouraging, the theatre remained closed.

After that fateful outburst on the declaration of war, Berton disappeared and Sarah had to begin tempering herself again. Guilt plagued her until she broke down. But nothing would keep her in bed, and she finally decided on a course of action, a prescription which was sure to assuage her conscience.

The harrassed young woman took a course in nurse's training, and found that her art studies in anatomy were useful as a basis. She drove herself to prepare for any emergency and even mastered minor surgical skills. She was now ready to wheedle a permit from the authorities to turn the Odéon into a hospital.

Through Girardin, Duquesnel got her a letter of introduction. It was signed Comte de Keratry. Her curiosity was aroused.

'Do you think,' she asked Petite Dame 'it could be a relative of the comte who came to the party the night you made me dress and go to Mama's party?'

'It certainly must be. There aren't many people by that name.'

They drove to the Tuileries to meet the Préfect of Police. A long list of supplies had been painstakingly prepared and stowed in Sarah's purse. Despite the distractions of the war, happier memories streamed through her mind's eye as they drove along.

She recalled the Grand Ball given for Queen Victoria only a short year ago. Her Majesty was the only English reigning monarch ever to come to Paris. Never was there brought together such a wealth and variety of many-shaped, many-coloured and much-embroidered, gilded, buttoned, be-medalled uniforms. Outstanding were those of the Hussar Generals of the Austrian Army. Sarah had remarked: 'See, the tunic and breeches are scarlet, embroidered abundantly with gold; the dolman is white, laced with gold and edged with stable; the busby is sable. Have you ever seen such a covering for a man?' She had been impressed by the predominance of shades of red, at the ball, from the pink burnous of a Moroccan sheikh, through all the hues of scarlet and crimson to the dark claret of the Empress's chamberlains. Her memories grew more vivid. A guard was saluting her just as her carriage halted. Behind him a semicircle of forty guards in brown and silver uniforms gave their traditional elliptical salute, then bowed concentrically. She looked round to see if other guests were there, to deliver their bows rotarily, as was their stern duty.

But today broke into yesterday with its blunt language, mixed odours of tobacco and grease, scratched cabs and irritable abuse. Her carriage had halted at the Tuileries, but the Palace was now headquarters for the Préfect of Police. She shuddered, squared her shoulders and took a fresh full breath.

'If you saw me now for the first time, would you say I was pretty?' she asked Madame Guerard, tilting her face in a pose of charm.

'*Mais oui, absolument.*'

'You see, those who hold the nation's purse strings won't part with a sou unless they're charmed into it. And I'll need tons of things. *Alors*, we shall try to make him part with a hospital.'

Sarah breathed deeply and as they entered, smiled angelically at the comte whom she found she had met at her mother's and who was now behind a huge desk. At her name, he jumped up quickly, pulling a long face: 'Ah you don't remember me.'

'But I do,' Sarah said happily. 'Ask Mme Guerard. She'll

tell you I had hoped it would be you. Now I'm in heaven because I know you'll let me have everything I need.'

'That's all! Well, *c'est la guerre!* Order away. I'm your slave.'

'Here's the list and, while we know you're being kind to me, it's for our country too, isn't it? Our brave army will need linens, food, medicine, blankets – it's all here.'

Sarah gave Keratry her list, then, at the moment of departure, she remembered something. Reading her hesitation, he inquired : 'What else can I do for you, beautiful Madonna?'

His sensitive perception earned a grateful smile : 'There's a stock of gunpowder in the cellars under the Odéon. If Paris were bombarded and a shell hit the building, it would be blown up with everyone in it.'

'Of course, we'll have to remove it now that the theatre will be a hospital. But you'll have to help with that. I'll need a petition, signed by the tradespeople and home-owners of the neighbourhood. Anything more?'

'Thank you for France and myself. You've been very generous.' She started toward the door, then stopped. Hanging over a chair was a heavy, warm overcoat. It hypnotised her. Mme Guerard took in the meaning and began to pull Sarah away : 'My dear, don't do that!'

Keratry, mystified by the pantomime, said : 'I would like to oblige you, but I don't understand, not at all.'

With her most charming manner, Sarah begged : 'Give it to me, will you?'

'My overcoat?' he asked in amazement. Sarah nodded assent.

'What do you want it for?'

'For my wounded when they're convalescent.'

Keratry could not control an explosion of laughter, but Sarah, when she had a course of action in mind, was determined : 'There's nothing so funny about it. It will be freezing in the Odéon foyer, and that's where the men will gather to smoke or play cards when they're well enough. Warm overcoats will be a Godsend, and not many men are as tall as you. Coats for tall men are hard to find,' she smiled, 'and this one looks so warm.' She ran her delicate hand over the silky fur lining. 'I was reminiscing on the ride here, recalling the Ball for Queen Victoria. You were one of the few men who stood out in spite of the glorious uniform. It takes a man of striking figure not to be effaced by the bright colour, medals, ribbons and cut of a smart uniform. Do you agree?' She had delivered the *coup de grâce*.

Keratry recovered his composure and began emptying the pockets of the coat which, a moment ago was his. He pulled his fine silk muffler out and pleaded: 'Will you let me keep this?'

Coquettishly pretending resignation, she gave in. Keratry rang for the orderly and laid the coat in his arms. With wrinkles of laughter still playing around his eyes, he said, 'Please take this to the carriage for the ladies.'

Twelve days later, Sarah had the petition completed and made another visit to Keratry. He was busy, and only when she entered his office did he jump up and, instead of greeting her, flung something into his closet and slammed the door shut. Then, quite breathless, 'Excuse me, please. After your last visit, I nearly had pneumonia. It's only an old ugly coat in there, but I'll keep the key to the closet if you don't mind.'

Sarah smiled sympathetically, 'You're so kind.' The war was going badly and neither of them were in a mood for levity. Home politics as well as foreign were reaching new crises every day. The German army was advancing toward Paris. One army was being formed in the Loire for another desperate attempt at surprise by generals Gambetta, Chanzy, Bourbaki and Trochu.

The Odéon was already operating as a hospital, and every day the ambulances crowded with wounded came, making the rounds, dropping off patients as though they were so much freight to be stored wherever there was room.

Keratry talked for a moment about the Emperor and Empress. The latter had been rushed away in an American dentist's carriage. No Frenchman dared to expose himself to protecting her, so high was the feeling against Napoleon III.

The great saving factor in the next weeks were the generous shipments of food; linens; tinned fish and meat; thousands of dozens of eggs; chocolate; grains of all sorts; tea and coffee. Everything which was available was sent from near and far; family and friends who had not been heard from for years now contacted the actress, giving her their whole support. Julie's stepmother, great-aunt Betty, a sister of her ninety-three-year-old grandmother, who was still living in Holland, sent three hundred night shirts through the Dutch ambassador.

Sarah turned the foyer of the theatre into a kitchen, thus serving two purposes. The oversize cookstove which held soup kettles big enough to make soup and herb tea for a hundred men at a time, warmed the large entrance hall, comforting the convalescents and was handy for serving bed-patients immediately inside the many doors to the auditorium.

Already, there were so many wounded that cots had to be placed on stage, close to the little room off the wings where Sarah and the nurses slept by turns, and which served as her office as well.

Madame Guerard and Madame Lambquin, another actress, who played mature roles, had been trained as nurses by Sarah. There was so much to do that the women slept only one night out of three. Otherwise, the only additional help she had was when a friend who was serving in the fortifications came at intervals to do the secretarial work. Dr Duchene, chief surgeon was on duty full time for the duration. The nightmare of the siege of Paris lasted four months. The women, old and young, waited for hours on end, standing in the wet, freezing weather to get bread, meat and milk for their families, now mostly children.

It was more than Sarah could bear as she occasionally glimpsed them from a window. Frozen blue in their worn garments, barely able to stamp their feet, itching for the moment when they could get their rations and rush home to the relative warmth of the bed covers. The severity of the cold broke a twenty-year record. Many a victim was carried into the hospital, stiff and silent from exposure.

And still, ambulances continued to bring wounded from the front. Sarah set up the officers' beds in the former dressing rooms, while additional cots were squeezed into the refreshment salon. A young casualty, now able to sit up, holding a bowl of soup, reminisced: 'Only three months ago I was having a cognac here with my girl.'

A consignment of canned meat finally arrived from the commissary. Of course they were opened immediately. But the gaseous fumes which rose and filled the room sent everyone running out. Sarah called them back and read the label 'Do not be alarmed by the bad odour on opening. Rinse several times in tepid water.'

It was useless. The meat only turned all colours and stunk worse than ever. Madame Guerard and Sarah decided to throw it out. Fortunately Madame Lambquin prevented it:

'In times like this we don't dare throw out anything, even rotten meat.' She replaced the meat in the tins: 'Send it back to the Council. If we don't return it, how will they know it's condition?'

As she never left the hospital, Sarah had sent her little boy to Julie's. Not only did this move solve an economic problem, but having the whole family under one roof gave them all a deeper sense of security, and Maurice had playmates in Regina and Jeanne. Marguerite was fond of the little boy but refused to look after the pets – all except the parrot, since he stayed in his cage and amused her.

Shells fell nearer Paris all the time and sometimes dropped close to the hospital and the nearby Luxembourg Gardens. Sarah saw a group of ragged dirty children run to grab the pieces of masonry in which the shells had imbedded themselves. George Boyer, a reporter who had taken refuge in the hospital, answered her unspoken question, reading the shock in her face:

'No mystery at all. They sell them to buy their turn in the queue when meat is distributed.' He pointed to a group who were lying under the stone walls of the Luxembourg. 'See how quickly they learn war tactics.'

Many a child's body was torn apart; Sarah would order the remains to be put into coffins and she herself followed them to the pauper's grave. When a barrage was going on, Julie would send messages that upset Sarah for days. Her heart could not stand the strain of the ear-piercing detonations, nor the happy squeals of laughter from the children.

Quite unexpectedly Madame Sand came to pay Sarah a visit. Sarah had heard she was ill, and there were rumours that the great author might even be imprisoned or exiled because she was again writing pamphlets in opposition to the war, scarifying Napoleon III. They fell into each other's arms, tears of joy dimming their eyes.

Sand's acquaintance with the Emperor dated back to the time when he was an obscure prisoner of Louis Philippe in the fortress of Ham. There, he wrote pamphlets and his *Extinction of Pauperism* attracted her attention. Her praise of it was repeated to the lonely prisoner by a friend.

At the time of the *coup d'état* eighty-eight members of the reactionary assembly and more than twenty-six thousand men were exiled or deported, among them Victor Hugo. No one was immune. For a time, Sand feared for her own safety.

She wrote him after the *coup*, reminding him that she had stood by him while he was in prison when he had no influential friends, and when his pretentions to the throne were regarded as ridiculous. Now that the former prisoner was a dictator, he could hardly refuse her an audience.

Upon their first meeting, he took her two hands in his and said:

'You who have the qualities of a man without having his faults, you could not be unjust to me. I care for the esteem of men, but I care especially for yours.'

George stated her position: 'I am as much of a Republican as you have ever known me to be and I shall never change.'

Then she presented him with a list – the names of her friends in exile: 'They will not retract their opinions either. I plead for the right of liberty of conscience.'

Everyone told her it was madness to hope, but George always attempted the impossible. She became a veritable nuisance to the Emperor but he looked over the lists and granted every man his freedom.

'It's so good to see you, I can hardly believe it,' Sarah cried. 'How are you? I heard you were ill and in danger.'

'None of it is true but I am tired. Is there a corner where we can sit? I promise not to smoke.' Arm in arm, Sarah led her to the sanctuary, the office-bedroom, but picked up a bundle of bandage tape on her way. Settled down, she held some of it out to Sand. 'We have so much to do and so few hands there isn't a moment to lose. Whenever we sit down, we roll bandages. Mind?'

'Of course not, *chérie*. How's your mother and little Maurice?'

'I'm worried about my mother. She wants to leave the country – afraid of the bombs. She can't stand confinement and hardship. I must find a way to get her out, quietly.'

'Do you know of any way?'

'No. Who could one trust? It's a matter of life and death.'

'True. But there is one, only one.' Sand looked quizzically at her.

'I haven't a clue.'

'Berton. He's the only one you can trust.' Sand dropped her voice, 'He would die for you.'

'But I've treated him like a savage! How can I ask him for anything even if I knew where he was?'

'That, my love, is what I meant by my work. If you wish him to come to you, I'll tell him.'

Sarah's eyes lit up as they had not done since her last stage performance. Trembling, she fell at Sand's feet and kissed her hands: 'Please do. A miracle has sent you. Please tell me more.'

'I don't do much but it is time-consuming. I send money

and food parcels to the families of the exiled writers – some writers are imprisoned – you can imagine their suffering. Now and then Napoleon allows me to come and plead for the release of one of my friends. In return, I promised not to slay him with my pen. It is all I can do at my age.'

With Berton risking his life against impossible odds, Sarah could now only set her teeth and continue waging her personal war.

It was Christmas Eve and to lighten everyone's spirits, she decorated the hospital with props from the attic: an icon of the Virgin, some festoons of leaves that she scrubbed and dusted with 'snow' from her cosmetic case, and stirred up a bowl of punch to serve with the Christmas pudding sent by the Ministry. A young priest from St Sulpice presided.

The dramatic highlight was the delivery and presentation of the Cross of The Légion d'Honneur for a young hero, Captain Menneson, tall and classic in face and bearing. Admitted only two days before, with a bullet in his shoulder, unconscious from loss of blood, his recovery was a miracle. Sarah counted sixteen bullet holes in his cape after she had gently removed it. Three bullets fell out of its hood as she helped him into his cot.

Without flinching, he had stood a target for three hours, spreading his cape out to screen the retreat of his men as they fired at the enemy in the Champigny Vines. Two days later, sufficiently recovered to smile broadly at Sarah, the young hero began to dress for his return to the front, stubbornly rejecting advice from the doctor. His sister, a nun, was summoned and together, they prevailed upon him to rest a few days longer.

January arrived bringing still more hardships; brutal biting winds and sub-freezing temperatures. Enemy flanks were tightening on Paris and food was almost a memory. Slightly wounded soldiers were numbed so quickly that they froze to death before help could reach them. Against this, Sarah's chief struggle with her conscience was in having to nurse German prisoners.

A German prisoner was well enough to tease Sarah: 'Ah *chérie*, it's obvious you've lost the war. Our army will be here in a fortnight and then you'll see how fat our women are.'

'I prefer to be slim and I hate fat women.'

'Admirable! You're quite courageous, but you have no food. I see there's barely enough to feed the wounded.'

'And why do you imagine that because you don't see it, we have nothing to eat?'

'Because if you did, you'd feed your own men better.'

Sarah burned. A plan was forming in her mind: 'We put it in their soup. I didn't suspect you were so curious or I'd have shown you the big chunks of chicken and beef.' She needed a long breath to control her impulse to strike him.

'Sure I'm curious. Let's see some of those chunks.' He scratched his grizzly three-days beard.

'Indeed! Do you like chicken?'

'Who doesn't?'

'Very well. You shall have a chicken dinner tonight.'

The German gave a nasty chuckle, 'This I *would* like to see.'

Sarah hurried to Felicie, a helper who was being instructed by Mme Guerard. She tossed the girl's coat to her: 'Put your coat on. Now listen carefully. Go and tell Marguerite to kill my parrot and dress him. Make as tiny a package as possible and slip it into your sleeve. Then hurry back here, understand?' She saw her off, to make sure: 'Now hurry!'

Sarah returned to Mme Guerard, a sharp glint in her eyes.

'The Bosche will have *Poulet à la Guerre* for his dinner tonight!'

'Poor Polly! A war casualty.' A tear dimmed Madame's eye.

No messages and no news were permitted to come in from outside for a civilian. Even nurses and doctors were considered civilians, but Sarah received a message through the diplomatic pouch of the United States Ambassador, who stayed on in Paris for the duration. A thin slip of paper with the delicacy of a primrose petal read:

'Everyone well. Courage. A thousand kisses. Your mother.'

It was dated seventeen days before, from the Hague. Sarah had hoped her family had at least arrived safely, wherever they were headed for, but never thought they had gone as far as Holland. She had assumed they would rest at Havre, where she had a cousin of her father's mother. Again, conflicts bore down on her, plaguing her: Why did they go to Holland, and were they still there? But there was no time to think of that.

Hope had fled when the bombardment commenced on 27th December, and in the midst of the flying shrapnel, Sarah and all hands rushed out to the entrance to help bring in the wounded from the ambulances before the cold and the flying debris could play their part in the tragedy.

Inside the hospital, beds of straw were improvised on the floor for the wounded, where already twelve long rows were sitting or lying, waiting to get well, and to return to the everlasting inferno.

Holding a small lantern in her hand, Sarah stepped into the ambulance to announce she had only two places left. The wounded men turned their faces toward the lamp, then turned them away again, closing their eyes, too weak to bear even that feeble light.

At midnight in the middle of January, the Brothers from the École Chrétienne came to ask Sarah for ambulances and assistants to help gather the dead and dying on the Chatillon Plateau. Anyone who was available and had shoes tough enough to walk over frozen ground with a faint light to search for bodies was pressed into service. The macabre scene was like one from Dante; the night air was so icy cold, the ambulances could hardly move on the slippery surfaces. Crawling slowly along, lit by the dim lanterns held in the stiffly frozen hands of those who took turns lighting the path, they finally arrived.

Carefully letting themselves down, not to step on anyone

in the dark, they picked their way, two to a team, whispering 'ambulance! ambulance!' One of each team had a lantern, the other carried a flask of brandy. When they heard a groan, they went in the direction of it. Sarah and the Brother who assisted her found their first soldier lying on a heap of dead bodies, his ear and part of his jaw blown off, while clots of blood, coagulated by the frost hung from the part of the jaw still there. Raising her lantern to look into his face, a wild look greeted her from the man's glazed eyes. She placed a straw into the brandy, drew up a few drops of it and blew them into the open cavity of his mouth, repeating this several times until she saw a little sign of life come back to him. Between them, the Brother and Sarah carried him to the ambulance over the dead, and over the slippery ground beneath their feet.

The next victim lay with his chest completely exposed and full of black holes. A shell had ripped off the coat front, scarring his flesh, leaving just the torn sleeves hanging at the sides from the shoulders. The blood was still oozing slowly from his mouth as Sarah approached and covered him with a gingham curtain from her eternal storehouse, the prop-room. She blew some brandy into his mouth, and when he surprised her with, 'thank you', she thought it must be his spirit speaking for him. They lifted him into the ambulance, but the effort was too much for him and the soldier began to haemorrhage, his dark blood gushing out, covering all the other wounded in the ambulance.

'Courage, sister,' the Brother told Sarah. 'We are doing all we can. The Merciful One will give you strength. Courage!'

They worked through the dark hours into the dawn after the worst night Sarah had ever known. The ambulances were crowded and still there were more men to be collected. Suddenly, Sarah was aware of daylight just as her lantern burned out; a dull, ghost-like dawn in which the living, and the dead and dying, were frozen together in an icy tapestry, each holding the other by invisible hands and unspoken words. She looked across the battlefield and surmised there must be a hundred persons in attendance; Sisters of Charity, civil and military male nurses, Brothers from the École Chrétienne, priests and a few volunteer women, all of whom gave themselves to the service of mankind. Looking further, Sarah saw by daylight, that which the night tried to hide: so many wounded, that it would be impossible to transport them all to the hospital, even though the ambulances continued making round trips without a halt. She cried out without realising it; the thought of their helplessness crushed her; many, with only slight wounds, were doomed to die of cold. In a wave of utter weariness memory again crowded out the present, substituting a bizarre scene in Sarah's mind. During her visit to de Ligne's Palace a masked ball was given. Some guests wore two masks. Several portrait masks had been made of persons at court and were worn under other masks. When the time came to uncover, the second mask was mistaken for the face. Yet all the time, the real face was still underneath and hidden.

'If only I could mask my heart so easily,' she thought.

A few days passed and another thin piece of paper was handed to Sarah with a message in her mother's handwriting, saying, 'We are all very well and at Hamburg.' At Hamburg! Sarah turned pale. Her mother, aunt and her helpless baby settled down in the enemy's country!

Rosine had friends everywhere, in Italy, Switzerland, London, Belgium, as well as Germany. There was only one possible answer – Rosine did it out of pique; to annoy Sarah and cause her anguish. She still envied Sarah her youth and vitality, and her important contacts. It never occurred to Rosine to be grateful to Sarah. She choked back the feeling of sickness welling up within her, that her mother could so easily go through life feeling no real responsibility to anyone or any country. Rosine had always led Julie from their childhood days on to the present – but how could Julie follow her now to the enemy's camp? Sarah bit her lip, forcing back her contempt.

The bombardment of Paris continued, compelling the

people to pull their belts in tighter still, and stuff more paper into their worn shoes to warm their feet, their socks being so worn now that they could not be mended. The morale of Parisians was at a low ebb as the latest rations were listed: Bread for adults, three hundred grams. Children, one hundred and fifty grams. Patriotism and anxiety led to bitter quarrels, some people advocating war to the bitter end, others pleading for peace. 'What good is fighting on, if we'll all be dead heroes, frozen and crippled,' one faction argued; while the others insisted they could not eat bread while the Bosche looked on, sneering down his nose.

The German prisoner, Frantz Mayer, to whom Sarah had served her pet parrot was fuming with anger. When she inquired why, he threw down the 'chicken' wing he had on this occasion been served, and refused to eat anything. 'I am here seventeen days in this infernal hospital. They told me Paris didn't have enough food to last two days before surrendering. I have been tricked!' What Frantz didn't know was that Sarah had bought some game birds from the Zoo, and kept them hidden in her dressing room, at the top of the Odéon. The Zoo attendant, didn't have enough grain for all the birds and animals, and hated to see them starve. It was all Sarah could do to keep herself from wondering what her landsmen would think if they knew the game she was playing to keep the German from knowing the truth. Sarah paid a high price for her pride! This, very few would comprehend.

The bombardment got worse, and now shells were flying in through the windows, breaking the glass into splinters and showering them over everyone within range of the falling debris. Sarah moved all the men down to the cellars, and Mme Guerard and the soldier she was moving were nearly killed as a shell flew at them, missing them by three inches, tearing through the cot from which she had just lifted the patient.

No sooner had they all been moved down than Sarah had to consider what to do next; the cellar was filling with water, in which large rats swam about, tormenting, everyone, and exhausting tempers and patience.

She moved the most seriously ill patients to the Val-de-Grâce Hospital, and for the others, she rented an immense empty flat in the rue de Provence. With all the moving, shortages, and resettling, thoughts of her family never left her for a second and she was almost out of her mind with anxiety.

Sarah needed money for the apartment, for linens and medicine, and blankets, because everything had rotted in the cellar when the water rose. She was afraid to use any of the mattresses or food, for fear of contamination by the rats. She needed help, and had heard that armistice negotiations were in discussion. Among the terms demanded by the Germans was the sum of two hundred million francs. Everyone shuddered at the figure, no less than their chagrin at the price of peace. Baron de Rothschild came to the rescue immediately, giving his signature for the full amount.

Sarah swallowed her pride, changed out of her uniform, and quietly told her Petite Dame: 'Take care of the hospital until I come back. I am on my way to apologise to an old friend.'

Mme Guerard looked at her, astonishment in her honest face:

'But why now, of all times?'

'Because I need money and the only man who has any is Baron de Rothschild.'

'Oh yes, he will help. The Rothschilds are always and ever kind.'

When Sarah came back, she found George Sand waiting to see her. They embraced as if a lifetime had passed. Sarah told her where she had been and how generous the Baron was:

'Look, all this money! Thousands of francs! He gave it to me without asking one question. I'm so ashamed.'

'You are my madonna, as I always said you were. You're irresistible to everyone, so how could he refuse? This is war, *ma chère*, and the price of celebrity. It is a scandal, of course, but you must ignore it.'

Looking out from the deep cuff-collar of her warm coat, her small hands tucked inside a tiny muff to keep them warm, the small figure of Madame Sand settled itself into a still smaller ball inside the drapes of her coat to make the most of its protection in the freezing room, far from the comfort of the stove. In the kitchen, the men who were able helped with the chores and there was no space for a private chat. The two women made the best of it, sipping a cup of broth from the soup-kettle brought in by Mme Guerard.

'I'm a fraud,' Sarah suddenly blurted out.

'What! What are you talking about?'

'Haven't you heard the rumours that I sent my baby to Germany deliberately! That I'm a traitor! A spy in the disguise of a nurse! But the worst is that I've had no news about my baby for two months.' Stammering, Sarah asked 'You . . . have you any news for for me?'

'No, *ma chère*, nothing.' Sand sipped her broth watching Sarah. 'The powers are negotiating the peace. As soon as that's settled, you can go find your baby and bring him back.'

But Sarah still looked disconsolate. Sand changed the subject: 'Soon, the theatre will open again and you can lose yourself in your work. You'll see, everything will be just as it was. No one can replace you there.'

Sand saw that her words had penetrated.

'I'm so weary,' Sarah said, sinking back into her chair, her eyes closed. But Sand could see a new expression coming into her face. Already Sarah is dreaming of her future, she thought.

It was a long time before Sarah opened her eyes again.

'Forgive me.' Sarah said softly. 'How is it with you?'

Sand's eye lit with wicked candour. 'Oh, you'll love this. Know what they're saying about me?'

'Oh yes. I heard they called you a witch and that you were burned in effigy because of your trips to Louis Napoleon.'

'That's right. They think me a traitor too! If only they knew how I despise that man! But I did receive some pardons for my friends and a promise that I would not be exiled. From him, that's a lot.' Sand was using her confidential tone again. This was what Sarah loved about Sand.

'You're a tonic. I feel so much better.'

'You cheer me up too. Sometimes I feel so old, I think of myself as a hangover from the *Ancien Régime*.'

'Have you any news from Berton?'

Sand took out a small cigar and lit it, deliberately tormenting Sarah. Through the smoke, she looked deeply into Sarah's eyes, 'Don't despair over Berton. I heard he's safe and by now, has a wide following! Plans, my dear.'

'Plans? What plans?'

'Why, to send Little Napoleon running for his life! It was unforgivable of him to have provoked a war for vanity.'

'You know something! I can sense it! Please tell me!'

'Oh well, I never could keep anything from you. Come. We're going to the Odéon.'

'The Odéon? Why? It's just a smashed up wreck!'

'Never mind. I'll tell you on the way.'

Like two conspirators they entered the deserted street. Hardly anyone was seen in daylight anymore except on urgent business. They hailed a cab. The horse's hooves sent flurries of muddy snow into the air with every step.

The astonished driver saw them go into the dilapidated building now full of holes and broken windows. Black crows flew silently in and out, too cold even to caw to each other. '*Mon Dieu*,' he murmured, 'What the war has done!'

They let themselves into the foyer of the Odéon, 'Am I hearing things?' Sarah asked.

Sand gripped her hand and pulled her along. The sharp tapping sounds grew louder as they entered the empty auditorium. The large hall was dimly lit with three lanterns and a long ladder reached from the floor to the royal box. At the top of the ladder stood a tall gaunt figure with a hammer and chisel in his hands. It was Berton chipping away at the letter N from the front of the box.

Sarah watched Berton in utter disbelief. She stood transfixed as he finished his work. Then he saw her. Instantly, his eyes lit up. He gripped the ladder and made his way down. Sarah slowly started toward him, then, magically it seemed, her feet barely touched the ground. She flew into his arms. Kissing her fervently, Berton whispered: 'How I wanted to see you! I'm so glad you're here.' Words were unnecessary.

Sand had waited discreetly but at last interrupted: 'Well, I guess I'd better go.'

'Oh, no, no,' they turned to her insisting that she sit with them and talk. 'Let's go to the Rond Pont. Come, join us in a toast.'

Sand laughed lightly: 'Thanks, but I have to confirm a rumour about my own brand of *apéritif*. Oh, how I've been itching to write this. Now at last I can tell my dear public that each evening, I drink a cocktail of the blood of aristocrats from their empty skulls which I store in my wine cellar. *Au revoir.*'

Snuggled against Berton's chest, Sarah whispered: 'But darling, how could you be so foolish as to have come here now. You know there's a price on your head.'

'I had to come. How could I stay out of Paris with you here. But don't worry. We've made our last plans. Tonight I rejoin my regiment. We will yet save Paris.'

'Ah Bertie, you smell so good. You're so warm. Oh, how I love you.'

He crushed her tightly to him fulfilling all the longings of the past.

Sarah went back to her duties. Instead of feeling relieved now that she had seen Berton and that the war would soon end, she was more irritable than ever. Dozens of false rumours were spread, fouling the air and strangling progress. The days of preliminaries were more unnerving than anything she had suffered before.

But finally, news of a twenty-day armistice was given out and a deep melancholy fell on the city affecting everyone, even those who had been the hardiest champions of peace. The ugly brand of shame and the vile breath of the conqueror burned on the cheek of every Parisian.

6

A Dangerous Journey
through Enemy Lines

One thought now possessed Sarah: to find her baby and bring him back. No word had come through for weeks, and knowing Rosine's love of travel and Julie's willingness to follow her sister, for all Sarah knew, they might even be in Russia. There was no great need for her to stay at the apartment-hospital. Madame Guerard and Madame Lambquin could manage without her, now that they had the money from the Baron de Rothschild, but, just the same, they did all they could to stop her from going. 'It is madness! The dangers are greater than ever at a time of armistice! What will everyone think of you now if you go over the lines? The French consul may give you a passport, but he'll be sure you're a traitor. You might be followed by someone and be killed. You won't be questioned, why you're going. All they'll say is Sarah Bernhardt is leaving France!'

She agreed everyone was right, and Mme Guerard's husband drew a sigh of relief, but Sarah's strength was ebbing. Her war duties had left her emaciated and deathly pale. If she put it off, maybe she would never see her baby again – the only thing she really lived for, Maurice.

She sent word secretly to his governess, a Mlle Soubise who had remained in Paris, thinking to herself that if this girl refused, she would not go. Happily, the young girl was delighted with the chance of adventures and travel in other countries, leaving the hardships of Paris behind. Even the prospect of great danger appealed to her youthful imagination.

Their passports signed, on the 24th of February they left Paris, only to be sent back with a brutal order to get permission from the German outpost at the Poissonières before they could be permitted outside the city. Arriving they were taken into a small shed and found a Prussian general seated there. Looking them up and down, an amazed expression came over his face. In a crisp voice he asked :

'Are you Sarah Bernhardt?'

'Yes.'

'And you believe you will cross easily?'

'I hope to.'

'Then let me tell you, you'd better stay inside Paris. You'll never make it.'

'I've heard all the reasons. I'm still going,' she said with determination.

The General called another officer and talked to him in German, after which both men left, the young women waiting unmoved. Fifteen minutes later, the second officer returned with an old friend of Sarah's, Réné Griffon, who tried everything he knew to talk her out of going, but it was no use. Seeing how stubborn Sarah was, Réné wanted to know exactly what the risks would be. The general's answer was decisive :

'Everything and worse than everything!'

Réné spoke in German with the general, to Sarah's annoyance, since she did not understand it, and imagined he was helping the general prevent her from going. Instead, a comfortable carriage drew up at the shed a few minutes later, with the general's impatient last words :

'There! I'm sending you to Gonesse to catch the provision train leaving in an hour. I'll send a message to the station master there to look for you – after that, you'll be in God's hands.'

She thanked the general and Réné Griffon, who stared after the departing carriage in utter despair. At Gonesse, Sarah was greeted politely in the Prussian manner, by a young, one-armed veteran, a recent casualty. He introduced himself and asked the two young women to follow him as the carriage drove off quickly, its driver refusing the money Sarah offered. A table was prepared for them and tea served to which they did justice, then they were escorted to their place in the train by the wounded soldier who saluted with his remaining arm as he showed them in.

The trip to Hamburg which should have been made in two days, took eleven, and as the Prussian general had predicted, everything happened. The train started and stopped innumerable times without plausible reason. It waited an hour at a time in the icy cold night, the passengers painfully freezing, while the German engineer, oilers and coalmen got down and drank beer on the siding, told jokes and laughed boisterously, spitting and pointing to the women, as they strutted in the manner of the conqueror. Sarah and Mlle Soubise bit their lips. Seeing their discomfort, the Germans grasped each other and waltzed around in circles, yelping in demonic delight.

The two young women thought it best to turn their attention to the passengers sharing their compartment. Until now, they had kept strictly to themselves, and though the other passengers were Frenchmen, they hoped to reach their destination without resorting to any more contact with strangers than was absolutely necessary. Hoping to show the Germans their dancing and wasting of time was a matter of indifference to them, Sarah spoke to one of the Frenchmen. Very happy to reply, he began to berate the Germans, telling her he had just been working on an invention which, if he had time to complete it sooner, the war's victory would have been France's. Sarah naturally questioned him, begging him to tell her all about it, imagining it to be some peaceful innovation. The Frenchman explained :

'It is a fire-proof balloon, covered with an impermeable outer wall, and can carry inflammable bombs, which could be fired a distance of even fifteen hundred yards, Yet we, up in the balloon, would be perfectly safe.'

'What for?' Sarah asked.

'What for? Why for war! Here, let me explain the technicalities so you'll understand.'

But Sarah cut him off, thoroughly disgusted :

'I don't want to hear any more about it. You evidently haven't suffered in any way from this war. I hoped you would come up with a solution for world peace, but your invention would foul the earth and the sky, destroying all of nature's handiwork and genius. I love to fly in a balloon, straight into the clouds, gently blown by the wind, but I will never again be able to do so without turning sick, remembering the thoughts you've given me in connection with it. Sir, you horrify me!'

A balloon! Sarah's mind raced back to an exciting episode – so remote it seemed now, it must have happened in her dreams – her first flight in a balloon. Giffard, the first and most famous balloonist, lunched in her studio as Clairin guided her progress in clay. Gaiety and puns spiced the young people's party. Clairin came up with an idea shortly after his meeting with the great sportsman.

'You know Sarah, there's one thing you haven't done yet. You haven't been up in a balloon. Here's your chance. Giffard is a confirmed Bernhardtist.'

'There's hardly any need for that,' Dumas *fils* put in wryly. 'Her head's always in the clouds, or vice versa. What she needs is ballast to keep her down.'

Clairin winked to silence him. Jealousy was risky. And Dumas Junior might arouse Sarah to provocation. Clairin had a special reason for wanting Sarah out of Paris that day. He was relieved that she had become so eager to fly that she had not heard the remark.

'Can you really take me up?'

'At your service. Immediately if you wish.'

She quickly turned to Clairin, 'Come with me, will you?'

He shot a smile to Dumas Junior and quipped : 'Who but a poor poet would not follow his angel into her natural element? Of course, my dear.'

While the trio were high up in the clouds, another drama was in action far below. A deadly duel challenged by an admirer, de Lagrenée, to defend Sarah's honour against newspaper smears, and O'Monroy, the author of them. By the time the balloon landed, the papers were screaming headlines about this latest scandal.

Finally, the train arrived at Creil, where it waited for two hours. Impatiently stamping their feet, so cold that there was hardly any sensation in them, since there were no heated compartments, or any heat at all except for the coal used in the locomotive, everyone stood up, and two Frenchmen opened the door to get out and walk around. With the opening of the door, they heard music in the distance and the sounds of people laughing as at a party. It began to get on Sarah's nerves, it seemed they would be there interminably. She got out and started in the direction of the music, stumbling in the dark on the slippery road.

Luckily, before she got to the house, a German officer came towards her and in German asked what she was doing there. She told him she was French and he repeated his question in perfect French.

'I'm a passenger on that train and we've been freezing for two hours while all this party music has been going on.'

The German officer was shocked, and explained he had no idea there were passengers in the carriages. The engineer told him he was taking cattle and goods and didn't need to arrive before eight in the morning, so he had given the men permission to dance and drink.

Sarah explained there were eight passengers and the officer apologised and sent for the other passengers, while he ordered hot tea for them at his expense: 'Come in and rest. I'm here on a round of inspection as part of my duties.' As they sipped the hot tea, one of the Frenchmen, the inventor, remarked sarcastically,

'Ah, we're the guests of his Majesty William. Very chic, indeed!' The others shushed him cautiously, reminding him they were obliged to the Germans for the hospitality of the moment.

Suddenly, the orchestra stopped playing and an uproar of men fighting and cursing was heard. One Frenchman opened the door a few inches, and Sarah heard and saw the officer give orders to two sub-officers who seized the train guard, the stoker and the engineer, kicked them brutally, hit them with the flat of their swords on their shoulders, and struck the guard down with the butt end of their guns. The punishment sobered the train staff, who were then despatched to their duties again, in a mean, surly frame of mind.

The passengers were told to board the train again, and Sarah held back in fear until she saw one of the sub-officers ordered to accompany the passengers until Amiens. Arriving there at six in the morning, a fine rain was falling, freezing underfoot as they made their way in the blackness through which the dawn had not yet lit up a path.

No one knew Sarah's identity, and as soon as the others stepped off the train, they got into various carts and conveyances which seemed to have waited expectantly for them, and they drove off. Sarah and Mlle Soubise inquired of the sub-officer where they could go to rest until time for their departure to Hamburg, and were directed to a house with a balcony a few streets away; there were no rooms available at any of the hotels.

Soubise helped Sarah walk to the house indicated to them, and they were ushered into a small room by a young woman in mourning.

'You may rest and warm yourselves here by the stove, but we have no room at all,' she told them. 'You can see for yourselves, the hall has been turned into a dormitory.'

Sarah looked and her legs gave way as she fell unconscious.

When she awoke, she heard someone addressed as 'doctor' and couldn't recall or collect her thoughts. Soubise smiled with relief when she saw Sarah's eyes move, and in reply to Sarah's question, she answered : 'You had an attack of fever and we've been here two days. *Dieu!* did you frighten me!'

The doctor then warned Sarah not to move for forty-eight hours before going on, and offered her a sedative. She took it willingly, turned to her pillow and fell asleep again, utterly exhausted.

When Sarah fainted, Soubise told the young woman who she was. Sadly, the young hostess went upstairs and made up her own bed for Sarah, showing Soubise a photograph taken of Sarah in *Le Passant*, which her brother, now dead five weeks, kept as a souvenir after seeing the play ten times. The brother had died a hero, firing at the enemy to the end. He was only twenty-two years old.

Soubise had curled herself up at the foot of Sarah's bed, like a little dog, and watched over her as she lay unconscious, dreaming nightmares of the war in her feverish delirium.

Two days later, Soubise gathered their few belongings together and they started on the next stage of their journey. Again there were the makings of more troubles as seven German officers crowded into their compartment. Seeing Sarah's eyes burn with anger, Soubise calmly whispered to her: 'Remember, please, we are going to find Maurice. Your baby is all that counts.'

Sarah calmed herself; when two of the officers began to argue, and stood up preparing to fight, the women held their breath. They were approaching Ternier, when suddenly, in the distance a locomotive whistled warning signals in repetition. Then the engineer tried to slow the train, but before he could stop it three explosions up-ended the carriage, throwing the people inside it against each other, as fire and a thick smoke burned their eyes and choked them.

Everyone assumed he had sustained some fractured bones. Sarah examined herself and found she could move her legs and arms but her head had knocked against the sword of the officer opposite her and was cut deeply. Her hand was covered with blood but whose blood it was, she couldn't tell.

Help came immediately, and they were dragged out through the shattered windows, placed in carts and driven to Ternier as the cold and penetrating rain fell silently, soaking them through to their skins. They spent a day in the Ternier hotel.

Cateau was to be the next stop on the way, but there were no trains, and the only alternative was by horse and a wagon of some sort, but there were no animals left – the

Germans having requisitioned all of them. There was just one young colt which had never been broken and was offered at an exhorbitant price, plus a deposit of four hundred francs in case the colt should die. A miracle then produced a two-wheeled wagon and the yard boy began to tease the colt between the shafts with the usual kicking, bolting and stubbornness. After paying for the wagon and the boy's services they sat on the ricketty conveyance and from eleven in the morning until five that afternoon, they covered only five miles. They were exhausted, but the colt looked ready to die.

Again they stopped and were fleeced royally for the necessity of resting for an hour, to let themselves stretch and thaw out, while the sorry little animal caught its breath. For this one hour of respite, Sarah paid seventy-five francs, about five pounds ten shillings in value at that time.

After an ugly remark from the matron of the house as to how many thieves had stayed there in the past six months, Sarah's party set out again for St Quentin. Tired to death, the sky gloomy and dropping moisture, she fell asleep, only to be suddenly awakened an hour later, the colt frightened and refusing to go another step. She saw they had stopped in the middle of a field which was ploughed up by recent heavy cannon wheels, the ridges glistening with icicles, and not five yards away a pack of growling dogs were pulling with their sharp teeth at a dead body, half of it still underground. Sarah snatched the whip from the boy-driver and began lashing at the wild dogs, until the boy leading the trembling colt by the bridle, found the road in the darkness. The moon finally rose, throwing the ridges into shadows, making Sarah believe each mound was a head crying out from beneath the black earth. For a moment, Sarah wondered how Julie and Rosine had managed this horrible, impossible journey with her baby. It was a good thing she didn't know it at the time.

Here and there, the boy-driver pointed out groups of people who came to look for their husbands or sons who had fallen, led by soldiers who saw them fall on the plains of St Quentin. Suddenly, the boy pointed out a figure in the dark:

'Oh, madame, see over there! A scoundrel stealing from the dead!'

The dark figure had a dim lamp and a large bag and was filling it with swords, boots, sword belts, brass buttons, anything he could tear off the dead men. Sarah with her usual impetuousness moved quickly. She grasped the colt's bridle and went deliberately in his direction. Seeing the advancing horse and wagon, the man put out his lamp, stretched out flat and pretended to be dead. She continued towards him, and just as she feared he would let himself be trampled, rather than be caught, he called out:

'Please, I'm wounded. You'll run over me!'

By the gig lamp, she saw a man at least sixty-five or seventy years old, with a long, thin face and dirty, white beard. In a rage, forgetting everything, she cried out accusingly:

'You're not wounded. You're robbing the dead. Leave everything and go, you miserable wretch, or I'll call the police.' She felt in her bag and took out her pistol and pointed it at him hoping she would not be forced to use it. While he emptied his sack and pockets, he begged her to let him keep some of the things, pleading poverty and asking for mercy. But Sarah was too angry for mercy.

Again, the little party continued; heavy-hearted and frozen, going through Busigny, a wood, and a quicksilver bog, almost sinking into it before getting to a road which led to Cateau and finding a room for the night, too tired and feverish to do anything but get into bed and send for the nearest doctor. This time, both women were sick; Sarah with a fever which paralysed her limbs, and Soubise with trembling and hallucinations. The doctor gave them sedatives, and next day they were treated to the luxury of a hot bath which restored their balance and flexibility.

From Cateau to Brussels, then on to Strasbourg and Cologne, the journey was uneventful, but the train from Cologne to Hamburg left suddenly, the doors shutting violently just as their bags were placed in the carriage, taking them away without Sarah and Soubise. Almost in a hysteria Sarah told her story to the station-master, who telegraphed the train about her bags and took her to the Hôtel-du-Nord, to his sister who considered it an honour to have Sarah as her guest. Sarah could do nothing but resign herself until the next day, there being no other train that day or evening.

Suffering only a broken brake which held up the trip to Hamburg, the train with Sarah and Soubise finally arrived and she gave the last address she had of her family – 7 Obere Strasse, driving up to the house where amazingly all her family and her baby Maurice still were, and who were so surprised at the visitors they could hardly believe their eyes. It simply could not be! Sarah's anguish over the hardships, brutality and impossible adventures of the last eleven days disappeared as if by magic. She cried tears of joy, infinite joy, as she hugged her precious little Maurice, her sisters, Julie and Rosine, happy beyond all words to see them all again.

In the excitement of arrival, Sarah forgot to ask how Julie and Rosine had made the trip, and what experiences they had had, because again, the maddest 'everythings' continued as the German Officer in Paris had predicted. Fire broke out in the house that night and the whole family had to escape in their night clothes, and were forced to camp out for six hours in five feet of snow. But they came through that and much more, safe and sound, according to the officer's second admonition – they were in God's hands.

The return to Paris, via Havre, though not so adventurous was difficult, for now there were six women and a baby boy, but Sarah squeezed them into what was formerly the signaller's cubicle, and they arrived at Havre at seven in the morning. Learning of their intention to continue on to Paris, the conductor told Sarah Paris was very dangerous : more revolutionary upheavals were in preparation, and she and her family would be under suspicion. Her countrymen were impatient and in short temper. But nothing could keep

Sarah away from her beloved Paris. Arriving in her home town, there was no carriage to be had, as all vehicles were requisitioned for the use of the German occupation staff. Only a milk cart passing by at the moment delivered the refugees to their home in two trips. Julie was so jolted about she refused to speak to Sarah for an hour.

As if degradation knew no bounds, reporters arrived like undertakers, to tell the world about France's most humiliating moment – the entry of the Germans; they waited on a balcony in the Avenue de la Grande Armée in the early morning of 1st March 1871.

At the Arc de Triomphe, two men in blouses stared through the mist at the Porte Maillot. It was from this gate that the entry was to be made. Otherwise, the entire avenue was empty, or seemed so. A thick fog blanketed the ground. At about seven thirty uneasiness was felt; the fog could be hiding troops. Foreigners gathered on the balcony but one reporter went down to inspect the Arc where trenches had been dug and gravel thrown during the barricade. Some thirty blouses, wretched and evil-faced, arrived, and eyed the foreigners with undisguised suspicion. They kept coming until several hundred had gathered, and except for these, there was no one else in sight.

Not one window was occupied. One of living history's greatest spectacles was about to be enacted, yet, except for the reporters and the blouses, there was no one to see it. The French hid themselves in grief. A few reporters represented the world, as a priest sometimes is the only mourner following a coffin to its grave.

Waiting seemed interminable when at eight thirty someone said : 'I see moving specks beyond the gate.' Up went the field glasses and there they were! The tiny specks grew larger until they became distinct – six horsemen galloping very fast. They grew sharper and larger with each second. They reached the gate and dashed through it. The one in front had been riding at a canter, and now broke into a half gallop, then into a full gallop and tore up the hill to a halt. The other five spread out right and left, occupying the Avenue.

As the single horseman neared – a Hussar officer, a boy hardly eighteen – everyone stirred in astonishment. His majestic carriage as he charged past, sword uplifted, head thrown back, eyes fixed straight before him, called out admiration from the balcony.

'By Jove, if that fellow's mother could see him, she'd have something to be proud of the rest of her time.'

The youngster raced on alone but at the Arc, the blouses stopped him. He waved his sword at them, slackened speed and passed round them and the trench which would have broken his horse's neck and his own had he ignored it. His gesture, seen through the archway, sword held high, made him look as if he were saluting the vanquished city at his feet. His five men joined him now. He gave them orders and they diverged.

The boy trotted round the Arc with the blouses glaring on. The occupation was over, that is, the moral effect was produced. That boy had done it all alone. The single reporter at the Arc was now joined by others. He asked:

'What is your name?'

'What for?'

'To publish it in London tomorrow morning.'

'Oh! That's it, is it?' he said with a tinge of contempt for newspapers that was typically German. 'Well, I'm von Bernhardi, 14th Hussars. But if you print it, please give my captain's name also; he's von Colomb.' With this, a squadron of the regiment came up and Lieutenant von Bernhardi's commander-in-chief took over.

The reporters stood among the blouses, wondering if they would have their necks wrung for talking to the enemy. Now more and more troops marched in, infantry and cavalry, but the mass of the German army was at Longchamp for the great review to be held that morning by the Emperor. By ten, the French began to trickle out into the Avenue, and in the afternoon, an estimated one hundred thousand, mostly blouses, were there to challenge the forty thousand Germans and their officers, and generals from Meiningen, Altenburg, Schoenburg, Waldeck, and many others. But the discipline of the enemy offset almost all provocation. One woman gave vent simultaneously to her appreciation of their conduct and to her indignation at being forced involuntarily to admire them, 'It is disgusting how distinguished they are!'

Nevertheless, episodes followed: punishment of women who fraternised, even slightly answering a greeting as they passed a German; cafés burned if they fed the enemy; wine shops wrecked for the same reasons. Foreigners too, suffered the same fate if they spoke to the Germans.

Because of the striking similarity of the name of the young Hussar, Bernhardi, and the fact that her family had taken refuge in Germany, Sarah suffered many calumnies of her landsmen's unreasoning vengeance.

However, in spite of the great uneasiness in the city, to the immense relief of the artists and public alike, the theatres opened again.

7

The Goddess and the Genius

Sarah reacted to the notice of rehearsals like a charger to the rein. The public stood about the billboards reading the posters that listed the plays to be given. When they saw Sarah's name, they muttered under their breath and made odious noises and signs. She watched and waited some moments, then, like a battle scarred veteran, advanced through their midst up the steps and addressed them in stern tones:

'Whoever told you these lies has done France and me a great disservice. I can prove my loyalty if I have to. Now, I beg you all to join with me in singing our country's National Anthem.'

Her voice, full of emotion and power, moved the crowd to a respectful silence. She began to sing the opening bars and it was too much for them. They could not believe that voice was ever used in the service of any country but theirs. A frenzied thrill swept through each Frenchman and all lifted their voices as in a convocation; she made them feel whole again; whole and healed.

She then entered the theatre to the ringing shouts of *'Vive Sarah! Vive notre Sarah!'*

One of her first successes on the re-opening of the Odéon was in a play by André Theuriet called *Jean-Marie* through which she was noticed by Victor Hugo, now back in Paris.

From the time of the demonstration in the theatre against Dumas, long before the war, she had harboured resentment against Hugo.

She believed the scandals and rumours which her snobbish family repeated – that rebel renegade! His poems, often quoted by the Satanists whose ideal he was, and especially the poem *Châtiments*, only confirmed the worst. If she had a choice, she could only prefer Dumas, in whose play *Kean* she had scored her first important success.

The Odéon was preparing a gala for Hugo and to celebrate, *Ruy Blas* would be presented. Sarah was overpowered with a desire to play the Queen though she knew well enough it was an immodest ambition. She tried reasoning with her duality: 'After all, seniority gave other artistes preference,' but found no peace.

Duquesnel agreed that he too had given it some thought, when she intimated her hopes of playing the role, but it seemed useless as Jane Essler the senior actress 'in vogue' was also a close friend of Hugo's, and quite naturally had the best chance at it.

Berton's activities with the leaders of the Commune kept him out-of-bounds. It was too dangerous for him to contact anyone, more particularly Sarah who was still a controversial figure. In the minds of the keen politically-conscious public, her adoration by the *élite*, and the luxuries with which she surrounded herself, told against her.

With rehearsals in progress in honour of the Master's return, Paris talked of nothing else. The buzzing in literary circles and salons everywhere proved too much for Berton and he left his anonymity to answer the call of the theatre. He must be part of the greatest event in the history of Paris, Victor Hugo's triumphal return! Infamy could not crush the Master.

Sarah was forced to stifle memories of successes during the royal empire, and for survival she adopted republicanism. Almost before she mentioned the word, however, the existing government was swept away by the introduction of the horrors of the Commune. She saw patriots set Paris afire 'to save the Nation'; saw some of her friends shot dead without a trial and nightmares disturbed her sleep by the daily threat of the return of the Reign of Terror.

Before the re-opening of the Odéon, she met Paul de Rémusat, the author playright. He tried to broaden her politically, but she rejected it all unconditionally. Her natural intelligence sought healing from the recent exhaustion and strife and found peace and escape in his poetry which she loved to read curled into a ball at his feet, her head nestled in his hand.

Paul was one of the moving forces behind the revolution and it was to his flat that the committee came to finalise their plans. He could quickly assess the pitfalls and revise it to assure maximum security. But for the prefix *de* in his name, he would have been offered the presidency, but feelings ran high against anyone whose name symbolised aristocracy. It fell to General Trochu instead.

'Never mind,' Sarah assuaged his pride, 'it is your writing that will imortalise you!'

Berton spent all his evenings at Hugo's home but Sarah refused to join him there if the subject was politics. She knew Berton's involvement with the revolution and hated it. Finally, it came between them, but only as lovers.

Until now Sarah's early career differed little from that of other actresses. She had stormed the citadel and it had flung her back reeling. Tormented, angry, ambitious, scornful, she had ignored defeat to scale the fastnesses of the Française, the Odéon, the Gymnase, the Ambigu – only to crawl away bruised like a wounded animal. But the hated apprenticeship was ended and now she made new plans. Sarah needed money, lots of it for the education of her son. She had pledged herself to raise him royally, had been interrupted by the war, but now she painted, sculpted, and posed for photographs which sold in the thousands. She made a game of earning money, another happy talent.

She no longer doubted her future but she must strive hard and in many directions; up from the depths poured an endless variety of talents and personalities. She learned that after her great success in François Coppée's *Le Passant*, Duquesnel's joy was incomplete only because his adversary Chilly was unable to appreciate his victory, as at that moment Chilly was watching over the body of one of his sons, dead at the age of twenty.

On his return to the office after the funeral, Chilly told Duquesnel to have the cashier return the money he had advanced for Sarah, 'and suppose we raise her to two hundred and fifty francs a month.' Two hundred and fifty francs a month was an insult, especially for one reared in luxury, and now a celebrity. The years of testing were behind her; the stage no longer a mystery or a terror; speech flowed smoothly, gestures captivated, talent and distinction were inseparable, and all were carried over into her private world which indeed was as colourful as her public one.

When a critic wrote that 'such a full mop of hair of an unheard-of-colour must be a wig, and that only false teeth could gleam so brilliantly,' she dressed quietly and appeared at his home. She surprised the scalper at his work, tossed off her hat and clapped his hand to her hair : 'Pull hard, pull!' Then she bit his hand and said : 'If you still doubt, you may examine my teeth further. Sorry I can't leave them; you see, we're attached to each other.'

The public licensed her eccentricities, unable to compromise its idol. Everything she did was imitated. From this time on, she never paid for clothes, accessories, or furniture, though the prices of her costumes and gowns were widely advertised. Courtiers and tradesmen competed to have her advertise their wares, and were considered highly successful if she consented so that they could tell clients 'this is the gown Mlle Bernhardt wore,' and 'these are the fans and shoes worn by Mlle Bernhardt.'

Sometimes her childhood devils spent themselves in target-practice and in hard riding through the parks accompanied by her growing son, both racing as equals.

One day when Prince Napoleon sat in her dressing room chatting with Dumas *fils* and Clairin, Coppée nervously entered, 'I believe I forgot my gloves, do forgive me.' He indicated the chair in which the prince sat. Prince Napoleon rose, 'Sorry, I didn't notice that the chair was unclean.'

Sarah slapped him furiously, 'Courtesy used to be the

province of kings, I didn't know princes were exempted. You have permission to leave.'

Photographs of her in her coffin, *à la morte* were sold everywhere and cartoonists were never so inspired. Following the line laid down by some critics, Vitu amused himself over her thinness, describing her as 'a needle made to look as neat as a new pin'; and 'there is nothing of the sorceress about her except the wand – herself!'

Newspaper circulation increased as the curious watched for the weird caricatures, and cartoonists' salaries rose with the products of their pens. Souvenirs of every sort and fabric, even to miniature caskets, became the rage and lobby kiosks did a thriving business at every performance. Only Sarah knew that under the stuffing and upholstery of the coffin, layers of love letters and faded bouquets added their scent and thickness to its padding – reminders of happy hours – waiting to console her in the silence of the tomb. However, for now, she would savour her success.

As box office receipts swelled whenever Sarah played, Chilly gave her the parts she wished whenever possible. Secretly, he too was a confirmed Bernhardtist. Auguste Vacquerie, related to Hugo and also in the theatre, felt certain Sarah could do the lead in *Ruy Blas* better than any other actress of the day.

She received an invitation from Hugo for the following day to be present at the reading, adding that he too, could see only one little Queen of Spain worthy of the crown, and she was Sarah.

He never missed a rehearsal; shaping, polishing, instructing the artists in interpretation of the meaning he intended. When it seemed something disagreed with his idea of the production, he patiently spent hours, nimbly jumping up, explaining and showing how it should be done. Finally delighted and grateful, he brought Sarah a huge bouquet of roses, presented in his ever correct form : 'to My Queen of Spain, from your humble valet.'

She stared at them, and thanked him, 'I know where you got them.'

'From my garden, Mademoiselle,' Hugo said, bowing gallantly.

'No, sorry to disagree, but they came from the garden of Paul Meurice. There's no other rose bush like it in all France!'

Anticipating all this, Meurice who was watching in the background exploded with laughter to Hugo's intense embarrassment.

'I told you she'd recognise them. I did tell you!'

The Master's recovery was lightning fast and *à point*.

'Mademoiselle, they are truly the finest roses in Europe! I offered to buy them but Paul would not sell. I then tried to steal them, but he caught me. I then had to beg him to let me have them. Knowing of their existence it was manifestly impossible to give you any others.'

Sarah was utterly charmed by his gallantry.

The opening night of Hugo's play, was the 26th January 1872 and it showered glory on the author, the stars and all who were connected with the production. Sarah rose to undreamed of heights. The audience was breathless, and the exultation and triumph resounded through Paris; the artistic Fête of the Odéon; the greatest First Night in theatre history. The performance was stirring throughout, the stimulation mounting as it picked up momentum line by line and act by act. It left Sarah dazed, and soon streams of admirers and well-wishers advanced to the stage after more than twenty curtain calls. An attempt to thank her audience ended in stage fright and she ran off stage sobbing, to the utter delight of everyone. The applause thundered, while she returned, to stand rooted in awe. The crowd separated itself and formed two orderly lines through which she saw Hugo and Girardin advance toward her. Petrified at her own loss of words, she knew she must find some way to express her thanks but no words would come.

Thanks to the genius of Hugo, all her life had expanded – and here she stood thinking how she would love to cry out her confession and repentance for the ill thoughts that she had harboured against him. How stiff she had been, how imperious at their first meeting. And with his sharp intuition he had grasped it, yet kissed her hand gently:

'Ah Mademoiselle, I see my greatest trial is to come in your prejudice against me!'

Now, before she could utter a sound, Hugo had dropped on his knee, raised her small hands to his lips and kissed them: 'Thank you, thank you. I say it with all my soul!'

He, the great poet whose universal genius thrilled the world, whose generosity flung pardons like gems to all who insulted him; it was Hugo who said 'Thank you.' She felt small and ashamed, but happy in the shelter of this great man. He then rose and shook hands with everyone, ready with the right word for each one.

Sarah wept, lacking the courage to embrace Hugo. Girardin comforted her: 'Now that you are crowned with laurels, don't let yourself become too intoxicated. No more risky jumps. You must be more yielding, docile, *compris*?'

Sarah could promise nothing. It was just as well.

Berton waited until last. After the crowd dispersed, he it was who served her the sweet taste of the sugar in the bottom of the cup.

'My angel! Superb! You'll never know the exquisite pain I suffered not to have been on stage with you.'

'Darling, I owe it all to you. I never would have had the part if you had not spoken to Hugo for me. *Mille merci, cher.*'

'Ah no. Hugo had no choice. It was a foregone conclusion. He never would have consented to anyone else.'

Meanwhile, she congratulated Berton on the coming production of his play, *Zasa*, in London. 'I'll give a *soirée* and we'll have a double celebration.'

But Berton refused. 'Let's go home quietly and sit and dream over an *apéritif*, like we used to, as if nothing had happened.'

'*Oui, mon cher.*' She felt two arms wrap themselves around her waist, and a whisper wooing her:

'So many kind words and not one for me? My Queen.'

That voice! She turned in embarrassment. 'Hugo! At last!' they embraced warmly.

The scene was caught by Clairin's swift pencil strokes and sent to the newspapers, captioned THE GODDESS AND THE GENIUS. This quick sketch launched Sarah's reputation as the Divinity. The public worshipped at her feet.

When Berton left, Sarah could not sleep. Mme Guerard had come to stay with Maurice on this most important of all evenings, and Sarah roused her gently, only to find her Petite Dame ready and avid to hear about everything that had happened down to the minutest detail. She made hot chocolate while Sarah talked, and at seven in the morning they took a cab to take Mme Guerard back to her flat. Still sleepless, Sarah rode around through the fresh morning air of Paris in the cab, telling herself again and again, life was finally worth the living.

At two o'clock, next afternoon, George Clairin brought his paints and a canvas to Sarah's dressing room and set up his easel, in preparation for his new painting of her, the most famous portrait of all, and her favourite. Delacroix, Gautier, and François Coppée dropped in also, not wishing to miss one moment of this, the most exciting event in their lifetime. Reporters by the dozen, as well as photographers, swarmed like bees through every part of the theatre, but were shooed away by guards with instructions to do so.

Sarah was generous with interviews, but refused to be smothered by crowds of newspapermen after having given them her whole morning. She now wanted a respite, to spend a few delicious moments with her close friends. She had dropped into her favourite position of rest on her divan when she recognised a delicate knock on the door. Jumping up, she ran to open it herself and fell into the arms of Madame Sand, who was now dressed in a smart, woollen, tailored suit with a shirt of a dark green colour; looking very chic.

The women cried with happy emotion as they embraced, then Sand greeted all the artists and poets, as familiar to her as they were to Sarah, all of them buzzing happily over the sparkling success of the evening before. Sand settled herself in the armchair offered to her by Coppée. Slowly, by ones and twos, the men left, discreetly leaving the two women to themselves knowing from experience Sarah's desire for privacy with her dear friend.

Left alone, the older woman lit a cigar, and beamed even more, as she contemplated the younger one:

'I told you, didn't I, that you were carved out for greatness, *chère*? Congratulations. It is only the beginning.'

After a thoughtful pause, she continued:

'Why was Hugo spared, you might ask. To restore France? To assist the next generation's advance in civilisation? One could go on endlessly pursuing logic. But my belief is that all the civilising institutions come about far more swiftly through the theatre. His forces had to join yours to achieve a total triumph. By stimulating the public emotionally, the tensions of months are released. Through the release comes an enveloping ambition to rise with the artist, and thus, new ideas, goals, relations are effected. Do send for tea, dear. And those roses, who sent them?'

'No one knows what anguish the actor suffers. Last night, I felt as though I were at the edge of a precipice. I felt the same way when I was doing your plays.'

'I know. I've had that sensation. Holding back the torrent for fear of the deluge. The torrent in your voice last night reminded me of another Commune, the one of 1848. I saw again in the inspired faces in the audience, the people looking just as they did then – grand, sublime, sincere, largehearted – the people of France united in the heart of France. You were the Spirit in Lutecia herself.' She saw Sarah overcome with emotion.

'It's not so bad. You'll get used to your laurels.'

'You look so chic in that lovely green wool.' Suddenly, Sarah asked, 'How did you start wearing men's clothes? Was it defiance or was it because you looked so neat?'

Sand laughed gleefully. 'You make me feel young again. I'll tell you gladly. When I came to Paris as a young

divorcee, I had no money. I had to give up all my posses-
sions, including my grandmother's home, to buy my freedom
from Casimir. Women's clothes were expensive, accessories
cost a fortune and everything was so expensive to clean. I
cut my hair and let it fall to my shoulder, so I looked like
a student in medical college. Besides, it was fun, I could go
to lots of places that were off bounds for women. I was
never detected.'

A few friends had dropped in for lunch, and were reading
the reviews. Lazily, Mlle Hocquiny remarked: 'Don't you
think Sarah should now join the Théâtre Française?'

'Oh no, I've never been so happy. Whatever time I
spent there, was a torture.'

'Still, tradition I'm afraid. It will be quite different now.
All the critics but Sarcey agree you were divine. Listen to
him:

> She is a scarecrow with a voice. Certainly the public
> is entitled to be informed of the reasons MM Duquesnel,
> Chilly and Hugo had for giving her the role in which
> she appears. She is not yet mature, does not move
> naturally, and seems to rely exclusively on her talent
> for recital.

'Imagine! Still at it! What shall I do?'

'Unimportant, but if it really annoys you, ask Berton to
find out. He knows Sarcey well.' Sand put in.

'Yes, I never thought of that. Of course.'

At that moment, Petite Dame handed Sarah a letter with
the large round insignia of the Comédie Française at the
corner. Sarah thought back: it was ten years to the day
that old Marguerite had brought her just such a letter for
the first time, while Julie nodded her permission. She paled
slightly and signed to Guerard to read it.

'It's a letter from Perrin, Director, and he would like you

to set the time for an interview on Tuesday or Wednesday.'

'Today is Monday, please answer that I'll be at his office at three tomorrow.'

The letter was sent and next day Sarah drove to the Odéon to show Perrin's letter to Duquesnel. She reminded him of how little the Odéon was paying her 'and the money from the Havre notary is almost used up'.

'Then, what will you do'?

'But that's why I'm here. Raise my salary and I'll stay.'

'You know I'm not independent. I'll have to see Chilly about it. Come back tomorrow and I'll tell you what he says. But promise me one thing, if he refuses, don't leave. I'll try something else. Promise!'

She was summoned to see Chilly next, and sat calmly waiting.

'How can you be so foolish as to want to leave,' he shot out bluntly. 'Where would you go? At the Gymnase? – only modern, not your style. It's the same at the Vaudeville. At the Gaité, you'd spoil your voice, and as for the Ambigu, you're too distinguished for that.'

Sarah sat unmoved.

'Then, we agree?'

'No, not quite. You've forgotten the Comédie.'

'Oh no, my dear, they've had enough of your quirks,' he laughed rudely. 'At dinner with Maubout recently some-one suggested you ought to go back and he nearly had apoplexy. He'd never work with you.'

'You might have told him I'm reliable now.'

'I did. I even taunted him that it would be good for that stuffy old ladies' home to have someone like you, a person with talent and will power. After a bit more, he argued that you had no talent and declared that you'll only enter the Comédie over his dead body.'

'Then you refuse to raise my salary?'

'I don't have to. Your contract runs another year and I'll hold you to it.'

'You might be wrong, sir!'

'Indeed! So you thought I was an idiot.'

'Oh no, I think you are at least a triple idiot.'

She flew down the stairs followed by Duquesnel who had sat quietly aside. He pleaded with her to come back but she doubled her speed.

Perrin, meticulous and correct, indicated an armchair with a dramatic gesture and the proper welcome.

'Lovely day. Have you thought it over? Mademoiselle.'

'Yes, I'm prepared to sign.'

He dropped the paper-knife he was toying with and dipped a pen into the inkwell. '*Voilà!* if you please.' As she took the pen, a large drop of ink splashed on the blank sheet before him.

'Please, don't throw it away. Let me have it. If that spot is a butterfly, I'm right to sign. If it's anything else, I'm wrong.'

'Oh, very well.' He handed it it to her.

Sarah folded the paper exactly through the centre of the blot, pressed it tightly together and slowly opened it, while Perrin looked on like a curious parrot. There before him, a handsome black butterfly spread its wings against the stark white of the paper.

'Well, well, imagine. You were right in signing. Congratulations.'

Ruy Blas continued its run, playing to packed houses and Duquesnel came while she was making up. 'I must lecture you, my dear. You were very rough on Chilly and most inconsiderate to me. Instead of coming back, you broke your promise. Paul Meurice says you went straight to the Comédie, is it true?'

'Here's the contract. Read it if you wish.'

'Mind if I show it to Chilly?'

'No, my pleasure.'

Duq was hurt. 'You shouldn't have done this without telling me first. You know you can trust me, yet you didn't. I haven't deserved this.'

Sarah was contrite. Duquesnel had been more than kind. It was her demon: impatience with its aftermath of regrets. She could not abide being taunted.

Duquesnel left with the contract and a few moments later

Chilly strode in waving it furiously. He shouted and stammered angrily:

'It's treason! Abominable! You had no right to do it! I'll make you pay damages! I'll sue you!'

All Sarah could do was turn away and excuse herself to Duquesnel, the man who had never done her an unkindness, who had always given her proofs of his friendship, and who had kept the door of her future open when nobody believed in her.

The next door opening to that future was to begin the following October with the signing of the contract which made her a member of the House of Molière. There were mixed feelings with this new venture. Among them the satisfaction of revenge for Mme Nathalie's spite against her, with all the lamentable publicity.

Remaining at the Odéon, meanwhile, on a very nominal salary of six hundred francs, Sarah's success continued, her press growing more favourable while her colleagues looked on in wonder mixed with envy.

Victor Hugo outdid himself, overwhelming her with eulogy:

'This is the first time this part has every really been acted. This young woman is truly a Queen! . . . She is really adorable. She has more than mere good looks; she has harmonious movements and an irresistible enchantment of expression. She is something better than an artist – she is a woman.'

Berton knew but one duty: when Sarah called, he dropped everything and ran to her side. So far, Sarah had heard only praise. Her friends came to bask in the joy of her success, each opening a paper to the column on the *Ruy Blas* performance. All but one critic agreed on Sarah's Divinity. That one was still Sarcey.

But Sarcey rebuffed Berton. 'Your protégée has blinded you with her pretty blue eyes. She's not the great success you think and she'll never be one.' His reviews continued to tear Sarah down. The Odéon managers began to feel discomfort over it, until one day Girardin, the greatest journalist in France, made it his business to track down the 'devil in Sarcey's pen'. A week later he had the answer. He went straight to Sarah. 'He has a very thin skin. Seems you rebuffed him at the home of a friend.'

'I never met the idiot in my life!'

'You did. Here's what happened; Sarcey said Camille Blanchet was a cow on stage, and. . . .'

In a flash, Sarah remembered and finished the story: 'Yes, yes. And I said I'd rather be a cow on stage than a pig in a drawing room! I had no idea *that* was Sarcey who was criticising one of my friends.'

'Well, my dear girl, that was he.' Girardin relaxed and mussed up one of the little fluffy dogs at his feet.

'What shall I do?' Sarah wondered.

'You can make friends with him. I hear he's susceptible to a pretty woman. You can explain it all away charmingly by telling him you didn't know it was he.'

'Simple. Indeed. I recall a student of my art school who admitted sitting in the class expressly for the purpose of picking the other students' brains. Never scratched a line, and didn't even own a brush. "Why should I soil my hands. I'm cut out for a critic's career," he boasted.'

Less than a week later, Berton saw the highly-polished, sharp-looking Sarcey sitting in a stage-box, wearing all his honours; shined up; smiling like a Cheshire cat when Sarah came out on stage. It was so obvious that Berton had a strong jealous reaction immediately. He said nothing, but watched as the weeks passed, noticing that Sarah treated him with more and more coolness, while Sarcey's column contained less and less vitriol when he commented on Sarah's performance. In fact, Sarcey's pen seemed to be going into reverse.

From habit, it was Berton who used to take Sarah home after a performance, but one evening she told him: 'I don't feel well, I'll go home with Blanche.' Berton attempted a protest, but Sarah was adamant: 'I'm ill. I must go straight to bed.'

Berton hurried to change into street clothes and hiding in

the doorman's box, waited in vain to see if she left immediately with her maid. Twenty minutes later, the page he had asked to watch for her at the front door, came to tell him Sarah had left. Hurrying to catch up with her, he was too late, but saw her drive off in a carriage with Sarcey, warmly wrapped up in his arms.

Berton remembered their first meeting, after her failure at the Ambigu. How sensitive she had become while she waited in the outer room of Doucet's office, and wondered if she should not leave and make straight for the Seine. Then, she was roused by a voice asking her to step into the office and ran into a tall, handsome young man who caught her and held her firmly to steady her. She looked up into two serious deep-set blue eyes that searched her face with real interest.

'Is not this Mlle Sarah Bernhardt?' the tall man inquired. He subtly overlooked her hesitant reply, knowing perfectly well who she was. 'I have just been talking to Doucet about you. Come in and we'll see him together.'

She followed him, not knowing who he was, nor why he knew who she was. Doucet quickly cleared her mind.

'This is Pierre Berton, junior. He would like to see you a member of his company at the Odéon.'

Sarah was overwhelmed. To have been singled out by the greatest actor of the day was an honour she never entertained. Doucet then went on to mention the possible difficulty with Chilly, but Berton quickly interposed:

'You need not be afraid of Chilly! I have spoken to Duquesnel and he is on our side. Chilly will have to agree.'

It was to Berton that she owed all. He had told her on the way home, after some further conversation:

'Since the day I first saw you in *Les Femmes Savantes* at the Comédie, I have believed that you would one day become a very great actress, but I believe also that you need someone to help you with the directors who do not understand your temperament. I have watched you for two years and I am prepared to help you at the Odéon as much as possible, with your permission.'

Berton was in love with Sarah from the first, – and from that moment – between Pierre Berton, the accomplished and successful actor, and Sarah Bernhardt, the débutante of twenty two – a sincere and enduring love began. Berton smoothed every knotty problem, became her personal dramatic coach, explained tactfully every *faux pas* and loss of temper and control, and kept her from losing friends or making enemies. How many times he reminded her : 'Remember who helped you when your flat burned out? The man you hated most during your childhood.'

Sarah's betrayal of Duquesnel was followed by her betrayal of Berton, two of the kindest, most loyal friends she ever had. She threw all integrity to the winds, but paid dearly for it. Berton still admired her genius, never flinching in his friendship, but was too deeply hurt to be anything more.

To celebrate the hundredth performance of *Ruy Blas*, Victor Hugo gave a supper party and called on Sarah just as she was entertaining George Sand and discussing make-up in her dressing room. Blanche opened at his knock and he entered with a grand flourish. Sarah held out her hands. He kissed them, then received her embrace on both his cheeks. Sand looked on, and responded gaily in her turn. Hugo was never without the right word :

'Ah, my fortune is twins! A double pleasure, ladies. Sarah, you become more superb with each performance. No author could wish for more,' he turned then to Sand. 'Would you dispute that?' Sand responded with a pout. 'But you know that already from the critics. The sparkle still clings to the theatre. We're turning back the war tides and dissensions.'

Hugo hurried away to let her finish preparations for that evening's performance. At the supper party, he placed Sarah at his right and Chilly next to Sarah in the hope of reconciling them. Mme Lambquin was on his left and next to her was Duquesnel. Opposite Hugo was another poet,

Théophile Gautier, the great friend of Sarah and Dumas. She enjoyed describing Gautier as the 'lion's head on the body of an elephant'; or the caricature of an oriental potentate with hands as white and delicate as a woman's; he had piercing eyes under heavily-veiled lids. In spite of this grotesque appearance, Sarah's admiration of him was immense. She collected choice morsels, *bon mots* dropped by Gautier, 'that stylist in a red waistcoat' as the Goncourt Brothers described him. He was now responding to another guest who was waxing eloquently on Molière, 'I couldn't say this in print, but Molière! Molière is an alderman writing plays. There's a crude foursquare sound-sense which is utterly artless.'

In contrast, one of those oddities which destiny indulges in, next to Gautier sat an odious individual, Paul de Sante Victor, the critic. He had the ugliness of a flabby face with a sharp short crow's beak nose, arms too short, eyes, evil looking and cruel, and a too stout body. Sarah knew instinctively that he disliked her and thoroughly enjoyed returning his hatred.

The illustrious Master rose to thank everyone for their cooperation on the reappearance of his work, and was just lifting his glass to toast Sarah, saying : 'As for you Mademoiselle, you have a voice of gold!' – and was interrupted by the breaking of a glass. It was Sante Victor who put his glass down so spitefully and violently that it broke, causing a momentary silence to follow.

Sarah retaliated, offering him her glass; 'Sir, take mine. Then you will know my answer to your thoughts, so clearly expressed just now.'

He could do nothing but take her glass but shot her a look of deadly hatred. He waited for his revenge in the future.

The Master finished his toast and Duquesnel whispered to Sarah to nudge Chilly, – it was his turn to speak. Seeing he did not rise, Sarah turned to see if he had heard. The colour was leaving his flushed red perspiring face. His staring glassy eyes were wide open, while his mouth was involuntarily opening and closing. Chilly finally stammered, 'My legs are being held, I can't move.' His finger tips were white against the purple of the rest of his hand. She took his hand. It hung inert, icy cold. Everyone's eyes turned in fright to the suffering impressario.

Sarah gasped; 'Get up!' but Chilly's head fell forward, his face on the plate before him. Everyone hurried to the stricken man, each muttering helplessly in disconnected phrases. His son and a doctor were sent for, and Chilly was made comfortable in a small ante-room. Sarah followed after, heartsick that she had so recently caused him grief. She had become attached to him, even though they frequently fought. She begged to ask his pardon but Chilly was unconscious.

While they waited for the doctor, each one commented in his own way: 'It is indigestion,' sadly, from Lafontaine. 'It is cerebral anaemia,' philosophically from Tallien who was always losing his memory.

Hugo said simply: 'It is a beautiful kind of death.'

The gloom weighed heavily. Everyone waited, fanning themselves in the room which had suddenly became very hot. Duquesnel told Sarah quietly; 'I'm afraid he'll not recover.' Sarah was stricken with intense grief as she gripped Duquesnel's arm. She begged him: 'Please send someone for my carriage. I'll get my wrap and be ready to leave,' As she reached the small room where the cloaks were, old Madame Lambquin bumped into her, dizzy from the heat and the wine.

'Oh, I nearly knocked you down, little Madonna. Excuse me.'

Sarah whispered into her ear: 'It doesn't matter, Mamma Lambquin, Chilly is dying.'

As she finished, Mme Lambquin who had been flushed a bright red, turned chalk white, unable to utter a sound. She reached for her cloak, then whispered to Sarah; 'Are you leaving? Please take me home. I must tell you something.'

Consternation seized the old actress as they drove to her home in the St Germaine. In a shaking voice she began:

'You know I have a mania for fortune-tellers. Last Friday

a woman who reads fortunes by cards told me I would die one week after a man dies, who is dark and not young, whose life is connected with mine.

'At first I was angry with her, because I'm a widow and I've never had a liaison. She then answered me: "in fact it is one of two men who are connected with you, one is dark and the other is fair."

'Now you tell me Chilly is dying and I realise what she meant. Our two managers, one is dark and the other fair – Oh! I'm stifling.'

They arrived at Lambquin's and Sarah helped the old friend of her war-time experiences up the four flights to her flat. She tipped the concierge generously, begging her to sit with her friend and give her every attention. Then she went home to her young son, deeply disturbed, and full of anguish and remorse.

It was dizzying to contemplate all that had happened under the roof of the Odéon. Could this possibly be the same building in which only a few months ago, she had nursed the wounded, sending cognac out to the women waiting in the bitter cold in queues, stealing a glance through the windows, fearful of seeing too much?

Was the theatre saying farewell to her in its own way? 'You've made me suffer the scourge of war, you denuded me of all trinkets, burning and destroying them in the name of mercy. Well, we're even now. You've got all I could give you, including the great glory you wanted. You don't need me now. No more!'

Chilly died in three days, never recovering consciousness.

After Chilly's death, Sarah was notified he had begun an action for breach of contract just before he left his office for the dinner. He had threatened her, she remembered, but she didn't think he would sue. She lost the case, but the Comédie Française paid the damages of ten thousand francs under a proviso in her contract.

Lambquin died twelve days later, confessing her sin of delving into the unknown to the priest who attended her: 'I am dying because I listened to and believed in the demon.'

163

From the evening which ended so tragically, began the famous legend of THE GOLDEN VOICE.

The news reports of the dinner read:

Sarah may be said to have reached the highest elevation of historic fame when she sat at dinner at the Grand Hotel with Victor Hugo and a hundred and fifty of the most distinguished men in France. She was the honoured guest, and the distinguished poet and host honoured her in a speech only he knows how to make, ranking her above Mlle Mars, the greatest artiste hitherto seen in the part of Donna Sol de Silva.

The article closed with the mention of Chilly's death and Sarcey's re-echoes of Hugo's praises. Death was never absent whenever Sarah's destiny reached a new pinnacle.

The axemen were ready when Sarah re-entered the Française in 1872. Théodore Banville dropped the first blow:

Make no mistake! The engagement of Mlle Sarah Bernhardt at the Comédie Française is a serious and violently revolutionary act. Poetry has entered into the house of art; or, heaven help us, the wolf is in the sheep-fold.

With Chilly's death, the season for the Odéon closed early and gave Sarah a short vacation before the Comédie début. The axemen were still able to get under her skin, and though Sarcey was friendly now, she resented the inference that he had made it easy for her to return to the Française, and that she was really going back in order to show that she was powerful enough to make her former enemies eat crow.

On 6th November 1872, Sarah's second début at the Comédie in Dumas' *Mademoiselle de Belle Isle* was a sell-out. She felt strangely relaxed and so confident that she permitted herself a glance in Julie's direction. As she watched, Julie turned deathly pale and after a few moments, left. The recent death of Chilly haunted her as she went through her role, unable then to do anything, and ran off-stage almost before finishing her scene. She ran into Croisette who had anticipated Sarah's reaction. She comforted her:

'Febré's attending her. She's had immediate care.'

By this time the doctor returned and found Sarah in tears; "Your mother had a fainting fit. They've just taken her home.'

'It's her heart, isn't it?'

'Yes, I'm sorry to tell you it is serious.'

Croisette tiptoed in and quietly told Sarah: 'I've sent Guerard to find out how your mother is. She'll hurry back, you may be sure. Now fix your make-up.'

Sarah knew Julie's condition would one day be fatal. She had an idea.

'When she comes back, tell Guerard to open the OP side, just a little and give me a signal like this if mamma is better, and like this if she's worse.'

In the fourth act the Duc de Richelieu was saying the line: 'Why didn't you say someone was listening, that someone was hidden,' when Mme Guerard opened the door to give the signal of recovery to Sarah. Forgetting all at that moment, Sarah said: 'It's Guerard bringing me good news.' The Duc covered up quickly and the audience never noticed it.

With the good news and the laugh over her fluffed lines, normality returned and she was applauded at the finish. Neither did she mind it when the honours for the performance went to Croisette whose Marquis de Pris was charming.

Glad to be home alone, she lit a candle and prayed. On her bed-table was a note from Sarcey:

It was ludicrous. Shall I ever understand you?
The first act was wonderful; in the others you spoilt the play.

How quick these executioners are to condemn, jumping to conclusions before learning the reason, she mused as she dropped into sleep.

With this sole exception, her success was so marked that she was accused of hiring people to applaud her : 'People are turned away at the box-office every time I play. Do they think I have money to burn?'

The multiple pressures undermined her health and Sarah began to vomit blood in dangerous quantities, fainting, oblivious to all for hours. On recovery, she pulled herself together and went on as if nothing had happened.

Perrin learned of it and came to see for himself, thinking it to be merely a prank to tease him out of his assurance. These two had already tested each other on minor matters and had clashed. He had to make sure so as to be prepared in case it was true.

Perrin found it all to be only too true. Sarah was ill, and he had trouble picking his way through the confusion of paint, plaster, stale food, dog and bird droppings, countless manuscripts and books, some letters, all strewn between easels and sculptures, the sculptures all the work of Sarah and all titled – *Young Girl and Death*, two yards high; *After The Tempest*, a sculpture of an old woman holding the body of her dead grandson; the tragic *Medea* and others.

Perrin, the model of propriety, put on the face of patience and in a paternal tone preached; 'You're killing yourself, my dear child. Why should you want to paint or sculpt? Is it because you must prove there's nothing you can't do?'

'Oh no, not at all. You don't understand. I must create a necessity for staying here!'

'B-but I don't understand!' he was honestly bewildered.

'Perhaps if I put it this way. I have a wild desire to travel; to see another sky, to breathe another air; bigger trees, mountains; anything. But instead, in order to keep to my contract, I grasp at any straw to chain myself. There's no alternative.'

Perrin was hardly aware of walking out and down to the street, so utterly confused was he. The great Sarah Bernhardt with all the adulation of the artistic world at her feet, with a great career ahead of her and *in Paris*, the culture centre of the world? Why was she not content?

For six years more Sarah was to continue to study anatomy, painting and sculpting.

Sarah's association with the Française was a succession of triumphs in comedy, each one overshadowing the last. Sarcey could only praise her talents honestly now. In his paper *Le Temps*, he apologised for his short-sightedness in giving her a harsh review for her performance in *Mademoiselle de Belle Isle*, explaining Julie's illness, and stating that, in the following production of *Zaire*, 'it was Our Sarah – the Sarah of twenty successes'. Just the same, the public still believed it was an artist's excuse to cover her eccentricity.

She yearned for more dramatic parts and had a discussion with Perrin which brought no results; she finally appealed to the Ministry of the Beaux Arts to give her more important parts to play because she was being stifled with no outlet for her tremendous resources. To overcome the disappointment in the emotional void left by her theatrical career Sarah began to raise hopes of fulfilling herself as a sculptress; to find the satisfactions there of a Michelangelo or a Cézanne. Sarah must always reach for the pinnacle. But changes were in the air.

Skirting the issue at first, Perrin came to Sarah's studio, pretended a casual interest in having her do a medallion of him; then, in the same off-hand manner inquired whether she knew the role of Phèdre. She gaped at him in astonishment.

'Well, so there *is* something that can frighten you!' He pressed her hand comfortingly. 'Work it up, I think you'll play it.'

'But . . . what about Mlle Rousseil?'

'Oh, she has refused to play Phèdre for the Racine fête unless she's assured of becoming an Associate in January. As you know, the committee cannot allow itself be be intimidated. She will certainly get the appointment but rules must be respected. If she changes her mind, you'll play Aricia again and I'll change the posters.'

Perrin was hardly out of sight when she nearly fainted with fear! She took a few steps to call him back, and couldn't. She was hysterical with fright. *Phèdre!* She play Phèdre! The ghost of Rachel and her still loyal audience sent Sarah rushing to Mounet-Sully, her opposite male lead. His confident voice and blazing look of assurance saved her.

'No, no. You musn't be afraid. I can see exactly what you'll do with it. Just be careful not to force your voice. Play it sorrowfully rather than furious. Much better for everyone – even Racine.' He was her only strength in the theatre but still her mind seemed obsessed with everything she had heard, over and over, about the great Rachel – the woman of inborn conflicts – of commanding figure and stately poise, who projected substance in her deep alto voice that resonated like a bass cello, rising in violent and wilful passion to a grandeur so intense that it held her audience captive. The most hardened wept. Rachel, idol of classic heroines still lived in the memory of all of Sarah's critics!

It never occurred to her that when the most difficult role in drama would finally be hers, she would not be given the normal period in which to learn and rehearse it. For a while, she wondered if this had been deliberately planned to embarrass her. If she refused, it was an admission of her inadequacy; if she accepted there was little chance of her making a success of it. Who could it be, she wondered, who hated her enough to plan her suicide? Sarah tore herself to shreds with conjectures and agitation, but she returned to the script. Racine's classic Greek tragedy, his last masterpiece, was the concept of Aphrodite as a 'Force of Nature' or as a 'Spirit working in the world' against which, it is an unarguable fact, it becomes possible to speak of Hippolytus as 'sinning'. By the same virtue, Phèdre may be tainted and become a 'sinner'. Theseus is identified with that hero's fabled expedition to Hades. Phèdre, his second wife and mother of two young children believes him dead. Theseus returns and hears rumours to the effect that his son, Hippolytus has dishonoured his stepmother. Hippolytus is in love with Aricia, and ignorant of Phèdre's feelings for him. He is absorbed by all manner of masculine exploits; hunts, horses, athletic competitions and is unsophisticated in the refinements of love. His father out of vengeance, disinherits Hippolytus who goes into exile to raise an army to make war on his father, and regain his and Aricia's rights. Phèdre suffers guilt secretly on added grounds. Her mother and sister have both sinned and she feels the gods themselves are against her. Consumed by her passion, Phèdre watches furtively the innocent couple who hardly exchange any signs of affection.

Suddenly to Sarah came a moment of clarity: an emotional memory brought back a scene – a distant parallel. She had played a role . . . death had played a role . . . there was a Salon party, a prince, all was staged, rehearsed . . . all was acting, and all were actors, and she had played the tragedienne! No one applauded, no one. But a someone who recognised 'the actress' had the compassion of the madonna.

Sarah sat down, penned a note and gave it to Blanche. 'Quickly, take it to Mme George Sand.' The small gesture released sufficient static to let the torrent do what it would, carried on by its own momentum.

Here was the mortuary, a frightened lonely girl walked in, her intense curiosity about happiness in death as she looked at the face of the fifteen-year-old Sleeping Beauty in the coffin! A young man who seemed shy and timid at first when he spoke gently of the young dead girl, who had died almost before she had lived. And then . . . HIPPOLYTE . . . the name . . . again the haunting parallels!

The end of that drama . . . the humiliation . . . Fate exacted a bloody price! Very well. One paid a price. She was paying for Maurice now. Her beloved princeling. She would pay a king's ransom and more if need be. She must redeem her pledge. She had forgotten too much in her struggle to keep a step ahead of the unstable, combustible world she had lived through. She counted her credits, successes, achievements. She had been luckier than most actresses. Only one thing lacked – money.

When Sand arrived, Sarah tried to make sense; to control the onrush of thoughts. She must make sense. She needed help. But Sand's highly developed intuition read her easily.

'I see tribulation in my madonna's eyes.' She passed her hand over her forehead, mimicking a crystal-gazer's gesture. A moment later, both exploded in laughter. Sarah waltzed round the room while the tension spun itself out. 'If I may be forgiven a bromide, "perpetual inspiration is as necessary to the life of genius as perpetual breathing is necessary to animal life." Have I divined correctly?'

'Indeed you have. Allah be praised! I marvel at it,' replied Sarah.

'Then we can quickly dispose of it.' She lit up a small cigar. 'Are you haunted, like Hamlet, by the ghost of Rachel? I knew it. Let me tell you about her. But please, order tea. We'll need it when I've finished.'

She arranged her legs under her. 'Rachel was as petty as you are generous. When she indulged in wit, it was to the detriment of her comrades. She could not endure handsome people on stage with her. Speaking of an artiste whom everyone was praising, she said: "You find her pretty? Well, I admit her classical profile, but such feet! She could easily sleep standing!" ' Sand watched her protégée's face. It was the face of a child – hungry, eager.

'Every artist of talent was an object of Rachel's hatred; she wanted to reign supreme. Her enemies – and they were numerous – thought one day that they had found her rival in Mlle Maxime, a young tragedienne of great talent. The entire press, knowing Rachel, agreed to applaud Mlle Maxime, in spite of the great tragedienne. Rachel bore her anger long and silently, until she found herself face to face with Maxime in Lebrun's tragedy, *Mary Stuart*. Rachel had the title part; Maxime played the Queen. Rachel approached Maxime, superb and impressive with real anger, to declaim her lines with a passion approaching unsimulated rage. Mlle Maxime drew back in fright. She was scared by the haggard eyes of Rachel, who, in a frenzy articulated with tones of disdain the last lines of her tirade : "I plunge my *poignard* in my rival's breast!" Mlle Maxime never rallied from the shock. It was a public execution, and before all Paris assembled.' She watched the change in Sarah's face and went on.

'You remember Beauvallet, whose voice frightened you as a débutante?' Sarah nodded. 'He was the only one who dared to withstand her. He wielded a terrible weapon which he did not hesitate to employ. The weapon was his voice. When Rachel had been particularly refractory, he would tell his comrades at rehearsal : "Well, we shall see tonight." So, in all great scenes they played together, Beauvallet would throw his formidable voice into the house in accents so powerful, so metallic, that Rachel, so exhausted and desperate to make herself heard, was crushed and defeated, she would promise never to offend again, if only he would permit her to be heard by the public. Beauvallet consented, only to have to discipline Rachel again. She always forgot her promise.' Sand puffed peacefully, then continued :

'She feared death as much as you have always faced it. During her last performance in America, she played Adrienne Lecouvreur. She was in the last stages of tuberculosis which killed her so young; she was making violent efforts to sustain herself until the fall of the curtain. Towards the end of the last act, when she cries : "No, I do not want to die!" she became suddenly oppressed with a vision of the hereafter. Deep anguish seized her which she expressed with such real emotion that the public, understanding her grief, sympathised with the unfortunate actress. It was not Adrienne Lecouvreur it was witnessing, but Rachel herself who was fighting with death. Whatever may be said about you, you are honest in your religion. Rachel was superstitious. I bring it up in order to make an important point. It is said that religion generally results in narrowing the mind, and killing inspiration. You are the best proof of the opposite.

'Once, it chanced that thirteen sat down at her table. Seized with fright, she flew from the dining room, but foreseeing the ridicule it would bring on her, she returned full of fear to her seat. The teasing began. "Laugh all you want. I believe in the fatality of numbers, especially thirteen. Do you remember the dinner at Victor Hugo's several years ago? We were thirteen at table. Within weeks, see what happened! Mme Girardin died in her zenith; Mme Arsene Houssaye, scarce in the prime of life, in the splendour of her beauty, and Alfred de Musset – dead; also the Comte d'Orsay and Perrée, such a good man! Dead too, my poor sister Rebecca; Gerard de Nerval committed suicide in the rue de la Lanterne over a gutter. As for Victor Hugo, his wife and two sons, they are worse than dead. They are exiled! The twelfth, whose name I cannot recall disappeared in a tragic manner, and here I find myself, the thirteenth, at table with all of you! What will become of me?" Alas, Musa Avis (the bird muse) as Paul de Sante Victor called her – it was not long before she flew away.' The effect upon Sarah was clear.

'So you see, though she was formidable in art, she was basically a mere mortal woman. I hope I have shattered and routed your spectre. And if you think I made any of this up simply for your sake, forget it. It's all to be found in the newspapers and daily despatches from wherever she appeared. Now, please, may I have my tea?'

'Then you think I can do it? They won't laugh at me?'

Sand sipped daintily. The tea was delicious, prepared by Petite Dame herself. George Sand was always special for her. Fresh croissants and jam, three flavours, all Sand's favourites.

'I'll tell you about Cézanne, his contempt for the Salon? He sent a canvas every year and always they refused it and sent it back. His townspeople asked him to a discussion on an art matter. They asked his opinion and promptly ignored it. Stung to a realisation of the contempt in which he was held, his knowledge of his worth suddenly rent the trammels of his customary humility, and he burst out

"Don't you know, all of you, that there is only one artist in Europe – myself!" '

'*Touché!* I shall try to earn your high opinion of me.'

'You shall. Simply play it as you yourself conceive it. You're not to let comparisons betray you, an original artiste. An actor or actress is as vulnerable as a new born babe; when you step out on stage, unlike other *milieux*, what you display is yourself; and to a critical audience who come to be titillated, excited. I dare you to do something new, they think; while on stage, nothing is hidden from view. You have fought them on their own grounds and have come off thoroughly baptised. May I have another cup of tea? My, I'm thirsty.'

Alone after Sand's departure, Sarah trembled. Another scene, this time evoked by the thirteen at Hugo's dinner, so feared by Rachel, recalled the two deaths that followed the dinner given her by Hugo. The theatre was a law unto itself, she knew, and Hugo had told her himself of his belief in the supernatural. She was yet to meet another great playwright who would confirm all and more.

She knew Sand was innocent of deliberate mischief. But she could not shake off the parallels and the allusion. Was Fate acting through Sand to warn Sarah? Was it an omen! She had betrayed Berton and 'Duq' her two most loyal friends. The Hugo dinner in her honour had been presided over by death. Was this role to be her punishment? Her undoing?

She poured balm on her conscience, 'I did it for Maurice. My salary almost doubled in the transfer.' She was twenty-seven, her son was ten – just the age when education cost a fortune. Academic tutors, fencing, riding, dancing lessons, pocket money, clothes, and soon he would reach man's estate; she had vowed to provide an endowment fund for him; he must be as independent as any prince should be.

Whenever she let herself remember her vengeance on all men for de Ligne's betrayal, she felt absolved of guilt. The term 'Prince of the Blood' always called out her most violent reactions. How he had wooed her, made promises, sent her a king's ransom in flowers and foibles, only to index her among 'obsolete matters'.

Ah yes, he had tried to renew their acquaintance. But he had forgotten her autocratic pride. She accepted his call, let him come to her studio; had invited every great and shining personage of the day; and after decorously introducing him to each guest, ignored him completely.

She opened the script at random. She let her eyes run down the page.

Know Phèdre then; let all her madness speak.
I love thee. Do not think that while I love,
Spotless in mine own eyes do I approve
Of what I am; nor that of the perverse
Passion that shakes my reason. I did nurse
The poison by an abject yielding. – Nay,
Of heaven's wrath the miserable prey
More than thou loathest me do I abhor
Myself.

Her little dog shuddered. A crash of china, tea and script smashed to the floor. 'How will I ever speak those lines! Fall on my knees and cry "Hippolytus! I love you. Kill me!" ' The little dog had scampered swiftly to the debacle and was sweeping up the crumbs with his pink tongue and lapping up the spilled tea. 'That's right, show me up! Show me what I'll be doing picking up and eating crumbs off the floor.'

She swore: 'Impetuous Satan!' picked up the script while the gloom dispelled. She let the little dog lick her cheek while she studied her lines.

'Whose fault is it if I want to fly with the eagles! May Molière forgive and help me. I fear Racine too much to ask him.'

The slag of genius had gone through another firing and testing in the self-sustaining furnace, and Sarah was sheathed in a shining new suit of armour.

The day of the fête, the 21st of December, bore down with

all its sinister threats. All the artists were busy applying make-up, gesturing, talking nervously to each other, some of them happier than others in hope of seeing Sarah's balloon burst and deflate. Regnier, sympathetic to Sarah, came to help.

'Courage, aren't you the spoiled darling of the public? They'll make allowances ... for your inexperience in important first parts.'

But the well meant comment sent Sarah into hysterics of sobbing. Another hopeful soul came to tell Sarah: 'Two hundred people were turned away at the box-office.' It had the opposite effect and now her teeth chattered. Perrin arrived and tried to console her. He powdered her nose playfully and completed her misery by blinding and suffocating her with powder.

Finally, Mounet-Sully, fully costumed and ready for his role approached. He had the profile of an Apollo and the figure of a Hercules, and his masculine vocal tones sent thrills through her whether he wooed her on stage or off. In a moment he restored her. 'I dreamed we were playing *Phèdre* and you were hissed ... and my dreams always go by opposites, so. . .' Sarah adored dreams.

Next, a *grotesque* greeted her. Martel dressed as Theramenes asked: 'Are you ill?' She looked up and saw an unfinished putty nose drooping, two black spots on either side for nostrils, a wide bar of red painted across his brow ran down his nose, and yellow wax dripped from his cheeks. Her tensions loosed, swinging wide to the opposite extreme as she broke into loud laughter.

That performance proved to be the final triumph in her drive towards mastering the classical drama tradition; she had stormed its citadel, the forbidding pinnacle she had dreaded, and now stood upon it, bowing to the applause that thundered around her.

The public was conquered. It had come with every opinion listed, to make comparisons, to judge. Instead, it was as though a mass hypnosis had enveloped them. For one evening they forgot everything in a new rapture. Without reservation they bathed in depths of emotions under the spell of an unyielding spirit who had hidden secrets of endless surpriseful beauty.

They too longed to enter the secret chambers where perhaps they too might learn those secrets. The applause continued and Sarah was irrevocably adopted.

The Queen of Paris bowed from Olympus.

The directors now looked around them. A new problem faced them. What next? Where could they turn to find new challenges, new worlds for their genie to conquer? The public was happy enough and could go on watching Sarah play the same roles in the same repertoire endlessly, but the problem was still Sarah. She was their golden goose and they had to watch and anticipate anything and everything for her sake as well as their own.

In Rome, Vaincue Perrin had expected Sarah to play the role of the young vestal Opimia, but instead she insisted on doing Opimia's grandmother Posthumia, the old blind Roman woman whose efforts to save her granddaughter failing, she stabs her and asks her pardon in a stunning scene.

Perrin at first objected, partly because of his love of order and balance. If Sarah played Posthumia, what role would Mounet-Sully play? He could no longer play the male lead if Sarah did not play Opimia. Casting about, Perrin found in the play, an old idiot, Vestaepor. Unnecessary to the play, a part which had been cut out, but which Perrin quickly rescued, it was to restore his beloved ideal of the two lovers, the two heroes, or the two victims. Sully created the part of the old idiot in his characteristic artistry, giving it the dimensions of a profound, Shakespearian classic.

Vitu wrote his praise of the play; a piece which had so little merit it would never have been noticed except for the elevation which the two artists gave to it:

Draped like an antique statue, her head crowned with long tresses of white hair under a matron's veil, Mademoiselle Sarah Bernhardt made the character of Posthumia the finest of all her creations. No contemporary actress could have rendered this figure with such nobility, sincerity and true sensitiveness. The tears, the real tears, of the public, proved to what a degree she had touched their hearts and minds.

Sarcey added his comments, glowingly:

She is not an actress in the ordinary sense. She is nature itself, served by a marvellous intelligence, a soul of fire, and the most expressive, melodious voice that has ever enchanted human ears. This woman acts from her heart, from the very core of her being. She is a marvellous, an incomparable artist; a creature apart, magnificent – in a word, an actress of genius.

Until 1877, this restive creature who could never find enough to do, even though she had already crowded several lifetimes into the past twelve years was always bored. She could satisfy her desires by indulging them, but she only hungered for more. The scars left by Julie's indifference would never heal.

Given no new roles to play for a year, she spent very little time rehearsing the well-known ones she played, and the repetition of doing something which no longer required any deep driving, soul-searing effort now sent her in search of other worlds. She wrote a book: *Into the Clouds*, which Clairin illustrated. In this, her début as an author, her creative ingenuity told the story of her ascent by an inanimate voiceless witness; a chair. Her public was delighted with it, and Sarah turned back to her painting.

Among her devotees, Sarah was far more than the interpreter of Phèdre, the demi-goddess whom she could incarnate at will. It was as Sarcey said: Sarah was not simply the incomparable artist, she was the artiste – she realised and understood in the most perfect sense the ideal of beauty.

Working at her newest passion, fashioning still stronger chains to keep herself tied down to her contract, she let painting now obsess her. All her friends happily aided their idol with instructions and again she launched into epics without studying; hoping only to tire herself into exhaustion.

On one of his visits to Sarah, Victor Hugo said admiringly:

'Ah, my dear, how I wish I could paint!'

'But of course you can,' she said simply.

'No,' Hugo protested.

'That's ridiculous. Anyone who can write or act, can paint if he tries. Come here now, here are brushes, paint and an easel. Try it.'

With her confident urging, Hugo dove into the paint. Not long after, his work in pen-and-ink medium was exceedingly good.

Just as Sarah was beginning to lose interest in painting, a year later, on 21st December 1877, she was billed to appear as Doña Sol in Victor Hugo's *Hernani*. Thankful for the new role, she refreshed her interest in the theatre by studying and rehearsing the new part. Her public as well as Sarah herself anticipated the event. It had not been presented for ten years, and at that time it was not very popular.

Playing opposite her again was Mounet-Sully whose perfect sense of the epic, romantic and poetic style balanced Sarah's natural gifts, and he made an impassioned rebel and lover to her Doña Sol. The duo triumphed again, brilliantly.

The generous author-poet-playwright again knew no bounds in his desire to thank the prima donna. Encased in a jewel-box lay a pear-shaped diamond pendant, hung from a fine gold chain. With this gift, Hugo sent the proof of his sentiments:

Madame, you gave us at the same time grandeur and charm. I was deeply moved, old fighter though I am;

and at a certain moment, while the public, touched and enchanted, applauded you, I wept. This tear you drew from me is yours, and I lay it at your feet.

Sarah adored the tear drop and wore it constantly, until one evening at a party given by the wealthy nabob, Alfred Sassoon, she lost it. When he offered to replace it, she told him:

'No one can give me back the tear of Victor Hugo.'

8

London Debut

The managers of the *Française* were in discussion with Hollinghead and Mayer of the London *Gaiety* who hoped to bring the French company to England for several months. The artists had heard the exciting news and were anxiously waiting for developments. Very few had ever been to London.

'Just what we need – a holiday!' they told each other.

Hoping to keep her health Sarah avoided all activities which might dissipate her energies. She came straight home from the theatre and stayed home. She gave her maid orders not to let anyone disturb her. But the maid could not stop a certain very tall stubborn, white-haired man from forcing his way into the foyer of her studio one day. 'But I insist, Madame will see me.'

'No, no. Monsieur, please go!'

Lost in her painting, Sarah did not notice the commotion going on in the hall. It was a child, Ann Marie, who was acting as a model who interrupted :

'Madame, a man is trying to come in.'

Angrily, Sarah turned from the canvas. She rushed out ready to send whoever it was flying, but ran right into the intruder. She only saw two piercing grey-blue eyes studying her. He exuded a strange authority which immediately halted her.

'Madame Bernhardt, permit me.' He took her arm as casually as if he were an old friend. Sarah allowed herself to be led back into her studio. For the next ten minutes he remarked upon and admired her many paintings and sculptures. Sarah invited him to sit down recognising method behind his tactics, but enjoying the mystery he created. Without wasting further time on amenities, he came straight to the point.

'I'm Jarrett, the impressario. I can make your fortune. Will you come to America?'

His French was stilted but Sarah liked the first part of his offer until she realised what he had really said.

'America! Never! Never!' she rose from her chair.

'Oh well, don't get angry,' he said soothingly. 'Here's my card in case you change your mind.' Jarrett was not defeated yet. Sarah was picking up her brushes. He would try once more.

'Madame, you're going to London with the *Française*. Would you like to earn a lot of money in London?'

'Surely. Why not, if I go. How?'

'By playing in small drawing rooms. I can make you a fortune.'

'Wonderful – that is, if I go to London. I haven't decided.'

'Then will you sign a little contract making me your exclusive representative. I'll then be able to go on with publicity.'

Without ever having previously set eyes on Jarrett, Sarah was so inspired with confidence that she signed. Jarrett honoured his contract to the letter. This was the first of a long series of contracts netting Sarah millions of francs; bringing her to every corner of the world and making her an international figure.

Sarah's dressing room was the inner sanctum for her special friends as well as for her furred and feathered ones. She had never outgrown her attachment to her pets and wherever she lived or travelled, she carried her menagerie with her. When a stray puppy of unknown parentage or ownership had the good sense to circle the attractive stroller on her walks through Parc Monceau, she brought it to the theatre to join the *élite*.

Along with the others of the company, she had been told that an agreement had been signed between the management and the London *Gaiety* directors, without consulting the artistes. Sarah was irked.

When the management finally called a meeting, Perrin saw the familiar look of rebellion on Sarah's face. He took her aside: 'What are you turning over in your mind?'

Suppressing her anger, she said: 'I'll tell you what! I'm turning this over. I won't go to London in a second-rate position. I intend to have all the benefits of a full associate for the entire period of the tour, and I'm not going on the same salary you pay me here.' There was something positive in her tone.

'I'll speak to the committee tomorrow,' he assured her.

He met her next day: 'I'm sorry, *chérie*, it can't be done. They wouldn't listen.' He threw his hands up in despair.

'Well, I won't go to London.' She stamped her feet and turned her back. 'That's all. Nothing in my contract obliges me to go.'

When the committee heard this, Got, one of the members, cried out: 'That's a relief. Let her stay here. She's a darn nuisance anyway.'

Perrin came back to Sarah's dressing-room hopefully, to see if this would change her mind, but she was adamant. Like a shuttle, Perrin started back to the committee in such a hurry that he tripped over one of her strays and fell into the arms of Madame Sand who was just then coming in through the doorway.

With a raised eyebrow she greeted him and smiled as the little dog scampered off.

Unable to wait until the door was closed, Sarah laughed gleefully: 'I have something to tell you!' She confided the terms of the contract with Jarrett.

It was almost time for the first curtain. Sarah, dressed for her role had been applying make-up when she was suddenly seized with a wild desire to play a prank on those little people who sat in conclave deciding other people's fate.

'I have an idea! Guaranteed to send them up the wall! Will you help me, dear?'

Sand was always ready. 'Anytime you say. I thrive on conspiracy. And I need a good laugh.'

They quickly cleared a space in the centre of the room, got some packing cases from the prop room and pushed them together to form a platform. A couple of large white sheets and a pair of candlesticks two feet high joined the other props.

'Hurry, they'll be here any moment. You can watch from behind those drapes.' Sarah whispered.

A moment later the stage manager came to give Sarah her cue and nearly had a stroke at the sight of the 'corpse' serenely laid out, her hands crossed over her bosom; the peace of death on her brow.

'Blanche! Blanche! where are you?' he screamed for her maid. From the next room Blanche came running. 'Yes, what . . .' Blanche fainted. Now the manager had to find help for Blanche. He threw water at her from a flower vase and she opened her eyes, only to become hysterical. The manager shook her and she dropped to her knees and began to pray, tears pouring down as she mumbled in pitiful fright.

The manager pulled himself together, sent a page to call Perrin while he strengthened himself to make the announcement of the cancelled performance 'due to the sudden death of Mlle Bernhardt'.

Meanwhile, back at the offices consternation broke loose when Perrin told the committee that Sarah would not go to London; Hollinghead had just informed them that 'We shall have to break our contract if Mlle Bernhardt doesn't come. She is the chief attraction.'

Quickly, the human shuttle was told 'Go back to her. She must come. Tell her we accept her demands. She wins.'

Perrin arrived at the theatre to find everyone aghast at the shock; the audience leaving in a daze, not even asking for refunds. He dashed up to see for himself. There was the body of his prima donna stretched out, true enough; two lighted candles flickering and sputtering, her maid beside the bier, crying. Perrin cracked his knuckles:

'What will we do now? The Tour will be cancelled and the Company will probably lose its standing and disband. *Mon Dieu*, what shall I tell the Committee! First the War, now THIS! What a catastrophe!' He paced nervously when he suddenly thought he had gone mad. A burst of convulsive laughter broke the silence. Sand came out of hiding. When

Perrin realised the hoax had been staged to make a fool of him, he was so outraged that he never again could speak to Sarah without feeling self-conscious. If possible, he avoided her.

Along with Sarah, Croisette had also been appointed an Associate with full benefits, not only for the tour but on a permanent basis. Peace was restored for the London departure but five days later at nine in the evening Perrin came to Sarah's, interrupting a dinner party. She greeted him coolly: 'Why have you come?'

'Read this,' he handed her a newspaper and pointed to an advertisement.

Drawing room Comedies of Mlle Bernhardt under the management of Sir Benedict: The repertoire of Mlle Sarah is composed of comedies, proverbs, one-act plays and monologues, written especially for her and one or two artistes of the Comedie Française. These comedies are played without accessories or, etc. Please communicate with Mr Jarrett at His Majesty's Theatre.

She read it and explained the contract: 'And what is the objection to my making money during my free time?'

'That has nothing to do with me. It's the business of the Committee.'

'Oh, that's too much.' Sarah cried and showed him a letter which had arrived the day before from Delauney.

Would you care to come and play *La Nuit d'octobre* at Lady Dudley's on Thursday, 5th June? They will give us each five thousand francs. Kind regards,
Delauney.

'Let me have this letter,' Perrin said, 'I'll show it to the committee,' but Sarah refused.

'You may tell them I showed it to you.'

There was much discussion for the next three days, but in the end a statement was given out to *The National* on the 29th of May:

184

Much Ado About Nothing. In friendly discussion it has been decided that outside the rehearsals and the performances of the Comédie Française, each artist is free to employ his time as he sees fit. There is therefore absolutely no truth at all in the pretended quarrel between the Comédie Française and Mlle Sarah Bernhardt. This artiste has only acted strictly within her rights, which nobody attempts to limit, and all our artists intend to benefit in the same manner. The manager of Comédie Française asks only that the artistes who form this 'corps' do not give performances in a body.

The committee had learned its lesson.

'Hip, Hip, Hoorah!' Sarah heard for the first time on the pier as soon as the company had landed. Above the heads of the crowd, a luminous forehead shadowed the most penetrating gaze that ever beheld her. An armful of lilies landed at her feet: 'Do walk on them, Mademoiselle.' Then: 'A cheer for Sarah Bernhardt!' and the crowd responded enthusiastically. It was Oscar Wilde whose plays she had longed to do. She was captured by the English welcome and an enduring love of England sprang up, one of the few of her entire life.

The long train ride lulled her to sleep until Madame Guerard woke her, 'We're in London, *chère*. Oh see, a red carpet; there!' Alighting, she was about to step on it when two porters swiftly rolled it up. '*Comment c'est drôle!*' Madame gasped. 'We must find out about their customs.' She helped Sarah into the carriage and drove to 77 Chester Square.

Her vanity suffered a second blow when the coachman proudly related watching the Prince and Princess of Wales stride down the carpet to their train for a holiday in Paris.

'Here we are, madame.' The coachman helped her out while the butler hurried to collect her luggage. The door of the house stood wide open and her first impression was that of a greenhouse, so high and crowded were the flowers that filled the room. She slid onto a couch and looked over the cards, neatly stacked on a silver tray, near the blazing fire. The topmost one written in a large clear script read: 'Welcome! Henry Irving!' At such a moment, it could never have occurred to her that Irving, the great English Shakespearean actor, and she, the great French star, would one day lay the corner stones of a new building on Wardour Street, not far from where she now sat.

At seven next morning she arose to find Jarrett already there with a long list of instructions. She sipped her morning tea while he hurried through the details but had only covered a scarce half-dozen when the butler announced: 'The press has arrived.' Jarrett handled them like a champion chess player. It went so fast that she hardly remembered when it ended and how she then found herself caught up in the social whirl. Her fondness for luxurious appointments was a constant distraction: the lavish table settings, gleaming sterling silver beautifully carved and chased; exquisite china and linens; the bell-tone crystal for toasts in French champagne. And those tall handsome Englishmen! She even loved the language. 'Smashing!' and 'Capital!' became her favourite expressions.

She had almost forgotten what she was there for, when she suddenly found herself confronted with her London First Night and a full house including many standing. An enthusiastic audience waited to watch her in that 'killing' scene, the second act of *Phèdre*. Suddenly she had a seizure of the trachea! Disaster! Already she had redone her make-up three times. She clapped a hand on her eyes to concentrate on her voice: *l-l-le balll*. Eyes open or shut, it was useless – her *le bal* rang neither high nor low. It was hoarse and smothered. Saying her lines as she fumbled with her rings, veil and cameo belt, she heard a page call 'Curtain!'

What followed she could not remember. Her nerves infected the others. The impatient Got mumbled: 'She's going mad!' Only the actress who played the nurse, Oenone, said :

'Calm yourself, all the English have gone to Paris. There's no one in the house but Belgians.' To which Sarah replied :

'How stupid you are! You know how frightened I was at Brussels!' and received the answer : 'It was all for nothing! There were only English in the theatre that day.'

The confusion was followed by the applause from the house which helped Sarah to get in control again. She stepped on stage, bowed and went through the play without the slightest error or betrayal of what she felt. The only one who shared that secret was Mounet-Sully who picked her up – unconscious, when the last curtain fell – and carried her to her dressing room. There he removed from her mouth the handkerchief she had stuffed into it to keep the blood from gushing onto the stage.

John Murray, the critic, in the *Gaulois* of 5th June 1879, said :

When recalled with loud cries, Mlle Bernhardt appeared exhausted by her efforts and supported by Mounet-Sully, she received an ovation which I think is unique in the annals of the theatre in England.

The Standard finished its article with these words :

The subdued passion, repressed for a time, until at length it burst its bonds, and the despairing, heart-broken woman is revealed to Hippolytus, was shown with so vivid a reality that a scene of enthusiasm such as is rarely witnessed in a theatre followed the fall of the curtain. Mlle Sarah Bernhardt, in the few minutes she was upon the stage (and coming on, it must be remembered, to plunge into the middle of a stirring tragedy) yet contrived to make an impression which will not soon be effaced from those who were present.

Eagerness to win the English public with her first appearance nearly killed her. A night of violent coughing and a great loss of blood forced the local doctors to contact the French Embassy. Dr Vintras of the French Hospital in London immediately ordered her family to be sent for. Unable to speak, she gestured NO. A pad was placed under her hand. She wrote : 'Send for Dr Parrot.'

Dr Vintras sat by all night slipping crushed ice between her lips. At 5 am the bleeding stopped and she was able to swallow a sedative that put her to sleep. Dr Parrot's arrival by the four o'clock boat found Sarah past danger and informing them that she would play that evening as scheduled. The doctors informed the directors that she was 'still critical' and must not exert herself under any condition.

To all this Sarah remained silent, but asked to have Mayer sent in and had a whispered conference with him. When the doctors left, she had her maid dress her quickly and escaped by a rear door to a waiting carriage. 'Say nothing but come to the theatre later,' she whispered to Blanche. 'Now, let's hurry!'

'Where are you going?' Mayer hung back stupefied.

'To the theatre, quick! I'll explain in the carriage.' They got in. 'Neither of the doctors would have believed me had I told them I'd been through similar crises before. The die is cast and we'll see what happens.'

She hid in Mayer's office to avoid the doctors and half an hour later Blanche gave her a letter from Dr Parrot, the kind man who had dropped everything to rush to her aid. It was a furious reproach with some drugs enclosed in case of a relapse. 'If you survive, it will be medical history,' he wrote.

The *élan vital* which nourished her renewed her whenever she exerted that stubborn will of hers. It gave her an astonishing beauty too, bewildering those who knew of her illness.

When the drugs which she had hastily taken in advance, wore off sometime after the performance, she listened in amazement and heard she had gone through the play in a semi-trance. Light as a feather after the opiate, Sarah had strolled back and forth gracefully while Croisette expected to go through her big scene in Dumas *fils'* play. Instead of the first line, Sarah delivered the last punctiliously, and left Croisette nothing to do but to walk off. Backstage, Croisette nearly collapsed.

'What's happened?' everyone asked.

'Sarah's gone mad!'

'But how? Why?'

'She's cut out the entire two hundred lines!'

Somehow the play was got through and it was reviewed in *Le Figaro:*

L'Étrangère is not a piece in accordance with the English taste. Mlle Croisette, however, was applauded enthusiastically and so were Coquelin and Febvre. Mlle Sarah Bernhardt, nervous as usual, lost her memory.

Only Dumas *fils* himself restored her when she apologised to him:

Oh, my dear child, when I write a play I think it is good. When I see it played, I think it's stupid, and when anyone tells it to me, I think it's perfect as the person always forgets half of it.

On the next date scheduled for this same play, Sarah was ill again, and as she was also to play *Hernani* the same evening, she requested a change of programme for the matinee in order to save herself. By 21st June 1879, sold tickets tallied one thousand four hundred pounds. Got, the dean of the Française said to the reluctant Mayer:

'Lloyd will play Bernhardt's role, and with Croisette, Brohan, Coquelin Febvre and myself, – hang it all – we should be able to make up for her absence.'

But Lloyd refused and *Tartuffe* was given instead, with disastrous results. Most of the audience asked for refunds and receipts totalled eighty four pounds instead of five hundred pounds.

Sarcey led off a wave of accusations branding Sarah as stupid and foolish, and lampooning the exhibition of art that she had brought to sell.

An old friend answered for her. It was Zola.

She is reproached above all for not having kept exclusively to the dramatic art, for having turned to sculpture, painting and what not. This is positively funny. Not content with finding her too thin and declaring her to be mad, they would like to regulate the employment of her days. Really! there is much more freedom in prison. Actually, people do not deny her the right to practise sculpture or painting; they only object to her exhibiting her work. . . .

Since it was impossible to attack Sarah professionally, the French press continued its attacks on her behaviour until it reached what amounted to a conspiracy. She managed to ignore it until some of the company players began to taunt her and this decided her to resign. She sent a copy of her resignation to the *Figaro* in Paris, but the management absolutely refused to consider it. This time the company knew the management was right and each one in turn spoke privately to her.

'Tell me you won't do it,' Lloyd pleaded. 'You're my best friend.' Coquelin and Mounet-Sully urged 'Fortunately, we'll make you change your mind. There's no greater stage than that of the Française. Where will you go?'

She sat silently when they left unable to deny any of their arguments. Still, she had sent off the letters and when she once decided a path, that was the way she took. These moments brought with them intense loneliness and she gave herself up to tears.

'Can anyone tell me where Mlle Bernhardt may be found?' she heard an old familiar voice ask. Sand had slipped in and was watching silently.

An utterance of joy escaped her as they hugged and hugged.

'Well, have you lost all your manners in this foreign land. Must I remind you to offer me tea after my long trip from Paris?' Sand broke the tension. 'And while you're about it, please order a carriage. You may show me the sights. I hear there's an Egyptian sphinx watching the Thames. Now, I want to hear everything, right from the beginning.'

'*A votre service.*' She rang for Blanche. 'Cancel all my engagements, bring tea, and be sure the trolley is loaded with all the best. Hurry, I have a guest.' She turned back to her friend.

'I've been exploding to tell you how I love London. From the moment I arrived everything's been so delightfully exciting and perfect.'

'Just as I thought. If I weren't a journalist myself, I'd never have guessed it.'

Sarah began with Jarrett, just as it had happened: 'He brought a list a yard long but it was a waste of time. He never got to read it. "There'll be thirty-seven journalists and you must see each one separately." ' 'Thirty-seven!' I replied, 'that's impossible. You can't mean it. I don't even speak English!' but he said, 'Madame, in dealing with journalists you must be businesslike. I'll be at your side and interpret for you. Simply be your natural charming self. Your lack of English may be a decided advantage. My English, as bad as the reporters' French made much work for Jarrett. Next day the papers printed that I was most enthusiastic about the beauties of London. Wasn't that remarkable. I had not even stepped out of my house.'

'I told you you were a witch.' Sand smiled.

'Later the same day Hortense Damian, the London favourite, came with plans for my introduction to society: a dinner that evening; a ride on a duke's estate, on and on as if I were dreaming. There's nothing like English efficiency and simplicity – it's their special gift – makes for perfection in everything.

'During the carriage ride the neat orderliness of the streets brought me my first pang. The contrast with Paris after the Kiss of the Commune. But Hortense distracted me

"See there, the changing of the guard!" She directed the driver to stop. The colourful pageantry, the staccato wooden-like movements, the silky tassels and brilliant uniforms brought tears to my eyes. I thought of my little boy playing with his soldiers and longed for him.'

'Hortense mistook my emotions. "I understand, it brings a lump to my throat too. Carry on!" she told the coachman. A bit further on she asked "Do tell me if it bores you. If you'd rather we can drive to the Zoo. Palaces and churches can be a bit much." I nodded and we drove home. I was beginning to be homesick, so I said I was tired.

'High tea was ready when we got to her home and her friends all gave me the warmest welcome ever. Women, thank God, are the same the world over. They chatted gaily with me in perfect French and for the first time I felt at home. You should have seen those trolleys, the clotted cream, crumpets and every imaginable pastry and biscuit, and so many fruit jams; when I build my house, the living room will be English!'

'I don't want to spoil your mood, but you seem quite happy now, so I'll risk asking – are you serious about your resignation?'

'Yes. I have no choice. Not that I know what I'll do next.'

'Then I accept it. I trust in your intuition to guide you.'

For breaking a contract with the *Française*, the custom required that the performer be tendered three summonses, regardless of who accepted them. The lawyer, knowing she was not at home dispatched these legal notices immediately upon receiving Perrin's orders. The maid accepted them, not knowing what they contained. The suit was lost by Sarah in advance.

A reporter wrote:

> To become a *Societaire* of the *Comédie Française* is a truly serious matter, seeing that the engagement is for twenty years and its conditions quite onerous; no member can resign until after ten years' service; then a year's notice must be given, and it must be renewed in the

course of the last year. A pledge must be signed not to perform on any stage in any country, or the resigning member loses the right to a retiring pension. Membership is the highest distinction which the stage can give in a country where the stage is held in peculiar honour, and it confers at once a social distinction and a security against those changes of fortune to which actors in other countries are so constantly exposed.

The lawyer took pleasure in going through Perrin's files, to find the many letters from Sarah – some written in anger, others at moments of a lighter mood – all of which he had saved. The attorney, smoothly and insinuatingly confidential, produced only those letters from Perrin to Sarah which proved his paternal devotion to the young débutante's highest interest. Also produced were Sarah's letters, but only those which were detrimental to her interest. Sarah had torn up all of Perrin's letters and had no proof to offer in her own defence.

The clever attorney's plea was so successful that he claimed and was awarded three hundred thousand francs damages, plus the confiscation of the forty three thousand francs withheld from Sarah's salary in the *Comédie* fund that was owed to her.

Barboux was engaged for Sarah's defence, but as he was also a friend of Perrin's, his defence was a mere formality. Sarah was furious, but she too had friends. Prince Napoleon's brother Jerome had begged innumerable times to let him be of service to her in reciprocation of the many evenings of exhilaration that he enjoyed in his royal box as he watched her. On her return to Paris, she tossed off a short note:

I am sued by that beast Perrin. You must interpose to save me. In memory of the past
Sarah.

She sent for her lawyer and handed it to him just as it was. 'Take it to Prince Jerome!' she ordered.

'But *mon Dieu*! Are you mad?' he stared at the lines in utter shock. 'Without an envelope?'

'Obey me!' she commanded imperiously. 'I know what I'm about.'

The advocate delivered the letter and the fine was paid. Sarah was an observer, and had learned from Jarrett to dispose of problems as quickly as possible. The future must be met – uncluttered.

With part of the money from her London appearances and the sale of her art, Sarah bought a few pets from the London Zoo. The cheetah horrified everyone, especially her other animals, as he bared his teeth, snarling, and taking stock as he slithered noiselessly from his cage. Petite Dame flew up the stairs, almost too frightened to watch from an upper window. In the garden, also freed, the furred and feathered newcomers flew or ran in all directions, screaming their protests, unable to find a safe branch or corner to hide in. Sarah's own dogs howled with fright. Only her monkey, Darwin, was delighted to have his mistress back, but would not leave his cage.

In total joyful abandon, Sarah too yelped, shrieked and barked in imitation of the cheetah and the other animals. George Clairin, come to welcome Sarah home, rocked with laughter, then quickly sketched the Hoffmannesque scene for the papers.

The only sober member of the new collection, a dividend from Mr Cross, the keeper, was a prehistoric type chameleon, truly a Chinese curio. He could change colour from pale green to dark bronze or to pencil-thinness from a fat ball. It sat royally as though peering through a lorgnette, focussing the right eye forward, the left eye backward, taking in the scene in cynical disdain. With apt genius, his mistress christened him *Cross-ci-Cross-ca* in honour of his donor.

Jarrett arrived, and as no one answered the bell, he strolled round to the back where the noise was enough to wake the dead. The tall impresario peered easily over the high wall. There Sarah, Sarah the moody, the eccentric, the impossible, was hardly discernible from her menagerie. He exploded into a loud and prolonged laugh until the tears ran down his cheeks.

She caught sight of him and stopped in her tracks. Jarrett was laughing! Never had she believed that Jarrett could laugh!

Mme Guerard hurried down to open the door. Relaxed and happy, Sarah joined Jarrett in the drawing room. After a few proper comments on her charming home, he came to the point as usual.

'I know you're the greatest actress in the world but I've been reading the papers. The press must make you suffer deeply. I can help you if you'll let me.'

'How? I've already resigned.'

'And you were right to resign.'

'Thank you. You do really mean that?'

'As the premier star, you were miserably underpaid.'

'But that wouldn't have been the worst of it if they hadn't slandered me.'

'Exactly. And now *they*'ve sued you for breach of contract.'

'It's too ludicrous! They can't stand anything I do, yet they object to my leaving.'

'Well, by accepting my proposal, you'll scoop them with one blow. Let me book you for the States. Here's my offer: two hundred pounds for each performance in cash. If the receipts run over six thousand six hundred dollars for a show, you'll receive in addition, half of everything above that figure. A special Pullman car with drawing-room and a piano for yourself, and a four-bed room for your staff. You shall have two cooks and forty pounds a week for hotel expenses. No pinching pennies and you won't need to paint or sculpt. If you agree, I'll give you one hundred thousand francs in advance.'

'*Formidable!*' Sarah stared.

'That is only part of it,' he followed up quietly. 'I'll teach you how to handle the press. I'll show you how to make them eat their own words. You'll become the most famous actress in the world with influence greater than a king's. No one will dare to contradict you. You'll be the vogue of the century. Everything you do will be copied as the mode of the moment.'

Jarrett's proposal went to Sarah's head like a whirlwind courtship by an oriental king out of the *Arabian Nights*. 'It's a fantastic dream! As I do need the money and have no other plans, *j'accepte*, Mr Jarrett.'

'You will never regret it. I am a man of my word, above all,' he assured her as he politely bowed himself out.

Guerard called her to dinner but Sarah was not hungry. She had no need of food and no need to think.

Jarrett's arrival in Sarah's life marked an end of preliminaries. His keen sense of business saw in her a means of realising two fortunes; one for Sarah, and through her, one for himself.

London was the doorway. In England, her genius crystallised. Critics, reviewers, society – each laid siege and claimed her for their own. And if she was autocratic before, it was England's blame that she afterwards became a veritable tyrant, a Pharaoh who believed, nay, knew she was the incarnation of the Sun God himself. She did as she pleased, ruled supreme in every detail – excepting only in her contact with Jarrett.

He alone brooked no contradiction. Always her uppermost concern had been for Maurice. Now through Jarrett's international connections she knew this dream would surely be realised. Jarrett never left room for doubt. She knew her pledge would soon be redeemed. She could lean on Jarrett as she had never done before. She could stop worrying about surviving long enough to provide for her son.

With those thoughts in mind, she hired the stage carpenters to crate her sculptures almost before she packed her clothes. They refused payment, 'We'll ask double when you return. You'll come back rich. *Bon voyage*.' Their confidence in their investment was no gamble.

There was nothing underhand about Jarrett. Most obvious to Sarah was as she put it 'he was Nature's model for the Rock of Gibraltar'. If she was moulded steel, he was pure granite, and she doubted if he ever had been a child.

In him she saw the man of principle and steadfast character which she hoped Maurice would be.

Though Jarrett objected at first, Sarah arranged that Maurice should go to America with her; her next port of call. Maurice had never been exposed to such a man, though she was the first to extol the male virtues of all her friends. But there was a difference. Jarrett was not an artist, made no pretentious to a knowledge of anything but business and integrity. His chief virtue was his unbending inflexibility; she never could wheedle her way with him. He never changed his mind once he had come to a decision. In short, Jarrett was the only man whom Sarah could not bend to her will. Here was a man who stood alone; fearless; blameless. He needed no marble gallery, no Hall of Fame. Jarrett set a pattern, an image for Sarah herself which she admired and strove to emulate. She saw that through him she would at once achieve two goals: an estate for Maurice, and even more important – an opportunity for her son to learn international business methods. All this decided Sarah to accept Jarrett's proposal for an American tour.

In London, he taught her how to meet and interview the press; which invitations to accept; and which excuses were acceptable when she had to reject invitations. On stage, due to fever and trachea trouble when she omitted two hundred lines of Dumas Fils play, it was he who taught her how to explain and continue her good relations with the great playwright.

He also got her a stall at the Albert Charity Fair in competition with duchesses and countesses. She not only sold all her art work but netted the largest receipts, £256, of which £110 came from the Princess of Wales for two kittens. Her autographs brought one pound each. The Prince of Wales was her best customer.

On the lighter side, cartoonists competed with their counterparts on the other side of the channel: her thinness was still the target: an example was – a near-sighted person approaches her: 'Take care, monsieur, you will sit upon me.'

'Good Lord, what a narrow escape,' exclaims the near-sighted one. 'I was nearly impaled.'

Her rivals would remark – 'She could take a bath in a gun-barrel. She could clothe herself with a shoestring.'

But Sarah could retaliate. After an argument with a Russian actress in whose face seemed to be reflected the ice-floes of the Arctic, the Russian broke down, having got the worst of it, and began to cry. *La Bernhardt* was called to attention, 'You were wrong to go so far. The poor girl is deeply moved. She weeps.'

'She weeps?' retorted Sarah. 'Come now, you deceive yourself; she is merely thawing.'

A duchess, rather sceptical, gave Sarah a commission for her sculptured portrait on condition that it be modelled before her eyes. *La Bernhardt* accepted and executed a 'speaking likeness' of the duchess in sight of the audience. The time for completion of this feat was twenty-five minutes.

She collected her fee, then revealed her secret: 'First catch your hare, that is, have ready a carefully modelled and well-baked medallion portrait of the person who has commissioned you. Then cover it heavily under some red modelling clay. When your audience is before you, merely make a few passes, remove the clay in handfuls, take a step back every few minutes to see how your "work" is getting on. Don't forget to look at your live model now and then. *Voilà la Chose!*'

Sarah's hunger for another sky and other people was to drive her on to America, the Promised Land. But there was yet another reason. Two years before a Dutch aunt had died leaving Sarah enough money to buy land and build a villa. In this beautiful home she lived with Maurice, her sister Jeanne, five servants and the ever-devoted Guerard. Sarah had no vices except her love of luxury. She furnished her house lavishly, kept two carriages – one for driving to the theatre – the other for visiting or holiday drives in the Bois. Lalique designed voluptuous expensive jewellery and Sarah went into debt to buy a serpent necklace and bracelet studded with jewels. Naturally all this did not escape the notice of the press:

The consummate actress is best seen in the native elegance of the daughter of Judah, when she neither acts nor dreams of her profession. All her gestures are simple and perfect; she is folded in her skirts, not dressed.

Mlle Bernhardt is a staunch Republican and held receptions when in Paris, at which the Deputies of the Extreme Left were as free as they were welcome. She might have aspired to the position of a French Lady Palmerston but for the circumstance that her drawing-room was frequented by members of the sterner sex alone. Women rule in France, but on certain conditions. In spite of her Liberalism, Mlle Bernhardt thinks the life of an English nobleman the ideal one for a man. 'To be an English *grand seigneur* with lots of money and Paris for one's residence – can the human mind imagine anything more delightful.'

Her great hobby was the building of a lovely home, and as long as that lasted she turned architect, and fascinated her bricklayers with as much ardour as if they were her Tuesday night admirers at the Théâtre Français.

Enter the house and you would say at once it was the home of an artist. It is in the artist's quarter; they dwell in sky-parlours at Batignolles or in the Pays Latin while they learn how to make their fortunes, and in the villas bordering the Parc Monceau when they have learnt that ofttimes arduous lesson. The streets are named after great workers with the brush – living or dead – one of them bears the name of Fortuny; and it is at the corner of this rue Fortuny and the avenue de Villiers that Sarah lives in a house built from her own design. It is half-studio, half-mansion. The drawing room window is large enough to illumine a cathedral, and there is as much skylight as roof. It has the same character within as without. The hall is frescoed in Chinese drawings and the antechamber is as a series of sketches in a public gallery with this difference – that it also contains an immense painting of the hostess. The large painting by Clairin renders the nameless charm of the woman better than any other. She sits on a couch as she sits in the *Étrangère*, an excessively frail but graceful shape, its outline half lost, half revealed beneath masses of drapery trailing far beyond her feet in statuesque folds. Above it, a thinnish face of intense power, with delicately cut features, framed as it were in a wild luxurious growth of hair, falling low on the forehead and forming a depth of shade to enhance the brilliance of the eyes. You praise her because she looks like the picture; you praise the picture because it looks like the life.

Not content with the laurels she has gathered on the stage, Mlle Sarah has pursued other arts with remarkable success. Monsieur Mathieu-Mensuier once induced Sarah to pose for him; she attentively watched the process and criticised the result in the free, easy, and independent way so characteristic of her. Her remarks were so correct that the sculptor said : 'You have an artist's eye, you should study modelling.' Impetuous, Sarah jumped at the idea : 'You mean that ? Very well, some clay, please.' She looked at the clock, time to go, she must give a performance and be applauded. She hurried away clutching her ball of clay. At the fall of the curtain she hurried home, hastily cast aside her diadem and royal cloak, and by 1 a m all was ready.

She was about to make her début as a sculptress when she realised she had no model – she had forgotten that most important item. Tip-toeing up to Aunt Brucke's room, she gently woke her, wrapped her in her blanket and posed her. Sarah had not yet learned the virtue of patience, and Aunt Brucke was helpless. Several short years later she exhibited a bust of Emile Girardin and completed a colossal statue destined for the façade of the theatre at Monaco.

Nor did this female Admirable Crichton stop here; not content with all this, she found time to acquire a very high proficiency in music and when in the humour, she has given delightful musical *soirées* at her villa. With the palette and brush, one of her most striking *chef-d'oeuvres* is of the *Medea* slaying her children.

Her constant companionship with the idea of death casts no shadow over her gaiety, and perhaps familiarity with the inevitable is preferable to a craven fear of it. It is told that she favours playing at croquet with skulls, but this is certain, that the skeleton in Mlle Bernhardt's home holds a post of honour; hers is the skeleton of a disappointed lover who took his life. His bony arms embrace the cheval-glass in her bedroom and when she studies a new part, she makes this gaunt prompter hold the manuscript in his fleshless hands. Two of her paintings in this mode are *Ophelia Morte* and a companion piece, *Les Fiançailles de la Mort*.

She not only indulged her family but could never refuse appeals from the needy. Merchants who knew her weakness brought their most tempting wares to snare her further into their debt, and never mentioned a price : 'Why concern yourself over that, Mademoiselle, you may have years to pay.' During her years at the *Française*, her home thus became a veritable museum and her debts reached staggering figures. She now resolved to rid herself of these vultures.

In the interim she accepted a month's contract to play at the London *Gaiety* from 24th May to 24th June 1880. Eight of the *Française* players formed a company with Sarah, including Jeanne who had begun to test her wings in the theatre.

This time London was a revelation of another sort. Those same axemen who formerly charged her with funereal fantasies, a monotonous voice and caprices, had followed her expressly to see her perform. The leader of the conspiracy, Vitu changed his tune.

The sincerity of my admiration cannot be doubted when I avow that in the fifth act Sarah Bernhardt rose to a height of dramatic power, to a force of expression which could not be surpassed. She played the long and cruel scene in which Adrienne, poisoned by the Duchess de Bouillon, struggles against death in her fearful agony, not only with immense talent, but with a science of art which up to the present she has never revealed. If the Parisian public had heard . . . or even hears, Mlle Sarah Bernhardt cry out with the piercing accent which she put into her words that evening: 'I will not die, I will not die!' it would weep with her.

Meanwhile, Sarcey and Lapommerge followed suit, the latter begging her to come back to the *Comédie*, promising her the fatted calf would be killed for the return of their prodigal child, while the former cried, 'What a pity, what a pity! Yes, I come back to my litany! I cannot help it. We shall lose as much as she will.'

On the 7th of June, he followed this with another review of *Frou Frou*:

I do not think that the emotion at the theatre has ever been so profound. There are, in the dramatic art, exceptional times when the artistes are transported out of themselves, carried above themselves and compelled to obey this inward 'demon,' (I should have said god,) who whispered to Corneille his immortal verses.

'Well,' said I to Mlle Sarah Bernhardt, after the play, 'this is an evening which will open to you, if you wish, the doors of the Comédie Française!' 'Do not speak of it,' she said to me! We will not speak of it. But what a pity! What a pity!

Then, suddenly, the management of the Française, nervously twitching over their mistake in letting their golden gosling escape through their stupidity, sent an emissary, Got, the dean, to persuade her to sign again as an Associate, and come back after her American tour to take up her position again.

But the managers could not have made a worse mistake in their choice of an ambassador. Got made a mess of things :

'You know, my little one, that you will die in that country. And if you come back you will perhaps be only too glad to return to the Comédie Française, for you will be in a bad state of health, and it will take some time before you are right again. Believe me, sign, and it is not we who will benefit by that, but you!'

All she said was :

'Thank you. I'll choose my own hospital when I come back.'

Free of the restraints and shackles of the Comédie Française, combining travel with her art, speaking and mingling with other people in another country, Sarah's health and nervous system recovered in tone. She slept and ate well, and for the first time in her life was told she looked round and rosy.

After London, came Brussels and Copenhagen, where, as the train came into the Danish station, she was gripped with fright on hearing shouts of 'hurrah!' rise from two thousand Danes who cheered her arrival, unaware of the terror their rousing voices caused her.

De Fallesen, manager of the Theatre Royale, and first chamberlain of the king, entered her compartment, bidding her to show herself, and gratify the public's curiosity. She looked out of the window and shrunk with fear again. The Danes, men and women, were so tall and so heroic in stature that she was over-awed; how could she with her slender frame, even rounded somewhat now, step out among these tall, blonde gods and goddesses without destroying whatever impression of her they might have.

The crowd separated itself into two walls, allowing her carriage to pass between the living hedge, while they threw her kisses and flowers, lifted their hats and shouted welcome. The road to Angleterre, her hotel, was lined with Danes, all the way to the entrance.

Happy she had come, Sarah did not disappoint them and

the press were generous in their tributes to her. The Danish king decorated Sarah with a high award.

In August she gave her last reception before her departure to America, to the regret of all her friends who would have to suspend their five-o'clock's in her studio. It was said the three most celebrated hours in Paris were one o'clock, when Gambetta smoked his first cigar; four o'clock when the Bourse dropped; and five o'clock when Sarah received for tea. Of the lot, by far the last was the most popular.

Clairin consoled them: 'We really have no right in our affectionate selfishness to keep Sarah with us. She is made for the world!'

Touched, Sarah looked up: 'But I'm sorry not to play my two favourites Adrienne and Frou Frou, not only here but in all France.'

'Well, why didn't you say so before,' Duq remarked. 'You had your first success with me and with me you'll have your last. Why wait. If you agree I'll book you in every large city and we'll give twenty five performances during September. I'll pay you fifty thousand francs for the twenty five appearances. If you accept, we'll sign the contract tomorrow and I'll give you half in advance so you won't have time to change your mind. As your ship leaves on 15th October, you'll have plenty of time.'

Everyone was delighted to have a 'Month in the Country' with Sarah. One hit on a happy plan: 'We'll draw lots and meet her by turns in the various cities, picnicking in the country, driving from city to city, basking in her triumphs until the tour is finished.'

Sarah signed another contract and under these conditions, the sacrifice of the five-o'clock causeries was accepted.

9

American Tour

On 15th October 1880, Sarah left on her first voyage to the
New World on the *Amérique*. Besides Petite Dame and
Felicie, her maid, Sarah's company included Pierre Berton,
Paul Mounet, a brother of the talented Mounet-Sully;
Angelo, a comedian; and Marie Columbier who went in
place of Jeanne who, taken suddenly ill joined them two
weeks later.

Hardly had Sarah adjusted to the departure when a
whirling snow storm caught the complaining vessel, jolting
it and pitching it sideways. Sarah was thrown to the deck
among a group of shocked passengers. Unhurt, she quickly
picked herself up and ran to a woman dressed in mourning
who lay unconscious near a gang-way. She raised the frail
woman slowly and helped her down to her cabin.

When the woman could speak, Sarah introduced herself
and asked: 'May I help you? I know something about
nursing.'

The sad-faced woman smiled gently: 'Thank you. I'm
Mrs Abe Lincoln, the widow of the late President. I'll be
all right. You're very kind and charming.'

Sarah, with characteristic curiosity, inspected the entire
ship, argued with the captain over the squalid, filthy
quarters for steerage passengers; the miserable food served
them, and especially the hopelessly inadequate lifeboats and
rescue equipment.

She made many trips down to the hold to bring food and
small comforts to the melancholy ones who so hopefully lived
on so little, only for the dream of setting foot in the New
World. To offset the monotony of the long voyage, she even
assisted at the birth of a new baby, and was touched when
she was given the honour of being its godmother.

But with all her activities, she was lonely and homesick, missing family and friends, and she cried for three days after the ship left Havre.

Jarrett helped her everywhere. It took all his diplomatic skill to free her hundred pieces of luggage immediately, because it nearly drove her mad to see her exquisite gowns handled by the dirty hands of the customs inspectors as though they were dish rags; and he paid half the customs bill.

As soon as she entered her hotel, more reporters swooped down upon her, and an ovation which continued into the night under her window, a serenade with the refrain 'Good Night Sarah, Good Night!' nearly drove her straight into hysterics. She didn't know which was worse: the reporters inside, or the jangling voices outside.

One thing saved the day! When Sarah set foot on the New Land the day was sunny: a good omen! No matter what happened, all would be well.

Next day at the official reporters' conference, Mercier, a French newspaper editor gave the cementing address in French. Sarah felt easier and relaxed. But it didn't last long. The awful moment of introductions arrived. She must catch the names 'Mr Pemb . . ., Mrs Herth . . .' half of one overlapped the next. Tired and tense after the tenth, she gave up; nodded her head, smiled and held out her hand which was thoroughly shaken. The air was soon dense with smoke and she began to feel her throat tighten, and without any warning she dropped – right into the arms of Jarrett!

'Quick! Air! . . . get a doctor . . . poor thing! So pale . . . loosen her corset! . . . she doesn't wear one! Unfasten her dress. . . .' Mme Guerard and Felicie surrounded her. Terrified, they would let no one touch her.

While Sarah recovered, Jarrett ushered the crowd out but she saw him in whispered asides with the reporters. Soon he came back to her and seeing a question in her eyes, he said: 'There will be a fresh one every ten minutes, from one o'clock on.' A petrified stare greeted him: '*Oui, oui, il est nécessaire!*'

Sarah knew when Jarrett had had enough so, with her two friends she went to her bedroom and slammed the door. She must have some sleep until the time for the interviews should arrive. On the other side of the door, she heard Jarrett's polished diplomacy persuading the visitors to wait, inviting them to have a drink at the Albemarle Bar below.

Not finding a lock or bolt on the door, the women pushed a bulky piece of furniture against it to ensure privacy. Then, a rustle of paper being pushed under the door was heard. Angrily, Guerard whispered to Jarrett: 'You don't know her! If she thought you were forcing the door open, against which she has pushed the furniture, she would jump from the windows!'

Sarah awoke refreshed in exactly one hour. She had the gift of being able to will herself to sleep, then to awaken at exactly the moment she wished. Quiet as mice, seated on a trunk, Guerard and Felicie watched for her to open her eyes.

'Are any people waiting?' she asked.

'Oh, Madame, there are at least a hundred!'

'Quickly. Help me take this off and find me a white dress please. Mr Jarrett will not wait much longer.'

Delicately perfumed and poised, Sarah swept into the drawing room. She smiled a little to see a wave of relief cross Jarrett's stern face. Then she looked round the room. Her first impression was pleasing. Busts of Molière, Racine and Victor Hugo were placed round the large room, among which were many vases and baskets full of fresh flowers. But her impression of the reporters was still wary. When she had entered, they continued to sit on sofas, chairs or on floor cushions and, in nasal bass voices, they still asked endless stupid questions: 'Whaddaya eat for breakfast?'

About to lose her poise, Jarrett quickly broke in: 'Oatmeal.'

'Whaddaya eat durin' the day?'

'Mussels.' Jarrett flung out again.

The reporter noted: 'Eats mussels all day.'

Sarah moved toward a woman reporter, thinking she

might rescue her. The reporter asked: Are you a Jew-CatholicProtestantMohammedanBuddhistAtheistZoroaster-TheistorDeist?'

Another woman stepped in to explain: 'This young lady is asking whether you are Jewish, Catholic, Protestant, Mohammedan, Buddhist, etc.'

Sarah quickly rushed to Jarrett: 'Heavens! must I go through this in every city?'

'Oh no! *Soyez tranquille.* Your interviews will be wired throughout the country. Now be patient and let the artists finish sketching you. They'll be printed in the papers too. Very important!'

'But . . . they're making me look like ugly caricatures!'

'Pay no attention. It's all free advertising.'

Sarah found a pioneer civilisation, its uneven development showing awkwardly through every seam. The two managers, Jarrett, and Abbey, his partner, had booked the artists to open at the *Booth* theatre, and had sold tickets at auction, most of them going for up to ten dollars a piece. Buyers fought for the tickets as they fought for land, gold, oil.

The successful bidders knew they would see a French actress; a new thrill! 'If the seats cost ten dollars, it must be terrific! Let's go boys! Take your girl to a real show and let her see a Frenchy kick her heels up!' Some knew almost nothing of comedy or theatre – they only expected to see an exhibition of vaudeville or dancing girls.

When the curtain went up on the first performance and Sarah did not appear in the first act of *Adrienne Lecouvreur*, they nearly created a stampede. As the act finished, a surly patron grumbled to his countrymen: 'Let's show these smart-aleck foreigners they can't do us! I'm gonna get my money back!'

In a body they approached Jarrett. But he was ready. He made them listen while he explained, then he gave his word to refund their money if after the next act they were not satisfied. They returned to their seats, their minds full of suspicion; the hackles standing up on their necks.

Hardly had Sarah stepped on stage when all was forgotten. Her voice, sweetly enchanting; her plastic movements, frail and insinuating, won them instantly. She was a faint breath of strange perfume: something they had never even dreamed existed; a subtle whisper that reached through their ignorance; a civilising embrace which for that moment met each one intimately in his own secret world. Each one was left with a promise that he too, whenever he wished, could enter this new world simply by remembering this moment.

The applause broke records. Sarah could barely extricate herself from the over-enthusiastic audience which now crowded towards her, shaking her hand as if it were an iron pump-handle.

Sarah's triumphs continued; ever-growing eager audiences waited impatiently wherever she toured. Receipts were enormous in spite of the language barrier, the plays being given in French, not a word of which was understood by the public. Not until she reached the French-speaking provinces in Canada did anyone know what was being said on stage.

Among the crude but *nécessaire* events which plagued Sarah was the style of advertising. She got her first shock-reaction when she saw her likeness painted on a float in ugly colours, advertising Madame Lilly Noe's Corsets. Its owner, a Henry Smith, paid a handsome fee to Jarrett for the 'exclusive'. Jarrett in turn, reaped a double harvest: 'It's advertising, not everyone reads the papers.' Sarah had a contract to fulfill; she was young and easily distracted and resigned herself to it.

She was intrigued by the differences in people from east, west and the middle states; the French Canadians; the mixtures in Louisiana, Georgia and Alabama, and above all, the Indians who were so different. But her sensibilities recoiled at the sight of the squalid and diseased conditions of the Red tribes, so recently a people of magnificent stature and independence, now reduced to begging, the last refuge of helplessness.

Sarah's native generosity would have got her into trouble if Jarrett had not kept a strict rein on her. She was interested in everyone and everything, and her French breeding charmed young and old alike. Her affect on the astute Spurgeon, the popular preacher then at the apex of his evangelical mission, was remarkable. When he was asked what he thought of her, he raised his arms in prophetic doom : 'She is the devil's greatest triumph!' As he turned from side to side enveloping his congregation with his hypnotic eyes, the rafters echoed his majestic thunder : 'This woman, a mere shadow, a bundle of bones! she can charm the mountains to waltz by the slightest gesture or whim, no matter how grotesque or ridiculous her acrobatics! She can provoke the heavens to thunder and storm! then laugh and walk away as if it never happened!'

'How colourful!' Sarah laughed when Jarrett translated for her : 'Maybe I am a sinful creature full of vice.' Chagrined at first to find the pastors up in arms, she learned to laugh it off. These all-powerful men of the cloth had girded themselves for battle by reading of the eccentricities of the 'foreign actress' in pamphlets and magazines. Their sermons always included diatribes against 'that monster' who had seduced every crowned head in Europe, and who had begotten four sons, each one fathered in turn by the Pope, Napoleon III, the German Kaiser and a condemned criminal accused of patricide. When they ran out of material culled from the pages of scandal sheets, the saintly men exhorted their flocks with their native eloquence, against this wicked woman.

To the immense delight of Jarrett, these sermons proved to be the best publicity he ever could have hoped for. Extra performances had to be added, with standing room booked solid at each one.

In New England, Puritan fury raised a hue and cry over 'The Bernhardt Question' and 'How to Save Our Husbands and Sons From the Damnation of this Enigmatic Woman!'

His most distinguished Reverence, the Bishop of Chicago, led all the rest by the virulence of his sermons. So potent was the result that Jarrett sent him a cheque :

'Sir, I am accustomed, when I come to your town to

spend four hundred dollars on advertising. As however, you have done the advertising for me, I am sending you two hundred dollars for your poor.'

It was not always easy for Sarah to ignore the scandals circulated about her. In answer to a reporter's blunt query: 'Madame, do you really have four sons?' she threw back:

'Four children and no husband? Indeed! Anyway, that's better than four husbands and no children, which happens here quite often in your country!'

Jarrett heard the *faux pas*: 'Permit me, mademoiselle. Next time you are in a delicate position, the diplomatic response is to turn the conversation elsewhere. Mention the ceremony in London at which you and Henry Irving had the honour to lay the cornerstone for a building on Wardour Street, and that they can see the brass plaques there which commemorate the occasion. It will not only impress your audience but they will repeat it later.'

Jeanne fell in love with Pierre Berton, the handsome leading man of the company, Sarah's former lover and now her loyal friend. She had been indulged, not only by Sarah with whom she had lived for most of her life, but also by all of Sarah's friends, and had grown up play-acting, believing she too would become a great actress. But Jeanne was destined for disappointment. No matter how much Sarah loved Jeanne, she could not give her talent.

Jeanne told herself she would shine more brightly in America where the public was less critical than in Europe, and where Sarah was only a name, no better known personally than Jeanne. She also hoped she would feel less inhibited. But Jeanne soon discovered that her contempt for the Americans back-fired.

She tried to hide her chagrin at this failure, which only intensified the other – the one caused by her frustrated passion for Berton. He, gallant as always, was kind and understanding, but made it clear that that was all he could do.

Jeanne hated Sarah for Berton's loyalty. She recalled a casual comment of Berton's that she overheard in the wings while talking to Hugo, and it now echoed loudly within her: 'The days that Sarah Bernhardt devoted to me were like pages from immortality. One felt that one could never die.'

One stormy grey day Sarah, describing the success in Cincinnati, was writing home, in her private drawing room *en route* to New Orleans. Pierre Berton was working on a play. Not knowing what to do with herself, Jeanne sulked in a corner. Almost at the end of her long letter, Sarah was just finishing with 'their bodies, so stiffened and numbed from the cold outside, and dried up by the suffocating heat inside, would at last be able to stretch and relax in a natural climate.' ... the words Jarrett had used, and now she almost fell asleep as she pictured the blossom-laden trees soon to be seen by the thousands, and thought of the smell of wild flowers growing in the green earth under the blue skies and sunshine, when a screeching halt of the train roused her. Ears erect, her dog came to attention. Knuckles quickly rapped on the door. In a moment, Sarah opened it and Jarrett silently entered: 'Please, what's happened! Something's wrong!'

'Well, it's this way,' he began. 'The river has swollen to such a height from the rains of the past twelve days that the bridge across the Bay of St Louis is unsafe. If we don't cross it now, we'll lose three or four days.'

No longer bored, Jeanne eyed the ceiling wanly: 'I'm starving for sunshine. We must go on!' Jeanne had really suffered through the long cold months. Sarah was touched. She would do anything to keep going. Three or four days more! It did seem a lifetime!

'There might be a chance to go on, but it's a risk you'll have to decide.' Jarrett continued. 'The engineer would take the risk of crossing, but he's just married and will go on condition that you give him two thousand five hundred dollars to send his wife and father in Mobile. If we all arrive on the other side, he'll return your money. If not, it will go to his family.'

Berton, furious with Jarrett for such a suggestion, inter-posed : '*Mon Dieu*, what are three or four days by comparison to the risk? Is money really everything in this country?' He turned to Sarah : 'My dear, you mustn't do this. Think of how many other lives you risk besides your own! It's insane!'

Jeanne saw a chance to end her frustrations, and take Berton and Sarah along with her : 'But it can't be that risky if the engineer is willing to take this train over the bridge. Here, they always exaggerate everything to make it more exciting. I'll die if I don't have sunshine right away. Do it for my sake, Sarah, please! You'll see, we'll cross safely and you'll get your money back. They'll say you're a bad sport if you don't!'

Berton again, tried to turn Sarah away from this mad-ness, in vain. Sarah had no defences against her family.

'Here's the money,' she said to Jarrett. She turned to Berton coldly : 'If you're afraid, you may leave the train.'

Impatiently, Berton went back to his writing, muttering : 'Women are mad creatures!'

While the train slowly backed down the track for two miles, and waited for Sarah's pullman and two coaches to be unhitched from the rest, she confided the situation to Guerard, Felicie and Felicie's husband Claude, and the comedian Angelo. The others knew nothing of it. Then Sarah saw Jarrett hand the money to the engineer, who mailed it to Mobile. The engine picked up momentum, every turn of its wheels raising suspense and fear in its passengers. Together they dared the fury of nature, now gone mad!

Only now as they approached the loosely shaking bridge, and saw the raging river tear under it, having already swept away homes by the hundreds with many of their occupants, only now, at this terrible moment did Sarah come face to face with her conscience! What had she done! Why should the river be more benevolent to her than to those others? Dear loyal Berton and Guerard! Felicie and her husband! All the rest of the staff, and even Jarrett! All for one selfish little girl! Suddenly, she felt suffocated. She ran to the open platform, and with mixed feelings, Jeanne quickly clutched her warmest coat and followed Sarah. Inside, Berton dropped his head heavily into his hands. Guerard looked on with compassion, praying silently.

With a full head of steam, the engine sped on and was now part way over the bridge: together, as if one unit, they swayed and slapped about in the whistling wind like an empty hammock. The train shook and heaved, tossed and groaned aloud; half way across, the bridge dipped so low that Jeanne grasped Sarah, shrieking hysterically: 'We're drowning!'

Burdened with guilt, Sarah began to pray, certain that the supreme moment, which seemed an eternity, was at hand.

By a miracle, the train just reached the opposite shore when a deafening crash was heard. The river had pulled away the bridge – girders, supports, tracks and elevations – as easily as if it were a few twigs of straw.

Everyone felt in a state of collapse. Those who were still able prayed their thanks for delivery.

At the station, Sarah, more dead than alive, had to accept the flowers and deputations from the crowds who waited in the dismal weather, to reward them with smiles for their patience. For once, it was almost next to impossible, but, reared upon crises, she rose to the test. When at last she found herself safely inside her hotel, she went into a dead faint. Guerard slept at the foot of her bed, protectively.

Next morning, the engineer who risked his life to bring Jeanne to the sunny south, came to return Sarah's money. She refused to touch it: 'Please don't remind me! Keep it! You earned it!'

If danger was over, inconveniences were not: the squalid dirtiness of the hotels; even the best of them harboured cockroaches, and when the candles were lit the rooms swarmed with huge mosquitoes, bugs and beetles that buzzed, hummed and pounced on her shoulders and stuck in Sarah's crinkly hair. Jeanne too, was frenzied with the horrors of everyday life in the 'sunny south' and refused to eat or sleep, afraid the bugs and mosquitoes would kill her while she was unconscious.

In spite of all the tragedy and dislocation of human life caused by the flood, Sarah found New Orleans the most interesting city of all those touched on her tour. The mixtures of people, so varied and so charming, all with smiles on their faces, all the women graceful, the shops attractive with cheerful window displays; hearing the *patois*-French wit of the open-air shopkeepers in the arcades challenging each other happily like boys. All this had an infinite charm although the sun *never* penetrated once throughout their stay.

Eight performances were given here where six only were intended.

One of her party, Ibe, the hairdresser, was almost out of his mind with fear after the second day of their arrival. This timid soul had the habit of sleeping in the large oversize trunk which served as his storage and workroom for the wigs used in the plays. Thus he never had to worry about a place to sleep or where his responsibilities were. Even at the theatre, he never left the trunk. In this, he was a kindred soul to Sarah. After an Italian tour, when she got back to the Continent, her coffin travelled with her and she never left without it wherever she went.

The second night in New Orleans, Ibe had gone to sleep as usual in his trunk when suddenly his shrieks woke the whole neighbourhood. Out of a sound sleep he was aroused by a heaving up of his mattress, and in his half-conscious state thought some disembodied ghosts were tricking him, hiding among the wigs under his mattress. When he was on his feet and fully aroused, he still saw the mattress moving up and down. Choking back his fears, he rationalised that it must be some cats or dogs that had got nto it. Timidly he raised the trunk-tray which held the mattress and shrieked with fear again. Inside he beheld two large snakes, fortunately they were non-poisonous.

Sarah's abnormal attachment to her 'own' was the cause of a conspiracy under her mobile roof during her tour. She had favoured Jeanne over Columbier in distributing parts

215

and often merely gave the latter understudies. The actress who had been her comrade since they were students in art school and the Conservatoire, felt slighted. By a secret contract with *L'Evenment*, she sent news dispatches to Paris of the tour, especially highlighting 'Sarah's eccentricities.' Columbier had a second secret besides the *Lettres d'Amérique*, she wrote a book entitled *Memoires de Sarah Barnum*, which was published after her return to Paris.

Sarah's intoxication with the New World, its vastness, the quickly changing panoramic scenes, soon dissolved every memory of discomfort, and busy with her personal success, she noticed nothing. Yet Jeanne was thoroughly unhappy. For seven months she had been touring and departure was not far off. She felt she had accomplished nothing here nor at home. Sarah still had everything. She had loyal Guerard, young Maurice, the most precious gift a woman could wish for was waiting in Paris. He had been sent home because Sarah feared his health would be undermined by the extremes of weather and the other hardships. She rankled over Guerard's and Berton's attempts to prevent Sarah from risking her life over the bridge. No one had even looked in her direction. She watched quietly brooding, enviously hoping something would happen to turn the tide.

In 1881, St Louis was repulsively dirty, poor and behind the times. For the first time Sarah was so bored that she pleaded with Jarrett to pay the indemnity to the theatre manager so they could leave immediately, but the ferocious upright man of sound principles held her contract up before her eyes in his powerful hand and said sternly, his steely gaze cutting through her :

'No madame, you must stay! You can die of ennui here if you like, but stay you must!'

Hoping to dispel some of the boredom Jarrett arranged a trip to an underground grotto where the guide had promised they would see millions of fish without any eyes. Sarah, Jeanne and Jarrett went, having to crawl through a low tunnel on all fours for what seemed an eternity through the cavernous dark, dimly-lit by a hand-lantern. At last the guide told them they had arrived and could now stand up. He struck a match and lit another lantern pointing its light to a deep natural basin at Sarah's feet. With relief they all stood up to look.

'You see,' the guide said lazily, 'that's the pond but right at the moment there's no water in it, neither are there any fish. You must come again in three months.'

Sarah's short temper changed only when she looked at Jarrett whose anger was stifling him so that his upper lip curled in a terrible grimace over his large front teeth, his eyes blazing their fury as though on the verge of madness. To think *he* had been taken in by this fraud! And subjected Sarah to it as well! To break the tension Sarah began to laugh only to succeed in developing hiccoughs, laughing and hiccoughing until the tears ran. They went back as they had come.

Relieved at the departure from St Louis, Sarah luxuriated in her magnificently appointed Pullman and was sitting on the outside platform watching from her rear view seat the constantly changing landscape as it ran past her on both sides like two rivers.

Hardly half-an-hour had passed when the conductor came out, stooped down quickly and turned pale. He took Sarah's hand, pulled her inside and said anxiously: 'Please go inside, madame!'

Rising quickly, she followed him expecting an explanation. He pulled the alarm signal, made a sign to another guard and without waiting for the train to stop, the two men jumped off. The conductor disappeared under the train firing a revolver to alert everyone on the train.

As Jarrett, Abbey and the others hurried out into the narrow corridor they saw with stupefaction an outlaw armed to the teeth being dragged from under Sarah's pullman, the guards pointing a gun to his temples, one on each side.

He confessed to being the accomplice of a gang of train robbers; seven men who were waiting at the 'Little Incline' to rob Sarah of her jewellery and money.

Jarrett then called the police who ordered a freight train to proceed, armed with eight state troopers, to the 'Little Incline' to catch the bandits. Her train then continued on, Sarah's pullman sandwiched in between the other two cars, and she was never allowed to be alone anywhere without an armed guard watching her. Jarrett rewarded the guard who caught the robber.

Hearing later that the gang of robbers had fought desperately for their lives, one of them being killed, the others imprisoned, Sarah was remorseful: she blamed herself. Jarrett had persuaded her to allow a jeweller in St Louis to display her jewels in his window as an advertising scheme. To the display, the jeweller added many of his own items, 600,000 francs worth including diamond-studded pipes and spectacles. She felt this display gave rise in the poverty-ridden city to the desperate robbery plan. Jeanne lost no sleep over Sarah's remorse. Jeanne suffered too, because Sarah was too innocent to see her sister's envy.

If Sarah's tour of the States had been a planned toboggan ride it could not have had more ups and downs, thrills, spills and chills; exasperation, consternation and incomprehension; exhilaration and exhaustion, torrid heat and freezing cold; pitiful poverty, formless opulence and ostentation. Oh, Jarrett left nothing out! He gave Sarah a ride for her money and America too was not disappointed in the advance billing and eventual presentations and showmanship, in and outside of the theatres.

During the first matinée of *La Dame aux Camélias*, she counted seventeen curtain calls after the third act, and twenty-nine after the fifth.

Thomas Edison staged a fairy-land reception which surprised even Jarrett. Sarah and Jeanne rode with Jarrett and Abbey in the first carriage. The others followed behind like conspirators, in the inky-blackness on an icy road that seemed endless.

Suddenly a shout of 'Hip-hip-hoorah!' went up at the same time as thousands of lights were lit, illuminating every tree, leaf, bush, roads, and paths along the garden walks, and the large mansion of the magician sprang into blazing light out of the darkness and stood as a background for Thomas Edison and his family, welcoming Sarah. Without a moment's hesitation, Sarah went up to Edison whom she had never before seen, as if drawn by a magnet, and offered her hand. 'Monsieur Edison, you are exactly as I pictured you.'

Momentarily awed by this striking woman, he held her hand much too long.

'How did you know it was I?' The genius almost blushed with boyish pride.

'There was no question. You resemble our Great Napoleon.'

He took her proudly by the arm and led her into the splendid dining-room. This two-day visit she would recall over and over, many times in the years that followed. There was something great about this simple, unassuming man that endeared him to Sarah forever. Thomas Edison too never tired of recounting this visit with all its tender moments.

A day before departure Sarah received a large bundle of letters from France. With them came some new photographs of Maurice, with all the news that could possibly be crammed into letters. One note of sadness wrung her heart, the news of the death of Gustave Flaubert.

Many gifts of jewellery accompanied Sarah back to France. A gold hair comb engraved with the names of the persons who presented it. From Salvini, the artist, a box set with lapis lazuli, and a forget-me-not in turquoise from Mary Anderson, the actress. One hundred and thirty bouquets were counted in her stateroom. On the last day, outside her cabin, dressed in an elegant iron-grey tailored suit, pointed highly-polished shoes, new hat and doe-skin gloves, stood Henry Smith, the corset advertiser, holding out a jewel box, grinning his grateful smile at Sarah. He brought back all the hateful nightmarish memories of every city which haunted her with crude publicity. It was too much to ask Sarah to control herself at this smugness.

Screeching like her cheetah, she had grabbed the box and was just raising it to throw it overboard when Jarrett caught it : 'My! it's magnificent!' he cried. But Sarah cried out to Smith : 'Go away, you knave! you brute! I hope you die under atrocious suffering!'

Smith disappeared rapidly and Jarrett stood admiring the extravagant piece of jewellery.

Among the letters received before departure was a long cablegram, asking her to give on her arrival at Havre a benefit performance for the families of the Life Saving Society; it was signed by the Society's president.

Anticipation of this performance lightened her voyage. Sarah's tour had lasted a little over seven months during which she stopped at fifty cities and played 156 performances for a total receipt of 2,667,600 francs.

Santelli, the captain, had promised Sarah she would surely arrive on the evening of the 14th of May. Sleeping by day and gazing into the black horizon at night she counted the hours and minutes. The voyage seemed endless. She became so impatient to see and hold Maurice in her arms again, that she thought she would go mad. At last she called the ship's doctor to give her a sedative and slept for twelve hours, shortening the voyage by this much.

Next morning, when she arose, she heard they were still twenty miles from shore, but the sun shone brightly. She quickly ran to her cabin to freshen her make-up and gather her things, hoping to kill more time. It was useless. She ran up again :

'How far now?' she asked Santelli.

'Twelve miles. In two hours we shall land.'

'You swear it?'

'Yes. I swear,' he smiled warmly.

Everyone now caught the nerves of arrival, each one urging the other to sit down, no one wanting to do anything but run back and forth, look to the shore and search the harbour which was now full of small boats draped with brilliant flags in all colours, and especially white ones. But finally, they touched close enough for the mail boat, the

Diamond, to receive its payload and return to shore. Soon, more than a hundred small boats surrounded the steamer and reporters came aboard.

But Sarah had one thought – Maurice! and there he was, waving excitedly from the quayside.

10

Paris Again :
Wealth, Marriage and Despair

Sarah had had no expenses on the tour, and came back with a million francs. She paid all her debts and breathed freely again. Jarrett's promises were kept to the letter and Sarah was now a master of publicity in her own right. She, knowing what the press wanted, gave interviews freely :

'Americans are warm and friendly, but the voices of their women . . . ugh.'

But not all her countrymen were happy with Sarah's success. Even before she had set foot in America, the jealous ones of the *Française* circulated vicious rumours about her, hoping she would be a failure there, to come back humiliated, and subdued, all the more swiftly.

Sarah tried to overlook the barbarous vulgarity in the yellow press, in its zeal to exploit her publicity value. Most of the time she was too busy, or too tired. She had long ago stopped reading the newspapers, but Marie Colombier's lies and exaggerated misrepresentations caused consternation to Sarah's friends. They aroused a wide-scale protest :

'This is scandalous! Sarah is a great international artiste! With all her alleged eccentricities, she could never bring herself to do anything vulgar! Her tastes are too aesthetic, she doesn't drink or smoke, and she may be extreme in her inclinations but that is because of her genius. Her sensitivity is well known. To throw mud at her now would be like insulting the "Tomb of Napoleon".'

Sarah's association with Jarrett and his partner, Abbey, was the key to the fortune she had dreamed of and had worked toward until she met the two astute impresarios. The mutually successful partnership prospered beyond their fondest expectations. As Berton and Sand had predicted her artistic genius, so Jarrett had fulfilled his predictions that she would not only be finished with manual drudgery, pinching pennies and selling autographs, but would be the undisputed queen of the world.

She endowed a fund for Maurice which paid him sixty thousand francs a year when he was fifteen; she had redeemed her pledge and dropped the shackles from her conscience. There was a noticeable lightness and sparkle in, her and little incandescent explosions seemed to play round her eyes. Critics searched for new dictionaries, having worn out the resources of their usual ones. How to describe the indescribable? She knew the wonderful feeling of having so much money that she need not have one home, one theatre, but two of everything. She filled her home in Paris with new furnishings, curtains, draperies of finest brocades, tapestries, and bric-a-brac collected from every corner of the world. She entertained like a rajah, and even had guests who stayed for months. Servants were nearly as plentiful as pets, and . . . her future was assured. In short, she ranked with statesmen.

The wild oats of genius had been sown . . . yet she fell into the simplest trap : such as only genius is blind to. A lesser woman would readily have seen through a jealous sister. But in Sarah's family, she herself had been the despised one, while Jeanne was favoured by all. It never occurred to her that Jeanne would be jealous of Sarah, let alone try to kill her. But genius must ever pay for walking on Olympus with the gods.

Jeanne's despondency led her to seek amusement in the life of the Paris Montmartre, and before long she discovered the pleasure of oblivion by drug-taking. Sarah tried in vain to check her downfall, but Jeanne wanted to die. She took Jeanne to health spas, for rest-cures, sat up with her night after night, tempted her with delicacies, but Jeanne turned away from everything – if she could not have Sarah's glory or her success, she only wanted death, she hated Sarah, and if this way happened to hurt her, if Sarah lost sleep and worried over her, so much the better.

Jeanne, who had become the centre of Julie's fond hopes after the death of Regina, had neither the strength nor the will of Sarah, she only had a talent for mimicry, and the life which nourished Sarah, and upon which she thrived, ruined Jeanne.

Having tried desperately to cure Jeanne; having had her promise to cooperate, Sarah discovered Jeanne wilfully hid the drug, only to take it again as soon as she was on the edge of recovery. In a fit of fury, Sarah horse-whipped Jeanne, and kept her locked in her bedroom, a prisoner for four days, without food or drugs in a heroic attempt to force a cure on her.

Sarah's contempt for any weak-willed individual rode rough-shod over Jeanne, but neither force nor kindness averted Jeanne's inevitable fate. Julie blamed Sarah for Jeanne's death, believing that the bad elements which influenced Jeanne had come from Sarah's circle.

The prodigious Sarah who had come home with a light heart on which rested the world's rarest honours, now felt all of these victories a heavy burden. Death was present as usual.

Sarah had only her son left. Maurice was developing into an admirable and distinguished youth who adored his mother: the most exciting, attractive woman in the world. He consoled his mother as her dearest ones swiftly departed, Flaubert followed by her dear Sand whose wisdom and wit had stood by her in her turbulent youth and now Jeanne! Rosine had gone travelling with a new gentleman and was never heard from again.

Sarah turned that side of herself that belonged to the outer world toward a new future. Ahead lay the path she must walk. She dared not look back for the pain it brought, but although she faced foreward, the past still held her fast. She swung back to a device that had saved her before: forging new chains.

Of the countless ones tendered her, gowned more extravagantly than ever, she rarely missed a dinner or soirée.

Jules Paul Damala, a Greek of a good family, had come to Paris to educate himself for the post of a diplomat, and had swiftly earned the title of 'the handsomest man in Europe.' The 'Diplomat Apollo,' earned this second title because of his easy triumphs among the beauties of Paris, and jealous husbands and lovers called him the most dangerous man in Paris.

He was a mixture of oriental and classic beauty, his passionate face dominated by deep, dark brown eyes and thick, softly curling lashes, and a silky-fine brown beard fashionably cut as prescribed in the early eighties for young men, outlined the delicate modelling of his cheeks, temples and chin.

Having conquered society, disported himself to his heart's content, laughed scornfully at all that was both holy and unholy, Damala was attracted to the stage, where, while he enjoyed acting, his physical attributes more than compensated for his lack of talent. Damala had little more to do than to present himself and exert a gentle charm to win his audiences.

Damala's greatest boast was that he had only to meet Sarah to add her to his lengthening list of victims. Yes, Sarah the Incomparable whose victims to her charms also counted by the hundreds : kings, playwrights, artists, and musicians. It was manifestly inevitable that Sarah and Damala should meet. The moment that they each dreaded did arrive. It was a dinner given in Sarah's honour, and she was more ravishing than ever.

At the introduction, Sarah in her most autocratic tone pretended ignorance of who he was : 'Damala?' to which he responded in kind, raising one eyebrow : 'Bernhardt?' His icy detachment, the equal of which she had met only once before in the hard-driving Jarrett, stunned her. He stoically received the fury shot from her eyes. Terrified, the hostess recovered enough to remind him; 'Sir, you are addressing the greatest actress in France!'

'Well! That makes me the greatest man in France!'

Damala had dared to mock the irate woman. All eyes were upon them. Sarah knew her reputation was at stake. To parry his insolence would only have played to his vanity. She turned away coldly: 'I've seen crowing cocks strut before.'

'But wait, madame. I'm also the wickedest man in all Paris.' Suddenly, as if by design he smiled. Sarah was dazzled. His oriental face lit up deepening the dark, mysterious eyes.

'That may or may not be.' She struggled to regain her composure: 'To me, you sound like a fool.'

She turned away. Behind her she heard a laugh. It struck deep into her – too deep – it struck her vanity. A man had dared to laugh at Sarah Bernhardt! She would never forget that!

Though Sardou's stature as a playwright had not reached the dimensions of Dumas or Hugo, as the author of *Madame Sans-Gêne* he was among the most celebrated of the modern school. An astute appraisal of Sarah's effect on his work was bluntness itself:

If we pronounced *Fédora* a masterpiece, we should risk being contradicted not only by our readers, but by the author himself. However thanks to the artist, Victorien Sardou has pocketed for this vulgar melodrama, a royalty exceeding a hundred thousand dollars, nor is its earning power yet exhausted. If Sardou ever repays his obligation to her, a fortune will change hands. . . .

But while Sardou stands in the front rank of dramatic authors, we shall be kept far from the highest ideals in plays. Yet, what talent this clever constructor shows! The principal actors of renown die away, but the plays of dramatic authors, if of value, are handed down to posterity. With Sardou's dramas precisely the reverse happens. The value of the work has quite disappeared, although the work is kept afloat by the artist, if in the fullest possession of her powers.

Shades of George Sand! Sardou resembled Sarah's great late friend so closely, not only in his ability to build plays which tapped her resources but he was deeply intuitive and highly interested in psychic matters. Sarah found immediate rapport with Sardou who, alongside Jarrett, kept Sarah from utter financial oblivion with his lengthening list of triumphs. But, her unmitigated grief and hunger for those she lost drove her into a parallel to match that of the days before she resigned from the *Comédie*. Sardou had traced the same steps as Sarah during the siege of Paris and had acquitted himself a hero.

Sardou was an eye witness to one of the most dramatic episodes in the history of France. On receipt of the news of the disasters of Worth and Forback on 7th August 1870, the Empress Eugénie moved from St Cloud to the Tuileries, where she lived in increasing terror of the mob, and held her last reception on 14th August. On the afternoon of 3rd September came the fatal telegram from Napoleon III 'The army is defeated and captured. I myself am a prisoner.' The next day saw that bloodless revolution by which the second empire fell and the third republic was established. As the clock of the Tuileries rang out half-past-three, the imperial flag was lowered. This was a signal for the Tuileries to be stormed. The soldiers on guard interposed little resistance. Before the mob broke in, Signor Nigra, the Italian ambassador, warned the Empress that she must flee. Escorted by Prince Metternich and Dr Evans, the American dentist, she left Paris in disguise that same night for Belgium, and later sailed from Deauville for England on Sir John Burgoyne's yacht.

Among the crowd assembled outside the gates that fateful day, were Sardou and a friend of his, a certain Armand Gouzien. The Empress was still in the Palace and the Imperial flag was still flying. The building was protected by a detachment of the Imperial guard. Sardou and his friend stood watching a man engaged in knocking the golden eagles off the gates. The crowd became dangerously excited, the gates were stormed, and several hundred persons, including Sardou and his friend, were swept into the gardens.

Foreseeing a collision with the troops, the two friends came to the front. Gouzien harangued the mob, saying that the Tuileries belonged to the people, and that the empire no longer existed. The Imperial Guard must not remain and he proposed that Sardou and he go and demand the withdrawal of these troops. But he urged them to keep in quiet order to avoid a bloody conflict. The crowd broke out into applause and waited patiently while Sardou tied a handkerchief to the end of his walking-stick, hurried with his companion to the soldiers and asked for the commander. Two men stepped forward : General Mellinst and M de Lesseps. Meantime, Eugénie had left the palace and the two ambassadors persuaded the General to lower the flag and replace the Imperial Guard with the National Guard and the Guards Mobiles. Thus, by intelligent and tactful handling, Sardou averted a debacle, and when the Mobiles arrived through the archway, it found all safely guarded and surged through the palace into the Place du Carrousel harmlessly.

A gala dinner was given in Sarah's honour on her return to celebrate her success in the States and to inaugurate her coming season in collaboration with Sardou and Deslandes. Among the actors who were to be in the new company were Philippe Garnier Dameny, and Decori, who were also attending the banquet. Everyone was eager to have Sarah's impressions of her American tour, and though she never allowed anyone else to make fun of Americans, she herself liked to tell an anecdote or two, imitating with her fingers how the Americans ate, and laughingly convulsed her listeners with her descriptions of American food.

'*Mon ami,*' she addressed Decori, 'you'd never believe it – Americans never take more than fifteen minutes to dine, and they eat in whatever order the food arrives. If the fruit is served first, that's where they begin the meal! Imagine!'

Sarah's *Fédora* was a new creation, a subtlety addressed in the manner of the great modern playwright Sardou, he who wrote for her as Mozart wrote for the piano.

After her success in *Fédora*, Sarah presented a new play by another young playwright, Richepin. The play was *Nana Sahib*. Still a little depressed over the loss of her family and many of her most illustrious friends, she was delighted when Richepin offered to play the male lead in his own play. Sarah's magnetism never failed :

'You mean you want to walk the planks with me?' she asked, a little astonished.

'I would do anything for you,' he answered. It was a prophetic remark.

Since her return from America, Colombier's book caricaturing Sarah had been completely ignored by the press and most of the public. Paul Bonnetain, the author of *Charlot* amused himself by writing the preface for it. Octave Mirbeau, Sarah's friend, whose pride and audacity matched hers, wrote a scathing article against Bonnetain's preface. Naturally, a duel followed. Bonnetain was wounded. Naturally also, a scandal followed. Suddenly everyone wanted to read *Sarah Barnum*. Sarah was beside herself. Her son took the matter into his hands. Angered, Maurice had to avenge his mother's honour.

He went to Colombier's home accompanied by Richepin and two friends. With difficulty they broke into the apartment. Frightened out of her wits Colombier ran into another room while Richepin, Maurice and his friends cut and slashed everything they could lay hands on, breaking lamps and furniture as well.

Richepin and Maurice came back bragging to Sarah of their accomplishment : her honour was avenged. So it was, but they overlooked Colombier's audacity. She was far from intimidated and immediately started suit for damages against Sarah while all the papers carried the account of the illegal entry and housebreaking. A cable of six thousand words was sent to the *New York Herald*, but that was the least of it. Colombier's book became a best seller overnight and the presses worked overtime turning out printing after printing to keep up with the demand. Cartoons showed Colombier drinking a whole bottle of ink.

Again Sarah had nightmares. She could think of nothing to do but to buy up every copy available, bankrupting herself, and still it was useless. Richepin then had another idea. He would write the same type of scandal about Marie Colombier : 'I'll teach that tart a lesson for causing you such anguish. I'll use her method, but this time she'll blush through three hundred fifty pages. She'll be the victim this time.'

Not knowing which way to turn, Sarah agreed. Richepin wrote a pamphlet levelled at Colombier under the title of *Marie Pigeonier*, and signed it Michepin.

The public amused itself for a while with the odorous competititon. They crowded the *Porte St Martin* where Sarah and Richepin were appearing together. The partisans of Sarah and Colombier took turns in making themselves heard. It was too much for the play. In addition, the critics were unanimous in adverse criticism of Richepin's acting and his play.

Jarrett was in command of Sarah's next tour, its farthest point St Petersburg. A young actor applied to him under the name of Jacques Daria, showing military credentials of service, evidence of good family background and asked to become a part of the touring company of Madame Bernhardt. Jarrett suggested he present himself to Sarah, and if she approved, he would arrange the business details.

Daria then, under Jarrett's name procured an appointment, arriving at her home with a bouquet of lilies-of-the-valley. When Sarah entered her luxuriously appointed salon, she stopped abruptly. It looks like him, she thought. Could it be possible? Her eyes changed colour: 'Well!' she exclaimed. 'Is Monsieur Daria really that wicked Monsieur Damala?'

His bouquet wilted under her fixed gaze. He stood uncomfortably but unwavering before her: 'May I explain?'

On guard, Sarah took the bouquet and allowed him to sit down.

He had, he explained, begged an acquaintance to arrange the first meeting with Sarah and now he was truly sorry he had been so insolent. He would like to try his hand at acting, and had written some poems if Sarah would care to have him read them to her. Reluctantly, she agreed to listen. At first he seemed like any struggling poet, but as he became absorbed in his material, greatness recognised talent.

Sarah wanted to send him away, but instead, she smiled graciously: 'You may rehearse one play and after we hear the verdict from the audience, your future will be decided.'

She had a plan. So far, she had won this encounter. She had succeeded in hiding the passion he had aroused in her.

The first play was *Hernani*, given in Brussels, with Damala playing Don Carlos to Sarah's Doña Sol, under his pseudonym Daria. His inimitable poise revealed a well-developed sense of drama. Yes, he had an air of distinction! She even took time to notice during the applause that her leading man fulfilled her hopes of male support; his resonant voice and far-seeing glance a perfect foil for her frail beauty. As the audience overwhelmed her with applause she fumed inwardly. The one whose admiration she so deeply wanted and expected was missing. Damala was smiling and bowing to the audience as if the applause was just meant for him.

The critics were quick to single out his talents. There was only one reason why Sarah agreed to his joining the tour. She would bring him to his knees. In St Petersburg, Emperor Alexander III himself presided over the banquets, the command performance and the special tours of Moscow in her honour. She left the great Czarist empire wearing a handsome decoration, a gift from the Czar. Not once did Damala acknowledge her as a woman.

On and on the company toured, playing triumphantly, as always. But by now Sarah was overcome with envy; the sameness of the repertoire began to pall on her. She thought she did not really love the young Adonis who had newly joined her company, but was piqued by his careful deference to her, while he gaily showed an animated interest in a young actress of the group.

Something was wrong. Sarah could not step down from her pedestal. On the journey from Trieste to Naples, she began to brood: Damala was the only man she had ever known whom she had to wait for. Must she take the initiative? He was a thorn in Sarah's pride, and she could think of nothing except to dominate this man who filled her whole life with one desire: that he should return her passion for him!

She had made certain plans, plans based on revenge. She had not forgotten the insult at their first meeting. But now, for the first time in her life she had planned to bring a man to his knees and he refused to kneel.

Chagrin was eating away at her insides. Sleepless nights plagued her. When she thought of him in her moments of solitude, a youthful restlessness obsessed her. In exasperation she decided she would do it. For the sake of her art she must have him. In Naples she would boldly invite him to midnight dinner.

She planned it deftly. The lure of Capri; its starry nights, the undulating mountainous horizons; an endless concert of mandolins; the seduction of nature herself would come to Sarah's assistance.

Before Sarah could carry out her plans, Damala reached the climax of his plan. He had played his role well off stage as well as on. He knew Sarah well enough now to fear that she might do something unexpected and spoil his well laid plans. He would have to work fast now to make good his original boast: that he was the greatest man in France . . . and the wickedest. He had watched his prey carry on at first like a woman of the world, seductive, assured. Admirers buzzed about her like bees round a honeycomb. Out of the corner of her eye she had kept a watch on his reactions; had thrown herself into the scandalous competititon which Marie Colombier had provoked; and now she was subdued, weary, lonely, bored with Angelo, and in the most romantic, earthy city in Europe, Naples. Here, the most unromantic felt the seduction tug at their hearts, stir up mysterious passions which they knew not existed, and drove them against their most sober judgment to wilful childish abandonment.

Damala studied Sarah with the concentration of a scientist; she was a specimen under his microscope and he knew her every emotion and thought. Now it was time to act. They were billed to play *Camille*. Damala slowed his tempo until the fourth act, their most intense violent scene : that scene would do his work for him. All he had to do was to whisper between his lines.

It was the scene in which he confronts Marguerite for breaking her promise to give up her wealthy lover, to abandon all her luxuries, and go away to live alone with him in any way that he could provide, such was her love for him. She then sent him a letter telling him she had changed her mind, without betraying the fact that it was his father who came and begged her to make the sacrifice. Armand is bitter, and when they are both at an exclusive gambling club, Marguerite asks a friend to find Armand and tell him Marguerite wishes to speak to him.

ARMAND : You sent for me ? [Armand watches Sarah compose herself. Pause]
(You haven't been your usual animated self since we got to Naples)
MARGUERITE : Yes, Armand. I want to speak to you.
(How kind of you to notice)
ARMAND : [Damala gloated as he saw Sarah's heart leap]
Go on. I am listening. Do you wish to excuse yourself?
(Aren't you well ?)

MARGUERITE: No, it has nothing to do with that. I have
no wish to go over the past again.

(I'm not sure. I miss my family so. And I've lost so
many friends, dear friends this year)

ARMAND: You are right. Your part in it was too shameful.

(So that's it. How stupid of me. I thought these
Neapolitan skies would mock memory)

MARGUERITE: Don't Armand. Try to listen to me
without hatred and without bitterness. Give me your
hand——

(Yes, almost. Only Egyptian skies rival them)

ARMAND: Never! If you have nothing further to ask of
me——

(I'd love to do Cleopatra with you [he said hotly])

MARGUERITE: Who would have thought that you
would ever have refused my hand when I offered it
to you? But it is not that that I wished to say.
Armand, you must leave here at once.

(Sardou is writing the play for me. We might do it)

ARMAND: Leave here?

(I can hardly wait. [Damala encircled his prey with
his voice])

MARGUERITE: Yes, immediately.

ARMAND: Why?

(Will you dine with me tonight?)

MARGUERITE: Because if you don't, the Baron de Varville will challenge you to a duel.

(Can't. I have an engagement with Angelo)

ARMAND: And you suggest that I should run away?

(I detest him. Do get rid of him and dine with me)

MARGUERITE: Armand, I have suffered so deeply in the
past month that I can scarcely find strength to say to
you what must be said. There is a burning pain here
that takes away my breath. For the sake of our past
love for the sake of anything that you have ever held
dear or sacred in your life, return to your father and
forget that you have ever known me.

(You know what that could lead to?)

ARMAND : I understand. You are afraid for your lover. It would be a thousand pities if a pistol shot or a sword thrust were to put an end to your present good fortune.

(Just what I'm hoping for. I'm expert in both, if I may be forgiven the boast)

MARGUERITE : You yourself might be killed, Armand. That is the danger.

[Sarah's spirits were picking up. She had just been saved the humiliation of kneeling to him]

ARMAND : And what difference would that make to you? Did you care whether I lived or died when you wrote me that you were the mistress of another? . . . But I tell you that between de Varville and me there is a quarrel to the death. For I shall kill him.

(I want you. I've wanted you for so long)

MARGUERITE : The Baron de Varville is not to blame for this.

([How Sarah gloated. She was still queen of hearts. Coolly, she whispered] a good entrance but I've heard better)

ARMAND : You love him! That is reason enough for me to hate him.

(Even before I met you, every time I heard your name, something echoed inside. My death knell)

MARGUERITE : You know that I don't love this man, that I never could love him.

([she could scarcely believe her ears. She did hear it. How long she had waited])

ARMAND : And yet you left me and went to him. Why?
(Answer me, I perish)

MARGUERITE : Don't ask me, Armand. I can't tell you.
(After your next lines)

ARMAND : Then I will tell you. You gave yourself to him because you don't understand the meaning of loyalty and honour; because your love belongs to the highest bidder, and your heart is a thing that can be bought and sold; because when you found yourself face to face with the sacrifice you were going to make for me, your courage failed you; because I, who would have devoted my life to you and my honour too, meant less to you than your horses, carriages and jewels around your neck.

([There was a pause in the acting here. Sarah whispered] What do you wish of me? [Then she had to breathe deeply. Emotional memory was active again. Hadn't she played this scene in reality? or was it a dream?])

MARGUERITE: Yes, it is all true. I am a worthless and ungrateful creature who has cruelly betrayed you, and who never loved you. But the more degraded you know me to be, the less you ought to endanger your life for me and trouble the peace of those you love. Armand, on my knees, I implore you before it is too late, leave Paris.

([She had played this scene countless times without feeling the slightest emotion, had done it automatically, relying on her artistry and technique; why was it changed now? While she spoke her lines, Damala whispered] I adore you. *Dame d'Amour*, I would die for you, with you, to please you)

ARMAND: I will, on one condition.

(I'll wait for you at the stage door)

MARGUERITE: I agree to it, whatever it is.

(No, that won't do)

ARMAND: That you come with me.

(Where then?)

MARGUERITE: Never!

ARMAND: Never!

MARGUERITE: Oh, my God, help me!

(The dining room of the Danielli)

ARMAND: Listen Marguerite, there is madness in me tonight. I am capable of anything, even a crime. I thought that it was hatred that was driving me back to you, but it was love, Marguerite, angry, remorseful, torturing love; love that despised itself and was ashamed, for there is shame in my loving you after all that has happened. Say just one word and I will forget everything. What do I care for this man? Only tell me that you love me and I will forgive you, Marguerite. We will leave Paris and the past, find some solitude and be alone with our love.

(Perfect. That sacred shrine immortalised by Sand and Musset)

MARGUERITE : I would give my life for one hour of such happiness, but it is impossible. Go, forget me. You must. I have sworn it.

([Sarah was in a whirl; luckily, the lines came automatically and her voice did the rest. She tried to cope] I hadn't thought of that)

ARMAND : To whom?

([He saw her turmoil] Dear, are you alright? [She had a long speech, so he went on] It will seem a lifetime until we're alone)

MARGUERITE : To one who had a right to ask such a thing.

(You're forgetting yourself. You're supposed to turn and walk away)

ARMAND : To the Baron de Varville?

(Can you blame me? See, already I'm your slave)

MARGUERITE : Yes.

ARMAND : [seizing her arm] Because you love him! Tell me that you love him and I will go.

(Not the dining room; too public; my suite)

MARGUERITE : Then, yes, I love him.

(True. In that case, my suite. I'll pretend a headache)

She anticipated one of her greatest scenes. Everything was perfectly arranged. Impatiently she went to the balcony where the table set for two challenged her.

The doorbell rang. It could be no one else. Nausea welled up in her. She steadied herself against the table. She took a deep breath. Standing there, she could feel his eyes

237

possessing her. For a moment they just stood still, waiting and wanting. Damala broke the silence : 'You're ravishing!'

From then on, the evening moved like no other she had ever known. As he revealed himself to her she began to realise that here was a wonderful warm human being longing to love, but even more to be loved. Gently she opened the door of love to Damala, which would never again quite close. She knew that she was right. She would always have to be Damala's lover. For the first time love had brought her a burden which she welcomed. Love had made her kneel.

A new freshness bloomed in Sarah, and it showed in her work.

The news of their son's career co-starring with the Great Bernhardt reached Damala's parents. He read parts of his mother's letter to her.

> We hear you are in love. If this is so and you are serious this time, please let us have news of the date of the event.

Sarah's eyes dimmed. She dropped her gaze. Damala enveloped her. No words were spoken. Sarah nodded her consent. She recalled Sand's words

'Love can only thrive when free of all shackles.'

The days passed as in a dream. Each day he revealed a new and beautiful part of his character. Sarah loved him desperately. It was inevitable that two such magnetic personalities would find fulfilment in each other. Marriage that had always seemed so repulsive to Sarah now was to be more desired than a king's ransom. Damala too, responded more ardently than ever.

There was no real proposal. One day Sarah sent a telegram to a London friend :

> *Mon cher*, I am visiting London for a few hours only, just long enough to get married and shall then leave the city immediately. My fiancé's name is Aristide

Damala. He is Greek, I am French. I'm calling upon your kindness to do all that is necessary so that I do not miss my train, for I am playing at Nice next Wednesday. I leave Naples tomorrow morning and will send you a telegram to tell you the time of my arrival.

London was one thousand miles from Naples and a little less than that back to Nice, but the thirty-eight-year-old Sarah went to London with her twenty-seven-year-old husband-to-be. They arrived in plenty of time to be married in St Andrew's, Well Street, only to be frustrated.

Damala had forgotten his papers and had to go back for them to the hotel. They missed the train which would have taken them back in time for the performance in Nice, but for the first time in her life, Sarah deliberately threw responsibility for her career to the winds. Her Damala was worth it. His love fulfilled her more than the applause of the multitudes.

Meanwhile Jarrett and the company waited impatiently in Nice for Sarah's return. The house was booked solid but all the money had to be refunded. She gladly paid the twenty five thousand francs indemnity for breach of contract.

Sarah and Damala caught up with the company in Spain on 5th April. They enjoyed the curious sensation created by the news that 'Sarah was a wife' – the Goddess had married not a genius, nor even a playwright – but an ordinary mortal, a mere man, a poor actor more than ten years her junior! But the company celebrated the occasion – a dinner arranged by Jarrett. Everyone outdid himself in toasting the couple.

The tour had to continue. Finding herself at a station with time on her hands betweeen trains, Sarah had a far-away look in her eyes. The wheels and whistles shrieked and hissed but could not drown out Damala's whisper: 'What is it, dear?'

'Do you suppose there's time for a phone call to Paris?'

He led her to the dispatcher's office, dimly lit but with a welcoming quiet. She waited twenty minutes for the call to go through to Maurice. She began to tell him but he stopped her; he had already heard : 'Yes, Mama, I know. The newspapers all carried headlines!' He hesitated. Sarah recognised the pleading beneath the self-assured voice. For a moment, tears welled up in her eyes. How awful, she thought, to be young. How could she reassure him. How could he know that his beloved mother was happy at last : 'Maurice, dear,' she said quietly, 'it's real. I love him and he loves me.' Vaguely she thought she could hear him sigh. 'When I come home, I'll tell you a love story like you never heard before.'

She could hear the receiver gently click. Once again someone dear was leaving her life and she wanted to cry out. Then she saw Damala and rushed into his arms. He hustled her aboard the train. Sarah was never more glad that she was on her way back to Paris once more.

She was never home long enough for Maurice to tire of her – rather contrariwise, he never saw enough of her even when she was at home. As he grew older he was more attentive than ever. Sometimes even to becoming a bore. Sarah tried to hide her tears in vain but Damala knew instinctively that he must not intrude. She and Maurice would have to settle this themselves.

So far, Sarah was reassured. Throughout the tour, Damala had been the devoted adoring husband keeping up his position with his practised, but natural-looking dignity, his attitude entirely that of the lucky man who had married the most wonderful woman in the world. Sarah squeezed his hand but the feeling of his nearness could not erase from her mind the pain she knew Maurice was suffering now. Even as a child he had been possessive. Every parting had been full of bitter tears.

Paris welcomed Sarah, and now she had a husband. Everyone turned out to see them it seemed to her, with a deeper even warmer applause than before. But Maurice did not come. Never once in response to her many calls did he answer. Maurice showed his disappointment openly and Sarah was hurt. But she was not defeated yet.

With misgivings, Damala agreed to move from their palatial hotel suite back to Sarah's home. It looked the same to Sarah. It welcomed her. Surely here, there would be a chance for her to win Maurice's love back again.

Quick footsteps approaching made Sarah's heart jump. 'Petite Dame!' she exclaimed, dropping her cape and rushing into the older woman's arms. Tears flowed copiously. Finally Damala exclaimed laughingly, 'Is this a homecoming or a wake!'

They all laughed together joyously. He knew immediately he would like it here. Maurice looked more handsome than Sarah had remembered. Tall, slender, pale, with blue eyes and waving golden hair.

Sarah immediately began to make plans for her family's future. How wonderful to have a family again! And a real man she could look up to! Her husband had talent and she would teach him the art she knew so well. Hadn't he been applauded for his sympathetic Armand in *Camille*? and as Don Carlos to her Doña Sol? The future would prove she was right to have married Damala.

Garnier had told her the *Ambigu* was for sale and if she would act quickly, it could be had at a bargain. Well, why not? she thought, it was just the thing! No more travelling. There was plenty to do right here at home.

Authors were putting out fresh materials; plays that gave the theatre a new lease on life. Even the audiences were sated with Hugo and the romanticists before him. Every word of Molière's and Racine's plays were known by her countrymen and it was a strain to do them before such jaded critics.

Yes, it seemed fated that she should buy the *Ambigu*. Damala would be the male lead and share duties with Maurice, who would be nominal manager. She could dispense with Jarrett. Thus she would combine career and motherhood and marriage. Everything would be in its place. Besides, it was time Maurice grew up and learned something about business.

She was right. Maurice welcomed the chance and at

first all appeared to go well. Only now and then, to Sarah, Damala criticised Maurice: 'You know, dear, I could have done much better if I'd handled it. After all, Maurice is hardly more than a boy. He'll learn, of course, since he has your cleverness and intuition. But I do think that in important matters, my decision should bear more weight.'

'You're absolutely right, my dear. But we must be patient. Maurice needs to be handled with tact. He's so sensitive.'

Damala made many compromises. He watched as Sarah indulged Maurice beyond all reason. Again, this time containing his anger, he remonstrated with her: 'It's no wonder he never does anything properly. He'll never learn as long as you continue to baby him. He's not as helpless as you think!'

Sarah forgot herself. Damala had gone too far. Maurice was to her, the holy of holies; she could think nothing or hear nothing wrong of him. For another thing, box-office receipts had fallen off and debts were piling up. Formerly, she could have packed up and gone on tour – always coming home with bulging pockets – to pay off her debts and have plenty left. She was not used to bickering over money. Much to her surprise, she found herself beginning to be irritable not to be able to travel, to have to stay in one place, even if that place were her beloved Paris. But stay she must!

Out of earshot, Damala praised her: 'She's divine! She's the sun, the moon and the stars!' He wanted Sarah badly, but his pride suffered when he saw how Sarah fussed over Maurice, and how critical she was of him. She was too sure of herself.

One argument followed on the heels of another, and one day Damala confronted her: 'I'm your husband, not your stage-hand. I won't have Maurice giving me orders while he acts as if I'm beholden to him for my living. Do you understand?'

'How dare you raise your voice to me,' Sarah shouted. 'And I've warned you not to speak disrespectfully of Maurice. He's the son of a prince, do you understand!'

'Very well. If that's the way you wish it, I'm leaving.'

'That will be a relief,' Sarah shouted. 'Now maybe I can get some peace, so I can concentrate on my work.'

'What, your work? You call that work? The way you stalk about on stage and screech in your high-pitched crow's squawk? Look at you! You call yourself a woman with that body? You're nothing but a fraud. If the dressmakers were not so clever where would you be?'

The next moment Damala just barely escaped being hit by a flying vase. It crashed against the door and fell in a hundred pieces.

'You're mad, really mad! I'll leave now before it's too late. And my sweet, I promise you, you'll be sorry.'

The time came when Sarah let the newspapers pile up unopened; unable to withstand the pounding of her inner conscience: Vanity! Vanity! it had been her undoing, hers alone. On the face of it, the reports sounded candid, even flattering:

Their tour of the provinces ended, Madame Sarah Bernhardt Damala returned with her husband to Paris. Sarah then decided to become manager of a theatre with the aid of her son; at the same time she undertook with Damala as co-manager, the management of another theatre. One enterprise of the kind is generally quite enough to manage successfully, but Sarah essayed two of them. These two theatres soon became insufficient for her insatiable persistence, for she acted at the same time in a third theatre, *Le Vaudeville*, where she created *Fédora* on 11th December 1882. Sarah followed with *Théodora* which she was obliged to perform continuously for a year. But during this period of comparative idleness, she found time to exhibit *The Infant Mars*, a bust in marble; *Henriette*, a cast of a bust; she also wrote a play and published a book. Surely this feminine body, so frail-looking, this ever-ailing woman will have spent during her career not only ten fortunes, but twenty women's lives. A robust horsewoman might have died of similar exhaustion. With Sarah it is

different : the nerves, dominated by a strong and powerful will, infuse her entire being with electrical activity.

To her, rest seems but another form of death : that
which is not paroxysmal means lethargy. She dreams of
the impossible, and, insatiable, she would centuple the
hours of her life by overloading those she is permitted to
live.

Sarah proposed taking lessons in order to play Shakespeare in English. She asked the teacher, 'I want to learn
English very very quickly.'

'Mlle Bernhardt, I would gladly give you lessons but
I can spare but half an hour every day.'

'Well then, you must try to let me have it from 2.00
to 2.30 am, for it is the only time I am not engaged.'

Daylight often surprised her before she thought of it;
that head seething with projects and plans; that
tornado of thoughts and deeds by which she carries a
world in her train.

Sarah decided to run the theatre alone with Maurice,
hoping somehow to recoup her finances. She threw herself
into rehearsals for the new plays of Mendès and Sardou,
but to a degree which even she thought impossible. For the
first time, Sarah was pretending – not on stage but in real
life – a role she detested. She raged, but she turned her rage
inward. Damala had done it again.

Knowing better than anyone how it hurt her pride,
Damala continued to stay away, and let people know about
it. Her public soon repeated what they heard : she thought
she could buy herself a husband and put him in her show-
case at the *Ambigu*. Who could blame such a handsome
young man? Of course it's natural for him to find young
distractions.

Now Sarah's pride was crushed. She knew a new and
terrible kind of suffering. But she also realised how he must
be feeling. She relented, and decided to go to see him.

He came home after Sarah went to him, pleading with
him to consider her humiliation; her position. She even

begged his forgiveness hoping to effect a reconciliation and scotch the scandals.

This suited Damala. It was what he waited for : to see the proud beautiful woman, queen of hearts, come to him on her knees so he could humiliate her still further. He gloated : 'I had Sarah on her knees last night, but I refused to forgive her. She needs more punishment!' After which to prove his superiority, he again deserted Sarah and openly took up a liaison with a Swedish girl.

The rumours and gossip began again : 'Sarah can't be much after all. Her husband betrays her right before her eyes.' The joke of the day was : 'I saw Damala at the theatre last night.'

'With Sarah?'

'Sarah? Of course not! Sarah is now his wife!'

Sarah dragged through the days, fighting her torn pride, humiliation in her once proud eyes, trying not to linger over regrets. But for the first time in her life Sarah's will failed her. She limped about like a hurt puppy trying to keep on in spite of all. Only on stage, in her role as an actress was she able to be what she had always been. This was the other Sarah, playing to the outer world, where feelings did not count, and where as an actress, her genius always triumphed.

Sarah's collaboration with Sardou required new attitudes, new approaches, new gowns, in brief : a new Sarah. It was a departure from the classic to the new mode of realism. Her successful adaptation to the new era was not a reflection of the inner Sarah. That inner part was still struggling in the battle of the many tragedies after the triumphant return from America. She had, thankfully, one release : on stage she could rage.

She came on as Théodora, a dark mysterious creature in flowing robes heavy with jewels and ornamentation. She strode across the stage with long supple movements, not a woman but a veritable tigress. She paced, like a caged animal back and forth; her lines given from her depths as though born in the jungle. A scented emanation surrounding her called forth the exotic; an attraction of disquieting moods which enveloped its captives while her voice – their usual opiate – lulled them into inertia. Sarah hypnotised her audience.

Sarah's art was reaching new dimensions in new plays, all great successes – but her box-office was insufficient to cope with her expenses. She had other troubles too. Many of her company wanted to leave, to spare her facing them backstage in her anguish, but Berton prevailed on them to stay. He had grown accustomed to watching over her, as though it was his duty. No one knew that Sarah's money shortages were due to Damala's blackmailing. He threatened to pose for the papers with other women if she refused. Worst of all, Sarah could not understand what had happened to change him so: she could not believe it.

Unrelenting, the gossip continued: 'It must be true she's terribly eccentric if her husband can't live with her for more than a week!'

Ridicule was killing Sarah. Lines came into her features and hollows deepened under her eyes. After a few months her face lost the girlish look that had been her great charm. For hours, morbidly inconsolable, she sat looking into space.

Then one day Damala returned with an excuse that he was ill, missed her terribly, and could not live without her. They had an angry scene, made peace – only to begin again.

This time, he left the company with an actress whom Sarah had dismissed because she suspected her of intimacy with Damala. He wrote to Sarah, and again she pleaded with him to return. He said he had lost eighty thousand francs while gambling and if she could send him the money, he would come back. Sarah sent the huge sum and he came back – but with the actress. Nothing could stop Sarah's fury now. She made a terrible scene, threatening the woman with physical harm and criminal proceedings, all in vain.

Coolly, Damala smiled: 'She's only come back for her wages.'

It drove Sarah straight into hysterics. But it was true. Sarah did owe the girl back salary, and raging, 'There are more worthy people who haven't been paid. You can earn

246

your keep another way,' she insulted the girl.

A week later, Damala proposed to Sarah that if she made him managing-director, he would feel a closer, personal interest in both the theatre and their marriage. Yes, it might be just the thing : kill two birds with one stone. She accepted and let him plan a tour of Europe. They had to leave the *Ambigu* with its mountains of debts : four hundred thousand francs which Sarah liquidated by selling at auction all her jewels, gifts, royal decorations, and even some of her art work. She would never get accustomed to this humiliation. Stories came back : the whole Paris population swooped down like vultures, fighting, bidding for her personal trinkets, honoured decorations : souvenirs of her happiest carefree memories.

Never mind! *quand même!* Sarah shut her eyes to this. This time she would surely make her marriage succeed. She packed her costumes and went off with Damala holding the reins. It would be a second honeymoon.

Close to him again Sarah discovered what had caused the change in her husband. He, like Jeanne, had become addicted to morphine and now she knew utter despair.

Damala was a complete failure as a business man. Seeing he was totally incompetent, Sarah knew she was all alone again. It cleared her mind. Still, she told no one, until at an hotel in Milan he was nearly arrested for exhibiting himself naked. Sarah made a quick decision. She wanted to disband the company; she told them she had dismissed Damala because of his lack of efficiency, making it impossible to continue the tour.

To her astonishment everyone shouted for joy. They all detested Damala; had known he had become a degenerate, and only tolerated him for her sake. They would work for nothing if she wished to reorganise and continue. Berton took over.

She breathed freely again, and on her return to Paris instituted a legal separation from Damala, paying him a monthly stipend for her release.

With a great effort, Sarah surmounted her melancholia and began to work on new plays. Out of her mysterious depths new art forms, new attitudes and new inspirations were born.

Every playwright produced plays in a new mode for her; comedies, dramas, tragedies, all in the modern genre. As if reborn, Sarah created a new vogue among her confrères who, touched by her genius, seemed to catch it like a disease. It was the birth of a new form in theatre technique and the public, finding refreshment, again flocked as before.

She alternated a season in Paris with tours of Europe and the two American continents, playing to ever-widening audiences.

It was the beginning of a new era. Skilled craftsmen, specially trained, designed fine jewels for clients who could afford the best, and they were ordered to create new decorations which rivalled the riches of the Medicis; these far outshone the sentimental jewellery which Sarah sacrificed with her past. America had a bumper crop of millionaires now, who were eager to show their appreciation of refinement and culture and they showered her with gifts. The days of pioneer woodsmen were gone and families came with their young children to see and hear the Great Bernhardt.

Although Sarah had disciplined her heart since parting with Damala, she kept track of him. For a short while he was able to obtain engagements with theatres who were willing to exploit his publicity value. The crowds flocked to see him out of curiosity. But now that he was a drug addict, without Sarah's genius to help him, he soon wore out his box-office value. The ravages of the poison which originally focussed on the defects of his character now destroyed the whole man.

In the midst of her new-world joys, Sarah's conscience pointed a finger. She could not turn away. She must go to him.

Sarah had a little house now on the Boulevard Pereire.

Maurice had married but lived close by and the two were still inseparable. Petite Dame, at her beck and call, kept some semblance of order in the confusion of Sarah's collections of trophies from all over the world. For these blessings she must give thanks . . . in her own way.

Sarah found Damala, barely able to recognise him. How to speak normally with nausea welling up in her? Somehow, he let her persuade him away from his filthy lice-ridden lodgings to go home with her.

Two months passed and Sarah never left his side. Sufficiently recovered, she primed him for her next Grand Tour to begin on 1st October 1887. Her friends exclaimed: 'It's a miracle!' What they did not know was that Sarah was counting on his youth, and that her moral support should make life worth fighting for. His life hung by a thread. Gambling for his life, she gave him the role of Armand in *Camille*: 'Remember our success on our honeymoon?' she wooed him.

But Damala was as fragile as a glass bubble. He could only arouse pity from the audiences and Sarah returned home with her invalid. Heavy-hearted, she gave him the tenderest ministrations: spared no medical assistance, but saw a repetititon of Jeanne's tragic end.

On hearing of his death, his family claimed his body and entombed it in Greece. Here, Sarah made one pilgrimage.

Berton and Richepin, one old and one new friend, observed solemnly: 'The widow wept bitterly.' Finally, Berton persuaded her to leave. 'How can you weep for him?' he murmured.

'I cry for his soul. There is only one Judge.'

Berton bowed his head. Sand was right. No one knew Sarah as she did.

The chapter on her marriage was closed.

Her maid quickly undressed the widow after her return and hid the black garments in an attempt to prevent Sarah from wearing them again. There was a glint in her mistress's eye which boded ill.

Sarah riffled through her mail slowly, pushed it aside, but

a thickish envelope caught her attention. It was postmarked
Surrey. A brief note explained that the writer's mother had
saved the enclosed clippings from *Punch* among her memoires,
and she had now passed on, perhaps Mme Bernhardt would
appreciate adding them to her collection. Sarah skimmed the
lines. A necklace of gems: sparklingly happy, exciting,
episodes strung themselves out. . . .

Che Sara Sara?
Avis per-rara!
Sculptress and paintress
Poseuse and faintress,
Swooning and swaying
Playing and praying,
For praise or for profit
On stages or off it.
Of actresses, actress;
Proud-benefactress –
Critics – appoking,
Canard provoking,
Paragraph – feeding –
Puffary – breeding –
Che Sara Sara –
Avis per-rara?
Poseuse? Pooh! pooh! Yet who so well can pose
As thou, sweet statuesque slim sinuosity?
Stagey? Absurd! 'The death's head and the rose?'
Delicious! Gives the touch of tenebrosity
That lifts thee to the Lumia level. Oh!
Shame on the dolts who hint of dulcamara
   Serpentine Sarah!
Oh, idol of the hour and of my heart!
Who calls thee crazy half and half capricious?
A compound of Lionne's and Barnum's part,
In *outrecuidance* rather injudicious?
Ah! heed them not! play, scribble, sculp, paint,
Pose as a plastic Proteus, *mia cara*:
   Sémillante Sarah!!!

Never before had her memories seemed so heavy a burden. I'm hardly more than a memory myself! she thought. Everything, everyone was now only a memory; her whole family, Morny, the two bourgeois bachelors, Sand. All the early playwrights and Musset, who wrote, 'The pen that shall do complete justice to the transcendent talent of Sarah Bernhardt is still uncut.'

Now, at last she was desperate. She felt she was lost. Disbelieving in her future she feared old age: to be an old actress, pitied by those who remembered her glorious youth frightened her. Old age in this guise rose as a pitiless threat. There was no way out. She could run nowhere. Every corner of the civilised world knew her. It held no refuge, no haven. She could think of no way out. None except suicide.

In her despair, Sarah took a large dose of chloral, determined to die. In this too she failed.

Sarah was crushed. Her marriage failure, the Colombier scandal, the rising debts, creditors hounding her like baying dogs at her heels. Maurice whom she had raised like a prince, who loved gambling and racing and wore expensive clothes made by the most fashionable tailors. Maurice, the most feared swordsman in Paris; his elegant manners and adoring gaze left her helpless. She forgave him everything. She knew she would have to work for him all her life.

Then Sarah had a dream: that more brilliant laurels than she had ever before were being placed on her head by unseen hands. She awakened, feeling better than she had since the day she arrived back on her native shore from abroad. Courage! Courage! Something inside said to her. Your past honours were only practice. Now you will see the real thing!

11

New Birth, New Love

The gentle Italian climate was a balm for grief and suffering of the soul. Sarah took the manuscript of her new Sardou play with her to study in Italy while she prepared herself for it. In Ravenna, another actress was searching museum records for the same reason which had brought Sarah there. A young woman moved silently, an air of mysticism in her deep eyes set in a dun-coloured face. She looked shyly at the striking figure of the other whose lovely face nevertheless expressed sorrow.

'Who is that slim woman studying the case, just over there?' she inquired of the museum attendant.

'That's Sarah Bernhardt, the famous French actress. She's studying the displays for her new play.'

'Thank you.'

The quiet, dark-haired young woman approached the golden-haired one. With diffidence she spoke two lines in perfect French.

'Allow me to introduce myself. I'm Eleonora Duse.'

'This is a pleasure, a great pleasure. How kind of you.' Sarah's eyes shone warmly. 'Please be my guest for dinner, that is, if you're free. We'll have so much to talk about. Naturally, your fame is well-known in my country which is addicted to tragedy as much as Italy.'

'*Merci*,' Duse answered. 'I have wished to see you perform and had planned to do so this season as I shall have an engagement in Paris. I had tried to attend one of your plays in my country, but always something prevented me. I'll be happy to have dinner with you, but as you are visiting my country, please be my guest.'

'Very well, if you'll be mine in Paris.'

That evening, the two women compared notes and discussed their opinions on how *Fédora* should be played. Duse had played it in Italian. Duse had a vast hand-picked library collected through years of touring. Though she was twenty five years younger than Sarah, she already had a reputation significant in theatre circles.

In Duse, Sarah found a kindred spirit, a tragedienne whose beginnings followed the tradition of Rachel, a sensitive child born into the world in a railway car, her young parents so poor they had no roof over their head. Duse had known a life so dire, and deprivation so final, that she never could become accustomed to comfort and security, though she made millions.

The season opened and each played *Fédora* in her own way. Duse played the Queen sober, thoughtful and dignified, a Queen who never forgot her beginning as a slave-temptress of the Emperor. Sarah's was the fiery proud Empress whose cleverness and loyalty outwitted her husband's enemies and saved his throne.

On the twenty-fourth of November 1887, Sarah appeared in Sardou's third play, *La Tosca*. It was most violent. Maurice Baring wrote:

It is impossible to go further into horror in theatre. A condition, it will be understood made possible only by Sarah's playing. If anyone else but she was charged with the role, it would never have come into existence.

La Tosca was a great success, and Sarah resolved to live. Again she toured Europe and America, paid her creditors, and made new plans.

She had faced her last demon, had fought satan on his own ground and had beaten him. She knew now as never before that she would never again dare tempt the gods. Berton never reproached her, still loyal, idolising, protective. She would soon become a grandmother, and she anticipated a new joy.

Swiftly she created three more women, all very young, only eighteen, and very different from each other. Barbier's

Jeanne d'Arc, robust and confident, followed by the role of the Virgin in Rostand's *La Passion*, then Cleopatra. Each one was given as though she alone was Sarah's masterpiece; each a unique entity already cast in the die of full womanhood. The honest simplicity of the Maid of Orleans whose peasant stockiness cut abruptly into the elegant tapestry of the Court of Charles VII was in no way mirrored in the spiritual beauty of the Virgin whose placid features were washed in the holy light of her mission. Cleopatra, the fierce tigress of the Nile, jealous, primitive and proud, renounced any resemblance to all known females. This was only a prologue to Sarah's longest tour – world wide – going as far as Australia in 1891, giving three hundred and ninety five performances in fifteen months.

On shipboard returning again, she remembered a wager that she had made with Rothschild, who reminded her before her departure of that memorable day in her studio when she had smashed his bust.

'You could never get Sardou to sit for you, I'll promise you anything you wish if you want to take a wager.'

'Indeed, and if he does will you buy me a dog when I return?'

The Baron had laughingly agreed. She formulated a plan and knowing of Sardou's fascination with spiritual matters, she had him tell her how it all came about. Meanwhile, she began to fashion a likeness of him.

The story went that, one evening as a young playwright he was hard at work scourging vice and rewarding virtue in the fifth act of a melodrama, when he suddenly heard faint sounds of music behind him. He whirled round in his chair. No one was in the room except himself. Nevertheless, the piano, a spinet, dear to him because it came to him from a sister whom he had lost, was sounding as if fingers were flying over the keys. He looked attentively at the keyboard, for the instrument was open, and he saw that the ivory keys were moving as if impelled by unseen fingers. He watched them closely. Though the keys were covered with dust, the spirit fingers that were moving them left no trace behind them. When the melody, an old air by Haydn, was ended, the piano again became mute.

Sardou pinched himself to make sure he was not dreaming, but he was wide awake. He went to bed but slept little that night. Next morning he hastened to visit a friend who was acquainted with all mysteries of modern spiritualism.

'It is very simple,' said the friend 'you are a medium but you have been unaware of your powers. There are many people like yourself.'

Sardou was surprised but soon found that it was the truth. He found himself capable of bringing about all sorts of remarkable phenomena; raps from tables; materialise spirits; receive messages from beings in the other world. Sometimes the spirits would seize his hands, and with inconceivable rapidity would draw wonderful designs of scenes and buildings which he had never seen.

While in exile, Hugo whiled away the weary days in Guernsey by conversations with the other world by means of table-tipping. Claretie chronicled the thousands of pages which Sardou advised Meurice later to publish. 'But,' Claretie questioned, 'I suspect that this unknown who wrote clever verse and prose was no other than Victor Hugo himself.'

But it would not have been possible to offer such a simple explanation to Victor Hugo; quite the contrary, it would have made him seriously angry. He firmly believed in these realities of manifestations and voices of the other world. He was as firm a believer in them as Sardou. Rather than discuss the matter, he said that 'facts could not be debated, and he accepted the phenomena as genuine.'

Sardou said the fashion, imported from America by Madame de Girardin into Paris, caught the attention of great men who dwelt on intellectual peaks, and accepted without question the mysteries of the abysses below. He showed no signs of irritation when he heard attacks upon or remarks against spiritualism.

'There are people with whom it is useless to argue. Their incredulity is proof against attack. If you prove a fact to them, they admit it but next day deny their admission. Fear of ridicule with them is stronger than the love of truth.'

'So you see what I mean when I say I took unfair advantage of him. He entertained me while I won my bet.'

The irritable, sensitive Sardou was compelled to sit for her twenty one times, when, in a burst of energy, Sarah insisted on immortalising his beautiful head. Her famous bust of the great playwright in black marble is her masterpiece, but the author resented her autocratic domination and zestful application to the difficult art which enslaved him against his wish. Sarah told him sweetly:

'It is the least I can do for you after the great successes your plays brought me.' She still adored playing tricks when the mood seized her.

When she returned from Australia, she began to write her memoirs. Once again, Sarah's inner resources performed a miracle of healing. For the next two seasons, she leased the *Porte St Martin*, wrote three plays, and closed a successful run in 1893. Sarah was busy in her dressing room one day when she was interrupted:

'There's a wild-looking man who wants to see you, Madame,' the doorman told her, looking harrassed.

'Who is he?'

'He said Jean Richepin sent him. He looks a true savage!'

Sarah laughed mischievously. 'Send your wild man to me. He's a boy named Rostand. A great poet.'

Her leg in pain from one of the falls during her fainting spells, she remained seated when he entered. The leg would swell and become infected and feverish if she stood up too long, so she folded her arms over the back of her chair, dropped her chin on her crossed arms and stared blankly, steadily, at her visitor.

The sensitive young author, intimidated beyond words just to find himself in the presence of the Great One, seated himself in the chair Sarah had indicated, not knowing what to do with his hat, gloves, manuscript, or hands. Rostand looked up blushing, waiting for a word of encouragement. But the head remained motionless, the eyes hypnotically holding his gaze. His long tangled hair in wild profusion over his reddened face seemed to drip with embarrassment. He waited. Where was the kindness and compassion everyone talked about? She who picked up stray dogs and cats, and would mother the world if only it would let her?

But Sarah's pose continued.

After two stammered attempts at telling her why he came, unable to get beyond the opening, he flushed and in a fit of exasperation, still clutching his belongings, he rose abruptly and with as much dignity as he could muster he headed for the door. This woman, he thought angrily, this piece of marble, she's an actress! Not only had his hopes been dashed, but he was as disappointed as a small boy whose ice cream had fallen off the cone. Not quite out of earshot, he could hear her ringing girlish laughter and her mischievous comment to Felicie:

'*Eh bien*, so that's Edmond Rostand, the poet?'

But Sarah did not have the last laugh. She had just left her dressing room and was painfully approaching her carriage when her coachman hurried up to her, taking her arm firmly as she leaned on him. Embarrassed, he indicated the carriage: 'Madame, a strange man is sitting in your carriage and refuses to leave!'

Recognising Rostand, she nevertheless commanded:

'Throw that stranger out!' Hardly able to hold back her hysterical glee at the painful expressions on everyone's face, she watched the young poet step lightly down beside her. Seeming to catch her mood, he bowed reverently:

'Madame, I'd rather not cause you embarrassment or have your son send me his seconds for knocking your coachman down again, so permit me to help you into your carriage.'

'But why?'

'Because I wish to read you a play.'

'Well, why didn't you say so! Of course, by all means!'

Suddenly realising a fleeting expression of pain crossing her face as she struggled to enter the carriage, he whispered:

'Permit me, madame.' His strong arm encircled her waist as he lifted her like a small child into the carriage. Settling himself close beside her, he covered her small hand possessively with his own. For some moments they drove in silence. Only a glance passed between them. Her mischievous mood had left her. In its place came an emotion Sarah had thought was buried forever. A smile that was at once contented and yet a little sad played about her face.

The carriage moved off into the park where the early spring blossoms fell in profusion into their laps. Gathering a handful of them, Rostand turned to her, grinning: 'Even mother nature applauds you.'

'There's something about the spring that always makes me cry.'

Rostand gently brushed the tears away: 'You are too lovely. . . .' She felt his warm lips pressed against her cheek. There was gentleness and strength in his embrace.

As evening fell, she admonished: 'We haven't even discussed your play yet! and here it is, almost time for dinner!'

'So it is,' he said gently.

Although Sarah had never been to the country inn that Rostand had selected to dine in, she immediately responded to its warmth and dignity. Any fears she might have had concerning Rostand were immediately dispelled. For the first time in many months, Sarah's stomach responded to food. She ate ravenously as he entertained her with gay chatter, recitations and nonsensical poems, and in every way gave her great happiness.

Rostand had read much about Sarah's early life not only out of admiration, but also to familiarise himself with the great woman of his time. He was richly armed with biographical lore from newspapers, magazines, war records and biographies of all the great companions of Sarah's early and middle career in art, theatre and state. He amazed her with his knowledge.

'Aside from your own biography, I soaked up every drop of ink spilled in your name.' He commented after reciting several episodes.

'And what was your conclusion?'

'Cleverer minds than mine have failed there. It has been

said that you are not a woman but a complex : you might fly to the moon, innoculate yourself with rabies, or marry a negro king. And speaking of kings, one of the drollest was the incident of Gambard, the negro king who searched and found you when you ran away from the *Comédie* the second time.'

'Oh yes,' Sarah laughed. 'I had forgotten that.'

'And did it happen just that way?'

'Yes, strangely enough. We heard the sound. . . .'

Rostrand interrupted. 'No, let me tell you and correct me if I'm wrong. You had pitched a tent near Nice on the spot where Empress Eugénie later built her villa, assuming you could count on privacy so far from town. It seemed safe enough as it was heavily overhung by dense shrubs and bushes. But it was useless, if anyone wanted to find you, they did so even if they had to finecomb the world.'

'Yes, quite true. He had come to buy my group sculpture, *After The Tempest*, and as he agreed to pay me two thousand francs more than Susse had offered, he was the successful bidder. He wrote out a cheque on the spot and was happy to have concluded his business. But what a colourful figure!'

Rostand went on : 'This was the age of literary giants, yet no one could match Sarah in ordinary talk.' Rostand looked up to see the smiling eyes. 'She could be eloquent on fifty current topics, with something original and interesting to say on each of them.' He stopped reading and added his own comment 'Who would not envy your comradeship with the entire male gallery of men of letters. But it is what you did for them, their achievements would long since have died but for your genius. Perhaps I can understand why most of them died so young.'

Sarah studied the young man : 'Why?'

'Because we forget them so quickly. They would have died of heartbreak long since. The public . . . well, listen to this : "It was Sarah Bernhardt more than anyone else who transformed with her magic touch, the theatre in France from the superior, intellectual toy of the cultured few to the amusement and recreation of the many. This she accomplished not only by her own special tastes – but by her personal genius in finding the 'common touch'." '

Sarah was aglow. 'You are so young to be so profound!'

'How I envy every moment you spent with Hugo, Dumas, Flaubert, Sand, Zola. *Ma foi* . . . now, would you fill me in on the discussions which touched on the mystical topics?'

'Why?'

'Well, I read about the many meetings and was fascinated.'

'No, I don't mind. I was curious about everything; the histories of French prophets included, especially as I played Joan of Arc. But as I was a practising Catholic, such topics are tabu, that is, séances and spirit contacts. But I wish I could have had the time to explore the writings of Nostradamus, as Hugo and Dumas did.'

Mysticism was a part of the liberal education Sarah received in her youth and later development from such great men as Dumas, Victor Hugo and Ernest Renan, all of whom studied the writings of Nostradamus. Along with George Sand and others, many an evening was spent at the Princess Mathilde's, even after her brother's exile. Her brother, Louis Napoleon, adored all manner of mystical phenomena and séances, and had often invited the Scotsman Home to perform for him.

Sarah remembered Morny's reference to these evenings, with the aftermath of 'nerves' and sleeplessness which he suffered, and how Julie left special orders with the staff to keep the youngsters quiet at these times. Sainte-Beuve and the Goncourt Brothers were among Princess Mathilde's favourite guests, and they almost always found historical parallels from which they derived laws which did work. In any case, prophecy was a topic that was discussed with familiarity beginning with the Ancients in the Old Testament down through the ages to Joan of Arc and Nostradamus, counsellor and medical advisor to Catherine de Medici, she whose husband, Henry II of France, read his own destiny in the great seer's thirty-fifth quatrain.

How often had Sarah's thoughts been interrupted and turned backward when she strolled through the Luxembourg

Gardens to sit beside the tree-shaded lover's retreat that that famous queen had built. She studied the group sculpture which walled it off for privacy, a romantic theme from Chrétien de Troyes' epics. Its charm and peace sustained her in many a difficult moment. She could not dismiss lightly anything which gave her strength or inspiration.

At Princess Mathilde's she seemed to feel the presence of those who had passed on yet seemed presently among them. Hugo pointed out; 'It would not surprise me in the least if our Sarah should be our next prophet. Let me explain. Like Nostradamus, she was born a Hebrew, and like him, she was educated as a Catholic. He was protected by Henry II and Catherine de Medici, and if we stretch a point, we could say that the Emperor did all in his power for Sarah, and had destiny not interfered, he would surely have made generous provisions for his favourite. However, Sarah has other royal protectors in every country of the world. Agreed?'

'An excellent point.' Sainte-Beuve put in, 'and don't overlook the fact that one of Nostradamus' first great friends was Julius Caesar Scaliger, philosopher-poet and first of all literary critics.'

Dumas laughed his heartiest : 'For shame, can't you forget for one evening that you're a journalist. Enough that you are the only soul among us who can afford to resign every lucrative position if it conflicts with your notions of liberty. I envy you, brother. But what interested me was that Nostradamus knew himself to be a descendant of the tribe of Issachar to whom it was given to discern and know the times. He wrote that he burned some ancient Egyptian books after having learned their contents by heart; these books had come to him by inheritance from one or the other of his grandparents. Now, what did the Hebrews carry away from Egypt in the Exodus?'

The princess put in : 'They could not have failed to possess themselves of all possible documents from the initiation chambers of the Egyptian temples; all the geometric, cosmographic and algebraic formulae subsequently used in the Torah and in the construction of the Temple of Solomon.

Then, one day the Romans destroyed the Temple of Jerusalem. But before the Temple was demolished, the documents had disappeared. When the Holy of Holies was entered, it was empty.'

'Were they ever found?' Renan asked.

The princess turned to Hugo: 'I don't recall the end of that history. Do you, Victor, do finish it for me.'

'They were never found. According to the biographers they were doubtless transmitted from father to son in that tribe of Issachar which had always lived close to the Temple and to the Kings of Jerusalem. Also, the builders of that Temple were said to have migrated to Provence.' The brilliant Hugo held his audience spellbound: 'In his preface, he wrote to his son, I did not desire to keep those volumes which had been hidden during long centuries; so after learning their contents, I burned them. You should read that part again,' Hugo impressed upon the princess. 'Nostradamus said: "that flame was more brilliant than ordinary flame, as though a preternatural lightning flash had abruptly illumined the house and threw it into a sudden conflagration." How I should wish to have such an experience.'

Renan, not to be outdone, added: 'Goethe must have had a somewhat similar experience, for he too had the gift. He wrote of Nostradamus: "Was it then a god who penned these signs," referring to his Oracles. He was the most illustrious figure of the fifteenth century, the most dazzling period of the Renaissance.'

Those who lived long enough, saw a succession of new Sarah's, as though the first was a basic soft clay model over which time placed new faces, personalities, ambitions. She also grew inwardly, the roots, as they reached new depths sent forth new riches to unfold themselves and illuminate her outer self.

'Fondle no such flattering hopes,' Sarah told Hugo. 'I want no life with a price on its head. One Jeanne d'Arc should be enough for us.'

Sand loved these quick retorts, and like Sand, Sarah's

latter fame transformed her from a maddening woman who outraged tradition, into a rather superior being who merited the highest regard. She had learnt restraint and enjoyed its rewards. Bursts of eloquence from her lips were jotted down by listeners as birds quickly flutter to catch the early fireflies before nesting at sundown.

But whether she was aware of how much she did use her intuition, it is impossible to say, for the French put high store in this faculty. That it played a great role in her life was a certainty, and many a morning she watched the dawn for her own special omen. She wrote in her memoirs: 'That night left me without sleep, for I wished to catch a glimpse in the darkness of the small star in which I had faith. I saw it as dawn was breaking, and fell asleep thinking over the new era that it was going to light up.'

Rostand next turned to a newspaper clipping on another topic: 'I can understand,' he said, 'with all your responsibilities and sculpting, painting, writing, that you were quite a critic in your own right. I like your comment at the beginning:

Nothing indeed is so disconcerting as the general aspect of a picture gallery while the eye ranges over good and bad paintings. Very fortunately for the amateur, after a few minutes the beautiful paintings stand out bright and encouraging. But the miserable daubs which are all round demand attention, fatiguing by their ever increasing number, ending by irritating the nervous system. . . . There are fifteen hundred canvasses too many in the Salon. Art should be elevated, not broadened.

Her description of a portrait of Modjeska is interesting and vivid. Here is a portrait by Carolus-Duran. It is superb. The head, with a smile on the face and with yellow hair, stands out upon a russet background, calm and lightly poised. This background is a *tour de force*. The long, slender hand plays with an eyeglass. A yellow rose relieves the delicate tone of the flesh. The white satin dress is a marvel of execution, especially in the shadows of the skirt. . . .

Sarah was visibly moved: 'You're wicked. You'll have me crying in a moment.'

This was what Rostand wanted. He pulled out another clipping,

> When artists who have succeeded when playing with her have lapsed into oblivion when away from this influence, or when they were trying to make their way alone, Sarah bears them no ill will; often she re-engages them or aids them in some way. One seceder had fallen into poverty and a friend came to ask Sarah's help in a benefit to be given for her. The first words were scarcely uttered when she agreed, 'The poor woman. Yes, but what shall I play. Never mind. Let them print the posters and I'll think of something.'
>
> From niggling beginnings, the magical name of Sarah Bernhardt worked the miracle and a bulging box office told the result.

'Enough, enough. Let's talk of something else. Please.'

'Now that we understand each other, would you mind telling why you married the man you did? I omit his name out of delicacy.'

Sarah dropped her eyes, and Rostand wished he had not pursued this topic. But Sarah bravely raised her head and told him:

'You are really kind, Edmond. And you're right, why indeed? I had just lost my family and George Sand. Then Flaubert died and . . . then Hugo and Zola died. Damala had my mother's demon in him. He stood aloof from me, as Julie did when I was little, and that was my weakness, only, I didn't know it then. I wanted her to love me, and I tried so hard, but it was useless. My father loved me but he died when I was thirteen. Since then, I look on thirteen as a bad omen.

'Even before we met I felt – though I denied it to myself – that he would be the means of my undoing, and yet, like the proverbial moth, the flame overpowered my better sense. I was surfeited with success, homage, flowery speeches and stately decor. Damala was the opposite extreme. I paid a high price for boredom and my loss of esteem for the gifts and talents bestowed upon me.

'There was so much about him that was familiar, the opportunism of Morny; the egotism of de Ligne; the gay spoiled butterfly existence of my mother and Aunt Rosine; and of someone long forgotten . . . during my art school days. . . .'

'Who? May I ask?'

'A young apprentice, it doesn't matter. I saw him in so many characters in plays. I was heartsick, alone with my glories, no one to share them with; just when I had earned the fortune my mother dreamed of . . . it would have made her so happy, she could have had everything her heart desired – even her baronial estate. But she was gone, she had died as she sat knitting . . . so young, only fifty one. I can see her before my eyes . . . how lovely she was especially when she would scold me in a petulant mood, her eyes blazing as the colour heightened. Her lotus-like hand swept across her lips as if to relax the muscles; French cramped her speaking a bit.'

'I see. Please don't go on if it's painful, *chère*.' Rostand whispered.

'It's all right. Well, I felt myself drawn to him against my will. Maybe if I'd been home with my son and Madame Guerard, and all the other distractions of Paris, it might not have happened. But, on tour, in Italy . . . the hours with nothing to do . . . waiting from one show to the next. . . . Maybe I had to learn I was not really a goddess. I always take my coffin on tour with me, to remind me I have feet of clay.'

'There you're going too far. I won't have it,' Rostand interposed : 'As you know, all goddesses, and gods of legend, had mortal weaknesses, but they were still superior to mortals. You are still the muse of poetry – how many poets would have languished and died, if you were not here, manifest, in the flesh? You distil magic essences wherever you go and whatever you do. But, there's still the question, why didn't you divorce Damala? How did you put up with him?'

'I couldn't put up with him, but I'm a Catholic. It seems it was my cross to bear not only his drug mania, but my sister's also. I knew how my sister suffered before her death, and that's why I didn't divorce him. I knew he didn't know what he was doing. I'm grateful to heaven that my son is a clean, honourable man.'

'How did you get back on your feet again? I know you were penniless.'

'Help came to me from the beautiful Alexandra, the Princess of Wales. She and the prince loved to chat with me after a performance in their private apartments. We talked about all the royalty of Europe as if they were my relatives as well as theirs.'

'How wonderful! They appreciated you as a woman as well as an artiste. I wish I could have known you as a child. It is unfair that I was cheated out of that.'

'If you had, you would have been my age now.'

'Exactly. And everything would have been in its proper place, historically. I would have been by your side all through it. How you suffered from your mother's neglect! Do you think of it ever?'

'Of course I do, but not with anger anymore. Life has been good to me. My mother was not made like me. I love my son. I loved my mother and sisters, but they were different. They were made to be loved and spoiled.'

'And you?' asked Rostand.

'I was made to work hard. If I do one little thing carelessly, mispronounce one syllable, or speak off-key in the slightest degree, it is blown up into a catastrophe, articles appear, and duels are fought. . . . Nothing is overlooked.'

'True, but maybe that's why you're such a great person. You always listened to the critics, and tried to please the public. Not many of us do. I wish I'd known you when you were a saucy, unbridled débutante at the Française.'

'Why?'

'Well, everyone says that now you're punctual for appointments, then they begin to make comparisons. I'm jealous.'

'But you don't know what a price I've paid. And now, it means I have almost no time for my private life, and I can never see all the people I want to. It means constant rehearsals and attention to my career.'

'Sarah, you're right. You must have your own theatre and stop touring. It's enough you've graced every theatre in the world, leaving the mark of your footprint on their boards. Paris, your home, should consecrate a theatre in your name. The Sarah Bernhardt Theatre.'

'It's enough, *cher*. France is too poor for that. Her wars have taken all her strength.'

But Rostand went on. 'I've heard the Théâtre de L'Opéra Comique, the one on the place du Châtelet, is available for lease. Shall I speak to them about your taking it over? Of course, only if it will bear your name in the future?'

'How strange. Did you know I gave my first performance there? And if they give it to me, I will probably give my last one there,' Sarah almost whispered.

'Speaking of theatre, I must say you do play male roles with more conviction than young male actors do'.

'I feel it is a new strangeness in my life, a new art. An unexpected horizon for me, while in my youth, I often played old women, and was lauded as much as for my young women.'

(Le Théâtre Sarah Bernhardt became a reality, and Sarah's premonition came true.)

At last, when dinner was over and the table cleared, Rostand began to read his play.

Although Sarah was prepared to like anything Rostand had written, she found herself entirely enraptured in the story. She already saw herself as Roxanne, the sensitive intellectual heroine. Sarah loved poetry and artistic phrasing. Never before had she had the opportunity of playing a woman such as this. Unashamedly, she wept for poor Cyrano. For Rostand, it was the greatest applause he would ever know.

Cyrano de Bergerac was an overwhelming success. Her performance of Roxanne brought tears and plaudits again and again from her audiences and sky-rocketed Rostand's reputation.

During the rehearsals and many conferences in preparation for *Cyrano de Bergerac*, their admiration for each other deepened. At first, Sarah tried to restrain her feelings of love and adoration for this so-young, young man. But gradually, he convinced her that souls alone know how to love, and that the body was only its expression.

He reminded her of the 'Great Woman of the Century' who had been her closest friend, George Sand.

'Her greatest artistic and spiritual fulfilment resulted from being loved by many far younger men than herself, Musset, Chopin, Manceau, Mallefille.'

'Yes, I recall her words, "Do we really ever get old? Something within us remains eternally alive, eternally young. One day it will help to reconstitute a more idealistic humanity."' She believed that our land was now under an eclipse, but would, through devotion to art, once more become the France of miracles.

'She told me that it was Liszt's influence which carried her into the study of mysticism. None of her earlier friends, not even Sainte-Beuve with his *air de soutane* and his delight in whispered secrets; all except Liszt were out of their depth in the transcendental world. His physical appearance was remarkably like the ideal he espoused. He was twenty-five at the time, the world's foremost pianist, society loved and spoiled him for himself as well as for his genius. His brow was luminous, like Dante's, his blue eyes set wide apart in a candid gaze, and George sat drinking in his music for hours. He was such a relief after the famous Magny dinners where she met with the Goncourts, Maupassant, Zola, Flaubert, Taine, Renan, Gautier and others.

'As though riding the crest of a high mystic wave, she joined in admiration of Lavater who believed in the progressive divinisation of man and who had a kind word for even the worst display of human weakness. She felt his influence, even from the grave. She believed, through his teachings, that nature was probably not created exclusively for man, and she would quote Goethe, "Hail to the unknown superior beings whose existence we surmise." '

Sarah paused. Rostand wondered whether to let her go on. He had not expected the conversation to take this turn, but he was fascinated. He said

'How simply the poet expressed it.'

'Yes, and how much better,' she smiled. 'Lavater's theory was eagerly accepted by the *littérati* – that all art is divine inspiration and that "Whosoever is not a prophet, is not a poet; all true art is an inspiration of the divine mind; all human language is remembered, not invented." But Lamennais said this was nonsense. He agreed that art is revelation but derives its contents from the contemporary ruling ideas, or from the faith, knowledge and scientific perception of a given historical epoch. Art must serve the truth of the epoch which it expresses and in the noblest and purest sense.'

'To sum it up,' Rostand interposed, 'art has no other aim than to manifest human progress. You've broadened my concept of the truly great woman Sand was, and you've won my argument for me.'

As though she hadn't heard him, she went on : 'She told me she recognised her final mission in society, that at last the immensity of heaven was opening up. What a career. She was utterly fearless. She always tried to find the higher meaning, the only one intended by God.'

Rostand, twenty-four years younger than Sarah, would weary himself with writing and planning dramas; then, thinking to leave them with Sarah while he rushed home to sleep, he would hurry to drop them off. No sooner did his eyes light on her than his love overwhelmed him. Again and again, he found new qualities that endeared her to him even more. Stimulated by their love, he was refreshed and ready for a full day's work.

They were so compatible, Rostand felt incomplete unless he was with her constantly. He proposed to her times without number; sometimes, if she put him off, through a poem, or sending flowers and gifts with pleas – begging her to become his wife. Sarah was determined this would never do. She loved him too much for that.

'Ah, no, Edmond. You must marry a girl who can give you children and perhaps bring another poet to France.'

'You can't mean that, not if you really know me. I must love the woman I marry, and I love you. You are more to me than life itself, than my whole future. If it doesn't include you, it is nothing!'

One night, Rostand was especially elated. New ideas were flowing from his pen as fast as he could put them down. In the morning over breakfast, he said :

'You have played Hamlet, the young Prince of Denmark who avenged his father's betrayal. I'll write the drama of another prince for you, our own L'Aiglon, who died so young and who lived in the melancholy shadow of his great father's memory. What do you say to that?'

'How exciting! I've always been attached to the legend of the Great Napoleon. What Frenchman could resist it! And there certainly is a striking resemblance between the two young princes. I should love to play L'Aiglon.'

Sarah looked every inch the king in the role of the nineteen-year-old son of Napoleon, the Duc de Reichstadt. She too had fathered a prince. She had reared him, protected him, educated him in the royal manner; had been mother and father to him, nay, more, she was queen of the world of art, diplomacy, charity . . . had received every great honour that the world's monarchs and governments could bestow. And the honour was theirs! She was in fact the emblem of royalty itself. She had mothered a prince of the blood and the adjective was more than fitting.

She had never ceased giving her blood. She studied Rostand's script and was reading his second act, scene one.

DUKE: Now I understand why I'm so restless at night. . . .

A VOICE: Cavalrymen never kill you decently, the swine!

DUKE: . . . why I wake up in a cold sweat – why I spit blood. . . .

(Dawn breaks, grey and stormy. In half-light, all familiar objects take on a sinister and fantastic air. The wheat turns to waving plumes, tussocks of grass become forage caps, and saplings beckon oddly in the wind)

DUKE: He sowed. I reap and garner. I'm the heir.
    Yet, though he sinned, pity me,
    Men who died! Have mercy, you with horrible flayed hands.
    Speak though it kills me! Speak!
    What do you want to say?

VOICES: Long Live the Emperor!

DUKE: I understand. The glory is the pardon.

Emotional memory pierced the script and it dropped from her hands. The scene she read was overlaid by another, . . . the scene, another battlefield . . . when the Brothers of the Ecole Chrétienne asked her to help collect the wounded and dying on the Châtillon Plateau. She too had reaped and garnered, a harvest of death . . . and terror . . . she had worked without sleeping for months after – afraid of sleep and its nightmares – guilt driving her, she knew not where, knew not how much of that destruction could be laid at her feet. How she would have covered each corpse with a double mask if she could have obliterated her part in it – one mask for death, one for life! Her hands went up and covered her eyes.

'What have I done?' Rostand asked with anguish.

'Not you! not you, my love. I've come full circle again. It is one of the mysteries of my destiny. Oh, please don't think me superstitious but send Dominga for candles. Tomorrow I shall attend the earliest mass.'

'Yes, yes, of course, but you haven't told me a word.

Haven't I yet earned your confidence?'

'*Pardonne, cher*. I fear to tell you, but oh, I fear a great and terrible war again. Ah, *mon Dieu* . . . and in my lifetime.' Sarah was caught in Rostand's arms as she collapsed in tears.

When she told him the whole story and her premonitions, he instantly offered to tear up the play but she would not permit such 'desecration'.

'It is a work of art, and art is living breathing life! And simplicity is the essence. My favourite philosopher, Kabir, said "Behold but One in all things; it is the second that leads you astray." I have seen him proven right over and over.'

Sarah now played her parts with no less an illusion of adolescence than when she played in *Kean* some thirty years before. The success of *L'Aiglon* revived the cult of nationalism in France immediately; copies of Napoleonic souvenirs were bought up like a flood of holy water, and showered Sarah and Rostand with glory.

Sarah who at fifty six would have been an anachronism if it were not for her genius; Sarah whose sucess in *Lorenzaccio* and *Hamlet* was incredible when one stopped to realise there was Mounet-Sully, an actor of genius, of sensitivity, and of handsome masculine proportions available for these parts; yet Sarah played the young Duc de Reichstadt with a sensitive, tender understanding beyond that of the author's dreams.

On the sixth of December, Edmond Rostand, Catulle Mendès, François Coppée, Haraucourt and Theuriet organised 'Sarah Bernhardt Day' by giving a dinner for six hundred at the Grand Hotel. Raymond Poincaré and the Princess of Monaco were among the celebrants. A cortège of two hundred coupés strolled the boulevards, circling the theatre, rendering homage to Sarah who, that night, played the second act of *Phèdre* and the fourth act of *Rome Vaincu*. The audience wept.

Again Sarah recaptured her success of the Comédie Française. Amid the plaudits and stately ovations paid to Sarah, Rostand's surpassed all. He followed her constantly and it was inconceivable to be in the presence of one without the other close by. His memorable tribute was simplicity dignified in eloquence:

The existence of Sarah Bernhardt remains the supreme marvel of the nineteenth century.

It was in December of 1890 that Sarah had given one of the most unforgettable of her performances. On 2nd December, she played De Musset's *Lorenzaccio*. All who saw it were agreed it was the most beautiful of all her creations. Jules Lemâitre said:

It was not to be compared with *La Dame aux Camélias* and the *Princess Lointaines*, all of which were rendered with beauty so movingly, but to that beauty Sarah added *Lorenzaccio*, a role extremely difficult to interpret, the genius of her most rare and most subtle intelligence.

Sarah's unique gift lay in her ability to form the 'inner-man' intuitively and instinctively. The greater the challenge, the better her intellectual and artistic gifts asserted themselves. She now realised the capital powers she possessed and threw off all discouragement. She nourished herself by this power, required still less food and rest to sustain herself.

It was this power which quickened poets and playwrights to work for her. On her audience, she exercised a fantastic fascination; she was an irresistible enigma, a mystery of endless conflicts and moods – all unexpected and seemingly uninspired – yet concrete and invincible. With every attack from her enemies, this enigma emerged ever stronger, ever greater.

In June of 1889 Sarah had played *Hamlet* in Shakespeare's country, at Stratford. After this, she toured Europe again playing her repertoire of young men interspersed with Rostand's Roxanne in *Cyrano de Bergerac*. She brought Rostand such fame through her interpretation that everyone concluded he must have written *L'Aiglon* in gratitude.

Maurice Baring spoke out: 'It is a certainty that Sarah Bernhardt made Rostand.'

Immediately after her triumph in *Lorenzaccio*, a few friends headed by Henry Bauer, decided to give a grand fête in her honour to mark the apogee of her artistic career; the date fixed was 9th December 1896. She was then asked by the *Figaro* to give its readers a glimpse into her mind at the moment of this memorable event. She sent the following spontaneous, vigorous account of her meditations:

'My dear friend,

You ask for nothing less than a full confession, but I have no hesitation in answering. I am proud and thoroughly happy at the fête to be given to me. You ask me to say whether I really and truly believe I deserve this honour. If I say "Yes," you will think me very conceited. If I say "No," you will set me down as quite blamable. Instead, I would rather tell you that I am very happy, and proud. For twenty-nine years I have given the public the vibrations of my soul, the pulsations of my heart, and the tears of my eyes. I have played one hundred and twelve parts. I have created thirty eight new characters, sixteen of which are the work of poets. I have struggled like no other human being has struggled. My independence and hatred of deception have made me bitter enemies; I have overcome and pardoned those whom I condescended to encounter. They have become my friends.

'I have ardently longed to reach the topmost pinnacle of my art. I have not yet reached it. By far, the smaller part of my life remains for me to live but what matters it! Every day brings me nearer to the realisation of my dream. The hours that have flown away with my youth have left me courage and cheerfulness for my goal is unchanged, and I'm marching towards it.

'I have journeyed across the ocean, carrying with me my ideal of art and the genius of my nation has triumphed. I have planted the French language in the

274

heart of foreign literature and this is my proudest achievement. My art has been the missionary whose efforts have made French the common speech of the younger generation. I know this to be true because teachers in foreign countries have told me so, and I have been openly blamed for my presumption by a German professor in Chicago. In Brazil, the students fought with drawn swords because an attempt was made to prevent them from shouting "*Vive la France!*" as they dragged my carriage along. In Argentina, students learned passages from Racine, Corneille, Molière, all of which they recited most correctly and with scarcely any foreign accent.

'When I arrived in Australia, the French residents were dominated by the Germans; our Consul was neither liked nor esteemed. Immediately upon arrival, I was received by the Mayor in his official robes; his wife and children offered me flowers and a military band played the national anthems of both England and France. This polite attention I owed to orders from England. The immediate effect was felt by my company and me through our great success, and when our steamer departed, she fired her parting gun and our own national anthem was sung by more than five thousand people massed on the quays. It was easily a scene not to be lightly forgotten.

'In Hungary the towns were decorated with French flags in spite of orders to the contrary from the government. Czechs went through their dances before me in their national costumes bedecked with red, white and blue ribbons.

'These are the victories that have gained me so much indulgence; I say nothing of the encounters at which you and all the Paris public have been present and now, after having finished my confession, I can still find one little incident in my own favour. Five months ago I refused an offer of a million francs to perform in Germany. If there be any carping critics to say the fête about to be given me is out of proportion to my talents, tell them I am the militant doyenne of a grand, inspiring, elevating form of art. Tell them French courtesy was never more manifest than when, desiring to honour the art of interpretation and raise the interpreter to the level of other creative artists, it selected a woman.

SB'

12

A Candle Burns Brighter at the End

Maurice handled Sarah's tremendous correspondence, sorting requests for seat bookings, concerts, letters to agents and theatres everywhere, negotiating contracts for future tours and dinners in her honour; the last just as important now, as Sarah was the greatest ambassador France had yet boasted.

Sarah's habit of rising with the birds, breakfasting early and daintily in her charming, lace-curtained boudoir, gave Maurice time to discuss present and future business with her. This was the time they loved best – an hour of un-interrupted privacy. His arms loaded with mail, news-papers, and telegrams, the long-legged, moustached, fashionably-handsome Maurice greeted his mother, always with affection lighting up his classic face:

'*Bon jour, ma chère.*'

Sarah returned his kisses and affectionate smile, her greeting in a voice dropped low, to a special pitch, in a key for him alone:

'*Bon jour, mon cher Maurice. Comment ça va?*'

'*Bien, merci, mère. Et vous aussi?*'

Sarah replied, then asked how his wife and children were, and turned to business. Maurice told her:

'There's another offer from Germany, requesting a week's engagement in Berlin. They will pay you a million francs.'

'Ah, that's nice.'

'You mean you'll go? You'll take it?'

'No, I won't.'

'But why not? You said you would if they got down on their knees and begged. That's what this offer represents.'

'I know. But I still hate them. I don't trust them. Write the usual "regret calendar is full, thank you". What else, dear?'

Maurice opened the newspapers and showed her the front page.

'See what the critics say. You've surpassed yourself.'

'I'm a bit tired. You read for me.'

'Very well, dear. They don't know how to honour you since your last tour. You're already a chevalier of the *Legion d'Honneur*, and here's a report of the official dinner given in your honour, in London, with a photo of you seated by the side of Lloyd George. Here also are the photos of your triumphant return reception at Le Havre, with your carriage and horses riding over pavements carpeted with flowers. I should have loved to see that. Here's a picture of the Order of Alphonse XIII, the Spanish King's decoration, as he presented it to you at the Palace.'

Sarah listened, slightly bored, then in a rich, jesting tone, she said:

'Yes dear. If I didn't remove those decorations when I go to bed, I'd wake up a tattooed woman.'

Maurice laughed with her. He never tired of her delightful jokes on herself.

'They can't wait to see what you'll do next, and I can't blame them.'

'Why?'

'There's someone would give you her whole fortune, a rajah's ransom, if you'd tell her the secret of your eternal youth. They feel that's why you also recovered from the illness of your leg. You see, you've really carried it off.'

'Have I? What else?'

'They think, perhaps now, your changing over from playing female roles to male roles has given you a new strength. Playing Lorenzaccio, Hamlet, L'Aiglon, all this and your amorous friendship with Rostand.'

'Oh, that reminds me,' Sarah interrupted. 'I hear you challenged Monsieur de Wendell, of *La Vie Illustrée*, to a duel. Will you never stop? I've told you publicity is my Beloved Monster.'

'For you, yes, *maman*. But you forget you brought me

up to be a spoiled gentleman. I'm your son, and I've a different sort of responsibility in this family since you have no husband. And I can't allow my mother's name to be scandalised. What would my father have said.'

A short respite between tours abroad and seasons in Paris found Sarah in her lavish Louis XV boudoir, scented with heliotrope and amber. She was queen in the midst of her own family, loved and adored by her granddaughters, Lysiane, the youngest, utterly inseparable from her 'Great', an affectionate added mark of respect, when she wrote to her *grandmère* on tour. At home, Lysiane cherished every moment she could be with her grandmother.

Lysiane adored coming up to Sarah's boudoir in the early hours of the morning, before the menagerie awoke, arms heavily laden with freshly cut roses from the garden, where there were more flowers than lawn. But that was Sarah's way. She adored a happy profusion, hating to see an inch of space uncovered on the walls or floors. No one ever learned to find their way through it without knocking something over, but Sarah slithered through as smoothly as a breeze. Sarah was approaching sixty five, Lysiane was seventeen. She knocked on the door:

'*Grandmère*, may I bring you your breakfast tray?'

'*Oui, ma chérie. Entres.*'

'*Bon jour, grandmère*,' she hurried to Sarah and kissed her on both cheeks, 'it is such a lovely day, so sunny and fresh, only one thing spoils it.'

'One thing! What's that?'

'Oh, there are already three newsmen and two photographers to see you.' Lysiane set down Sarah's tray, and began to fluff up the mountain of lace and satin cushions behind Sarah's back. Wrapping a chiffon bed-jacket round Sarah's shoulders, and putting the tray in front of her, Lysiane asked:

'What shall I tell them?'

'I wish I could see them all, but this morning my leg hurts. What shall I do?'

'I'll send them away if you like.'

'Not yet, *chérie*. See who they are while I have my breakfast, then come and tell me. Send in Romilda to straighten up my room in the meantime.'

Lysiane went down to the foyer where the group of reporters and others sat waiting patiently, hoping to spend a few moments with Sarah. One of them was saying:

'She played the role of a queen, but her friends always said she ruled her court with a rod of iron wrapped in silk. If a man complimented her, she brushed him off gaily, but with an order: "If you love me, write a great poem and dedicate it to me." To the painters, she'd say, "Paint a masterpiece to show you're truly inspired by me. How can I look up to you otherwise". The incredible part of it is that it worked! Look at Dumas Fils, Clairin, Sardou, Rostand, Ollivier, and I don't know how many others. Even Sand wrote three plays she never would have if she hadn't seen Sarah.'

Lysiane circulated through the group with a pad and pencil, noting the names and papers they represented. She came back to Sarah, who had finished her orange, tea and toast, still eating lightly and daintily as always.

'*Grandmère*, a man is waiting who says his name is Barnum, and he's an American you met in the States.'

'Ah, yes,' Sarah said softly, rolling her eyes up to the ceiling. 'A great showman. I remember him well. You may ask him to wait, but first arrange the drapes so that a narrow shaft of light comes in just where those roses are, on the table there. This time, I don't want to be the star. Now, give me my glass, I want to see how I look.'

Lysiane loved this. Running back and forth, doing a thousand things as Sarah called them off, running up and down the stairs to see who had come to interview or visit, smoothing the covers, the dust-ruffles, handing Sarah make-up. None of this ever lost its excitement for the imaginative young girl. Finally, things seemed to suit Sarah, the armchair was on the side she thought was her best profile, and Lysiane went to call Mr Barnum for his interview.

A few moments later, Barnum, the owner of the greatest circus on earth, followed Lysiane to Sarah's room, just as she was hiding the long, graceful hand-glass under the pillows. Lysiane announced Barnum and left. Sarah greeted him in English with the flavour of France in the syllabication.

'How nice of you to come to see me,' she said graciously, holding out her hand to him.

'Thank you for receiving me, madame. I have never forgotten you since I saw you in *Camille*. You are still the most talked about artist-visitor in our country. We all hope you will return soon.'

'Ah, thank you, take this chair, Mr Barnum. Thank you for your wonderful countrymen. They were so *simpático* when I was there. And I do hope to go again. How do you like *my* country, Mr Barnum?'

'Naturally, I agree with everyone, France is a beautiful country, very beautiful.'

'And are my countrymen treating you with courtesy?'

'Oh yes indeed! No complaints about the service here. Yes, indeed. Everybody here has been more than charming ... and the food and wine! That is something we don't have back in the States. I'm thinking of taking home a French chef with me.'

'Well, that is a compliment. I'm happy to know there's something which we can offer you. What else would you like to take home?'

At this, Barnum looked at the floor, a slight embarrassment coming into his manner.

'By the way,' he drawled, 'how is your health, madame? We've been reading reports that you haven't been well. Is it true you've been in bed for weeks?'

'Yes, it's true. It's kind of you to be concerned. But, my doctors despaired over me so many times, I cannot blame them, you see, but I will survive.'

'What are you saying?' Barnum fumbled with his watch, not comprehending.

'Well, I laughed at their predictions many times, but not when I was a young girl. Then, I took them seriously. I even wanted to die and tried to kill myself. But the *Bon Dieu* didn't want me then. We are in his hands, *oui?*'

'I'm sure he'll decide the millions of people in our world deserve consideration too. They all wish you to get well, so they can see you again.'

'You give me courage, Mr Barnum. Thank you.'

'Would it be too much, madame, if we talk about your doctors?' Barnum said hesitatingly.

'If it amuses you, certainly. I would not have expected you would wish to.'

Barnum fidgeted with his watch chain, twirled it in his hands nervously, then, leaning towards her, asked:

'I hear, I hope you'll forgive me, I've heard it said your doctors talk about amputating your leg to save your life. Is it true? Now, if you'd rather not talk about it . . .?'

'No, I don't mind, but I didn't know you would take it so seriously. I thought Americans dismiss news of me as publicity. I am touched, Mr Barnum.' Sarah said, a little sentimentally.

'But madame, you see it really is otherwise.'

'Yes, *merci*. My gratitude! What else can I do for you Mr Barnum?'

'Well, I have an offer to make, an offer of a business nature.'

Sarah brightened up so that Barnum felt a little uneasy. With intense interest, she asked:

'How wonderful! And just when I need money. It costs millions of francs to keep so many people in such a large house. Please, do tell me what is your offer?'

Courteously, Barnum came to the point:

'It isn't anything complicated. You know, madame, I own a circus.'

'Yes, your circus is famous in the whole world. I have been accused of kissing one of your bears,' Sarah laughed, a lilting happy laugh. 'I cried when I first saw it in the papers, years ago. Lucky my son was home. He would have defended me with his sword.'

Sure, that's how it is with important people like yourself, madame,' Barnum said while Sarah was still laughing musically. He waited for her, then:

'Now as I was saying, if the doctors should decide to amputate . . .' he stopped, waiting to see her reaction before continuing. Sarah looked steadily at him:

'Yes, go on.'

'If it is agreeable to you, I'll sign a contract with you now for ten thousand dollars, to buy your amputated leg after the operation.' Barnum ended breathlessly, his face turning a pinkish-red. He took out his large, crisply-laundered handkerchief, and mopped his brow and hands.

Sarah gave him her penetrating, panther look, then, unable to control herself, she again burst into fresh, delicious laughter, her head on the huge mountain of pillows.

'Ah, *monsieur*, you are too kind, but you don't know what you are saying. Have you seen my leg recently? It has been in a cast, and no one would believe it is the leg of Sarah Bernhardt. You would lose on your bargain, and I would regret your investment. *Merci*, just the same.'

'Then, madame, I will pray that you'll perform another miracle and not need to lose your leg. Good luck, madame.' As Barnum rose and held his hand out to her, Sarah took it and said sweetly:

'Thank you, Mr Barnum. I do feel much better and am ready for my next tour to your country. The operation can wait until I return. I have a contract and must keep my word.'

'And I'll be among the first to welcome you. Good-bye, and thank you again.'

During the following years, the love that Rostand and Sarah had for each other deepened until they became inseparable. Material success crowned their romance. It was hard for

Sarah to realise as she stood before the mirror in her dressing room that fifteen years had really elapsed since she had first played *L'Aiglon*. She was pleased to see that the costume still fitted her becomingly. Her hair was cut short, its curlyness fluffing into a golden halo softly crowning her fine brow. Satisfied that the crisply elegant uniform with its marks of distinction – medals and honours – were all correct, she swung round: 'I must give my best performance this matinée, Felicie. All my severest critics will be scrutinising me from their box.'

'*Oui*, Madame.' Felicie knew that Lysiane, Sarah's grand-child and some school chums were to see the matinée. Adolescents were so hard to please. Also in the box would be Sacha Guitry's children, watching their godmother. Changing the subject abruptly, Felicie said:

'Madame, weren't the peace parades impressive!'

'Yes, indeed.' Sarah said without conviction.

'But madame, every king and emperor in Europe gave his pledge. Surely. . . .'

'I hope this generation will grow up in a peaceful world. War is so hideous, and life is so precious.'

Felicie could see that the conversation had depressed Sarah. Hastily, she began brushing the short cropped hair and murmured, 'Madame looks so beautiful today. Lysiane will think she has the most wonderful *grandmère* in the whole world.' Her tone soothed Sarah. 'And now, as you still have a few minutes before curtain time, do rest.'

Suddenly they could hear wild shouts from the street below. Felicie hurriedly opened the window. The distant words became plain. It was war! Sarah didn't even open her eyes. The inevitable had happened. Now, Sarah felt she had lived too long. She was suddenly too old and tired to face life in wartime again. Poignant memories chased one another through her consciousness, until she was glad when Felicie touched her gently, 'Madame, it's time to go. . . .'

Sarah rose. She summoned all her strength for this, her very best . . . her very special performance.

A moment later, Rostand came dashing through the door.

One look told him she knew. He cradled her in his arms, 'Ah, my dearest, be brave. We're together! We'll always be together. I'll always take care of you.'

'Please call Maurice.'

Rostand despatched a messenger but almost before he left, Maurice arrived. They tried to persuade Sarah not to go on. It was futile. Sarah was rigid with determination. This might be her last performance, she thought, and . . . it would be her greatest. Pushing the two men aside, she started toward the door, but her face suddenly contorted in pain. She held her leg, unable to move. The tears began to flow.

They helped her back to the divan. Maurice waited until the pain subsided. 'You're coming home with me, mama. That's why I came. I have the carriage waiting. The doctors insist you must rest.'

'Oh those doctors! Don't they know rest is death! I'm ready. Help me. I'm going on!' Maurice's pleas were useless.

Rostand stood speechless. Sarah would actually go on! When he realised she was on her feet, he spoke, but it seemed not to be his voice. The whole world seemed changed :

'Where does it all come from . . . so much courage!'

'My love,' she smiled sadly. 'I have faced death seven times. I had hoped to die on stage. Earlier in my career, when the laurels were just beginning to cluster around my brow, Lemâitre said : "*Mourir en scène!* One beautiful night, die on stage with a tragic cry in a grand gesture!" But . . . I never could carry it off, even though I tried suicide.'

The men were terrified! So that was what she intended!

Quickly, Maurice interrupted. He must stop her at all costs. 'But I won't let you torture yourself! I won't let you commit suicide! Tomorrow you go into the hospital. It's all settled!'

'You're right, my dearest one. Of course. The leg must go. Very well. Cut it off! If this is the way my light must go out. . . .'

'It won't go out, mama. I can promise you that.'

Rostand turned away, his eyes burning. A moment later, he turned back, placed a tender arm around her and carried her down to the wings. Sarah stepped on stage, hesitating. A thunderous applause greeted her. It was just the right play for such a day: France's entry into war. The sadly courageous, yet tender tragedy of Napoleon's heir touched every heart. Despite war hanging over their heads, Sarah galvanised her audience. No one guessed that it would be the last performance she would give standing up.

A chill fell over the theatre as the crowds left and the lights dimmed. Sarah collapsed when the curtain fell for the last time.

The two patient men tucked her into the carriage, enfolding her in blankets like an infant. Rostand caressed her cheek, 'How did you do it? It's unbelievable!'

Maurice shot him a look, . . . 'You fool! You'll spoil everything! She may change her mind.' But Sarah's tone was resigned.

'Since childhood, I've had to prove myself worthy over and over. It's become a bad habit now,' her eyes twinkled bravely. 'No matter what I gave them on stage, they always wanted more and I had to please them. Everyone was a top critic from Sarcey down to the littlest lisping child. Every syllable, every intonation. . . .'

Sarah's voice trailed off wearily, but Rostand still marvelled.

Uraemia had developed from kidney trouble, infecting Sarah's leg with poison. The hapless doctors had no cure. In her many falls on stage, falls which, though they had been rehearsed were spontaneous when in the grip of a role, left her bruised and sore, the bruises acting as focal points for the infection. Warnings by her doctors were futile. She who had conquered so many insuperables, had risen out of desperation and crises unnumbered times, she would not listen!

Sarah had to face the amputation of her left leg.

With the amputation, miracles continued for Sarah. Her light did not go out. She quipped with the doctors before the operation, 'It would be admirably practical. You see, as I'll have one leg already in the grave, I'll only need one step, *n'est ce pas?*' But the doctors rejected her suggestion. They determined to save her.

Rostand, Maurice, the whole family, and most especially Lysiane, never left her side for a moment, each jealous of the time the others took when the special patient was finally allowed visitors. Petite Dame had passed on, and Sarah dreamed she hovered over her protectingly. Maurice looked into his mother's eyes, his own as blue as hers, and held her fragile white hand; he clasped it gently, willing his strength to flow through, to penetrate her body and soul, as though to let go meant . . . he could not bear to think of that.

Maurice recalled her courage during an earlier bout with surgery. On the 10th February, 1898 the actress entered a private hospital on the rue d'Armille where she would undergo an operation : during a performance of *Les Mauvais Bergers*, she had felt a sharp pain internally. The applause and curtain calls over with, she returned to her dressing room and immediately fell on her face to test what it was that had caused the pain; she must make sure that it was not her imagination, and she went on testing and making sure through the remaining forty performances of the run of the play. Then she called in Dr Pozzi who found serious internal trouble and advised surgery to be arranged for in June.

Despite the urgency, Sarah organised a provincial tour, but this time her will was bested; her condition became critical and the doctor ordered her into hospital immediately. She had kept this from her son until the last; it was quite a shock for Maurice. 'Are you afraid, mother?'

'Afraid? No, there's no danger with Pozzi. It's just a stroke of bad luck, I had a wonderful run of success last year, too much in fact, and now this is a set-off.'

'When is it to be?' he asked.

'On Wednesday, and don't be afraid yourself, I'll tell you all sorts of funny stories when I'm convalescent so you won't be bored. I've plenty yet that you haven't heard.'

When Maurice arrived at the little hospital in the Ternes quarter of Paris, which was a converted private house with a courtyard in front, he met his mother's friends and they all entered as if for one of their usual teas. The patient's room was on the first floor overlooking a small garden shaded by a few trees. The great artiste lay on a small iron bed, her golden hair completely covering her pillow; smiling and gay as usual, perhaps a bit paler, if that were possible.

She had by-passed a moment when a surgeon's knife could have abruptly ended thirty years of heroic ardour, wild passion, triumphs and melancholy but the rare vitality which always vanquished each combination of adverse circumstances scored again. She greeted her guests warmly and as if on stage :

'I kept telling myself that this is the price I have to pay for that great day I had two years ago. I always said something of this kind was bound to come. Ask Seylor if I didn't.'

Seylor was Sarah's faithful companion for the last ten years, never absent for a day : 'Didn't I tell you so Seylor?' she prompted her timid friend. 'When you kissed me and said how happy you were over my "glory" as you called it, and I said "Everything has its bad side as well as its good. See if I don't pay dearly for today!".'

It was not Seylor's idea to share the stage with the illustrious patient so she nodded briefly; the actress continued : 'It lasted an hour and a half yet I felt no pain either then or afterwards. I have had no fever at all, and at this moment, my temperature is normal; for two days the chloroform sickened me, gave me touches of nausea but that was all. My only pain was what I inflicted on my son by running the foolhardy risk, instead of going into hospital immediately. Poor boy, it's the only time I made him suffer of my own free will.' She followed her guests eyes as they looked round her room – full of portraits of Maurice from his babyhood until the present, and the marble bust which she made of him : 'Look, there, his first shoes and shirt.' The first, tiny white shrivelled patent leather; the second, a miniature that would only fit a doll. 'When I travel, I take them with me and as they never leave me, I felt I must have them here. I believe they bring me good luck.'

It was natural for her to have an audience, so she continued to the delight of her listeners: 'As a child, I was both reserved and fractious so I was seldom taken out as my more dependable sisters were, and sometimes even during holidays I was left at the Convent. The spirit of rebellion overcame my sadness and one day we heard that all the schools except ours had been given *bon bons* in celebration of the baptism of the Prince Imperial. I proposed that we should run away.

'The plan was that I, being on good terms with the sister in charge of the gate, should pretend to have a hole in my dress under the armpit. While she examined the hole, I raised my arm toward the cord which opened the gate and pulled it open. My confederates rushed out with me after them. You can imagine how far we could have gone with three pieces of soap in a bag and seven francs in money. The sisters had no trouble in finding us because a traitress was eager to denounce me as the ringleader – Amelia Pluche – I shall never forget her name. I was sent home in disgrace and shared the holiday with my family.'

The laughter rose and echoed through the corridor; Sarah was anything but a post-operative case; she watched the tears roll down Maurice's cheeck and told another anecdote: 'I was bored one day so I climbed the wall separating the Convent from the cemetery and as if in answer to my boredom, there before me was a grand funeral in progress with the Bishop of Versailles delivering a sermon to a huge crowd. I immediately began to imitate his gestures, mimic his dignified tone, and succeeded in distracting the attention of the crowd.

'You can imagine the scene; of course I was immediately expelled but owing to influence no doubt, I was soon back. Another time I was sentenced to three days solitary confinement for an offence, and before anyone knew it I ran out and climbed to the top of a chestnut tree. Unable to find me they set the watch dog on my scent; he promptly took up his position at the foot of the tree and barked, but there was no way of getting me down as the only man in the convent was the old gardener who would not trust himself at such a height, and the ladders were too short. To all the sisters' commands and threats I replied: "I will die here! I want to die here!" Finally they promised on oath that my sentence would be rescinded and I slithered down with the agility of a monkey. I was good at gymnastics because my mother always put this first owing to my early delicate constitution.'

Sarah laughingly continued, now enjoying her reminiscences as much as the others: 'After my departure from the convent, my mother provided me with a finishing governess, Mlle de Brabender – a very superior woman who had educated the Grand Duchess Marie of Russia. She adored me and used to take me to art school and anywhere else I was supposed to go. Mother gave me the bus fare for both of us, but as we both hated coming into contact with all sorts of people on the buses, I saved up the money and we walked instead, until I had enough to go by taxi, which was about every other day. I still avoid crowds when I can so as not to inhale other people's breath – partly I suppose because of my tendency to tuberculosis – mostly because of an aesthetic sense; in this respect I have always been ferociously unsociable.'

Dr Pozzi dropped in at this, his face alight, his manner that of a man who had just been relieved of a tremendous burden. He stayed just long enough to convince himself that all was well, received the congratulations of the gathering and left.

Sarah told of her difficulties as a débutante in the Conservatoire. 'I had a speech defect – speaking with clenched teeth which I inherited from my mother – and to cure me of this habit, my teachers gave me little rubber balls which prevented me from closing my mouth. I hated all that, but as I was committed, went through with it; Seylor, get the clippings from that drawer.'

Her friend handed her a scrap book. 'Here, listen to this. It's by Sarcey who used to make me cry every time he wrote something about me:

No role was ever better adapted to Mlle Sarah Bernhardt's talents than that of this melancholy queen. She possesses the gift of resigned and patient dignity. Her diction is so wonderfully clear and distinct that not a syllable is missed.'

'Mother, please.' Maurice begged her to rest and turned to Louise Abbema. Louise knew, she thought, just what would do the trick, but she only succeeded in part: 'Sarah, you've forgotten there's a tour suspended which awaits your recovery; and if you don't play, how many will be out of work and hungry? Besides, I'm selfish enough to admit I like my position as your friend; the status and glory which make me the envy of people whom I detest. Please save yourself, dear.'

Sarah only laughed and went on: 'You should have seen the Russian attitude to me – those of the people who were murderously anti-semitic – and from whom I had to be protected; after which I gave a performance and the curtain had not yet closed when I was seized with one of those sudden attacks which had begun to recur too frequently. I collapsed in Berton's arms with blood pouring from my mouth. I blanked out for some hours, but next day we left together, the whole company for our next 'port of call'.

It was more prudent to let the indefatigable woman follow her own genius, and they all applauded her story of the wild gallop over the face of Europe which by now had become an institution, recurring annually and bringing higher and higher prices for each performance.

The slim blonde Lysiane stood by her father, looking on with the helplessness of adolescence. She thought of the exciting matinées when she had whispered animatedly to her chums: 'My grandmother is that handsome prince in the

291

white uniform!' Then the happy tea parties when a few actors dropped in, still made up and costumed to add still more colour to the three-room apartment at the top of the Théâtre Sarah Bernhardt. How they would giggle, their skirts fluttering with every move while they gobbled up delicious sandwiches and richly stuffed pastries.

Sarah did not join her friends Guerard and Sand. She awoke in a flower-filled room – as she always loved to see a room – overflowing with joy and beauty. So many bouquets arrived that special assistants, all volunteers, had to be taken on to handle and sort the cards, letters and telegrams which then had to be answered. Sarah sent the flowers to all the other patients and Maurice even took a car full to a veterans' hospital.

Surgeons and doctors were hard to come by. The war had created shortages as usual. Even nurses were all at the front; nothing but aides and apprentices were left. But for Sarah, all went as though peace and plenty abounded, and nothing could be more natural.

Friends gathered daily, flowers and cablegrams came from heads of state including one from President Wilson, with an invitation to visit the White House immediately she was able to travel.

Maurice and Rostand looked silently down at Sarah for what seemed a lifetime. She was breathing gently. Conversation might be the straw which would break the delicate thread of life. Her eyes opened, but Rostand quickly silenced her, 'All's well. There's no need to speak. Rest quietly. We're all here.' He turned to the others. They nodded their tacit agreement.

Sarah was content. She had a heady sensation and felt she must talk, 'I thought I was dreaming, but it's true. . . .'

'You're not to talk, my dear. When I want you to speak, I'll write the lines. *Compris?*'

Sarah bowed to her master.

Soon she found new strength in the loving ministrations of her family and friends. Her room rang with laughter when a cortège of them arrived to escort her home. 'I know why you all prefer to be my weak friends rather than my strong enemies.'

'Ah, we feel a *bon mot* coming.'

'Fear that Maurice's seconds will rouse you out of your lazy morning sleep.'

'*Touché!* True enough. Only three years ago Maurice terrified Pioch after his article in *Gil Blas*! Very wise of him to have retracted!'

Her departure from the hospital was almost another fête day. Flowers and telegrams poured in while impassable crowds cheered, watching Sarah carried, sitting in a chair to her son's car. She waved gaily and smiled happily. They drove off in a shower of flowers, as if departing on a honeymoon.

France needed Sarah as never before.

Six months later found Sarah so well recovered that Rostand wrote a new play for her. Other young playwrights lent their talents, among them Louis Verneuil, who wrote *Daniel*, the story of a drug addict in which Sarah scored again. Her home was again the happy beehive everyone knew. Lysiane, Dominga, Claude, and hosts of others ran constantly up and down the stairs, bringing trays, announcing visitors, reporters, photographers and impresarios with contracts for future engagements. Sarah turned no one away. She even signed a contract to make films. She had misgivings at first but the impresario Leon Abrams agreed to bring cameras, lights, and other equipment to her home. Thus she would be spared the need to travel. The largest room was cleared out to serve as a studio and Sarah was paid five thousand francs each time she posed.

Sarah needed money badly. She was now the owner of a retreat on Belle Isle, her island estate which had formerly housed a fort. Then there was Maurice's family and her own little house in Paris. She wrote articles in her spare moments for several newspapers during her convalescence, and taught aspiring novices the art of acting. After listening to a reading, her impatience with short cuts was tendered to one pupil:

'Why should you study such pieces? It's only too easy to be common – we need no study for that. Art is exalted. We must seek to cultivate higher moods; the finest literature only is worthy of your efforts, and that alone will in life lift us to the plane of artistic emotion. Do not imagine all emotion is artistic. As students you should seek to express the moods and emotions which are universal, true of all ages, and all races because they come from the heart. Art knows no time – no individual. First the fundamental, lastly the particular. Art does not concern itself with personality until motivation and reactions of emotion are defined.

'Remember that art is greater than its expression. At most we can only suggest it and we can do that by reaching out to the universal forces that are working through all mankind. When we find the key which is common to us all, then we are touching universal art. Only great literature can help us in that.'

Sarah had recovered through the love of her family, but the greatest motivation came from the public who wished to see her in their favourite plays. Emotional memory played its part and they hungered to be moved by her art.

Now that she was herself again, Rostand could hardly wait for her to go into rehearsal. 'My dear, you must return to the stage. Even your doctors agree it is the best medicine for you.'

She hung back, wondering how much of it was true. Perhaps . . . she had to be sure: 'Indeed! They don't know how it feels to be old and crippled! What, I ask myself, is the purpose of my living on, a burden to myself and everyone around me. My son must lift me from my bed to my chair each morning, then when evening falls he must lift me again from the chair into bed.'

'If you only knew how happy he is for that. If you could have seen his face when your fate hung in the balance during our wait at the hospital! And his subsequent relief! You don't know how much he loves you. Please don't torture yourself.'

'Thank you. That should be enough, except. . . .'

'Except what?'

'I'm penniless. The roses you sent this morning are simply magnificent . . . and such divine perfume. They fill the room, but they must have cost a fortune.'

'But that's such a tiny tribute! There's no equivalent by which true art can be measured.'

'If only I had half the money that was spent for flowers and cables. . . . The good Baron de Rothschild again paid for my hospital bills. I wish I could have a hospital again for the wounded.'

'Money cannot produce artists but it can protect them. That is the privilege of the rich. And now, aren't you curious about the play?'

'You're too kind. You spoil me.' Sarah riffled through the manuscript, her fingers lingering on the pages, when Maurice, followed by Lysiane and Felicie burst into the room. In his hand he held a long white envelope. His excitement was catching. Sarah eyed him with that tenderly proud look – her special one for her only son : 'Yes, dear?'

'A cablegram from President Wilson! You're to give a performance in the White House to sell Liberty Bonds. And this is from our Ministry of War. You're to play for the soldiers at the front! *Voilà!*' He handed her the cable and letter with the seal of the Ministry.

Sarah fumbled under the mountain of cushions : 'Where are my glasses? They want me to play in this condition? Who signs it?'

'The letter was requested by Marshal Ferdinand Foch. He wrote the Minister that you gave him the will to live when he was a patient in your hospital forty years ago. He's certain you can still do the same for the soldiers under his command now.'

'So it seems,' she said dreamily. 'Yes, I remember him. We'll do whatever we can for our beloved France. If they can remember me, I can at least do this much for them.'

Rostand cheered her on, 'You'll be a symbol of courage on two counts!'

'*Vive, mes frères amputés!*' Sarah laughed.

Rostand went to the foyer outside Sarah's bedroom and came back with a distinctively chic hat box: 'And now, I have a surprise for you too.' Sarah's eyes were as large as a child's at its first party. Rostand took out a blue velvet hat with a curved brim and high crown, topped with frothy ostrich plumes, their tones blending with the velvet. In Cyrano's grandest flourish, he bowed: 'With my compliments, madame!'

'Why, how delightful! Just what I need!' Sarah's hand slid under the cushions again to search for her mirror, while the other hand stroked the silky plumes sensuously: 'Here, Lysiane, hold my mirror.'

Lysiane was already by her side, also stroking the plumes childishly. Sarah put the hat on. It was perfect. Her colour rose and she was radiant. Rostand had triumphed! Everyone beamed.

'It is becoming, isn't it?' she nodded her head, letting the plumes swirl about gaily. 'You see, I've always said artists can do anything. I love it, and I couldn't have done better myself. But I have to ask, why did you choose just this one and not another?'

'Well, remember when I first met you last week,' he teased, 'When we went riding in the park and I was supposed to read a play for you, only I didn't because you were too distracting?'

'Certainly I remember. It was spring.'

'Well, my dear, you wore just such a hat.'

Sarah's hand slid under the cushions again . . . for her lace handkerchief: 'You're still a dangerous man!' She dabbed at her eyes.

'I agree. We have a reservation at Maxim's tonight. Will you do me the honour, madame?' he bowed again mockingly.

Sarah looked slowly at each face. There was approval on each one. 'I accept – on one condition.' Curiosity patiently showed itself on the faces. 'On condition that Maurice pledges himself never to fight any more duels!'

'I promise! Absolutely!'

'Very well, you may all kiss me and leave!' she ordered imperiously.

Maurice kissed his mother and left with the family. Felicie had to dress Sarah for her next public appearance.

Paris again clamoured for her, and Sarah, acceding to their pleas, set a date for her return. The crowds, with flowers in every hand ready to shower her, milled about the theatre, blocking every entrance. Her chair could barely pass through as wave after wave of well-wishers showered her with rose petals, laughing and crying. Sarah's pulse skipped again and again. Never had she been so moved. Rostand placed her chair in the centre of the stage. The curtains were parted slightly and the chair pushed through into the spotlight. Sarah's first audience since her amputation applauded her in a standing ovation. The cheers rose, echoing and resounding louder and still louder. A few sat down but rose again. One had to be part of this growing momentum or leave. It was impossible to sit. In fact, one was hardly aware of standing. Rather, it gave one a sense of being levitated up towards the frescoed ceilings.

Amid the swelling emotion, pages laden with bouquets, boxes and baskets, gifts from heads of every state in the world, and many artists, ringed them round Sarah until she was almost lost in a huge bouquet of roses and blossoms of all colours. Sarah bowed and gave her most dazzling smile across the footlights as the applause continued and the scented air rose fresh and pungent.

Up the aisle to the stage, and through the sea of blooms, a small woman dressed in pale grey picked her way. In her slim arms she held what appeared to be all the white long-stemmed roses in Paris: 'Pardon, Madame Bernhardt. These are from Eleanora Duse with her compliments. I am her secretary,' she spoke in a gentle voice. A page stepped up. While everyone watched, the sensitive young woman cradled the loose mass of roses onto the outstretched arms of the page, then began transferring them by handfuls to Sarah. Many dropped at her feet. When she finished, there were at least two hundred roses all about her, some clinging by their thorns to her gown as if embroidered there. Sarah had difficulty in acknowledging the thundering cheers. This was what Paris loved! Sarah smiled most happily. It seemed the theatre was never so brilliant.

Speech was impossible, and Sarah waited patiently for a lull. At the first opportunity, she broke in: 'These roses are a gift from Italy's famous tragedienne, Eleanora Duse. *Vive La Duse!*'

Duse was now world renowned. She had expressly ordered her secretary not to deliver the roses tied or boxed, as if they were prisoners. 'Take them yourself and let them fall about her alive and free, that they may breathe new life into her to keep her forever alive!'

Sarah's countrymen applauded for half-an-hour in Duse's honour. The walls of the theatre were ready to burst. Finally, Sarah's pleas quietened them: 'It's time to raise the curtain. . . . The artists are waiting. *Merci, mille fois.*'

Once Sarah regained her hold on life, she was again in full command. She acted seated, her genius equal to every crisis. Her voice, her arms, and her marvellous face subtly projected her art.

With the need for money greater than ever, she accepted tours which took her to the United Kingdom for sixteen weeks in addition to those in America. The 'treasury' had to be restored.

In 1917, she submitted to another operation in a New York clinic. She was seventy three but was soon up, delivering inspiring speeches to the crowds gathered before the library at Fifth Avenue. Lyrical and steady, her voice rose as she pleaded with them to buy Liberty Bonds:

'I will not die! I hold on to life because I wish to see the defeat of the Kaiser before my death!'

Still menaced by uraemia, Sarah hung on, and the following year, shared in the joy of seeing the Kaiser defeated and her beloved France once more liberated. On her return to Paris after the war, Rostand died. Sarah collapsed. But life would not let her grieve . . . and now more money was needed.

She continued to play, always seated, as a new generation of authors began knocking at her door for inspiration. Her voice was just as golden, her remarkable memory clear, infallible – she not only continued to play but recited poetry, gave lectures, and even read prayers to the bereaved mothers and widows of the war.

Sarah seemed to radiate a spiritual brilliance. She held audiences with her voice, her febrile gestures, her eloquent eyes. Through them shone the tortured soul of *Phèdre*, the less tragic but eternally powerful souls of *Théodora* and *Tosca*; the sensitive soul of *Lorenzaccio* and of *Hamlet*; the sentimental soul of *Camille*, among the many that haunted the inexhaustible capacity of the great actress who gave to each their singularly brilliant existence.

There were new glories crowning Sarah's head, and though these brought untold millions of francs, they were never enough to pay for all of her expenses, especially the island retreat, Belle Isle, and Maurice's family. Against her life-long rejection of all things German, she was forced to accept engagements there, unable to refuse the attractive fees. She was surprised at their wooden appreciation.

The most important films she made were *Camille*, *Queen Elizabeth*, *Tosca* and *Jeanne Doré*. After the completion of her first film, she cried happily: 'Now I am a film. If only Rostand could see me.'

Once more Duse acclaimed her:

'At last, there is one woman who has been able to raise our business above the mundane; who leads the mass to the respect of the beautiful, and obliges them to bow before art.'

Sarah acknowledged Duse: 'She is the only artist who requires no costume or make-up to play a role convincingly.'

With the war's end in 1918, Sarah's energies were still formidable. Her genius, still burning brilliantly refused to let her rest, and anyway, for her, rest was always a kind of death. Lysiane had married one of the young playwrights, Louis Verneuil, but was still close to her grandmother. She was writing Sarah's biography.

After the first night of Sarah's last tour in America, a critic wrote: 'For half a century everything has been said about her that could be said': then added Victor Hugo's words; 'One does not analyse genius; one prostrates oneself. . . .' Nothing in the past two hundred years could be compared with it.

In her travelling chair, she toured the devastated areas of France and beyond its borders through Belgium and Spain. She allowed herself only a brief respite: an afternoon at a *corrida*. Her enthusiasm was undimmed and she cheered with the joy of her girlhood.

Sarah returned to Paris and between performances began a book on the art of acting, but her impatience with the idea of putting art between sets of rules prevented her from finishing it. The rebel in her was still untamed. Unable to rage on stage any more, or to rise to a pitch of frenzy after which she could tear across the planks exhausting herself, she had to learn patience, creating; consuming herself through the only world she knew, a world which she had created and which now rescued her from every crisis. She gave forty eight performances in thirty two towns.

On 24th September 1922 she played *La Gloire* in Paris, and immediately after presented two plays in Italy. She felt tired but did not stop, hurrying back to Paris for a performance of *Athalie*, the same play by Racine which first awoke her ear to the beauty of the human voice. Uraemia was ebbing her strength but she refused to rest. Her struggle against the consuming poison grew as she continued to believe she would win. Her belief in herself never waned. *Athalie* was the last of her performances, standing like two marble pillars, one at each end of her career.

Sarah's condition worsened but she began rehearsals for *Un Sujet de Roman*, a play by Sacha Guitry, while her film work continued. She fainted during one rehearsal, and this time gave the impression that she was resigned to the inevitable. But those who assumed she was accepting her condition were mistaken.

When Sarah could not go down to her film work in the

studio below, she ordered the cameras to be brought up to her bedroom for the following months. Her answer to queries on her health during March 1923 was: 'I'm so happy to be working.'

On 23rd March, Sarah collapsed while dining with a friend, and though three physicians were called in, they could not agree on a diagnosis. Next morning, to everyone's amazement, Sarah apologised, 'Sorry to interrupt the work schedule.' But she did admit feeling too weak to continue.

Her condition deteriorated rapidly that day. By six in the evening, five eminent doctors signed the bulletin of the grave news to the world, which stood by mournfully. On 24th March, she was in greater pain, her last agony – delirium! Between reciting parts of plays which ran through her mind, other visions played their roles . . . she was twenty again, fresh and enthusiastic over the adventure of life. Who was it said, 'Life is worth living, seriously but joyfully?' But see, here was the Prince de Ligne, Berton, Damala, Jarrett, Rostand and her whole family. And here were kings and queens – all her royal friends!

It was true; life had been a wonderful adventure. She knew every corner of the world and it knew her.

In her delirium she faced one group and they applauded her. She bowed, and when she lifted her head, there was another. She bowed again, only to find herself facing still another audience. A meteor of roses pelted her, fell at her feet . . . how sweet the scent. . . . Now her family came toward her: 'Let's go home, dear. Let's go back to Paris. Maurice is safe. He's such a good boy.' 'I know. I missed you all so terribly! My baby, my darling. *Je t'aime. Je te donne ma vie.* We have such a beautiful home planned. Come dear.' Sarah gave Julie her hand. 'Sand! Where is Sand? I thought I heard her laugh!' 'Here I am. You don't think I'd miss this? You must have dinner with me, just a few intimate friends, twenty or thirty as usual. Like old times, *comme il faut.*'

The voices trailed off. Sarah regained consciousness. In the few brief moments of respite, she spoke lucidly to her doctor: 'How slowly I'm dying. But I know I have been delirious because there's a hole in my memory.' Sarah could eat nothing and hope was leaving.

Maurice wandered about aimlessly unable to believe the truth, while Lysiane wept rivers of tears. Sarah's menagerie were ominously silent, strangely well-behaved for spoiled, garrulous pets.

By morning of 25th March, a glimmer of fleeting hope returned when the delirium left and Sarah was calm. But this glimmer soon fled when it was realised that her nervous energy had been sapped by the delirium. She whispered: 'Is my coffin in good order?'

Now, no one was permitted to enter the room except Maurice and his two daughters. 'You know my love for flowers and nature, Maurice. I hope there will be many flowers. . . .'

For a fleeting moment hope dazzled Maurice.

'Flowers . . . funeral,' she was saying. 'Do you remember, Maurice, at the funeral of Edward VII, when the floral piece did not arrive and it was my turn to step up to the grave and place my offering? Do you recall how quick thinking, thanks to Jarrett's lessons, saved the day?' A broad smile lit her marmorial visage. Maurice did remember. She had nudged him to find a fresh wreath a distance away, which saved the day. It was no occasion for polite apologies.

Newspaper offices and transatlantic cables hummed without ceasing. Reporters clustered round the garden and smoked endless cigarettes, sprawled wherever there was an inch.

Sarah's last passion was spending itself as the millions who had been stirred by her, waited passionless. . . . A pall hung on the world as the minutes ticked . . . sometimes too fast. As hoped dwindled the Curé of the Church of Saint François de Sales administered extreme unction at three in the afternoon. As if she had just waited for this moment, the fire died in Sarah's eyes and she lost consciousness.

At seven thirty, the doctors consulted again. It was only too apparent that death was a matter of minutes away. How much longer depended on Sarah. She gave up. Nine minutes past eight, the word was given out : 'Madame is dead!'

Her home was inundated with flowers, so full, it was impossible to move without stepping on bouquets everywhere underfoot.

A million mourners accompanied the funeral cortège to Père Lachaise cemetery where the travelling companions – Sarah and her coffin – found rest under a simple grey stone. She broke the last precedent : She was the first actress to be buried in consecrated ground in France.

No one could earn money in that family except Sarah. She worked until the last moment – even on her deathbed. How would Maurice and his family live? Maurice outlived his mother by only five years.